FERRIDAY

A

Concordia Parish Library
Ferriday, Louisiana

The Baljuna Covenant, Published October, 2016

Interior Layout and Cover Design: Howard Johnson
Editorial and Proofreading: Shannon Miller, Stephanie Peters, Karen Grennan
Photo Credits: Front and back cover images: Ganbat Badamkhand, Ulaanbaatar, Mongolia.
Interior: Classical Mongolian Script, (Numbers and Symbols), Mongol Tolbo font, kindly provided by Batjavkhaa Batsaikhan.

 **SDP Publishing**

Published by SDP Publishing, an imprint of SDP Publishing Solutions, LLC.

ISBN-13 (print): 978-0-9968426-7-9
ISBN-13 (ebook): 978-0-9968426-8-6

Library of Congress Control Number: 2015957309

Printed in the United States of America

To Leslie, Lauren, and James

Formerly there were champions, who had set up a throne; with great labor they opened a way through the thorns; swearing, they drank from the dirty water.

—**NAI-HSIEN,** fourteenth century Chinese poet

PROLOGUE

1937
OUTER MONGOLIA
BALASYKUTUL MONASTERY

Mikou sat motionless on the temple floor, his heart pounding. The youngest of the monastery's monks, he recited quietly to himself.

I take refuge in the Buddha, hoping the sentients gain understanding.
I take refuge in the Dharma, hoping the sentients find wisdom.
I take refuge in the Sangha, hoping the sentients achieve harmony.

He sank into his meditations, one by one releasing his earthly ties. Closing his eyes, he did not see. Ignoring the fragrance of incense burning on the altar, the salty sweat dripping from his upper lip, and the stone tiles beneath him, he did not smell, taste, or feel. As much as he tried, however, he couldn't help but hear.

Through the bricks and mortar of the temple walls, he heard the rattle of rifles and canteens. He heard the wind sweep through the grass, the incessant chirp of cicadas, and the distant call of a hovering hawk. Reverberating loudest, however, was the silence, the silence of three hundred monks as they stared over the steppe and contemplated the stark beauty, the silence of three hundred monks as they turned toward the soldiers and accepted their fate.

There was a whistle and call to attention. Then, it began. Nine resonating volleys. One volley marking each of the punishments for disobedience; one for each state of consciousness; one for each of the levels of heaven; and one for each level of hell: the number of the eternity. While the echoes of the last volley dispersed over the steppe, there was only more deafening silence as his three hundred brethren slipped from this life into the next—without cries of pain, without protest.

He opened his eyes. Next to him, Arahat, an elder monk, sat in similar repose, deep within his meditations. How long would they stay here? *Why weren't they doing anything?*

The elder monk suddenly rose and walked across the temple floor, his yellow robe billowing behind him.

Mikou followed Arahat past the stone Buddha to an unmarked tile, which they slid aside. From the exposed nook, Arahat removed an ornately carved wooden box.

Mikou slipped from his robe. He took the box and started to run, but came to an abrupt stop. He turned.

Arahat remained on his knees, facing the great doors.

"Master, if you stay, they'll—"

"Go!" Arahat said. "Remember your duty. *Remember our duty.*" The elder monk slipped back into his meditations, his face going irretrievably slack.

Mikou bowed and then ran down the hallway and out through a side door.

The northern wind, laced with the stench of gunpowder, carried him past the great tree toward the river. Clutching the box tightly to his chest, he thought of the sacrifices the other monks had made, that generations of monks had made, all for the box he now held. The preservation of the covenant, the covenant that had changed the world, now resided in his hands.

Behind him, there was a crash and the sound of splintering wood, the monastery's great doors giving way. A single, echoing blast rang from the depths of the monastery.

Arahat.

Moments later, he heard the side door slam open and a shout for him to stop. He ran faster, the river and reeds not far away.

Mikou's right knee exploded in pain—a gunshot sounding. He fell, hitting the ground hard, the box slipping from his grasp. Ignoring the pain, he returned the spilled contents of the box. Propping himself up onto his left leg, he hobbled toward the reeds.

Another gunshot sounded, the bullet tearing through his left thigh. This time, as he crumpled to the grass, he held onto the box.

Coming to rest on his back, Mikou gazed up into the cloudless blue sky. He remembered his training and slowed his breathing, trying to fill his thoughts with the surest sign of nirvana—love of enemy. As much as he tried, however, he couldn't.

A gray-jacketed soldier walked down the hill. Mikou, watching the soldier's approach, pried open the wooden box. His fingers slid over the contents, settling on an ivory-handled knife.

The covenant had survived the fall of the Mongol Empire and centuries of Chinese oppression. Mikou vowed it would also outlive the Soviets. Pushing aside thoughts of nirvana, he vowed to survive. He vowed to preserve the covenant.

ᠨᠢᠭᠡ

Do not let my death be known. Do not weep or lament in any way, so that the enemy shall not know anything about it.

—Genghis Khan

1

James Andrews, an archaeologist from the University of Virginia, peered down from the aging Russian transport helicopter as it approached Ulaanbaatar's International Airport. As the helicopter touched ground, a nearby terminal door burst open. Men emerged, running toward them, holding television cameras and microphones.

"Zail! Zail! Kharaa! Kharaa!" the pilot warned, his voice booming over a loudspeaker.

Despite the warnings and spinning rotors, the men continued forward, pressing up against the helicopter door. Among them was a shaman wearing a feathered headdress.

Andrews sat with the Mongolian members of his dig team. They'd just spent the last month on Burkhan Khaldun, Mongolia's holy mountain, searching for Genghis Khan's tomb.

"What are they doing?" Andrews asked.

"I don't know, but we have Ulaanbaatar's finest," a member of the dig team said. "Reporters from the *Ulaanbaatar Gazete,* the *National Broadcaster,* Channel 25." He pointed. "There's someone from the BBC."

The rotors came to a stop. The dig team stood and slid the door open. Weighed down with bulging duffel bags and backpacks, they jumped to the tarmac, shielding their eyes from the bright lights of the cameras.

"Dr. Andrews! Dr. Andrews!" the reporters called out, extending their microphones. "Is it true you found Genghis Khan's tomb?"

Andrews stared back, incredulous. "No."

"What *did* you find?" a reporter shouted.

"At the base of the mountain, we found some roofing tiles, the likely remains of a late thirteenth century temple dedicated to Genghis Khan," Andrews said. "The tiles have been taken to the Mongolian Institute of Geography for examination."

A reporter pointed. "What's in there?"

Andrews looked down at a small cooler clutched in his right hand. "We found a random fragment of human bone," he said.

"Random?" the BBC reporter said. "Could you clarify?"

"It was found with no identifying markers or other remains and none of the artifacts that Genghis Khan was reportedly buried with."

"Are you saying it *doesn't* belong to Genghis Khan?" a reporter asked.

"Yes," Andrews replied.

"You say that with conviction," someone said.

"Descriptions of the location and manner of Genghis Khan's burial vary widely," Andrews said. "It's impossible to separate truth from fiction. But I am sure of one thing. Great care was taken in his burial. I doubt his bones, even after almost eight hundred years, would be scattered randomly."

"Then, why did you keep it?"

"We'll leave it with the Mongolian Institute. If DNA testing indicates the bone belongs to a member of the royal family, it would suggest their burial ground might be nearby."

The Mongolian dig team members had made their way through the reporters. They now stood by the door leading into the terminal. Relieved the month of hard work was over, they were looking back at Andrews, smiling and waving. *"Bayartai,"* a few yelled out.

"Sain suuj baigaarai!" Andrews called back.

From the group of reporters, the shaman stepped forward. His face leathered, he stared down at the cooler. "This human bone," he said, his voice flat. "Did you find it in the Restricted Area . . . in the area of the Great Taboo?"

"Yes," Andrews said. "On the mountain's second plateau."

With a shriek, the shaman dropped to his knees. He

broke into a chant and looked skyward, his eyes rolling into the back of his head.

The reporters glanced at one another before clamoring forward, shouting questions.

A black jeep, its windows tinted, had pulled up just beyond the reporters. Its passenger door swung open.

Andrews stepped around the shaman. Pushing through the reporters, he made his way to the jeep and hopped inside, slamming the door behind him.

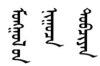

1170 Central Asia

In the shadows of Burkhan Khaldun, two boys, unaware of each other's presence, were hunting, arrows drawn. Entering a clearing, they spotted each other and froze. Long after their prey had scurried away, the larger boy spoke. "What clan are you?"

"Tayichiut," the smaller boy said. "And you?"

"Jadaran."

The boys slipped their arrows into their quivers. The Jadaran boy reached into a pocket and then held out his hand. His fingers were wrapped around multiple, small white cuboidal objects—sheep knucklebones.

The smaller boy eagerly removed a similar collection from his own pocket.

The boys threw the bones onto the ground and then looked up at each other and smiled.

It was late in the afternoon, but the summer's heat still hung heavy in the air. Against the base of a large tree, the boys continued throwing and gathering the bones, tirelessly keeping tally until one or the other raised his arms in victory. It was near nightfall, the bones' convolutions barely visible, when a distant horn sounded.

The Jadaran boy scooped up his bones and slung his bow

and quiver over his shoulder. "I have to go," he said, picking up his empty knapsack.

The smaller boy removed a marmot from his own knapsack. "I distracted you," he said, extending the animal. "Otherwise, you would have killed your own."

The Jadaran boy held the animal up by the scruff of the neck and nodded his approval. "I'll see you tomorrow?"

"Bring your knucklebones," the smaller boy said.

The Jadaran boy slipped the animal into his knapsack and ran from the clearing.

"What's your name?" the smaller boy shouted.

The Jadaran boy spun. "Jamuka," he yelled. "And yours?"

"I'm Temujin."

2

The tombs of the Mongols have no mound; they are trodden over by horses. At the tomb of Chinggis Khan, arrows have been stuck into the ground so as to make a fence, more than 30 li wide. Horsemen patrol it so as to guard the site.

—**P'eng Tay-ya,** Chinese envoy, 1232
First written account of the burial site

In a squeal of smoking tires, the jeep accelerated across the tarmac, leaving the transport helicopter and reporters behind. Shifting gears, Baabar Onon looked toward Andrews, smiling. The Mongolian had piercing dark eyes, high cheekbones, and a strong chin.

"It's good to see you," Andrews said as they grasped forearms.

The two had met during Andrews's first summer in Mongolia, eight years earlier. Andrews had been excavating Avarga, the Mongol's ancient capital. Baabar had just finished his undergrad studies and was working the dig site for extra money, contemplating grad school. At Andrews's suggestion, Baabar enrolled in the political science program at the University of Virginia. For the next two years, they shared an apartment in Charlottesville and spent their summers in Mongolia, digging and traveling the countryside.

"Is it true?" Baabar asked.

"That we found the grave?" Andrews asked. "Unfortunately, no. Where'd you hear this?"

"One of the television stations tweeted that you'd be

arriving at the airport at five with Genghis Khan's remains. Once one of them did, they all did."

"Did any report a source?"

"Not that I recall," Baabar said. "Knowing them, they probably made it up just to fill a time slot."

Baabar turned from the tarmac onto a road heading toward downtown Ulaanbaatar.

"I was beginning to think I might not see you this trip," Andrews said.

After graduating from the University of Virginia, Baabar had returned to Mongolia where he worked as a political writer for the *Ulaanbaatar Gazete*. A year later, he won a seat in the Khural, the Mongolian national parliament. Between the Khural's spring and autumn sessions, Baabar typically joined Andrews during his summer digs and sojourns across Mongolia. This summer, however, as he neared the end of his four-year term, he'd been too busy campaigning for a second term.

"I wish I could have made it to the mountain," Baabar said, nodding. "One day there can make you forget everything."

Andrews didn't ask what Baabar wanted to forget. His friend needed a break from Khural intrigues, not to rehash them.

Baabar glanced toward Andrews, raising an eyebrow. "I understand you had a woman up there."

Like most of his countrymen, Baabar was a member of the Mongolian Buddhist sect, which incorporated many ancient shamanistic practices. Women weren't allowed on the holy mountain without a shaman's blessing.

"An archaeology instructor from UCLA showed up," Andrews said. "I presumed she was okay. She and her two students had a hiking permit from the institute."

Baabar's brow knit. "I hope nothing illicit was going on up there."

"No . . . I . . . *We*—"

As Andrews stammered, Baabar started laughing. Andrews jabbed at Baabar's shoulder.

"If something illicit was going on, you have to tell me about it," Baabar said.

Andrews looked forward and shook his head, smiling to himself. "How'd you find out about them anyway?"

"There was a group photo in the society's newsletter."

The Asian Historical Society had funded Andrews's dig. Parker Winthrop, the society's representative in Mongolia, had visited the mountain two weeks earlier and taken photos.

"I couldn't help but notice she was attractive," Baabar said. "And you *were* standing rather close to her."

Andrews took a deep breath. "Are we going to grab something to eat?"

Baabar smiled. "Sure. How does Khara Khorum's sound?"

"Perfect," Andrews said, sitting back. "A cold bottle of Borgio, *aaruul, bansh*. On the mountain, I would have given anything for them."

They drove in silence for a few moments before Baabar turned. "What do you have planned for next summer?"

"Is another digging permit in the cards?" After years of denied applications, Andrews had finally received a digging permit for Burkhan Khaldun, largely due to Baabar's influence with the Mongolian Institute of Geography.

Baabar flashed a confident smile. "I *am* over twenty points ahead in the last poll."

"Delit' shkuru neuvitovo medvedya," Andrews said in Russian.

"Don't worry, I'm not counting my chickens," Baabar said.

Both were fluent in Russian. Andrews, the son of a former US ambassador to the Soviet Union and China, had spent twelve years of his childhood in Moscow and Beijing. Baabar, an orphan, was the adopted son of a Russian couple who'd immigrated to Mongolia in the early nineties.

"The elections are looking good then?" Andrews asked.

Baabar nodded. "The party hopes to gain several seats. It won't give us a majority, but analysts think we may break through in the next election cycle."

Andrews turned and looked out his window. "To tell you the truth, I'm not sure if I'll apply for another digging permit.

We excavated every location where my research suggested the grave might be and then some. If I went back, I wouldn't know where to start."

"I hope you haven't given up on Baljuna," Baabar said.

Andrews shrugged. "I haven't had a choice."

As a young man, Genghis Khan and a small band of followers were attacked and pursued across the steppe. After a long and harrowing flight, they arrived at the Baljuna River. While drinking the Baljuna's muddy waters, Genghis Khan toasted his men and vowed if they were delivered from their tribulations, he would rule fairly and share his wealth. Genghis Khan and the band survived, and the clan prospered. The bonds forged at Baljuna proved to be the glue that held together the future Mongol Empire. With time, the covenant became legend.

Most scholars believed Genghis Khan was buried on Burkhan Khaldun because he was born there. Andrews, however, believed Genghis Khan chose to be buried at Baljuna because it was the birthsite of the Mongol Empire. Andrews had documented his theory along with the highlights of his and Baabar's travels over the Mongolian countryside in a book, *In Search of Baljuna.*

"I've researched every document that's been written about Baljuna," Andrews said. "We've followed every clue from every manuscript. All our efforts haven't brought me one step closer to finding it. Like most stories about Genghis Khan, I'm starting to believe it's fiction."

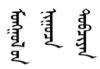

1170 Central Asia

Temujin and Jamuka sat in the upper branches of the large tree in the clearing. It was night. Over the past month, the two boys had met regularly to play knucklebones or to hunt or fish. Earlier in the day, they'd ridden up into

Burkhan Khaldun and spent the afternoon exploring the mountain.

"My father is khan of the Jadaran," Jamuka said as they stared up at the stars. "And I am the oldest son. Someday, I'll be khan."

"Can you imagine it?" Temujin asked. "You'll never have to worry about having enough food or milk or horses. You'll never live in fear."

"My father fears many things," Jamuka said. "He fears there will not be enough rain. If there is not enough rain, the grass will not grow and the animals will not eat. If the animals die, the clan will grow hungry. And if we are hungry, then so are others. Bands of men will come looking for food. My father believes we will live in fear until the day when all the clans are united. Only when the clans are united, as they were in the beginning and as they were under Kabul, will we live in peace."

A few generations earlier, Kabul, the former leader of the Borjigin clan, had united the steppe clans. He and his army were defeated, however, after warring with the Golden Emperor, the leader of the kingdom encompassing the lands and cities south of the Gobi. The Golden Emperor and his army disbanded the Borjigin clan and killed Kabul and his family.

"Why doesn't your father unite the clans?" Temujin asked.

"He doesn't think it's possible, at least not in his lifetime," Jamuka said. "There are too many clans. Each clan has a white-bone leader who believes it's his destiny to rule the steppe. He believes the clan leaders will only step aside for someone who clearly possesses heaven's mandate, for someone chosen by Tengri."

Tengri, the Mongol God, resided in the Eternal Blue Sky along with the spirits of those who'd gone before. Together, they watched over the people of the steppe.

"Your father doesn't possess this mandate?"

Jamuka shook his head. "When such a leader appears, my father says his abilities will be clear to all. He will become more than Gur Khan."

"More than khan of all khans?" Temujin asked. "How is that possible?"

"With heaven's mandate, this leader will become ruler of both earth and sky, a true Chinggis Khan," Jamuka said.

"*Chinggis* Khan?"

Jamuka nodded. "My father believes it is my destiny to rule earth and sky, to become . . . a Chinggis Khan."

3

*I have seen the tomb of Chinggis Khan. It is on the side of the
Lu-kou-ho; mountains and rivers surround it. It is reported that
Chinggis Khan was born there and that for that reason, on his death
he was buried there; I do not know if it be true or not.*

—**Hsü T'ing,** Chinese envoy, 1236

Andrews stood in Abbey Conrad's office on the downtown
campus of Ulaanbaatar University.

"I told you they're making a big deal out of it,"
Abbey said.

On the office computer, Andrews and Abbey were
watching a newscast of the helicopter's arrival. On the screen,
Andrews stood by the helicopter, answering questions. The
shaman dropped to his knees. The reporters swarmed forward.

"I underestimated the importance of finding remains on
Burkhan Khaldun—any remains," Andrews said. "I should've
said we found nothing."

"Which is what you tried to do," Abbey said. "Come on,
let's see what you've got."

They walked down the hallway into the lab. Using sterile
technique, Abbey placed a towel on a workbench. Andrews,
donning a pair of gloves, removed the bone from the cooler
and set it on the towel.

"That's it?" Abbey asked. "I imagined something more."

"Like an entire skeleton?"

"In full battle regalia," she said.

Abbey took measurements and pictures. After snapping
her last photo, she slipped on a pair of gloves. "I'll get some

of the marrow in media," she said. "I can start analyzing it tomorrow."

Andrews watched as Abbey deftly curetted the marrow from the bone. A Yale-trained PhD scientist, she'd moved to Mongolia eight years earlier to set up the country's first molecular biology laboratory. After falling in love with the country, she'd taken a permanent position at the university.

Abbey turned. "No hikes this summer?"

Each summer, Andrews typically led four or five day-hikes, which were sponsored by the Asian Historical Society. Parker had suggested the hikes as an opportunity to glad-hand donors. The hikes were an unwelcome intrusion on Andrews's busy summer schedule, but Abbey's frequent presence made them tolerable.

Andrews shook his head. "Being on the mountain for the whole month made it impossible to get away for just a day."

"And you're flying back tonight?" she asked.

He nodded.

Abbey divided the curettings between separate cups. Capping one of the cups, she placed it into a plastic bag, which she handed to him. As part of Andrews's agreement with the Mongolian Institute of Geography, he was required to turn over all organic findings to Abbey's lab for analysis, but there was no stipulation that she couldn't give some back.

"Thanks," he said.

Abbey continued her work, drilling a core from the bone. "On the mountain, I saw you had company," she said.

"Hayley Robbins, an archaeology instructor from UCLA," Andrews said. "She and her students were traveling the countryside doing research on Genghis Khan when their jeep got stuck."

"They didn't know you shouldn't attempt to find Burkhan Khaldun without a guide?"

"No," he said. "I guess they learned that lesson the hard way."

Abbey picked up a test tube filled with growth media and dropped in the core. Giving the tube a small shake, she held it up to the light. "It appeared she was pretty."

"Who?"

"The archaeologist," she said, turning toward him. "*Hay*-ley."

Andrews's temples burned.

"How long was she there?" Abbey asked.

"Two weeks," he answered, angry that he appeared embarrassed. "She and her students helped with the dig. In fact, *Hay*-ley and I were digging together when I found the bone."

Abbey looked away. Setting down the tube, she tore off her gloves. "Let me walk you out," she said.

Andrews followed her into the hallway. When Abbey came to an abrupt stop, he almost ran into her.

Reaching out, he pushed back her shoulder-length hair. "What's wrong?" he asked.

She turned toward him, her brown eyes glaring, accusing. My God. Was she jealous?

"James!"

They both turned. Parker Winthrop stood in the doorway to Abbey's office, watching them. The former marine, unshaven, had a crew cut, his black hair peppered with gray. "You should see this," Parker said, pointing into the office, where the television broadcast was still running on the computer. "The Mongolian interior minister is commenting on your find."

"Be there in a second," Andrews said.

Parker remained in place. He raised an eyebrow. "The bone," he said. "Who do you think it belongs to?"

"Probably a peasant shot by the Soviets for trespassing," Andrews replied.

In 1924, Mongolia was the first country to fall behind the Iron Curtain. The Soviets, to prevent Burkhan Khaldun from becoming a rallying point for Mongolian nationalists, designated the mountain and surrounding territory as a Highly Restricted Area. The Soviets used it to build missile, tank, and jet bases until their collapse in 1990.

Parker gave a thoughtful nod before disappearing through the doorway.

"What makes him think he can just walk into my office

like that?" Abbey asked. She stepped forward, but Andrews held out a hand. "I called him," he said. "He's giving me a ride back to the airport. Baabar had to take off."

"Next time, I'll give you a ride," she said. "Just please don't ask him to come back here again."

Andrews nodded. "Sure."

Abbey took a calming breath. "Well, I guess this is it, for another year."

"It is."

She extended her arms. They embraced.

"How's that biochemist down the hall?" he asked.

"Fine, I guess," she said. *"Why?"*

"I thought you two were—"

"What? No!" Abbey said, stepping back.

"What about that English literature professor?"

She shook her head. "There's been nobody since—" She glanced toward the open doorway where Parker had been standing.

"But, that was six years ago."

She nodded.

Although Mongolia was located on the other side of the world from her family's home in Connecticut, Andrews had never imagined Abbey being lonely, certainly not unattached. During the hikes, there had always been someone at her side.

"I—I had no idea," he said.

Abbey stepped forward and kissed him gently on the cheek. "And you don't now," she whispered.

4

*The Mongol conquests were not only the most far-reaching in world
history; they also had the most radical consequences.*

—**Leo de Hartog, 1989** *Genghis Khan: Conqueror of the World*

Andrews stood in the front of the main lecture hall of
the University of Virginia's Archaeology Studies
Building. It was the Tuesday after Labor Day, the
first day of fall classes. The hall was full. After the stir in
Ulaanbaatar had hit the world news, enrollment for his
course, Introduction to Modern Asian History, had doubled.

On the lecture hall screen was a map of the eastern
hemisphere as it had been divided in the twelfth century. "In
1162, at the time of Genghis Khan's birth, the Mongols were
a multitude of warring tribes," Andrews said, circling Central
Asia with a laser pointer. "Asia was an amalgamation of small
kingdoms. Europe was rooted in the Dark Ages. Just over a
century later, by the time of the death of Genghis Khan's
grandson, Kublai Khan, the Mongols had combined the
kingdoms in Southeast Asia, Xinxiang, Manchuria, and Tibet
to form China. They'd united multiple, warring Slavic city-
states into modern-day Russia. They'd established alliances
and drawn the boundaries for the countries of Afghanistan,
Kazakhstan, Hungary, Syria, Poland, Turkey, and Iran."

Andrews turned from the map and scanned the students.
Most were freshman. They all stared attentively back, taking
notes while tapping away on laptops or tablets. If any were
hungover from their Labor Day weekend festivities, they were
hiding it well.

"Most importantly, however, as the Mongols marched across Eurasia, they soaked up the best technologies of the people they conquered and applied them on a larger scale than anyone before," Andrews continued. "Using European bell casting technology and Song Dynasty gunpowder, they made cannons. Using Korean printing technology, a simplified Uighur script, and Chinese paper, they mass-produced agricultural manuals, almanacs, atlases, novels, and textbooks on mathematics, history, and law. Not held back by the archaic whims of priests, imams, or rabbis, they used Indian mathematics and Persian astronomy to build the best calendars and maps the world had ever seen.

"In his book, *Genghis Khan and the Making of the Modern World,* Jack Weatherford said, 'On every level and from any perspective, the scale and scope of Genghis Khan's accomplishments challenge the limits of imagination and tax the resources of scholarly explanation.'"

Andrews paused. "In 1995, the *Washington Post* conducted a survey of historians to determine the most influential man of the millennium. Genghis Khan won, hands down."

"Over Columbus?" someone asked.

"A distant second," Andrews said. "But even Columbus's discovery of the New World was a byproduct of Genghis Khan's success. After the fragmentation of the Mongol Empire, trade along the Silk Road disintegrated. Columbus's voyage was an attempt to re-establish a trade route between Europe and China."

Several hands went up.

"And yes, Genghis Khan was also believed to have more impact than George Washington, Churchill, Lenin, even Charlottesville's own Thomas Jefferson," Andrews said.

As hands dropped, the students began talking among themselves.

"Okay," Andrews said, sensing the skepticism. "Who can tell me what sparked the Renaissance?"

Hands popped up. "Printing and the dissemination of information . . . the end of feudalism . . . a de-emphasis of the church . . . nationalism," the students answered.

"Very good," Andrews said. "But where did all these new ideas regarding governing and philosophy come from? Why did Europe's monarchies do away with armored knights and walled cities? Why did Michelangelo paint the way he did?"

No one replied.

"The Mongols brought ideas on participatory government and a secular state to the West, concepts they'd already put into practice," Andrews said. "Walled cities became outdated after the Mongols built elaborate siege machines and catapults that were able to circumvent the most fortified walls. Knights became obsolete after Mongol warriors slaughtered tens of thousands of Eastern European soldiers. European artists, influenced by Persian and Chinese art brought by the Mongols, began experimenting with using light and depth in new ways."

Pacing the front of the lecture hall, Andrews stopped. "In 1620, the English scientist Francis Bacon concluded three things led to the Renaissance: the compass, gunpowder, and printing. The Mongols brought all three to Europe."

He walked to the podium. "Genghis Khan is the greatest conqueror the world has ever known. He conquered more than twice as much territory as Alexander the Great, Hannibal, Napoleon, Attila, or Caesar. The reason we'll spend the first several lectures of this course focusing on the Mongols, however, extends far beyond simple conquests."

Andrews advanced the screen to the next slide. The word *Chinggis* appeared.

"In some academic publications and Asian references, you'll notice this spelling for Genghis," he said. "For our purposes, I'll continue to use the conventional westernized spelling and pronunciation for Genghis Khan. But this spelling is actually a closer transliteration of the Mongol pronunciation of his name."

He advanced to the next image, the course reading list.

"Among the books I would like for you to read, you'll notice a biography, *Genghis Khan: Life, Death, and Resurrection.* Its author, John Man, said: 'To research the effects of the Mongol Empire today is to become the historical equivalent of a radio astronomer, listening for whispers of the Big Bang.'

"In this semester, I ask that as our discussions move into current events and we attempt to understand modern-day Eurasia, you keep in mind the influence of the Mongols," Andrews said. "To forget them would be the equivalent of being John Man's astronomer, gazing up into space and attempting to understand the existence and movements of the galaxies . . . without considering their origin."

5

*When they are carrying the body of any emperor to be buried
with the others, the convoy that goes with the body doth put to the sword
all whom they fall in with on the road. When Möngke Khan died,
twenty thousand were killed.*

—**Marco Polo,** 1300

Following his class, Andrews walked from the lecture hall to the molecular biology laboratory. Sara Johnson, the lab's chief technician, sat next to the DNA gene sequencer.

"I can take over," Andrews said.

After Andrews had flown back a week earlier to Charlottesville, he and Sara had begun analyzing the bone. They'd successfully extracted DNA and amplified a Y chromosome, indicating the bone belonged to a male. They'd then begun sequencing the Y chromosome at fifteen separate sites, searching for the Khan markers—specific DNA sequences believed to belong to Genghis Khan and his male descendants.

"Thanks," Sara said, stretching and yawning.

"How was camping?" Andrews asked.

Sara and her fiancé, Ron, had spent the Labor Day weekend hiking in the Blue Ridge Mountains. "It was great but tiring," she said. She motioned toward the gene sequencer. "It looks like you came in."

Andrews nodded. "I ran a couple of the DNA markers. I wanted to make sure we finish the testing before I leave for the ICA next week," he said, referring to the annual meeting of the International College of Archaeologists. "I was asked to give a presentation on this summer's dig. Other than

30

photos of empty excavation sites and a few fragments of tile, I don't have much to talk about. The bone is my only organic finding."

"Where's the meeting this year?" Sara asked.

"Paris."

She sat up. "Are you serious? You lucky dog. A summer in Mongolia and now a week in Paris. No fair."

Andrews shrugged. "I just go where they tell me."

Sara tore a paper off the sequencer and handed it to him. "With the two markers that you ran that makes a total of three matches. Twelve more to go."

As Andrews looked at the paper, Sara stared up at him, her chin in her hand.

"What is it?" he asked.

"Whatever happened to that visiting professor you were dating?"

"She's no longer visiting. She went back to Florida."

"Did you know she was leaving?" Sara asked.

"By definition."

"But you dated her anyway?"

Andrews nodded.

"You do that a lot."

"Date?"

"No," she said. "Date people who are leaving. Before her, you went out with that pediatric resident. I really liked her. What happened to her?"

"She's practicing in Phoenix."

Sara smiled, her point made. Over the past few years, she and Andrews had spent countless hours together in the lab. The normal boundaries between faculty member and lab technician had long ago disappeared.

"You dated a third-year surgery resident," he said.

Sara leaned back and held up her left hand, her long black hair draping over the back of the chair. "But Ron was never just a boyfriend," she said, admiring her engagement ring. "He's different. He always was."

"It's a college town," Andrews said. "People come and most people go. Except for a precocious few, marriage is something that'll happen in the future, after they settle down."

Sara nodded absentmindedly, still looking at the ring.

"Have you heard from Abbey?" he asked.

Abbey had also extracted a Y chromosome from the bone and begun testing for the Khan markers.

Sara sat up, a concerned look on her face. "Did you two have a fight?"

"No. Why?"

"It's strange," she said. "Besides me, Abbey Conrad is the only other steady female in your life. But she lives in Mongolia. And you only go there for a month every year."

"Abbey's strictly a colleague, a friend."

"Really?" Sara said. "Every year, you always manage to keep a dialogue going after you come back. Either you leave something with her or she gives something to you."

"As part of my hiking and digging permits from the Mongolian Institute, I'm required to turn over any organic findings to her for analysis," Andrews said.

"So, nothing happened this trip that wasn't *strictly* friendly?" Sara asked.

"Nope."

Sara gave a disappointed nod. She stood and pointed toward the sequencer. "It's in cycle four," she said. She picked up her bike helmet and backpack. "It'll need new primers in about ten minutes. By the way, something came for you." She gestured toward the break room.

Andrews walked into the room. On the table was a single white rose sitting in a vase. An envelope, previously opened, was attached.

James, I'm sorry. Still friends? Abbey
P.S. DYS389I, DYS389b, DYS390, DYS391.
All four sites match! Wow! ☺

Andrews pulled out his cell phone. He took a picture of the rose and sent it to Abbey, typing in the caption, *Friends, Always. Thanks, James.*

"It's illegal to read other people's mail," he shouted.

"Sorry," Sara said. She was standing in the doorway, watching him. "I thought Ron sent it. And it *was* addressed to the lab." She smiled. "When do you leave for your conference?"

"Saturday afternoon."

"I'll make sure I finish the testing before then."

"Thanks, Sara."

"No problem." With a wave, she left.

Andrews sat at the break room table by the computer. After logging into his e-mail account, he began typing.

```
To: abbeyconrad@ubu.com
From: jandrews@uva.edu
Subject: DNA results
Abbey,

DYS437, DYS438, DYS439. All match!
I have to admit, I'm surprised.
Eight more to go.
James
```

Based on the combined work of the two labs, they'd determined the sequences at seven of the fifteen Y chromosome sites: DYS389I, DYS389b, DYS390, DYS391, DYS437, DYS438, and DYS439. Thus far, the sequences at each of the seven sites matched with the Khan markers.

As Andrews hit "Send" on the computer, his cell phone buzzed. It was Abbey. He checked the time. It was almost midnight in Ulaanbaatar.

"Shouldn't you be sleeping?" he answered.

"I was just crawling into bed when I got your message," she said. "I see you received my peace offering."

"I didn't know we were at war."

"We're not," Abbey said. "It's just we didn't have the smoothest of goodbyes. I don't want there to be any hard feelings between us."

"You don't have to worry about hard feelings on my end," he said.

"That's nice to hear, James, Thanks."

Abbey suddenly laughed.

"What is it?" he asked.

"I'm reading your e-mail," she said. "The DNA findings are surprising."

"I agree."

"Did you send the bone for carbon dating?"

"Yes," he said. "The results should be interesting."

"They should be."

Neither spoke for a few seconds.

"Well," she said. "I just called to say I received your—"

"Abbey," he interrupted.

"Yes?"

"Do you ever think about coming back to the United States?"

"Sure . . . sometimes."

"We've talked about bringing in a PhD molecular biologist to run the department's lab," he said. "You'd be perfect. But if you're not interested in Charlottesville, you could work wherever you wanted. Your research is world class."

"That's nice of you to say," she said. "And thanks for the offer. But if my research is world class, it's because of where I do it. Right now, I enjoy my work here. I'm sure I'll move back someday, but I'm not quite ready—not yet, at least."

"If you're ever interested in Charlottesville, let me know," he said. "I'll do my best to make it happen."

"I know you will," she said.

"Good night, Abbey."

"Good night, James."

Andrews ended the call. He remained at the break room table, staring at the white rose. His thoughts turned to his first meeting with Abbey. It had hung over them, shadowing everything since.

It was a Friday night, his first summer in Mongolia. Parker had taken him to an Ulaanbaatar nightclub filled with expatriates. Strobe lights flashed as Nirvana's "Lithium" blared from speakers.

After walking through the club, he and Parker stood

side by side on a balcony looking over the dance floor. Parker had introduced him to an agricultural scientist consulting for Mongolia's herding consortium, research analysts from Chase Manhattan and Goldman Sachs, an evangelical minister from World Missions, and an engineer from Mobil. From their perch, Parker had pointed out an engineering team from Monsanto, three congressmen from the United States House of Representatives, and groups of businessmen from Australia, Germany, and Japan.

"What are they all doing here?" Andrews asked.

"They can see where the future battle lines will be drawn," Parker said. "They want to be part of it." He turned. "Over the next two decades, what country do you think will have the greatest rate of economic growth?"

"China?"

Parker pointed a forefinger downward. "Mongolia. This place is going to take off like a son of a bitch. Mongolia has huge reserves of copper, gold, silver, and uranium. They have 10 percent of the world's coal. Some believe they also have huge oil deposits. The multinational oil companies, investment banks, and large mining companies—China Shenhua, Rio Tinto, Billiton—are just surveying the situation right now, literally and figuratively, but they'll figure it out. When they do, they'll go to town. Some say it's analogous to the California gold rush. But I think it's more like Berlin after World War II. Everyone is circling. They want to make sure they get a sector, their piece of the pie."

"What about the Mongolians?" Andrews asked. "It's their country."

"Road kill," Parker said with a flick of his hand. "There's too much money involved. The few Mongolians who see what's coming will sell out and get rich. Most don't stand a chance."

"Seems rather pessimistic," Andrews said.

"It's *realistic*," Parker said. "China has over five hundred times as many people as Mongolia. At best, Mongolia will remain Mongolia, but in name only. Christ! The United States is worried about being overrun by China. What do you think will happen to Mongolia?"

"Then, why is everyone else here?" Andrews asked.

"They all have their reasons," Parker said. "The right-wing aide agencies moved in after the Soviet collapse and have been doing everything they can to foster democracy and capitalism. The missionaries are in their typical, self-righteous fervor, trying to convert the country to Christianity. The multinationals don't care who's running the country. They simply want to get their stake in early enough." He pointed toward the three US congressmen. "And they're here because Mongolia is strategically as important as hell. It's an island of democracy and capitalism situated between Russia and China. Zamyn-Üüd in southeast Mongolia is only 260 miles from downtown Beijing. The US doesn't know exactly what they want to do, but in the growing cold war with China, they love the possibilities. Do we protect Mongolia? Do we ask them to join NATO?"

"What's your interest in Mongolia?" Andrews asked.

Parker grinned. "You've read the society's mission statement. To use history to build a better—"

"No," Andrews said. "Why are you here? Parker Winthrop?"

"Do you know how much some of these consultants get paid?" Parker asked, jerking a thumb toward the nearest group. "It's mind-blowing. For the next few years, I plan to keep my ear to the ground, continue making contacts, and see what happens."

"Winthrop Consulting?" Andrews said.

Parker looked down toward the dance floor, suddenly distracted. "Yes, something like that," he said. "Come here. There's someone I want you to meet."

Andrews followed Parker down the stairs and through the crowd to a woman. She was looking out over the dance floor, moving in rhythm with the music. Her short black dress hugged the curves of her hips. When Parker tapped her on the shoulder, she turned.

She had brilliant brown eyes and short, spiked hair.

On each ear were multiple rings along with a diamond stud through her right eyebrow.

"This is Abbey Conrad, a molecular biologist," Parker shouted above the music. He turned toward Abbey. "And this is James Andrews, an archaeology grad student from Charlottesville. The society is funding his dig in Avarga."

Andrews and Abbey shook hands. Parker suddenly reached into his pocket and pulled out a ringing cell phone. "I've got to take this. I'll be right back." He walked away.

"Did I hear that right?" Andrews asked. "You're a molecular biologist?"

"In training," she replied.

"From where?"

"Yale."

"Really?"

"And you're an archaeologist," she said, ignoring his surprised look. "You must be here for Khan's tomb and his treasure."

He shook his head. "When Genghis Khan died, the Mongols didn't even have a word for 'tomb.' It seems unlikely he was buried in one. Also, he was too practical, too Mongolian, a nomad. He didn't hoard wealth during his life. I doubt he thought he'd need it for the afterlife."

Abbey nodded thoughtfully.

"Too much information?" he asked.

"A bit," she said. "But don't get me started on automated thermal DNA cyclers."

They laughed.

"Would you like to dance?" he asked.

Her eyes briefly registered surprise. As she looked up at him, he imagined she was wondering if he was like the other expatriates at the club, interested in mining Mongolia for his own benefit: exorbitant consulting fees, untapped natural resources, minds to indoctrinate, or souls to convert. When she nodded, he felt as though he'd passed some sort of test.

They danced for a few songs before deciding to get a drink. As they walked toward the bar, however, someone asked Abbey to dance. To Andrews's surprise, she accepted.

With a nod in his direction, she walked back to the dance floor.

Andrews bought a beer. He found an open spot at a counter that overlooked the dance floor. As he sat and nursed the beer, his gaze settled on Abbey. She was mesmerizing. Unfortunately, he wasn't the only one who thought so. For the remainder of the night, she was surrounded by a seemingly never-ending string of suitors. If he wanted to talk to her again, he would have to stand in line.

Late that night, he checked his watch. He still planned on driving back to Avarga, where they would start digging early in the morning. Deciding to call it a night, he headed toward the door. Abbey appeared, blocking his path. "Would you like to dance?"

A new song had started. He glanced toward the dance floor. "No one from your entourage is interested?"

"I can go check, if you'd like?" she asked.

"That's all right, but are you sure? It's a slow one."

"I love the Pretenders," she said. She took his hand and pulled him into the middle of the crowded dance floor. Turning, she wrapped her arms around his neck. He circled his arms around her waist.

"An archaeologist who doesn't search for treasure and who likes to dance to Green Day and Nirvana," she said, recalling the previous songs they'd danced to. "That's a rare combination."

"Not as rare as finding a molecular biologist in Mongolia from Yale with nine earrings and one of these," he said, tapping the stud through her eyebrow.

Abbey playfully brushed his hand away. "Only seven," she said. She moved closer, setting her cheek against his chest.

They remained that way for the rest of the song, moving slowly together. When there was silence, she looked unabashedly up at him, her eyes gleaming with tears. "Told you I love that song," she said. She brushed at a wet spot on his shirt. "Sorry."

"You okay?" he asked.

"I'm fine," she said.

While the DJ fumbled at the controls, they remained on the dance floor, the crowd pushing them together, him watching her, her pretending to watch everyone else. After several moments, she finally met his gaze and smiled, acknowledging his nearness and comfortable with it.

"I still owe you that drink. Or better yet . . . let's get out of here," he said, the alcohol giving him a burst of courage.

Abbey gave an abrupt laugh. *"Leave?"*

When he realized she was looking past him, he turned. Parker Winthrop stood behind him.

"Thanks," Parker said, patting him on the shoulder. "I'll take over from here."

During Andrews's first two summers in Mongolia, for every humanitarian cause, political movement, drought, or famine, the Asian Historical Society had a fundraiser. For every coming or going, special occasion, accomplishment, or milestone within the small expatriate community, there had been a party. And Abbey and Parker were at the heart of them all, with Abbey playing the role of queen bee.

Two to three times a week, Andrews found himself making the drive back and forth between Avarga and Ulaanbaatar. He went because he was young, and the fundraisers and parties seemed important and exciting. With time, however, he came to believe Abbey was playing a role with Parker. Always the center of attention and always reveling in it, she was the pampered debutante: fun-loving, entitled, and carefree. Andrews wondered if Abbey was trying to prove she was more than just a bookish molecular biologist. He wondered if for her everything was also exciting and new.

After Andrews's second summer in Mongolia, Abbey and Parker split up. The breakup cast a shadow over the expatriate community. The parties came to an end.

Andrews continued staring at the white rose. He recalled his recent goodbye with Abbey. "And you don't now," she'd whispered in his ear.

Even now, the memory of the press of her lips against his cheek, her breath in his ear, pounded through his chest.

Abbey's once-spiked hair was long. Her piercings were gone. She wasn't as flamboyant or chic as she'd been that first summer, but she was still beautiful, even more so.

1171 Central Asia

"First one across the river will become ruler of the steppe," Jamuka said.

It was winter. Temujin and Jamuka stood at the edge of a frozen, winding river, their breaths condensing in the air above them. Each wore bones strapped to the bottoms of their shoes. They sprinted across the ice and slid, crashing simultaneously into a snow bank on the far side of the river. The boys lay in the bank, laughing.

Temujin removed an ivory-handled knife from his belt. The knife was studded with blue stones. He spread out his hand. With the knife's tip, he carved a line on his palm.

Jamuka grabbed Temujin's hand and sucked the blood away. When the bleeding stopped, Temujin handed the knife to Jamuka.

Jamuka held the knife above his own hand. When his hand began to shake, he set his jaw and jabbed the knife into his palm. Temujin sucked the blood away.

Temujin then gave Jamuka a cypress arrowhead. Jamuka presented Temujin with a whistling arrowhead made from a calf's horn.

"We've exchanged gifts and shared the food that cannot be digested," Temujin said as they slapped hands. "We're *andas*. A bond that can never be broken."

6

The Chinese are in the process of making a peaceful conquest of the Russian Far East.

—**Pavel Grachev,** *Russian Defense Minister*

Baabar stood in a crowded second-floor room of Ulaanbaatar's Government House alongside deputies from Mongolia's other major political parties. They were witnessing the signing of the Goodwill Treaty. In the middle of the paneled room, Mongolian President Tuminai Mandir sat with the Chinese foreign minister, who glanced nervously toward the sound of chanting coming from the window.

"This is a monumental day for our people," Mandir said, louder than necessary. "Another step away from the darkness of Soviet repression, another step forward with our brothers to the south."

The treaty guaranteed eighty trillion tugriks in yearly assistance from China. In return, the export taxes on raw minerals shipped to China and tariffs on imported Chinese goods would be eliminated. The number of Chinese work visas would also no longer be restricted.

Signature pages lay on the blotter. Mandir signed each and slid them across the table. With a tentative smile, the foreign minister nodded and then also signed.

There was a sudden commotion at a window, where several Chinese delegation members were looking outside. The foreign minister strode to one of the windows. The others did likewise.

The scene spread before them was Beijing's colonial nightmare. Grand Chinggis Khan Square was filled. One Mongolia banners rippled over a sea of people. Demonstrators waved the flags of the Chinese autonomous regions that had been increasingly pressing Beijing for independence: Eastern Turkmenistan, Inner Mongolia, Xinxiang, Taiwan, and Tibet. Near the equestrian statue of Damdin Sükhbaatar, the leader who'd declared Mongolia's independence from China in 1921, dozens danced around a burning Chinese flag.

"One Mongolia?" a Chinese delegation member snickered. "What does that mean? Are they proposing we give them Inner Mongolia?"

Demonstrators near Sükhbaatar's statue lifted a wheelchair-bound man onto a platform. Baabar swelled with pride. It was Navaandorjiin Mikou, the elderly founder and chairman of the Republican Democracy Party, Baabar's party and the chief rival of the current majority party, President Mandir's Communist People's Revolutionary Party.

The crowd quieted.

"When the Soviet curtain was pulled from our country, it presented opportunity," Mikou said, his amplified voice resounding over the square. "It also exposed our nation's soft underbelly. When we should have sought to protect our native industries, we welcomed in the wolves. Asked to compete with subsidized Chinese manufacturing, our prized cashmere, leather, and wool industries have collapsed. We did this at the behest of the international donor agencies: the Asian Development bank, the World Bank, the IMF."

The crowd erupted into a chorus of boos.

"These ideologues knew nothing of our country and nothing of our heritage," Mikou continued. "They came with money in one hand and a whip in the other. Like good sheep, we've followed our masters' commands. We've built an open, free market with unchecked capitalism. We've built a market that's less regulated than any country in the world. *But where has it led us?* Today, our country receives the highest levels of aid per capita of any in the world, but a third of our people live below the poverty line."

There were more boos.

"Our country has become China's warehouse for natural resources. They buy our raw materials for a pittance and sell them back for profit as manufactured goods. When we raise export taxes, they smuggle our cashmere, copper, gold, and wool from the country. Their workers infiltrate our ranks. They own our businesses. They poach our wildlife, pollute our rivers, and cut our timber."

The crowd roared its disapproval.

"When the Soviet curtain was lifted from our country, it presented opportunity. Little did we think it would not be for Mongolia," Mikou said. He raised a bony fist toward Government House. "President Mandir! Do not be seduced by the enemy. Their tongues lure us forward with promises, but their teeth are razor sharp."

The Chinese foreign minister turned and glared at President Mandir, who in turn nodded to his security advisor. The advisor spoke into a walkie-talkie.

Within moments, the high-pitched screech of whistles filled the square. Police rushed into the crowd.

Seconds later, there were gunshots followed by screams. A few policemen dropped.

Then, as if on cue, a wall of protestors formed. Several held Molotov cocktails. Lighting them, they rushed forward and threw them into the air.

Behind the second floor windows of Government House, Baabar stood frozen with the Mongolian and Chinese delegation members. They watched as the flaming cocktails rose high into the air . . . and arced toward them.

7

*Near the ruins of the dead city of Khara-Khoto in the Gobi Desert,
the great Khan's bones lie in a silver coffin, which rests upon
the seventy-eight crowns of Princes and Khans who he conquered.*

—***Montreal Gazette,*** October 31, 1927

overnment House alarms sounded. Guards led the
Mongolian and Chinese delegation members from
the second floor room deeper into the building.
Baabar broke away from the others. He ran down a stairwell
and through a front exit. Emerging into the square, he was
enveloped by clouds of tear gas, the smell of kerosene, and
the wail of sirens. Ambulances and police cars raced back and
forth as screaming protestors ran in every direction.

Baabar scanned the pandemonium, his gaze fixing on
a lone firefighter moving steadily through the crowd. The
fireman, his back bent, pulled a hose from a truck parked at
the base of Government House. The fireman lifted the nozzle
toward the burning façade. A protestor tackled him. As the
fireman tried to stand, other protestors knocked him back to
the ground.

Baabar rushed forward. With a sidelong dive, he knocked
two of the protestors down. Before Baabar could climb to his
feet, however, others were over him, cursing him, kicking and
punching.

There was a shrill whistle. The assailants ran off.

The fireman was on the ground, a whistle between his
lips, wincing as he held his right leg. He thrust a forefinger
toward the hose.

Baabar ran and picked up the hose. Opening the valve, he directed the emerging arc of water toward Government House.

For the next several minutes, he beat back the fire. The flames gradually dissipated, giving way to black and then white smoke. When additional firemen arrived, one of them took the hose.

Disheveled and wet, Baabar looked around the square. The injured fireman had been carried away. Most demonstrators were gone. The majority of those that remained huddled over the injured.

A woman stood several feet away, watching him, a camera and press credentials dangling around her neck. "Representative Onon," she said. "Do you have a minute?"

Baabar ran a hand over his ribs, flinching in pain. He began walking toward Government House.

"How would you describe what happened here today?" the woman asked. She extended a handheld tape recorder.

They stopped as several policemen sprinted by.

"Unfortunate," Baabar said. His suit was scuffed and torn. He slipped off his jacket and loosened his tie. "This was an opportunity for the Mongolian people to speak, for the world to hear. This was not the message we wanted to send."

"Do you agree with the speech of your party chairman?"

"Of course," Baabar said. "As a member of parliament, I did everything I could to prevent the signing of the Goodwill Treaty. But I don't agree with this." He looked over the square. "We're a small country. We have to work together to accomplish our goals. We must work within the law."

They began walking up the steps.

"Today started as a peaceful demonstration, but only turned violent *after* police intervention," the woman said. "Why would Mongolian police crush an anti-Chinese demonstration? How was Government House's response any different than Beijing's to protests in Inner Mongolia, Xinxiang, or Tibet?"

"I'm not sure," Baabar said. "But that's the beauty of our democracy. There are some who would rather see the country burn than grant concessions to Beijing. These people need to know there's an alternative. National elections are in a few days. If they don't like the direction the country has taken, they can vote for change."

"If your Republican Democracy Party became the majority party, would you assume an anti-Chinese stance?" she asked.

"We would maintain our current *pro-Mongolian* stance," Baabar said. "As long as China recognizes Mongolia as an independent, sovereign nation, our relations with Beijing will be the same as they are with Washington, Moscow, or any other foreign government."

They reached the top of the steps. Baabar stopped and looked up at the bronze statue of Genghis Khan. "But if China thinks they can roll over us, if they think we'll be their next autonomous region, they'll discover our desire for independence is far greater than they could ever imagine."

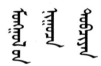

1171 Central Asia

Temujin lay motionless in the grass, staring intently toward a burrow. He held his fingers to his lips and made a series of whistling noises.

From the burrow, a marmot's head appeared. Temujin nocked his arrow. As he did, he heard his father's voice.

Wait.

Temujin whistled again. The marmot rose farther into the air. It was fat, its fur thick. Standing on its hind feet, the animal stretched, searching for the source of the noise.

Not yet.

His father had taught him the importance of knowing the weakness of his prey. The marmot's weakness was its curiosity. Temujin made a small chirping sound. The marmot's head swiveled toward him.

Now!

He released the arrow. Running after it, he found the marmot next to the burrow, the arrow through its chest. Temujin turned, expecting to see his father walking behind him, nodding his approval.

Instead, the grassy plain was empty.

A week earlier, Temujin and his father had been hunting when they stopped to eat with a group of travelers. While sharing food with the travelers, three men, Temujin's father became sick. The travelers had poisoned him. Before the three men rode off, leaving his father to a painful death, they told Temujin they were brothers of a man his father had killed in battle.

Temujin knelt on the grass and removed his arrow from the marmot. With his knife, he gutted the animal and threw the entrails aside. He carried the carcass to his horse, adding it to a string with four others.

His younger brother, Khasar, suddenly appeared over a rise, riding quickly. "The Tayichiut are leaving!" Khasar yelled.

Temujin jumped onto his horse. The brothers spurred their horses toward the camp.

Before Temujin left the valley that morning, it had been filled with gers—the clan's circular tentlike dwellings. As the brothers rode into the valley, only two gers remained.

Temujin's mother, Hoelun, stood with his younger brothers and sisters outside one ger while his father's first wife stood with his two half brothers, Begter and Belgütei, outside the other. They watched as the Tayichiut rode slowly away.

His father had left behind two wives and seven children. It was steppe custom that when a man died, his wives and children would be absorbed into the clan. With the oldest of the children being only twelve, however, the clan's burden was too much.

Temujin stopped at his mother's side. She sat on horseback, looking down at his father's *sulde*, his horse-tailed spirit banner, in the palm of her hand. She watched the banner's longhaired strands dance back and forth in the breeze, nodding her head and smiling, lost in a distant memory.

"Mother?"

Hoelun looked up, her gaze suddenly lucid. "Stay here," she said. "Watch the others." With a yelp, she spurred her horse forward. She held the spirit banner high and circled the Tayichiut.

A clan elder and friend of his father, Charaqa, rode to the front of the Tayichiut procession. He spoke with Kiriltuk, the leader. Charaqa made frequent gestures back toward the family and up into the Eternal Blue Sky. It appeared the elder was making a good argument for them. Then, Kiriltuk began yelling. When one of Kiriltuk's men raised his spear, Charaqa rode hard away. Kiriltuk and several men took off in pursuit.

Charaqa rode past the family. While the other family members cheered, Temujin leaped from his horse and grabbed a spear. Running ahead, he positioned himself in Charaqa's wake.

"Temujin!" his mother screamed from across the field. "Stay back!"

Ignoring his mother's plea, he focused on Kiriltuk. Once again, he heard his father's voice. *"Wait . . . wait . . . Not yet . . . Now!"*

Temujin hurled the spear. It sailed toward Kiriltuk, narrowly missing him.

Kiriltuk raised his whip and swung at Temujin. Temujin dodged the blow and the remaining horsemen, then turned and watched as they descended on Charaqa.

A Tayichiut warrior released an arrow, striking Charaqa in the back. The elder toppled from the horse.

The family rushed to Charaqa's side. Hoelun tried to staunch the flow of blood, but it seeped inexorably onto the grass.

As the light dimmed from Charaqa's eyes, Temujin turned to the north and watched Kiriltuk and the Tayichiut ride away. He felt the cool wind on his face and shivered, knowing the cold air meant winter . . . and that being alone during winter, without a clan and without a father, meant death.

8

*Genghis Khan was hunting and saw a solitary tree. The sight of
that tree pleased him, and he sat for an hour under it. Within himself
he was moved by it and thus gave his orders: "This place is suitable
for my burial; remember it."*

—Rashid al-din, 1306, Persian historian

Andrews sat at a desk in the front of a classroom in the
Archaeology Studies Building. Students from his Introduction to Modern Asian History class filed inside for
their first Q&A session.

When everyone had settled, Andrews leaned back in his
chair. "Any problems so far?"

The students glanced at one another. When no one spoke,
Andrews stood. "This is a history class," he said. "By definition,
we'll be retrospective. You'll learn the basic framework of
Asian history. But if there's one thing I hope you take away
from this course, it's that you gain an understanding of how
the world works."

He began pacing the front of the room. "We have a
textbook. It provides a two-dimensional account of history—
one person's perspective as he moves through time. I also
assign a lot of outside reading. It's advanced reading, often
controversial. I want you to see there are other viewpoints on
the past. I want you to ask questions. I want to have debates.
These will add the third and fourth dimensions. Only then,
when you see history in motion, nations and cultures moving
and grinding against each other, can you appreciate how the
world works."

Andrews fell back into his chair and smiled. "There," he said. "I'll get down from my soapbox. These Wednesday afternoon sessions are designed to be informal. As they say, there's no such thing as a bad question. You can ask me about anything: reading material, lectures . . . current events."

A student raised her hand. "The genetics paper that reported Genghis Khan's Y chromosome markers is confusing," she said. "I'm not a biology major. I mean, I know men have an X and Y chromosome, and that women have two X chromosomes, but how did they find Genghis Khan's markers, particularly if they didn't have his actual remains? And what exactly are these markers?"

"Excellent questions," Andrews said. "First, genetic markers are DNA sequences that are at specific sites on specific chromosomes. Theoretically, they could be any sequences at any sites, but geneticists have selected certain areas to analyze because the sequences at these sites are passed down from generation to generation with little variation; in other words, these sequences have a low mutation rate—often on the order of one mutation every ten or twenty generations. Geneticists have examined these sites on people throughout the world, creating huge databases. With these databases, they've been able to determine previously unseen relationships between groups of people."

He pointed at the female student. "You might have DNA markers that are different from anyone in this room. Your markers, however, may be identical to a whole community in Ireland, which would indicate your ancestors came from there. This community in Ireland may have similar markers to a community in Norway, which would indicate they migrated from there. With this type of analysis, geneticists have been able to trace the migration of civilizations through time, all the way back to the cradle of civilization in Africa. In fact, with this analysis, they've been able to prove that the cradle of civilization *was* in Africa."

Andrews stood. "Before I answer how the Oxford researchers found Genghis Khan's markers, I want you to tell me exactly what they did find. If you'd like, you can read from the summary in the syllabus."

The student looked down and read. "'The researchers examined the Y chromosome of 2,123 Asian men. In 8 percent of their study population who lived in widely disparate locations from the Pacific Ocean to the Caspian Sea, they found certain common genetic sequences at fifteen Y chromosome sites. The unusually high frequency of men possessing these sequences could not be attributed to chance. They concluded these men were linked by a common male ancestor, who lived approximately eight hundred years ago.'" She looked up. "That's what I don't understand. I mean, I understand 8 percent of Asian men in the study had the same fifteen Y chromosome markers, indicating a common male ancestor, but how did they conclude that ancestor lived eight hundred years ago? And how did they conclude it was Genghis Khan?"

Many students nodded their agreement.

"First, it's important to realize these 8 percent had similar, but *not* identical DNA sequences," Andrews said. "The sequences were similar enough that the researchers were able to conclude the men shared a recent common male ancestor, but different enough to indicate some time had elapsed since that common ancestor lived." He paused. "Does that make sense?"

The students nodded. "In other words, in the generations since they shared a common ancestor, there was enough time for mutations to develop," someone said.

"Exactly," Andrews said. "As I said, these fifteen locations on the Y chromosome have been extensively analyzed. Geneticists know the mutation rates at each site. Knowing the mutation rates, the Oxford researchers simply tallied the number of mutations that had accumulated among these men. Determining the time since they shared a common ancestor then became a simple mathematical computation: number of mutations divided by the mutation rate. Their calculation came out to thirty-four generations, or about eight hundred years." He walked out from behind the desk. "Now, knowing that, can anyone tell me why the Oxford researchers concluded this common male ancestor was Genghis Khan?"

The students looked down, scanning their class notes.

"Genghis Khan died in 1227," someone said. "The time frame correlates."

"What else?" Andrews asked.

"The highest concentration of men with the fifteen markers was in Mongolia, where Genghis Khan and his sons spent the majority of their time," a student said.

"But the markers were also found elsewhere: multiple locations throughout China along with Kazakhstan, Kyrgyzstan . . . Uzbekistan," another student said. "All locations within the boundaries of the Mongol Empire."

Andrews nodded. "In the thirteenth century, travel to all those locations would have been impossible for anyone except the Mongols. Anything else?"

"The proliferation rate," someone said. "The researchers concluded this common ancestor currently has sixteen million living male descendants."

"Yes!" Andrews said. "Over the last thirty-four generations, this male line has increased from one man to *sixteen million*. This is an extremely high rate of proliferation. For many generations and in widely disparate locations, Genghis Khan's male descendants held positions of power, allowing them to have many wives and dozens, if not hundreds, of children. They not only became khan but held the positions of Dalai Lama, emperor, sultan, shah, and emir. His descendants ruled the Ilkhanate, the territory between Afghanistan and Turkey until 1335, China until 1368, and parts of Russia until 1847. It wasn't until 1920 when the Soviets ousted Genghis Khan's last ruling male descendant, Alim Khan, from his position as emir of Bukhara in modern-day Uzbekistan."

He turned again toward the female student. "So, what can we conclude?"

"In our 8 percent, given the similarities between their fifteen Y chromosome markers, we can conclude they shared a common male ancestor," she said, looking down at her notes. "Based on the number of mutations that have accumulated, or the differences between their fifteen Y chromosome markers, we can conclude that approximately eight hundred years have passed since this common ancestor lived. And, given the distribution of the markers through Eurasia and their high frequency, we can conclude that only one line, Genghis Khan and his male descendants, could account for such a marked and widespread dissemination of genetic material."

The student looked up, smiling.

Andrews raised his hands. "My work here is done."

* * *

"Here's to my world-famous brother," Ben Andrews said, holding up a glass of beer. "You finally found ol' Genghis."

Andrews was having dinner with his younger brother Ben, a clinical professor of cardiology at Columbia University. They were at Pietro's, their favorite hangout as students.

After their dad had served abroad as a diplomat, he'd returned with his family to Charlottesville, taking a position as dean of the law school. The brothers had both attended the university as undergrad students. While James stayed and earned his PhD in archaeology, Ben left for med school at Columbia, which had transitioned to a residency, a fellowship, and then a job.

"A herder wandering the mountain, someone making a pilgrimage, if we're extremely lucky, one of his descendants," Andrews said. "But ol' Genghis, I don't think so."

"The newscasters sounded pretty sure you'd found him," Ben said.

"Once we find the bone doesn't have all the Khan markers and the time of death is different than Genghis Khan's, this whole episode will be forgotten," Andrews said. He raised his glass. "We do, however, have something to celebrate. Happy birthday!"

Ben was in town to meet with their family lawyer. As James had two years earlier, he'd receive the money that had been allotted to him in their parents' will. Their parents had been killed in a car accident ten years earlier.

"Thanks," Ben said.

The brothers, both with sandy hair and the same penetrating blue eyes, looked around the restaurant. "I miss this place," Ben said. "The smell. The pizza. I miss Charlottesville, not only Mom and Dad, but the slower pace, the touch of southern hospitality, even the damn brick buildings."

"After Manhattan, it must seem pretty slow."

"These days I'd settle for something slower." Ben smiled. "Tell me. How's the female situation? Have you found someone willing to spend a romantic summer night camping in Outer Mongolia and cooking over a fire of dung chips?"

"Not yet."

"Who's the blonde?"

"Blonde?" Andrews asked.

"The one on your mountain, in your society photo?"

After making a donation to the Asian Historical Society, Ben had been placed on their e-mail list.

"An archaeology instructor," Andrews said.

"I never had an instructor who looked like that," Ben said. "Are you going to see her again?"

"You mean professionally?"

"I mean . . . is she single?"

"Nope, married with three kids," Andrews said, summoning his best poker face.

Ben started laughing. "You're a terrible liar. Come on, the truth."

Andrews had never been able to keep a secret from Ben. "No," he said resignedly. "We have no plans to see each other."

"It's okay to have a relationship that lasts over a month," Ben said.

"So I've heard," Andrews said. "Believe me, this wasn't going anywhere. She's from Los Angeles. A long-term relationship wasn't feasible."

"Feasible?" Ben said. "That sounds so clinical."

"Not everyone meets his soulmate as a college freshman," Andrews said. "Speaking of which, how's Samantha?"

"Great."

"And the kids?"

Ben opened his wallet and pushed it across the table.

Andrews flipped through pictures of Ben's two kids. "They're getting big," he said. "Mom and Dad would have loved them." He slid the wallet back.

Ben paused to look at the photos before pocketing the wallet.

"Have you thought about what you're going to do with the money?" Andrews asked.

"Not really, but we are looking at a new condo," Ben said. "And we have so many bills." Taking a swig of his beer, he met his brother's gaze. "Hey, don't look at me like that."

Andrews raised his hands. "I'm not."

"You are," Ben said. "Trust me. You have no idea what it's like to live on the West Side with a wife and two kids."

"You're right. I don't. It's just this is the last of Mom and Dad's money."

"Not all of us can live like monks," Ben said. "What did you do with your money? You put it in their endowment, didn't you? You didn't spend a damn penny on yourself."

"The law school was Dad's life," Andrews said. "It's how he and Mom chose to be remembered."

"Jesus!" Ben said. "You can be so damn self-righteous. You realize they gave the money to you—not their endowment."

"Look at who we are," Andrews said, leaning forward. "Look at what we have. We owe it all to Mom and Dad."

"Yeah, look at us," Ben said. "I was born in Moscow. Most kids go to Disney World. We toured the goddamn Kremlin. That's not normal."

Andrews sat back. "I'm not going to fight over this," he said. "Do what you want with the money. Seriously, I'll never mention it again."

"Mom and Dad lived their lives," Ben said. "It's time for us to live ours."

Their waitress brought their bill. Ben flipped money on the table, but Andrews pushed the money back and slapped down a credit card. "It's on me," he said. "Now that I know how strapped you are."

The waitress took the card and walked away.

"You're unmerciful," Ben said. "You know that?"

"I'm a big brother," Andrews said. "It's my job."

Despite his best efforts, a smile crept across Ben's face. He shook his head. "Some things never change."

Andrews returned the smile. "No, they don't."

The brothers sipped their beers. Their mutual gaze settled on the corner table. The night before their parents left on their fatal east coast car trip, the family went out for dinner at Pietro's.

"It seems like it was just yesterday," Andrews said.

Ben nodded. "When they announced your find on national television and showed videos of you getting off the helicopter, all I could think about was how proud Dad would have been."

"No. If we're going to bring Mom and Dad back, it would be for something you've accomplished: graduating from medical school, marrying Sam, having kids. They would have burst with pride at any of those events."

Andrews pushed the pizza tray toward Ben. "You remember the Kremlin? You were pretty young."

Ben picked up the last piece of pizza and took a bite. "Just snapshots," he said. "But I definitely remember Beijing. And all those field trips Dad took us on."

"His excursions."

Ben nodded. "Dad thought he was training two future statesmen, not an archaeologist and cardiologist."

"I'm sure you're right," Andrews said. "Still, would you have traded the Forbidden City and Kremlin for Disney World?"

Ben looked toward the corner table. "Since you put it that way. No, I wouldn't have traded them for anything."

9

There came into the world a blue-gray wolf whose destiny was heaven's will.

—The Secret History of the Mongols

Baabar spent the morning of the day before national elections volunteering at a soup kitchen. In the afternoon, he had a meeting with local businessmen, which was followed by a party fundraiser and dinner. It was late at night when he drove home, relieved the campaigning was finally over.

He passed through Ulaanbaatar's business district, assaulted by a dizzying array of neon signs and billboards. A quarter century of capitalism had brought a plethora of restaurants, shops, and bars to the area. Transitioning to the relatively barren residential district, largely untouched since Soviet days, he turned into the parking lot of his apartment building—one of several drab, gray, block-like structures.

Inside the building, he walked down the first-floor hallway and unlocked the front door of his one-bedroom flat. He stepped inside. In his kitchen, he came to an abrupt stop.

The light was on. A man sat at the table, reading a newspaper. "Relax," the man said, holding his hands up in surrender. "I just want to talk."

The man appeared to be in his midforties. He had thick eyebrows and jutting, black hair streaked with gray. He appeared Slavic, but spoke perfect Mongolian. He motioned toward a kitchen chair. "Please, sit," he said, smiling. "I was just doing a little reading." He held up the day's copy of the *Ulaanbaatar Gazete*. A photo of Baabar fighting the fire at Government House was on the front page. "Nice picture, eh?"

"If you need to see me, make an appointment at my office," Baabar said.

"Trust me," the man said. "You don't want me at your office."

On the kitchen table were a neat stack of 8½ x 11 papers, two empty glasses, and a bottle of vodka. The man set the newspaper aside. He poured vodka into the glasses and slid one across the table toward Baabar, who remained in place.

The man raised his glass in salutation and downed it with one gulp. He then slipped on a pair of bifocals. Pulling the stack of papers toward him, he began reading. "In 1994, the Khural's speaker channeled over thirty million dollars in funds from USAID to road construction. The money was used to purchase equipment for the state's road works. Two months later, the road works were privatized. The speaker's brother then bought the new, privatized company for the equivalent of one million dollars, a price based on a valuation performed *before* the thirty million dollar investment."

He turned over the top paper on the stack and continued. "In 1997, the Minister of Finance signed a bill eliminating export taxes on raw Mongolian cashmere. He claimed he did so at the behest of the aid agencies. A week after signing the bill, he was given twenty thousand shares of stock in China's Asian Cashmere, a leading cashmere processing firm and the principal beneficiary of the lower cost of raw cashmere. Subsequent inquiries with the aid agencies revealed that none of them made the request."

The man glanced above his bifocals at Baabar before turning to the next paper. "From 1995 until 2000, the dean of Ulaanbaatar's medical school accepted fifty million tugriks in bribes to admit students. He extorted another fifty million tugriks from students to simply sign their diplomas and allow them to graduate."

The man took off his glasses and smiled. "Ironic, isn't it?"

The three men he referred to were not only current members of parliament, but also fellow members with Baabar on the Committee for the Investigation of Governmental Corruption.

"Where'd you get this information?" Baabar asked.

"Mongolia is a small country," the man said. "People see Khural members living in gated neighborhoods, wearing expensive Italian clothes, and driving Mercedes. They see them taking education tours with their families and enrolling their children in foreign schools. They're outraged." He nodded toward the stack of papers. "This is a byproduct of that resentment."

After the fall of the communist state and collapse of socialism, Khural members oversaw the privatization of state assets, along with the distribution of large amounts of foreign aid. The parliamentarians were exposed to temptations they couldn't resist. Corruption had been rampant.

"Why don't you bring this to the authorities?" Baabar asked. "You did all the work."

"You *are* a member of the corruption committee, aren't you?"

When Baabar became a member of parliament, he naïvely hoped he'd accomplish great things. After seeing that corruption had to be eliminated before anything of substance could be achieved, he'd jockeyed for a position on the committee.

The man pushed the papers forward. "Everything has been verified," he said. "Included are names, telephone numbers, even signed statements."

"Where'd you get this information?" Baabar asked. "*Who are you?*"

The man shook his head. "I realize I'm placing you in a potentially compromising position," he said. "I believe, however, someone with your intelligence and abilities will be able to take advantage of the situation."

"What if I'm not re-elected?" Baabar asked.

The man smiled. "We both know you will be. The only question is whether or not your RDP will gain a majority." He nodded toward the stack of papers. "This may help."

"You do know the elections are tomorrow?"

"Time is of the essence," the man said, nodding. "It's good to know your party is well connected at the ministry."

The man was right. Mikou had connections everywhere. Baabar recalled something Mikou told him on the night he'd first won his seat in the Khural. Mikou had pulled him away from the celebration and reminded him of the work ahead. "Radicals swim against the current; traditionalists swim with it, while corrupt leaders swim where they are told," the elderly chairman had said. "Good leaders pick a spot on the opposing shore and swim toward it, never losing sight of their goal. You need to learn when to swim with the current . . . and when to swim against it."

Baabar walked across the kitchen and sat. He reached for his vodka and downed it with one swig. *"Bez truda ne vytaschish y rybku iz pruda,"* he said, speaking in Russian.

It was time to swim against the current.

Baabar watched the slightest hint of understanding pass through the man's eyes before they went dull.

The man, catching Baabar's observing gaze, realized he'd given himself a way. He smiled and then began laughing, reaching for the bottle of vodka. "Very good, my friend," he said, refilling their glasses. "And let's hope, we don't drown."

1172 Central Asia

Temujin braced against the cold, pulling the collar of his full-length fur *deel* tighter around him. He and Jamuka were on horseback, forming a line with boys of similar age, their backs to the mountain, the snow-laden valley spread before them.

"Last night, the men of the tribes formed a large net," Jamuka said. "They're now riding this way, driving the animals toward us."

Each winter, the Jadaran joined the other large tribes of the central steppe for a hunt. This year, Jamuka invited Temujin. Temujin was grateful for the invitation. The winter had been harsh. His family had survived on their own, but their food reserves were dwindling.

Temujin looked down the line of boys. "Why do we get the first chance at the kill?" he asked.

"It prepares us for war," Jamuka said.

In the distance came the sound of hooves. A rising plume of snow appeared at the mouth of the valley. As the ground shook, the boys' horses began to whinny and buck. Temujin saw fear in the other boys' eyes, but they held their positions.

"Here they come!" Jamuka called out.

A herd of white-tailed antelope bounded in front of them. Temujin and Jamuka let loose their arrows.

Two antelope dropped, their snouts driving headfirst into the snow. The other animals leaped frantically back and forth, caught between the approaching horsemen and row of boys.

"Keep shooting!" Jamuka yelled. "We'll collect them later."

A snow leopard, its smoky-gray fur dotted with black rings, darted past Temujin and up the mountain.

Temujin gave chase. To his surprise, he found the leopard not far up the mountainside, panting near a tree. The animal, its fur matted with sweat and dirt, was exhausted by the nightlong pursuit.

Temujin raised an arrow.

There was a sudden, shrill cry. Temujin looked back toward the valley. Jamuka stood by his fallen horse surrounded by a pack of wolves. He was thrusting his knife back and forth as the wolves, worked into frenzy by the hunt, nipped at his back and ankles.

Temujin stormed down the mountain.

The largest wolf, its teeth bared, leaped at Jamuka and knocked him to the ground. Jamuka held the wolf back, his hands buried in the animal's thick collar of fur. The remaining wolves swarmed Jamuka's horse and began tearing at its flesh.

Temujin shot arrow after arrow as fast as he could raise them to his bow. Nearing Jamuka, he grabbed his ivory-handled knife. Standing on his saddle, he steadied himself and dove.

* * *

Jamuka's father rode up to the base of the mountain. Ong Khan, the head of the powerful Kereyid tribe, was at his side.

Jamuka stood among the carcasses of several dead wolves, frantically scanning the ground around him.

"Did you do this?" Jamuka's father asked.

"Of course not," Ong Khan said, laughing. "He's just a boy."

Jamuka continued looking back and forth. When the largest of the wolves rustled, the two men drew arrows.

"Wait!" Jamuka shouted, raising his hands.

The wolf's head sagged awkwardly to the side, its neck dripping with blood. A boy emerged from beneath the animal. He was covered in blood, a knife clutched in his hand.

"I didn't kill them," Jamuka said. "Temujin did."

"Temujin?" Ong Khan said. "Yesugei's son?"

Jamuka's father nodded.

The boy wiped the blood from his face and looked up at the men.

"I'm sorry to hear about your father," Ong Khan said. "I was his *anda*."

The boy's head dropped.

"You're with the Tayichiut now, right?" Ong Khan asked.

The boy shook his head, his eyes downcast.

"Did your mother remarry?"

The boy didn't respond.

"Who are you with?" Ong Khan asked.

"No one," the boy said, looking up, his eyes flashing. "We're alone."

"Alone?" Ong Khan said. "But—"

The boy broke into a run, whistling for his horse. "Hurry, Jamuka! We can still get the leopard."

Leaping together onto the horse, the boys rode up the mountain.

10

*The East has known only three great men: Buddha, Confucius,
and Genghis Khan.*

—Urgunge Onon,
Introduction to *The Secret History of the Mongols*

"In 1253, the French king sent an envoy to the court of
Möngke Khan, Genghis Khan's grandson, to establish an
alliance." Andrews stood once again at the lecture hall
podium. It was Thursday, his second lecture.

"In a series of letters, the envoy documented his
travels, describing his safe and pleasant passage from
Europe to Central Asia," Andrews continued. "He wrote of a
sophisticated postal system, the use of paper money, elaborate
rest stops, and more silk and wealth than he thought existed
in the entire world. In the khan's court, he described cordial
debates between Christian, Muslim, and Buddhist clerics
on creation, the nature of God, what happens to the soul
after death, and good versus evil. When confronted with the
dilemma that Christians, Muslims, and Jews all believed in
the same God, but followed the respective commandments
of Jesus, Mohammed, and Moses, the Mongols concluded
that to achieve universal peace, religious doctrine must fall
secondary to the needs of the state."

A student raised his hand. "When you talk about the
Mongols, you make them sound like intellectuals with
enlightened views on the world. But I'm having a tough time
getting beyond my image of them as bloodthirsty barbarians."

Andrews smiled. "Let me ask this," he said, stepping out

from behind the podium. "Does this sound like a barbarian? Genghis Khan believed all men were created equal. He held himself and his family to the same laws as everyone else. He eliminated the Mongols' archaic feudal system and established a meritocracy where rank was based on deeds and loyalty rather than birthright. He established participatory government, universal education, freedom of speech, human rights, and rule by law. He abolished torture. He tried to establish a world order with a universal alphabet, paper money, and free trade. A Shamanist, he established a secular state with freedom of religion and ruled over Christians, Buddhists, Muslims, Hindus, and Jews without discrimination."

"But in our reading, it says the Mongols massacred *entire* cities," a student said.

Andrews nodded. "After decades of constant turf warfare, Genghis Khan learned that if you didn't kill your enemy, he'd be back the next day: kidnapping your children, raping your women, and stealing your animals. Scholars who have examined this issue generally believe he was no more violent or cruel than other leaders of his time. He did, however, operate on a much larger scale."

"So we should look past his atrocities?" a girl asked.

"As students of history, it's not our job to forgive our subjects, but to understand them and learn from their mistakes," Andrews said. "Yes, by our standards, sitting here in lovely Charlottesville, the Mongols were cruel. But even today, we turn on the news and are appalled by world events: beheadings, genocide, slavery. The United States has launched missiles into civilian centers. We've tortured prisoners. Not too long ago, we dropped atomic bombs on Japanese cities, killing tens of thousands of citizens. As much as we'd like to, we can't impose our code of ethics on the world. We can't even do it on our own country. And we certainly can't do it on thirteenth century Central Asia."

Andrews returned to the podium. "You've all heard history is written by the victor. To be more precise, history is written by people with different religious backgrounds, political beliefs, and ethnicities. Intentionally or unintentionally, history is recorded through their biases. With respect to the portrayal of Genghis Khan and the Mongols as barbarians, it's propaganda, pure and simple."

"Are you serious?" someone asked.

Many students laughed.

"Genghis Khan was the only Asian leader to invade Europe and win," Andrews said. "The West has never forgiven him. He's been denigrated more than any figure in Western history. In Asia, however, he's a Mongolian King Arthur. His reign is considered a Camelot. His image is on their money and stamps. It's been used to sell energy drinks, cigarettes, candy, vodka, and beer. Genghis Khan is not viewed just as a bygone figure—world history's greatest conqueror and Mongolia's founding father—but as a religious and cultural icon, a living, spiritual connection with their Eternal Blue Sky."

Andrews again stepped out from behind the podium. "Fear was Genghis Khan's greatest ally. The Mongols only had to camp near a city and the opposing soldiers would flee. Genghis Khan encouraged this fear. His victories magnified it. Scribes of the time wrote he was a friend of the devil, adept at magic, and immortal. The Mongols' hearts were said to be made of iron. Their horses were said to be so big they ate trees.

"After the fall of the Mongol Empire, this negative propaganda machine kicked into high gear. Comte de Buffon, an eighteenth-century French naturalist, described the Mongols as being 'strangers to religion, morality, and decency . . . robbers by profession.' In the 1800s, the Mongols were developmentally linked to the orangutan. Scientists introduced the term *mongoloid* to describe someone with Down syndrome, a term still used today."

Andrews, standing in the middle of an aisle, held out his arms. "Is this starting to sound familiar? Throughout history, we've seen it happen so many times. The propaganda machine is activated, and distant peoples are turned into a faceless, mindless enemy—someone to be defeated at all costs. In today's world, the cost of absolute war means annihilation.

In today's world, we have to learn to live with other cultures, to understand them, not vilify them."

He returned to the podium. "In less than one generation, the Mongols progressed from being nomads to rulers of the largest and most diverse kingdom in world history. Their empire is more applicable to our own American empire than any. The lessons to be learned regarding their rise and fall are invaluable, but we ignore these lessons. *Why?*"

Andrews paused, scanning the students' faces. "As future business leaders, scientists, and diplomats, the decisions you make might impact millions, maybe billions. What are you going to base those decisions on? Whatever is trending on Twitter? The latest national poll? Or will you search for the truth? You may think the jump from where you're sitting right now to CEO or ambassador is a big one. It's not. Learn to look through the propaganda and hype. Learn to understand other people's motivations, their histories and cultures. Only through understanding will you be able to make the right decisions."

Andrews glanced up at the wall clock and pulled a paper from his pocket. "Let me leave you with an excerpt from the Canterbury Tales. It was written around 1390 by Geoffrey Chaucer, when Genghis Khan was still considered a romantic figure by the European gentry."

Lifting the paper, he read:

This noble king was called Genghis Khan,
Who in his time was of great renown
That there was nowhere in no region
So excellent a lord in all things.
He lacked nothing that belonged to a king.
As of the sect of which he was born
He kept his law, to which that he was sworn.
And thereto he was hardy, wise, and rich,
And piteous and just, always liked;
Sooth of his word, benign, and honorable,
Of his courage as any center stable;

Young, fresh, and strong, in arms desirous
As any bachelor of all his house.
A fair person he was and fortunate,
And kept always so well royal estate
That there was nowhere such another man.
This noble king, the Tartar Genghis Khan.

1172 Central Asia

Temujin and Jamuka raced their horses across the sunbaked steppe, their bows held in front of them. Jamuka was the first to release. His arrow sailed toward a tree, narrowly missing it. When Temujin released, his arrow struck the tree with a resounding thud.

The friends pulled up their horses. Jamuka removed a piece of dried meat from his saddle and tossed it to Temujin.

"Again?" Temujin asked, slipping the meat into his pocket.

"I'm out," Jamuka said.

Temujin pulled two pieces of meat from his pocket and extended one.

"You won it," Jamuka said. "It's yours."

"You need something to eat."

Jamuka reluctantly accepted the meat. "Tell me," he said, taking a bite. "I'm bigger and can shoot farther, but you always beat me. Why?"

"I only shoot when I know I'll hit the tree."

"How do you know?" Jamuka asked.

"I don't know. I just do." Temujin smiled. "It must be a dark spirit."

"Don't say that," Jamuka said. "Yesterday, our shaman cast a spirit from a man. The spirit caused the man to kill one of his wives and a newborn daughter."

"Where did the spirit come from?"

"One of our enemies," Jamuka said.

"Is that what your shaman said?"

"Yes."

"When the spirit left the man, where did it go?" Temujin asked.

"Into a goat."

"Why would the spirit possess a goat?"

"The shaman's spell was strong," Jamuka said.

"According to your shaman?"

"He speaks with Tengri."

"What did the goat do?" Temujin asked.

"Nothing."

"And the spirit stayed in the goat?"

"Yes," Jamuka answered. "The shaman then killed the goat and boiled it, trapping the spirit inside."

"Was the man punished?"

"No."

"He killed his wife and daughter, but he *wasn't* punished?" Temujin asked.

"It wasn't his fault. He was taken over by the dark spirit."

Temujin looked skyward and held out his hands. "Spirits could inhabit us at any time, but they don't."

"Don't tempt them."

"The man's spirit was weak," Temujin said. "He *must* be held responsible. Otherwise, no one is responsible for their actions. Anything can be justified."

11

Genghis Khan was buried with a young camel. Afterward, the grass over the site was replaced and ten thousand horsemen trampled the ground. When the Mongols wished to offer sacrifice, they took the mother of the young camel to the area. By watching where she stopped to wail, they knew where to leave their offerings.

—Yeh Tzŭ-chi, 1378 Chinese historian

Andrews entered his office, carrying a cup of coffee and a letter. He cracked open the window, letting in a light breeze. At his desk, he logged onto his computer. Sitting back in his chair and sipping the coffee, he picked up the letter and reread the bottom three lines.

Request for promotion to Professor: Deferred.
Current status: Associate Professor.
Next evaluation: Two years.

Before he left for Mongolia this summer, his academic review committee had interviewed him for consideration of promotion to full professor.

"Your last publication in a credible academic journal was five years ago," a committee member had said. "And that was based on your work as a PhD student in Avarga. This incessant treasure hunt for Genghis Khan's grave is not really an academic endeavor. It's more *commercial.*"

The committee member had been right. During Andrews's first two summers in Avarga, while unearthing foundation after foundation, he'd generated plenty of academic material, enough to earn his PhD. But there was something missing. None of the telltale signs that the Mongols actually lived in Avarga were there. There were no pieces of furniture, dishes, utensils, or toys. There were only buildings, empty buildings. The Mongol's first city was nothing more than a collection of warehouses for storing booty and tribute, booty and tribute that were no longer there.

A single bound copy of his PhD thesis existed. The thesis, detailing his findings in Avarga, was buried on a backroom shelf in the University's archaeology library. Meanwhile, copies of his travelogue, *In Search of Baljuna*, sat on the bookshelves of every Asian scholar. Because the travelogue was published in the popular press and not a peer-reviewed, scholarly journal, however, it was held in contempt by the academics at his institution.

Scholarship for the sake of scholarship no longer interested Andrews, but as his once-promising career ground to a halt, he wondered how much more time was he willing to waste. Six years of his research had been directed toward finding the tomb. Was it time to move on? Ben was a full professor of cardiology at Columbia with a wife and two kids. Baabar would soon be a twice-elected parliamentarian. Both were younger than him. By the time his father was his age, he was a full professor with tenure and associate chair of UVA's law school.

Andrews tried not to compare himself with his father or to Ben and Baabar, but he couldn't help himself. His life was more than his work, and his work was more than just his research, but since returning from Mongolia, he'd been overwhelmed by the sensation that he was falling terribly, irretrievably behind.

He turned to his computer and began going through his e-mail. There was a department notice from Sara.

```
To: Archaeologydept@uva.edu
From: sjohnson@uva.edu
Subject: Lab break-in
```

Colleagues,
    I came in early this morning and
there was a young man in the lab,
looking through a refrigerator. When I
confronted him, he claimed he was in the
wrong lab and hurriedly left. I've filed
a complaint with campus security.
    He didn't appear to be a drug-seeker,
looking for syringes, needles, etc...
but I thought this would be a good
time to remind everyone to lock the
doors after using the lab. Also, please
inform me or campus security if you see
unauthorized individuals in or around
the lab. If you recognize him from the
attached surveillance photo, please let
me know.
Thank you,
Sara Johnson

Andrews clicked on the attachment. It was a black-and-white image of a young Asian man. He had a backpack and wore a T-shirt, shorts, and a faded Virginia baseball hat. He looked like a typical student, but Andrews didn't recognize him.

He continued through his inbox, stopping at a message from Abbey.

To: jandrews@uva.edu
From: aconrad@ubu.com
Subject: X chromosome Khan markers

James,
    Just about done with the bone's Y
chromosome markers. Will send final
results to Sara.
    Also, we just finished sequencing the
X chromosome marker sites. 3,500 people!
We're starting to go through the data.
Wish me luck,
Abbey

Abbey was searching for Genghis Khan's X chromosome markers. While Genghis Khan passed his Y chromosome to his sons, he passed his X chromosome to his daughters. The Oxford study that detected the Y chromosome Khan markers concluded "social prestige" allowed Genghis Khan's male lineage to expand at a rate "comparable to the most extreme selective events observed in natural populations." By finding the X chromosome Khan markers, Abbey wanted to not only compare the degree of social prestige accorded to Genghis Khan's daughters with that of his sons, but to gain insight into the fate of his daughters, which was largely unknown.

Andrews's office door swung open. Sara stepped inside. "I just finished with the last marker," she said.

"*And?*"

"All fifteen markers match the Khan markers," she said.

"Are you serious?"

She nodded. "Either the bone belongs to Genghis Khan . . . or a close paternal male relative."

Andrews sat back. "That's mind-boggling."

"It is," Sara said. "Can you believe it? You just may have found Genghis Khan."

As much as he wanted to, Andrews couldn't argue with her.

"Are the carbon dating results back yet?" she asked.

"Not yet," he said, glancing at his watch. "The lab told me to check with them at one."

Sara pointed to the computer. "Did you see my e-mail?"

He nodded. "Did this guy threaten you?"

"No, but it *was* a little creepy. When I came into the lab, he was just standing at the refrigerator with the door open. He was clearly looking for something."

"I didn't recognize him," Andrews said. "But I'd think they should be able to identify him. It's a good image."

"I hope so," Sara said.

A breeze came in from the window. Sara stepped toward it. "I love your view."

"Of the parking lot?"

"No, beyond it through those trees," she said. "You can see the gardens in the Rotunda." She opened the window the rest of the way and sat on the sill. "I remember when I first started working here. I thought I'd spend a lot of time in the gardens, just sitting and reading. I never have."

While Sara remained at the window, Andrews's attention returned to his computer.

"Maybe this weekend," Sara said. "Ron is on call. I'll find a good book and just spend the whole day there reading." She turned. "How's your talk coming?"

"Good."

"Are you going to have time for sightseeing?"

"There's a group going to Versailles," he said.

"It sounds wonderful. Is Abbey going to be there?"

He looked up from his computer. Sara was watching him, smiling. "No," he said.

"That's too bad." Sara looked back out the window. "Do you think she can find the X chromosome Khan markers?"

"If the bone belongs to Genghis Khan, she may not have to," Andrews said. He sat back and sipped the coffee. "But with respect to matching the Oxford study and their results with the Y chromosome Khan markers, I think finding the X chromosome Khan markers in the general population is a long shot. There's no way his daughters could have had as many offspring as his sons. And, we just don't know that much about the daughters. If we had a better idea about how many there were and where they lived, Abbey would be able to concentrate her search."

"You'd think that kind of information would be available," Sara said. "I mean, we're talking about Genghis Khan's daughters."

"You would," Andrews said. "The problem is a concerted attempt was made to keep the daughters out of the history books. The Mongols' first written history, *The Secret History of the Mongols*, describes a speech Genghis Khan gave after uniting the steppe tribes. He was dividing the administration of his new nation among his followers, when he turned to his daughters and said, 'Let us reward our female offspring.'

The pages following that statement were removed from the original text."

Andrews took another sip of coffee. "What we know about the daughters has been pieced together from non-Mongolian sources: diplomatic reports to the Chinese court, Armenian and Persian chronicles, letters to the Vatican, and the memoirs of Marco Polo," he continued. "The daughters' exploits were carved into the stones of Confucian and Taoist temples. Fictional accounts of the daughters even appeared in the rhymes of Chaucer and Milton, plays of de la Croix, and arias of Puccini."

"They sound extraordinary," Sara said.

Andrews nodded. "Mongol boys were trained to hunt, herd, and fight, but girls were trained to run a household. While Genghis Khan sent his sons to conquer distant lands, he sent his daughters to rule them. Four of his daughters married leaders of kingdoms between Northern China and Central Asia. They became queens of the Silk Road, ruling more people for longer periods of time than any other women in history."

"If the daughters only married into the kingdoms, were they really able to rule?" Sara asked.

"Genghis Khan made sure they did," Andrews said. "After the marriages, the native kings were given the 'honor' of serving in his personal guard. The sons-in-law were removed from their homeland while the daughters stayed behind to rule. Under their rule, trade flourished. Some have even said that without the daughters' leadership, a Mongol Empire wouldn't have existed. Trade exposed the Mongols to what lay beyond the steppe and was the main impetus for moving beyond it."

"So what happened to them?" Sara asked.

"In the power struggles after Genghis Khan's death, they came under attack," Andrews said. "Nobody knows exactly what became of them. But Genghis Khan's sons and grandsons probably viewed them as a threat. Most, if not all of the daughters, are believed to have been killed."

ᠵᠢᠷᠭᠤ ᠨᠢᠭᠡ ᠵᠢᠷᠭᠤ

1173 Central Asia

In a swirl of frosty air and snow, Temujin and Jamuka entered Temujin's ger. No one was inside. In the middle of the ger, a small fire burned, its smoke spiraling up through a small hole in the roof. On either side of the fire, sleeping mats were laid out.

They walked to the altar in the back. From the altar, Jamuka lifted the ivory-handled knife they'd used to become *andas*. He unsheathed the knife and held it up, admiring the shimmering blade.

"It was my father's," Temujin said. "On the day I was born, he used it to kill a man. The man was a Tatar. His name was Temujin."

"Your father named you after an enemy?"

"My father respected the Tatar. When I was born, my father looked into my eyes and saw the Tatar looking back. He said the Tatar had the look of a horse before it's broken. He believed the man's spirit had passed into me, not his *sulde*."

Jamuka set the knife down and scanned the ger. He pointed toward a row of sacks along the wall. "What are those?"

"Elm seeds, garlic, and onions," Temujin said. He removed a handful of seeds and proudly held them out. "This summer was our biggest harvest."

"You *eat* these?" Jamuka said. "Where are your meat and milk?"

Temujin's cheeks burned with shame. The winter had been tough. The family had already slaughtered their last stallion for meat. Wolves had killed their last mare.

Temujin walked to the sleeping mat belonging to his older half-brother, Begter. From beneath the mat, he removed a piece of dried meat. "Here," he said, tearing the meat in half.

As they began eating, there was a scream.

Begter, standing at the ger entrance, ran and tackled Temujin. The other family members rushed in. Khasar jumped on Begter's back. Belgütei grabbed Khasar in a choke hold and tore him away.

"Stop it!" Hoelun screamed. "*Stop it!*"

When the boys continued fighting, Hoelun grabbed an arrow and swung it wildly.

The boys froze.

Hoelun snapped the arrow in half and threw it to the ground. "If we behave as individuals, we'll die," she said. She grabbed an arrow from each of the boys' quivers and held them together. She tried breaking the bundle, but couldn't.

She handed the bundle to the boys. Each tried unsuccessfully to break it.

"We're no different than these arrows," she said. "Apart, we're easily broken. Together, we're unbreakable."

12

The emperor is carried with an immense treasure by several men to a certain place, where they lay down the body and flee at the utmost speed, as if the Devil pursued them. Others seize the corpse and proceed in the same way to another place; and so on, until they reach the place where it is to be buried.

—Jourdain de Séverac, 1330
Dominican monk and explorer

Andrews stood outside Old Cabell Hall. Black-shuttered windows looked out from the redbrick colonial on a lush, green lawn and sunbaked sidewalks. White columns and a stuccoed arch framed an entrance where a sprinkling of students filed in and out. The hall was scheduled for demolition the following summer. Most classes previously held in the building had been moved into the Archaeology Studies Building.

Andrews entered the building. He walked through the hallways, remembering his many years of strolling the shadowed corridors. In the faculty offices, he stopped in front of a narrow office door and knocked, glancing up at the quote above the doorway.

History is after all nothing but a pack of tricks which we play upon the dead.

—VOLTAIRE

Through the door, he heard a familiar, reedy voice. "Come in."

Professor Emeritus P. Arthur Herald stood in the middle of a cramped office, squinting through bifocals at an open book in his left hand. The Mongolian scholar, wearing his familiar tweed jacket and bowtie, snapped the book shut and turned. "James!" he said, his face lighting up.

Andrews stepped forward. The two shook hands. Herald eagerly motioned Andrews toward a chair. As Herald shuffled around his desk, Andrews sat and surveyed the office.

Nothing had changed since his first visit to the office as an undergrad. The sweet fragrance of Virginia tobacco, emanating from an open tinfoil bag on Herald's desk, permeated the room. Decades of yellowing journals and books lined the shelves. On the wall behind the desk was the framed April 1964 edition of the Soviet newspaper *Pravda*, its lead article warning against attempts to glorify the barbaric Genghis Khan as a "historically progressive personage." Overseeing the office in the back corner was a mannequin dressed as a thirteenth-century Mongol warrior.

Professor Herald had become a Mongol scholar in the sixties, when it wasn't fashionable or practical. Mongolia was inaccessible, hidden deep behind the Iron Curtain. The Soviets were doing everything they could to crush Mongolian nationalism, killing or jailing a generation of Mongolian academics. Meanwhile, Western scholars viewed the early Mongols as simple nomadic warriors, unworthy of serious study.

Herald made his name among scholars of Asian history with an English translation of the *Tobchi'an*, aka *The Secret History of the Mongols*. Battuulga Dashdevinjiin, a Mongolian scholar, uncovered a copy of the book, which had only been rumored to exist. Commissioned by Genghis Khan to document his life and the rise of the Mongol Empire, *The Secret History* was handwritten in original Uighur script and composed in the equivalent of Mongolian poetry. To prevent the book from being destroyed by the Soviets, Dashdevinjiin had it smuggled through a series of academic colleagues to Herald in Charlottesville.

Andrews's gaze moved to a framed list next to the *Pravda*

article. The list contained the names of the Mongolian scholars killed by the Soviets. The last name on the list was Battuulga Dashdevinjiin.

Herald eased into his chair. "Tell me about this bone you found," he said. "I stopped by the lab earlier. Sara told me the bone's DNA markers matched exactly with Oxford's Khan markers. Could it *really* belong to Genghis Khan?"

"I thought it might have," Andrews said. "Until ten minutes ago."

Herald looked confused. "Even though the bone's DNA matches Genghis Khan's DNA, you can't say it's his?"

Herald was many things, but not a molecular biologist.

"In the time frame before and after a mutation developed in Genghis Khan's male lineage, his paternal male relatives, including his immediate ancestors and descendants, would have had the exact same sequences at all fifteen sites," Andrews said.

"Then the bone could just as easily belong to his father or a son," Herald said.

"Yes," Andrews said. "Or a paternal cousin or brother."

"You said you *thought* the bone might belong to Genghis Khan. What changed?"

"I just came from the carbon dating lab," Andrews said.

Herald smiled. This was something he understood. "How old is it?" he asked.

"Seventy-nine years."

Herald's smile dissipated, his brow furrowing. "But . . . seventy-nine years ago, a royal burial on Burkhan Khaldun would have been impossible."

"The Soviets must have buried one of Genghis Khan's descendants there," Andrews said.

"Even then, is it possible these DNA markers wouldn't have changed over the course of almost eight hundred years?"

"It seems unlikely, but apparently none did."

Herald walked to the window and looked outside. "Fascinating! You've found a bone that's seventy-nine years old, but its DNA matches Genghis Khan's DNA from eight hundred years ago." He turned from the window. "Can these markers be correlated with specific traits? Aggressiveness? Intelligence?"

"I'm afraid not," Andrews said. "The sequences are on junk DNA—sequences not involved in gene coding. It's analogous to a book. Junk DNA would be the part of the book you can't read, like the actual paper or binding."

Herald nodded thoughtfully. "So, what's next?"

"I'll apply for another digging permit for next summer. If I get a permit, I'll go back to the second plateau and do more digging."

"De Rachewiltz's site?" Herald asked.

On the mountain's second plateau were a group of rock formations that Igor de Rachewiltz, a renowned Italian scholar, believed were ancient tombstones.

Andrews nodded. "This summer, we excavated a few of the rock formations. At the time, I concluded they were natural, but that's where we were digging when I found the bone. It was in a pile of rubble and dirt—the accumulated flotsam from several formations."

"And if additional excavation of the site doesn't work, what then?" the old professor asked.

Like Andrews, Herald had researched the world's literature, searching for clues to where Genghis Khan was buried. Herald had concluded long ago, however, that because Genghis Khan did not want his tomb found, no one would ever find it. Firm in these beliefs, he'd been able to move on with his research, spending his career analyzing the Mongols' impact on world events. Many times, he'd urged Andrews to do the same.

Andrews shrugged. "If that doesn't work, I'm not sure."

"James, you've read more about Genghis Khan's death and burial than anyone alive," Herald said, his gaze narrowing. "Use what you know against him. It's a battle. You against him!"

Although *The Secret History* went into great detail on many events in Genghis Khan's life, it was silent on his death and burial, stating simply, "In the Year of the Pig, he rose to Heaven." Without other contemporary Mongolian sources,

Andrews had turned his attention to the writings of those impacted by the far-reaching Mongols.

In the European, Russian, Chinese, and Persian histories, accounts of Genghis Khan's burial were as numerous as the number of storytellers. The accounts were contradictory and at best cryptic, if not purposefully misleading. Various historians reported Genghis Khan was killed in battle, died after castration, or succumbed to lightning, malaria, poison, typhus, or magic. Most scholars agreed, however, that Genghis Khan died in 1227 after falling from a horse during the conquest of the Chinese city of Xi Xia. Chinese scholars believe he was then buried at his command center in northern China's Gansu Province. The overwhelming number of reports and most credible, however, describe a funeral procession back to Burkhan Khaldun and a burial near the source of the three rivers—the Kherlen, Onon, and Tuul.

"Genghis Khan was a ruthless adversary ," Herald said, turning and scanning his bookshelves. "To look back on all these writings, it's not a riddle that can be solved, but a maze leading further from the truth. Genghis Khan manipulated the histories. He's manipulated all of us."

1173 Central Asia

Temujin and Jamuka ran across the steppe, laughing. It was night, the moon full and radiant. Jamuka was carrying a skin of fermented mare's milk over his shoulder. In the clearing, they climbed the tree and shared drinks of the airag until the skin was empty. With their heads swimming, propped in the tree's upper branches, they looked up into the star-filled sky.

"Do you think our ancestors are up there watching?" Temujin asked.

"Yes," Jamuka said. "Along with Börte Chino and Qo'ai-maral."

The people of the steppe were believed to be descendants of the blue wolf, Börte Chino, and the doe, Qo'ai-maral.

"Everyone is watching," Jamuka continued. "Everyone except for those that Tengri condemns to wander the earth."

"Where are they?" Temujin asked.

"All around us."

Temujin stared hard into the night sky. After a few moments, he shook his head. "No," he said. "I don't believe they are. I don't believe there are dark spirits waiting to inhabit us . . . or that Börte Chino and Qo'ai-maral are watching us. And I don't believe we're descendants of a wolf and doe. Tengri put us here. He's watching us, waiting to see what we do. When we die, he'll judge us by how we lived our lives. If we're worthy, we'll gain acceptance into the Eternal Blue Sky."

In the distance, a horn sounded. Temujin turned toward Jamuka, who was breathing deeply, his eyes closed. Temujin tapped him on the shoulder. "It's time."

Jamuka woke. The boys climbed down the tree. Temujin held out a handful of knucklebones. "One last game?"

The following day, the Jadaran were breaking camp and heading east. The boys weren't sure when or if their paths would cross again.

In the moonlight, they threw the bones against the base of the tree. Seeing the results, they turned to each other and pressed the matching scars on their palms together.

"*Andas!*" Jamuka said.

"A bond that will last forever," Temujin said.

Leaving the bones on the ground, the boys walked in opposite directions from the clearing.

Temujin glanced frequently back. When Jamuka's shadow had blended into the night, he came to a stop. He could still see the shadowed outline of the large tree against the stars. "Goodbye, Jamuka," he called out.

Jamuka's reply came a few seconds later, feathery and light, wafting over the clearing. "Goodbye, Temujin."

13

From age to age, they have kept their true history in Mongolian expression and script, unorganized and disarranged, chapter by chapter, scattered in treasures, hidden from the gaze of strangers and specialists.

—**Rashid al-din,** thirteenth-century Persian historian

It was one a.m. as Baabar stood in the main conference hall of the Ulaanbaatar Hotel. Thousands of members of the Mongolian Republican Democracy Party watched in anticipation as Nambaryn Jambyn, the party's vice chairman, walked solemnly toward the central podium.

"The election results are in," Jambyn announced.

Cheers of exultation were followed by calls for silence.

"I'll start by listing the number of seats won by each party," Jambyn said. He waited for the hall to quiet before he began. "Independent party . . . five seats. Green party . . . two seats. Civic Will Coalition . . . one seat. Mongolian Democratic Union . . . seven seats."

There was nervous laughter throughout the hall. In the previous election, the People's Revolutionary Party, the holdover from the one-party days of communism, had maintained their majority in the seventy-six-seat Mongolian parliament. The majority vote entitled the communists to appoint the prime minister and Khural speaker, and dictate national policy.

"Communist People's Revolutionary Party . . . twenty-one seats."

Baabar raised his arms and howled. Others keeping tally did likewise.

"Republican Democracy Party and Mongolia's new majority party," Jambyn's voice boomed. *"Forty seats!"*

The hall erupted. Banners waved back and forth as confetti poured from the ceiling. The hall broke into a chant, "R-D-P, R-D-P, R-D-P."

As party members danced in the aisles, it was several minutes before Jambyn, banging his gavel, brought the assembly to order. "Now, I'll list the election results from each constituency," he said.

Another round of cheers shook the hall.

Jambyn, smiling, smoothed the sides of his perfectly coifed hair. Shuffling through a stack of papers, he again waited until it quieted before speaking. "The winner of Ulaanbaatar's northern district is . . . Baabar Onon."

Despite being projected as a landslide winner, Baabar felt a wave of relief. Hoisted onto the shoulders of those around him, he raised his arms in victory while the hall applauded. From his perch, Baabar spotted Mikou in his wheelchair. The party's founder and chairman smiled and waved.

Attentions shifted back to Jambyn. After Baabar was lowered, he walked to Mikou's side. "You did this," he said. "You're responsible for all of this!"

Mikou was a former monk. He was a full Brahmin by the age of fourteen when the Soviets raided his monastery. Shot twice in the legs, he hid in a patch of reeds in a nearby river, before eventually escaping to a monastery in Tibet, which the Chinese destroyed a decade later. While his Tibetan brothers stayed and rebuilt, Mikou could no longer forgive the sentients. Filled with anger, he made his way into the world, determined to change the ways of men.

At the podium, Jambyn announced the next winner. As the hall broke into another round of applause, Mikou shook his head. "This is about the future," he shouted. "It's about what our people can be—a truly democratic union." He motioned Baabar closer. "And your indictments of the members of the corruption committee might have had something to do with it. None of them were re-elected. Victories in those three districts allowed us to gain a majority and avoid a coalition government."

The night before, Baabar had taken the information from his late-night Russian visitor and turned it over to the minister of justice, one of Mikou's old friends and someone sympathetic to the RDP. By ten a.m. that morning, the minister had verified the information. By eleven a.m., the minister had made his indictments—an hour before the polling places had opened.

Mikou paused, looking into the younger man's eyes. "I don't suppose you'll tell me your source?"

Baabar shook his head. "I'm sorry. I can't. At heart, I'm still a journalist."

"But remember, you're not," Mikou said. "This information was given to you for a very specific reason. You're a public figure now. Someone obviously wanted to manipulate the elections." He smiled, motioning toward the crowd. "I can't argue with the results. But they also may be trying to manipulate you. If so, it's vital you figure out how and why as soon as possible."

14

In the year of the burial, trees and grass grew beyond measure over that steppe, and now the wood is so thick that it leaves no passage and they do not know the original tree or the place of the burial, so much so that even the old keepers of the forbidden precinct do not find their way to it.

—**Rashid al-din,** thirteenth-century Persian historian

Late Friday afternoon, Andrews sat in his office working on his presentation for Paris. His phone rang. "Hello," he answered.

"Dr. Andrews, this is Matt, the post-grad from Dr. Marcus's carbon dating lab."

"What can I do for you?" Andrews asked. During his visit to the lab the day before, the student had given him a verbal result with the promise of a hard copy later.

"I called to apologize," the student said. "I was going through your results with Dr. Marcus and we discovered that I made a logarithmic error in my calculations. The estimated time of death is 798 years ago, not 79.8 years."

"Are you sure?" Andrews asked, stunned.

"We're sure. It's 798 years with a margin of error of ± 15 years, establishing a time of death between 1203 and 1233. We've rechecked the calculations three times. I'll send you a hard copy of the results, but Dr. Marcus wanted me to let you know about the error right away. Again, I'm sorry."

"No problem," Andrews said. Ending the call, he dialed Abbey's number. After several clicks, he heard her voice. "Hello," she said, groggily.

Andrews looked at his watch. It was Saturday morning in Ulaanbaatar, 5:30 a.m. "Ugh!" he said. "I'm sorry. I forgot what time it was there."

"That's fine," she said. "Is everything okay?"

"Yes, I sent an e-mail yesterday with the bone's carbon dating results."

"I saw it," she said. "I'm sorry, James. I was hoping—"

"The lab made a mistake," he interrupted. "The bone is 798 years old, not 79.8. With the margin of error, the time of death is between 1203 and 1233."

Abbey laughed.

"Can you believe it?" he asked.

"No, I can't. Could it be anyone else?"

"Jochi was Genghis Khan's only son that died during that period, but he died and was buried in present-day Afghanistan," Andrews said. "History doesn't say anything about Genghis Khan's paternal cousins, but none played an important part in his life and none were likely to have been given a royal burial on the summit of Burkhan Khaldun. His grandfather, father, and brothers—none died during that time. The bone could belong to somebody else, but right now, I can't think of who."

"This will certainly make for a more interesting presentation in Paris," Abbey said. "When do you leave?"

"Tomorrow."

"I should tell you," she said. "I also have some interesting news. It's regarding my X chromosome study."

"You found the Khan markers?"

"No," Abbey said. "Not yet. We're still crunching the numbers. But once we do find the markers, we'll compare their population distribution to the Y chromosome Khan markers."

"To compare the degree of social prestige accorded to Genghis Khan's daughters to that of his sons?"

"Yes," Abbey said. "Similar to the Oxford study, we're detecting the Y chromosome Khan markers in about 8 percent of our male population. As expected, most of these 8 percent have accumulated at least a few mutations. We found one individual, however, who was an exact match for all fifteen Y chromosome Khan markers."

"What's the likelihood of that?"

"Of Genghis Khan's sixteen million living male descendants, I calculated that only two should still have the exact same sequences at all fifteen sites. With our sample size, the likelihood that we would find one of them is–"

"Zero."

"Pretty close," Abbey said. "But the mathematics isn't the interesting part. Ask me who it is."

"Who?"

"Our very own, newly-elected, second-term parliamentarian," Abbey said.

"Baabar? Are you serious?" Andrews had learned of his election win and e-mailed his congratulations. "You know, he's adopted."

"I saw it in the questionnaire he filled out for the study. Does he know anything about his real parents?"

"No," Andrews said. "Baabar told me his adoptive parents knew nothing about his real parents . . . or at least they told him nothing."

Andrews shook his head and laughed. "All those summers we spent looking for the grave, all that time, Genghis Khan was standing right next to me."

"Or maybe the closest thing," Abbey said.

"If the media gets hold of this, they'll have a field day," Andrews said. "I can see it now. Vote for Baabar Onon: Genghis Khan's reincarnation."

"That's why I haven't told anyone yet," Abbey said. "The idea of a reincarnation is obviously ludicrous, but if something like this gets out, particularly in a Buddhist country, it could get out of control. My hope is to find the X chromosome Khan markers. Once we determine they don't match Baabar's markers, we can shoot down any speculation about reincarnation. Someday, we'll all laugh about this."

15

There is a fire in his eyes and light in his face.

—The Secret History of the Mongols

Needing to clear his mind, Baabar went for an early Monday morning run. He'd spent the weekend celebrating the RDP's victory. The summer of campaigning had paid off. But now it was time to get back to the work that mattered—governing.

After the run, he headed for the shower. Passing the kitchen, he recoiled in surprise. His previously unsolicited visitor once again sat at his table.

"Congratulations are in order," the man said. "I hear you've been named chairman of your corruption committee."

Baabar looked toward the windows. None were forced.

"There's no need to thank me," the man continued. Another stack of papers sat on the table. The man reached out and slid the top sheet across the table.

Baabar picked up the paper and read. There were six names. All were Khural members. Two were senior members from the RDP.

"Will it be a problem?" the man asked.

"I need to know who you are," Baabar said. "I need to understand why you're giving me this information."

"To borrow a phrase from one of your party's campaign slogans, I'm someone interested in *a stronger Mongolia.*"

Baabar looked down at the list. "Sarnai Laagan is in line to be prime minister. Puson might be the next president."

"It's important that you're fair," the man said. "By transcending party politics, it legitimizes everything you do."

Baabar dropped the sheet. "I can't do this," he said. "I'm done."

"Okay," the man said. He gave a nonchalant shrug. "Do what you want." He pointed a forefinger at the paper. "But make no mistake. Laagan, Puson, and the others *will* fall. If you don't come out with this information, some other smart, young Khural member will latch on to it and use it to *his* advantage."

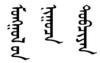

1175 Central Asia

Temujin pushed past the felt flap of his family's ger. His younger brother Khasar followed. The boys were dirty and lean, their hair long and unkempt. They were dressed in the furs of small animals they'd killed: marmots, rabbits, dogs, and rats.

It had been four years since the Tayichiut had abandoned them. During that time, harsh winters had been followed by summer droughts. Food was scarce.

Temujin and Khasar neared a small hill. Crouching, the brothers crept slowly through the dry brush. At the base of the hill, they rose, arrows drawn.

Begter sat lazily on top of the hill, eating a handful of seeds. Seeing his half-brothers, he jumped to his feet, the seeds falling to the ground. He looked toward his bow and quiver.

"Don't!" Temujin said.

The day before Temujin had returned home with a lark and fish. Begter—who was three years older—had taken both.

"As the oldest, it's my right to take the lark, the fish, and whatever else I desire," Begter said.

"I won't allow it," Temujin said.

"If you'd like, I'll give you two birds . . . and two fish," Begter said.

"You cannot return *everything* that's been taken," Temujin said.

Begter was now of age. It was his right to take a wife. He'd chosen Hoelun. The night before, he'd slept at her side. Begter glared at Temujin. "You must learn to accept the way of things."

The night before, Temujin and Khasar lay awake, listening. They could hear them: his mother and Begter, together.

"Your way or nature's way?" Temujin asked. "Your way works out best for only you. Khasar is our best hunter, but you take the biggest portions."

"And Temujin is the smartest, but you insist on leading us," Khasar added.

"I am not the lash in your eye," Begter said. "Without me you'll have no companion but your shadows."

Temujin stared at his older brother, knowing he could not endure another night. "Then so be it," he said.

Temujin and Khasar remained in position, arrows drawn. With a mutual nod, they let loose their arrows.

For a moment, Temujin wished he could take this back. He watched Begter struggling, pulling futilely at the quills, his hands covered in blood.

Begter looked up at his half-brothers, his eyes wide, questioning.

Temujin released a second arrow. As Begter fell, Temujin turned and walked away, knowing he could not spend the rest of his life taking orders from Begter, knowing this is the way it had to be.

16

For a dispersed nation, this is a fine place of refuge; and for a peaceful nation, this is a good pasture-land. For deer and stags it is a fine hunting place, and for an old man a good resting place.

—**Genghis Khan,** while passing through a meadow
near the bend of the Yellow River

Abbey gave a Monday morning lecture. At noon, she attended a lunchtime conference. It was early in the afternoon when she walked into her office for the first time that day and turned on her computer. She checked her e-mail. There was a message from James, sent last night.

```
Abbey,
    Arrived a few hours ago. I'm at the
Hôtel de Crillon in downtown Paris. The
history here is unbelievable. The Nazis
used it as their Paris headquarters. Ben
Franklin stayed here. Outside, a three-
thousand-year-old Egyptian obelisk stands
in the Place de la Concorde, where Marie
Antoinette was guillotined.
    I'm on my fourth espresso of the day,
trying to adjust for the jet lag. I
present at the conference in the morning.
Wish me luck!
    Hope all is well,
    James
```

"Abbey, can you come here?" It was Munhtaya, Abbey's chief lab tech. She stood in the office doorway.

"Sure," Abbey said.

They walked together down the hallway into the lab.

"Since we finished sequencing the bone's Y chromosome markers, I was planning to put the DNA samples into storage," Munhtaya said. She opened the refrigerator. "But they're not here."

After the tests for each of the fifteen markers had been run, they'd kept the remaining DNA in vials in a tray labeled *Burkhan Khaldun.* The tray was gone.

Munhtaya opened the freezer compartment. "And then, there's this," she said, pointing. The container with the bone, also labeled *Burkhan Khaldun,* was gone.

"Is anything else missing?" Abbey asked.

"Only the bone samples," Munhtaya replied. "Nothing else. No equipment. No specimens."

"Was the lab door locked when you came in this morning?" Abbey asked.

Munhtaya nodded.

Abbey's mind raced. Munhtaya was extremely reliable. There was little chance she would have misplaced the samples. Someone must have taken them. *But why?*

"It's a good thing you gave a portion of the bone to James," Munhtaya said. "If we need more, we can just ask him."

Abbey pulled out her cell phone. She scrolled through her contacts, stopping at the number for the lab at the University of Virginia. It was early Monday morning, almost two a.m. in Charlottesville. No one would be there, but she had no other number for Sara. And James was in Paris.

She tapped the phone.

After a few electronic clicks, the international call went through. Several rings later, Sara's voice sounded on an answering machine. "You've reached the University of Virginia archaeology department's molecular biology laboratory. No one is here right now. If you leave your name and . . ."

When the machine beeped, Abbey left a message. "Hi, Sara. This is Abbey. When you get in, please give me a call on my cell. My number is—"

There was another electronic beep. "Abbey?" a voice said. "It's me, Sara."

"Sara, hi," Abbey said, surprised. "What are you doing there?"

"I came in to advance the sequencer," Sara said. "I started a run before I left work. I probably should have waited until morning, but my fiancé is on call tonight and I had some extra time. Why? What's up?"

"To be honest, Sara, I'm not sure," Abbey said. "But something happened here. James's bone and all of our amplified DNA samples from the bone are missing. They may have been stolen."

"Who would take them?"

"Good question."

"If you need more DNA, we can send some," Sara said.

"Thanks, we may take you up on that. But Sara, can you humor me for a second?"

"Sure."

"Where are you in the lab right now?" Abbey asked.

"In my office, reading," Sara said. "The sequencer still has a few minutes before it finishes its cycle."

"Can you check to see if your bone samples are still there?"

"They are," Sara said. "I saw them in the freezer yesterday."

"Please," Abbey said. "Like I said, humor me."

"Sure. Can you hold on?"

"Yes."

Abbey heard the creak of a chair. "That's weird," Sara said. "There's someone in the lab."

"Who?"

"It's *that* student," Sara said.

"What student?"

Sara didn't respond. Abbey heard a clunk as Sara set the phone down.

"Sara!" Abbey shouted. "Stay in your office! Call security!"

Sara didn't respond.

Abbey heard a door opening and Sara's voice, now distant. "What are you doing?"

Moments later, there was a scream followed by a loud thud and the sound of approaching footsteps. There was heavy breathing over the line.

"Sara?" Abbey said.

The line went dead.

Abbey hurriedly redialed the lab number. After a few rings, the answering machine message clicked on and there was Sara's voice. "You've reached the University of Virginia ..."

17

ndrews wore a gray suit, crisp white shirt, and yellow silk tie. He felt refreshed after a full night of sleep as he stood outside the Les Aigles Room of the Hôtel de Crillon. He looked out through a plate-glass window onto the Place de la Concorde, watching the bustle of traffic make its way past the Quai des Tuilleries and across the Seine, heading toward the columned Palais Bourbon. He straightened his tie and turned on his cell phone. His presentation was scheduled to start in five minutes. He quickly checked his messages. Over the last ten minutes he'd received two calls from Abbey.

"James!"

Andrews looked up. His mouth dropped open as the long-legged figure of Hayley Robbins strode toward him. Wearing a charcoal blazer with a knee-length skirt and open neck blouse, she looked as if she'd stepped from the pages of a fashion magazine.

They hugged. Hayley, her long blonde hair braided back into a ponytail, kissed him on the cheek and then stepped back, assessing him. "You clean up well," she said.

During Hayley's two weeks on the mountain, they'd spent almost every waking moment together. The attraction between them had been undeniable. Their relationship had remained platonic, however, until two nights before she left. After everyone had fallen asleep, she slipped into his one-man tent. They made love into the early morning hours. The next night, her last on the mountain, they waited until the others had fallen asleep and then grabbed blankets and walked to a deserted area of the summit, where they started a fire and made love under the stars.

"I thought you weren't going to be here," he said.

"When I saw you were scheduled to present, I knew I couldn't miss it." She smiled, biting her lower lip. "To hell with my travel budget."

They hugged again. "It's good to see you," he said. A conference door swung open. Remy Therriault, a French archaeologist and the moderator for the morning lecture session, emerged. "James, there you are." Hayley squeezed Andrews's forearm. "Maybe we can do some sightseeing afterward." She gave him a quick kiss on the cheek.

Remy watched Hayley walk past him into the conference room before turning toward Andrews. "My friend," he said, winking. "You're almost late, but perhaps I see why." He waved Andrews forward.

They stepped into the darkened conference room. It was full. At the front, Tomas Bjork, a Swedish archaeologist, was speaking. Hayley was making her way toward an open seat in the back row. In the middle aisle, two men sat on the floor, holding television cameras. Several men, apparent reporters, stood in the back, holding microphones.

"The excitement over your presentation extends beyond our little academic community," Remy whispered, motioning toward the cameramen. "Come, this way. Tomas will be concluding any minute now."

As Andrews followed Remy along the back of the crowded room, a man stepped forward, blocking Andrews's progress. "Can I have a moment?" he asked. The man, who was Asian, wore a press badge.

"Dr. Andrews is about to present," Remy said. "I'm sure he'll gladly answer any questions afterward."

"This will just take a second," the man said.

Remy glanced skeptically at his watch.

"Please," the man said. "It's *very* important."

Remy turned toward Andrews, who shrugged.

"All right," Remy said. "But it must be brief. James, lend me your flash drive. I'll load it into the laptop when I introduce you to save time."

Andrews handed the drive to Remy, who continued along

the side of the room. Andrews and the Asian man slipped out a back door.

In the corridor, the Asian's meek demeanor vanished. "Listen!" he said, shoving a cell phone into Andrews's hand. "It's a matter of life and death."

Andrews watched the Asian walk away. He then looked down at the cell phone. The timer was running. He tentatively raised it to his ear. "Hello."

"James, this is Parker."

"Parker, what's going on?"

"Abbey and I are in trouble. We've been kidnapped."

"What?"

"They're making me give the phone back now," Parker said. "But please! Do exactly as they say."

There was a rustling noise followed by a woman's scream. "Abbey!" Andrews called out.

There was a man's voice. "Professor?"

"Yes," Andrews replied.

"Listen carefully," the voice said calmly, speaking in accentless English. "You will report to your colleagues and the assembled media that the bone you found *does not* belong to Chinggis Khan. It's imperative this information reaches the international media."

"Why?" Andrews asked.

There was clapping from the conference room. Andrews cracked open the door. In the front of the room, Remy was thanking Tomas.

"Following the presentation, return immediately to your room," the man continued, ignoring Andrews's question. "You'll receive further instructions. Don't speak with anyone. If you do not comply with these demands, your friends will be killed."

The line went dead.

Remy now stood at the podium by himself. The television camera lights were on. The first slide of Andrews's presentation—the group photo Parker had taken on Burkhan Khaldun—was on the large screen behind the podium. If Remy advanced to the next slide—a summary of the bone's test results—it would be impossible to convince the audience the bone didn't belong to Genghis Khan.

Andrews stepped quickly into the room.

"And without further ado," Remy said, spotting him. "I present Dr. James Andrews."

Andrews took the podium. "Thank you, Remy," he said. His hand slid along the side of the laptop and hit the power button. As he squinted into the bright lights of the cameras, he pulled out the flash drive. He looked up at the screen behind him, feigning surprise when he saw it go black. He hit a few buttons on the computer but to no avail.

Remy returned to the podium. "It was just working."

"I'll be fine," Andrews said. "I only had a few images."

"I'll have someone from IT take a look," Remy said, walking hurriedly off.

Andrews turned toward his audience. "As our esteemed host said, my name is James Andrews from the University of Virginia. This summer, I led an excavation on Mongolia's holy mountain . . ."

Andrews proceeded to give the highlights of his month-long dig. A couple of minutes later, Remy returned with a skinny, bespectacled young man in tow. Andrews waved them off. "I'm fine," he mouthed.

As the two men sat, Andrews looked back toward the audience. It was time to present the lab results. If he was going to convince the room full of archaeologists the bone didn't belong to Genghis Khan, this is when he would have to lie.

"We were able to extract thirty-nine of forty-six chromosomes from the bone," he continued. "One of them was a Y chromosome. After amplification, analysis of the Y chromosome demonstrated nine of the fifteen Khan markers. Subsequent carbon dating analysis performed on the bone indicates the bone is *seventy-nine* years old."

There were murmurs throughout the room.

Andrews looked toward Remy. The Frenchman's face had darkened. In the back, Hayley sat with arms folded, also unable to hide her disappointment.

"Because the bone was found on Genghis Khan's purported burial ground, media reports have incorrectly suggested the remains were his," Andrews said. "Based on lab analysis, however, we can state conclusively: the bone does not belong to Genghis Khan."

Andrews scanned the room, summoning a feeble smile. "I can take questions," he said.

The room was silent.

Remy stood and cleared his throat. "James, you stated the carbon dating studies indicate the bone is seventy-nine years old. At that time, Mongolia was in the midst of the Soviet Purges. Stalin was doing everything he could to crush Mongolian nationalism: imprisoning or executing a generation of Mongolian scholars, destroying historical documents, and killing Genghis Khan's known descendants. Travel on Burkhan Khaldun would have been prohibited. If the owner of your bone died on the mountain, *who is he?*"

"Since the bone contains nine of the Khan markers, it likely belongs to one of his descendants," Andrews said. "But who that is or how he died is unclear."

A reporter raised his hand. "You're telling us you went to Mongolia, spent a month digging, and found a seventy-nine-year-old bone that *might* belong to one of Genghis Khan's descendants?"

When Andrews nodded, the reporters glanced toward each other and shook their heads. One laughed. As the cameramen turned off their lights, Andrews felt a stab of panic. If his results weren't broadcast, Abbey and Parker wouldn't be released.

"Look!" Andrews said, stepping from behind the podium. "The international news media circulated inaccurate reports that Genghis Khan's tomb had been found. This may not be big news in the West, but the location of his tomb is of *profound* importance to the Asian world."

"Genghis Khan was Mongolia's founding father," a reporter said. "Shouldn't they know where he's buried? We French certainly know where our kings are buried. Americans know where Washington, Jefferson, and Franklin are buried."

"The Mongols were nomads," Andrews said. "When they died, they believed their souls transferred to the horse-tailed banners they carried with them during their lives. Since their spirits had moved on, the dead were often left on the open steppe to be reclaimed naturally. They used these spirit banners more than monuments or tombstones to remember their dead."

"Has his spirit banner survived?" a reporter asked.

An elderly British archaeologist stood. He turned and scowled at the reporters. "Excuse me, but this is an *academic* meeting," he said. "An academic meeting of the International College of Archaeologists. It is *not* a press conference. And it is certainly not a freshman lecture hall!"

Remy stood. "I apologize. As moderator, I take full responsibility for the media's presence." He smiled. "I admit I viewed this as an opportunity for the College. Although Dr. Andrews's find hasn't turned out to be what was anticipated, I still view this as an opportunity. One of the missions of our college is to educate. I can't think of a better way of doing it . . . or a better instructor. So, if no one objects, I suggest we let Dr. Andrews answer the gentleman's question."

As Remy sat, everyone's attention returned to Andrews.

"Genghis Khan had a white-tailed horsehair banner for times of peace and a black one for war," he continued. "The white banner disappeared shortly after his death. His descendants built a monastery for the specific purpose of flying the black-haired banner, which was reportedly kept at the monastery for hundreds of years until the Soviet Purges, when the monks were executed and the banner destroyed."

"That's the second time the Soviet Purges have been mentioned," a reporter said. "We know about Stalin's Purges in Russia and throughout the Eastern bloc, but in Mongolia?"

Eyes in the room turned toward the British archaeologist, who fidgeted in his seat but remained quiet.

"In 1924, Mongolia fell behind the Iron Curtain," Andrews said. "Although the Mongol Empire was no longer a threat, Stalin believed it still served as a model for the formation of a Pan-Asian coalition—a coalition that could threaten their supremacy in the Eastern Hemisphere. To circumvent an Asian uprising, the Soviets tried to crush Mongolian nationalism. Stalin's men destroyed hundreds of monasteries and killed thousands of monks. They exterminated or exiled a whole generation of Mongol intellectuals. In all, over thirty thousand Mongols were murdered with countless more imprisoned in Siberian gulags."

Andrews stepped back behind the podium. "Ironically, while Stalin was attempting to destroy Genghis Khan's legacy, he was also trying to learn everything he could about him. He studied Genghis Khan's battle techniques and his philosophy for governing. He even sent several expeditions into Mongolia to find the grave."

"Joseph Stalin was a *student* of Genghis Khan?" a reporter asked.

"He was probably Stalin's idol," one of them cracked.

While many in the room laughed, Andrews looked toward the cameras. They were back on. For better or worse, he had everyone's attention.

"If the grave is found, what would that mean to the Asian people?" a reporter asked.

"Ever since Mongolia emerged from behind the Iron Curtain, their transitions to democracy and capitalism have not gone well," Andrews said. "A third of their people live below the poverty line. If Genghis Khan's tomb is found, the artifacts could be used for a world tour. The tour would not only be a source of revenue for the country, focusing attention on the Mongols' remarkable history and current plight, but a source of pride, an instrument for change."

After a brief moment of silence, Remy stood. "Are there any more questions?"

When no one replied, Andrews nodded. "Thank you."

As the archaeologists in the room politely applauded, Remy and the IT man stood and walked toward the podium. "Sorry," Andrews said to Remy as they shook hands.

"*C'est la vie,*" the Frenchman said with a shrug.

The screen behind the podium suddenly came to life, a brilliant blue. The words "Logging on" appeared.

The IT man stood by the computer, glaring at Andrews, irritated. "Everything is fine," he said with a thick French accent.

"Sorry," Andrews said.

While Remy began introducing the next presenter, Andrews slipped out a side door.

He heard doors opening behind him, but didn't look back. Moving quickly ahead, he passed through several hallways. In the lobby, he bypassed the elevators and ran up the stairs to his third-floor room. Inside, a note and cardkey sat on the bed.

Leave your cell phone on the bed. Take this cardkey to Room 202 and wait for instructions. Leave your bags. They will be brought to you. We're watching. Go now!

He opened the closet and picked up his black leather computer case. His laptop was gone.

Andrews pulled his cell phone from his pocket. Abbey's calls must have been related to the kidnapping. As he raised his thumb, considering returning her call, there were a few sharp raps against the wall. They *were* watching.

He dropped the phone on the bed and picked up the cardkey. He left the room, taking the stairs to the second floor.

Outside room 202, a Do Not Disturb sign hung from the doorknob. He ran the cardkey through the lock. When the lock clicked, he opened the door and stepped inside. The door closed behind him.

The room contained a single bed, a nightstand, and a desk. He didn't see a phone. On the bed was another note.

Stay here until further notice. Do not make any noise. Lock the door. If anyone knocks, do not answer. If you do not comply with these instructions, we will consider it a breach of our contract.

18

Genghis Khan was a doer.

—Washington Post, 1989

Baabar stood in a hallway at Government House, waiting outside the office of Representative Sarnai Laagan, a seven-term parliamentarian from Erdenet. The office door opened. Mikou wheeled himself through the open doorway. Laagan, a tall bombastic man with broad shoulders and a sweeping grin, followed behind.

Baabar stepped forward. "Thanks for meeting with me," he said to Laagan.

"When the chairman of the Committee for the Investigation of Governmental Corruption calls for an appointment, it's probably a good idea to meet with him," Laagan said, winking at Mikou.

Mikou's attention, however, was focused on Baabar. When Baabar met his gaze, Mikou calmly bowed his head. "Gentlemen," he said.

Baabar and Laagan watched as Mikou wheeled himself down the corridor. "I asked him once why he doesn't have an aide push him around," Laagan said quietly.

"Why rush when you're content with where you are?"

"Yes," Laagan said, looking with surprise toward Baabar. "That's exactly what he said."

"He enjoys the time alone," Baabar said.

Laagan motioned Baabar into his office. Laagan moved behind his desk and sat. "So, what can I do for you?"

Baabar sat in a chair facing the desk. He removed an envelope from his pocket and slid it across the desk.

As Laagan opened the envelope, Baabar stood and walked to a window. Just like that, he thought, he could ruin a man's life. He'd turned over the second packet of information the Russian had given him to the minister of justice. He'd included the information the Russian had provided on five of the six individuals, leaving out the information on Laagan. Once again, the minister had used his considerable resources to verify the information. As before, every claim in the stack of papers his Russian visitor had provided was correct. The information, its accuracy and depth, was mind-boggling. Most perplexing, however, was its source. Baabar concluded it had to have come from inside Government House.

Outside, rain pelted Chinggis Square as workers hustled up and down the steps of Government House, their heads covered. The scene reminded him of the day of the demonstration against the Goodwill Treaty—the moment the shooting had started. The fire damage to the façade of Government House had already been repaired. Government House's other shortcomings, however, would not be so easily fixed.

When Baabar turned from the window, Laagan was staring at him, wide-eyed. "How?" Laagan gasped.

The information in the packet about Laagan had not been verified. But now, seeing the terror in Laagan's eyes, Baabar knew it was true. He shook his head. "I can't say."

"Who else knows?" Laagan asked.

"No one on the committee," Baabar said. "Not yet, at least."

"This happened *fifteen* years ago," Laagan said. "Before I was with the RDP. Before the party even existed."

Baabar nodded.

Laagan's gaze hardened. "I nominated you to be the party's representative from the northern district," he said. "I nominated you for the corruption committee."

"That's why I haven't submitted the information," Baabar said. "But trust me, I'm not the source."

Laagan stared down at the papers. "Can it be controlled?"

"It can be. But it'll require . . . sacrifices."

* * *

Baabar was working late that night in his apartment when his cell phone rang. "Hello," he answered.

"London," a voice said before the call ended.

Instead of returning to his work, Baabar grabbed his jacket and stepped outside. He walked from his apartment and headed north through the residential district's sparsely lit back alleys. Looking ahead, his gaze settled on one of Ulaanbaatar's tallest buildings, a twelve-story apartment building several blocks away.

A figure appeared in front of him, wearing a black skullcap and gray overcoat. It was the Russian. He motioned Baabar into the shadows.

After Baabar insisted on no more surprise visits to his apartment, the two had decided on a meeting protocol. If the Russian wanted to meet again, he would call Baabar, say the name of a European city, and hang up. Baabar would then leave his apartment and take a direct path toward the twelve-story building. The Russian would meet him somewhere along the way.

"Why didn't you charge Laagan?" the Russian asked.

The minister of justice, earlier that day, had indicted the five Khural members on charges of corruption.

"Laagan will resign from his post tomorrow morning," Baabar replied. "He's out. In the process, I haven't made another enemy."

"How do you think this looks?" the Russian asked. "A prominent member of your RDP resigns the day after you indict *five* other Khural members."

"Puson was from my party," Baabar said.

"You have to be above partisan politics; otherwise, you'll lose all credibility."

Baabar glared back.

The Russian shook his head. "We have another round

or two of indictments, then we'll move on to other areas." He removed an envelope from his coat and extended it.

"Other areas?" Baabar asked.

"*Zhizn' korotka, a del mnogo,*" the Russian said. So much to do and so little time.

Baabar reluctantly took the envelope.

"Your country has a great deal of work ahead," the Russian said. "Cleaning out the Khural is just the first step."

1178 Central Asia

Temujin woke. He sat up and looked around the ger, thinking he'd heard something. The others lay sleeping on their mats. The fire was out.

He stood. He stirred the fire's embers and stacked more wood. As he blew on the embers and the wood caught fire, he heard a noise. He walked across the ger and peeked past the felt door.

Several unfamiliar men were leading the mares away. Temujin grabbed his bow and quiver. He slipped through the door and nocked an arrow. As he raised the arrow, he heard a low whistling. He turned toward the sound.

A large man stood next to the entrance. The man held a wooden staff, which was swinging toward him.

Temujin woke some time later. He was back in the ger, his head throbbing. His mother was above him, pressing a wet cloth to his forehead.

"The mares!" he said, sitting upright.

"They're gone," Hoelun said.

Temujin groaned, holding his head. "How long have I been out?"

"All day," she said.

"Has Khasar returned?" His younger brother had left the night before on a hunting trip.

"Yes," his mother said.

"Then we still have the stallion?"

"Yes, but—"

Temujin stood and began walking toward the entrance. Hoelun followed. "You're not going after them," she said. "We'll get by without the mares."

Temujin turned toward her. "Do you really think we'll make it through winter without their milk and without their meat?"

"We've made it through worse," Hoelun said. She reached up and set her hand against his cheek, her eyes misting.

"What is it?" he asked.

"You're beginning to look and sound like your father."

A jolt of pride surged through Temujin, a smile crossing his face. Just as quickly, however, the smile was gone, replaced by a look of determination. He continued toward the entrance.

"And you're unfortunately just as stubborn," Hoelun said. "Before you go, let me get you some food."

"I'll be fine, Mother," he said.

"Then take this," she said. She walked to the altar and picked up the ivory-handled knife, extending it. "Your father would have wanted you to have it."

* * *

Temujin tracked the thieves to the east. After three days, he came upon a boy with a herd of horses.

"I'm looking for a band of men that rode past here," Temujin said. "They stole my horses—eight chestnut mares."

"What's your name?" the boy asked.

"Temujin."

"I'm Bo'orchu," the boy said. "What clan do you belong to?"

"I—I'm Borjigin," Temujin replied.

"Borjigin?"

Temujin nodded.

The boy eyed him for a few moments before setting aside

his milking bag. "Men with eight mares passed through here this morning," he said. "I'll show you their path." He walked among his herd and returned with a horse. "Here, take this black-headed gray. Yours is tired."

The boys tracked the thieves for three more days. At dusk of the third day, they arrived on a ridge overlooking a camp. Ten men sat around a fire. In a nearby field, Temujin's mares grazed alongside a dozen other horses.

The boys, realizing they would have to wait until nightfall before reclaiming their horses, rode a safe distance from the camp. Collecting roots and berries from the bank of a nearby stream, they sat and ate.

"Why did you tell me you were Borjigin?" Bo'orchu asked. "Everyone knows the Borjigin were defeated when they warred with the southern kingdom. Everyone knows the Golden Emperor will not allow them to exist, that they can't exist."

Temujin stared into the stream. It was a few moments before he spoke. "After the Golden Emperor defeated the Borjigin, Kabul and his family were killed and the clan disbanded," he said. "But my great-grandmother survived."

"Did she have Borjigin blood?"

"She was Naiman," Temujin said. "After the clan disbanded, she married a Tayichiut. I was raised in the Tayichiut clan."

"How are you Borjigin?"

"Seven months after my great-grandmother married the Tayichiut, she gave birth to a son," Temujin said. "My father's father. He was the son of her Borjigin husband."

"The husband was killed?"

Temujin nodded.

"Then you have a *direct* male bloodline. Do you know who your great-grandmother was married to?"

"Yes," Temujin said. "My great-grandmother was . . . married to Kabul. She was his third wife."

Bo'orchu's mouth dropped open.

"My father told me before he died," Temujin said. "He made me swear I'd never tell anyone except my own sons. He thought I should know, but was afraid that if word spread, men from the southern kingdom would hunt us down."

"Why are you telling me?" Bo'orchu asked.

Temujin's gaze returned to the water. "I'm tired of being ashamed of who I am," he said. "I'm tired of hiding."

* * *

Late that night, the boys rode their horses back to the field, which was now bathed by the pale light from a crescent moon. The fire was surrounded by at least two dozen men, eating and drinking.

Leaving their horses at the edge of the field, the boys crept slowly across it.

Temujin heard a sudden thud. He turned. In the moonlight, he saw Bo'orchu on the ground. Above Bo'orchu was the shadowed outline of the large man, holding his wooden staff.

The man stepped toward Temujin and swung. Temujin leaped back, barely avoiding the staff as it whistled by.

The man swung again. Avoiding the blow, Temujin lunged forward, stabbing with his knife. The knife's tip caught the man's thigh. The man, grunting in surprise, temporarily straightened. It gave Temujin a moment to gather himself and stab again.

Despite the man's large size and being injured, he moved surprisingly fast. Avoiding the knife, he grabbed Temujin's wrist and twisted. The knife fell to the ground. The man, still holding Temujin's wrist, continued twisting.

Temujin collapsed to his knees in pain. When his arm was about to break, the man suddenly let go.

Temujin looked up. Bo'orchu was on the man's back, clawing at his eyes.

The man, again reacting quickly, flipped Bo'orchu over his head. Bo'orchu landed hard on his back.

The man raised his staff, preparing to strike an immobile Bo'orchu.

In one swift motion, Temujin lifted his knife from the ground and thrust it into the man's abdomen.

Temujin caught the glare of the fire in the man's eyes. The man's eyes flashed with anger before they rolled into the back of his head, and he collapsed to the ground.

Temujin helped Bo'orchu to his feet. The boys looked from the man's prostrate body toward the camp.

The thieves sat around the fire, still laughing and talking. None had taken notice.

The boys, backing slowly away, slipped into the darkness.

19

Andrews paced the hotel room. No longer wearing his jacket and tie, the collar of his dress shirt was open, his sleeves rolled up. Following instructions, he'd stayed in the room until further notice. He'd waited for the remainder of the previous day and through the night without a word. It was now four a.m.

He walked to the balcony door and peeked past the drapes. The well-lit American Embassy, just west of the hotel, was tantalizingly close. Suppressing the urge to jump from the balcony and run to the embassy, he turned and poured himself his last cup of complimentary coffee.

Sipping the coffee, he sat on the edge of the bed and watched the television. Earlier, during a moment of defiance, he'd turned it on. When the screen had flickered to life, he'd muted the volume and switched to a twenty-four-hour news channel. All the while, he'd waited for a disapproving knock on the wall. It never came.

On the television, the top story of the moment continued playing across the screen: an oil spill off the coast of South Africa. The now familiar footage from a helicopter hovering over a listing tanker appeared. Andrews's attention wasn't on the crewmen waving from the ship's bow, however, but the words scrolling across the bottom of the screen.

```
AP News: University of Virginia archaeologist
reports remains found in Mongolia do not
belong to Genghis Khan.
```

Andrews pumped his arm in exultation. His results had been broadcast. Abbey and Parker would be released.

The words Breaking News Report appeared on the screen. Video of a seagull flopping helplessly in a pool of sludge was replaced by flames pouring from a building into the night sky.

Andrews stood, an uneasy feeling settling over him. There was something familiar about the building.

The camera panned back. The fire's location appeared in the bottom right corner of the screen: Charlottesville, Virginia.

Andrews recognized the Archaeology Studies Building. His heart racing, he hit the volume button.

"The fire, which is believed to have started last night around two a.m., was extinguished, but not before there was extensive damage," a reporter said.

The broadcast switched to daytime. Students stood outside the building, pointing up at the charred façade. The camera swung to a reporter. "Firefighters eventually extinguished the blaze," she said. "No students were harmed; however, a university employee was fatally injured. Relatives of the woman killed in the fire have been notified. Officials, a few minutes ago, released her name."

The reporter, assuming an appropriate air of solemnity, looked down at a piece of paper. "Her name is . . . Sara Johnson."

The words hit Andrews in the gut.

"Ms. Johnson was a laboratory technician in the university's archaeology department. She—"

There was a knock at the hotel room door. A paper slid beneath it. Andrews swept it up. There was a handwritten note.

Open the door

He looked through the peephole. The Asian stood outside. In a flash, Andrews recalled Sara's words.

It was a little creepy. When I came in, he was just standing at the refrigerator with the door open. He was clearly looking for something.

The man in the hallway wasn't the Asian from the surveillance image. Andrews realized, however, it was somehow all connected: the Asian student, the kidnappings, the fire . . . Sara's death. He threw open the door.

"Back!" the Asian said, raising a gun.

In a rage, Andrews rushed forward. The Asian stepped quickly aside, driving the gun's butt into his face. The blow knocked Andrews to his knees. The Asian grabbed him by the collar and dragged him back into the room. "Get up!"

Andrews climbed slowly to his feet, squeezing his bleeding, broken nose.

The Asian pushed Andrews across the room. He pulled back the balcony curtain and opened the door. "We're going out this—"

"Drop it!"

They turned.

Andrews was shocked to see Abbey standing in the open doorway. "*Abbey?*"

Her gaze and the gun remained locked on the Asian. "Drop it!" she repeated.

The Asian tightened his hold on Andrews's collar, pressing the gun against his temple.

"Shoot him, and you'll be dead a second later," Abbey said. "But either way, in a few moments, a dozen gendarmes will come through this door." She looked toward the open balcony door and nodded. "In fact, they probably have a rifle trained on you already."

The Asian turned toward the balcony. From outside, Andrews heard a soft, but insistent voice. "Down!"

The Asian obediently dropped to his knees. He set his gun on the floor and raised his hands.

Abbey stepped forward from the open doorway, gun raised. As the door began closing behind her, a hand appeared, grabbing the door's edge. Instead of policemen coming through the doorway, it was Parker. Also holding a gun, he walked to Abbey's side. "Hello," he said.

There was a brief look of surprise on Abbey's face. As she turned toward Parker, he grabbed her gun and wrenched it away. Abbey let out a cry of pain.

Parker tossed the gun aside and grabbed a handful of Abbey's hair, forcing her head down.

"*Parker!*" Andrews said, stepping forward.

Parker's gun jerked toward Andrews, who stopped. The Asian was beginning to stand. In one swift motion, Andrews drove the heel of his palm into the man's temple. The Asian flopped awkwardly back through the open door onto the balcony, unconscious.

"Do something like that again," Parker said, looking down his gun barrel at Andrews. "And I'll kill you."

"What the hell's going on?" Andrews asked.

Parker smiled. "I guess we have a few moments before my colleague regains consciousness," he said. He bent over and leveled his face with Abbey's, tapping the gun to her forehead. "Do you want to answer his question or should I?"

"And then what?" Abbey said. "You'll shoot us? Or do you—"

"Shut up!" Parker said, forcing her head farther down. "You're wasting time."

Parker turned toward Andrews, forcing a smile. "The long and short of it is, the Asian Historical Society is a CIA front." He nodded. "And yes, Abbey and I are also CIA. We've been CIA from the beginning."

Andrews shook his head. "No," he said. "Professor Herald would know."

Parker started laughing, his fist still buried in Abbey's hair. "Do you want to tell him this one?" he asked, giving her head a shake. "Or should I?"

Abbey, straining against Parker's fist, raised her head. Making eye contact with Andrews, she mouthed something unintelligible and glanced toward the balcony. Andrews followed her gaze toward the Asian, who was standing.

"If you won't tell him, I will," Parker continued. "The old professor is also CIA. We're one big happy family!"

Abbey suddenly threw all her weight against Parker, ramming her shoulder into the side of his knee. Parker grunted in pain, momentarily relaxing his hold. Abbey stood and drove her elbow into Parker's gut. "Run!" she yelled.

Andrews sprinted toward the Asian. There was the spit of Parker's gun and a searing pain in his back, but his momentum carried him forward.

Andrews collided with the Asian.

The Asian, attempting to stand, lifted Andrews into the air in a bear hug. He backpedaled until he slammed into the balcony ledge.

Together, they toppled over the ledge and fell into the darkness.

1178 Central Asia

After backing away from the thieves' fire, Temujin and Bo'orchu searched the moonlit field for the eight mares. There were now many more horses in the field. Unable to find the mares, they rounded up the entire herd and headed west, riding hard through the night.

At the morning's first light, the size of their herd became apparent. There were well over one hundred.

"We have to keep moving," Temujin said. "They'll be coming."

They continued west. It wasn't long, however, before Bo'orchu pointed behind them. A pack of horsemen were quickly approaching.

The boys jumped from their horses and ran into the herd, slapping the horses' rumps and yelping. The horses galloped off in every direction. The boys then hopped bareback onto two of the stallions. They rode away, low and quick. As they passed over the crest of a hill, however, their hearts sank.

Ahead, more horsemen were approaching, at least forty. Outnumbered and surrounded, the boys pulled up their horses, prepared to surrender.

But the approaching horsemen didn't slow. They rode faster, passing the boys at full speed, their fists raised and whooping.

"They're Jalayir!" Bo'orchu yelled to Temujin. "They're friends!"

Temujin and Bo'orchu watched, ecstatic, as the Jalayir descended on the thieves.

After the thieves had been cut down, a Jalayir horseman rode back toward them.

"This is Qachi, khan of the Jalayir," Bo'orchu said.

Qachi was a large man with a round face. He shook hands with Bo'orchu and then Temujin.

"Twenty of our horses were stolen," Qachi said, a smile forming. "We sent scouts to track them. They returned and reported two boys were herding them back, that *two boys* had stolen all of these horses . . . from horse thieves."

Barely able to contain his excitement, the Jalayir khan looked to the nearby field, where the horses were now peacefully grazing. "I had to come see for myself." With a loud roar, Qachi slapped his thigh and began laughing.

20

Andrews lay on his back looking up at a streetlamp. His head felt as if it would split. He pushed himself to his feet. The Asian was on the sidewalk next to him, immobile, his head turned at an unnatural angle.

"Say goodbye, James."

Andrews looked up. Parker was on the balcony, his face contorted in anger, his gun raised. There was a spit of compressed air.

Andrews's hands went reflexively to his chest, searching for the wound.

There were two more spits. Parker, his body quivering, fell from view.

A young man with blond hair materialized from the darkness, holding a gun. He seemed familiar. "Dr. Andrews," he said. "Step this way out of the light."

Andrews dabbed at his nose, flinching in pain. The effort left a patch of bright red blood on his shirtsleeve.

"Hurry!" the blond-haired man said, looking up at the balcony. "There may be more of them."

Andrews remained frozen in place, his vision growing blurry. He blinked, trying to focus. He followed the man's gaze up to the balcony. As he did, his knees wobbled and gave out.

Once again, he was on his back, looking up at the streetlamp. The blond-haired man was hovering over him.

"Where's Abbey?" Andrews asked.

The man spoke with someone out of Andrews's field of vision. Moments later, he felt himself being lifted and heard a woman's voice. "James, you're going to be okay."

He tried to reply, but drifted into unconsciousness.

1178 Central Asia

Representatives from several steppe clans came to the Jalayir camp to reclaim their horses. Afterward, Temujin and Bo'orchu journeyed back to Bo'orchu's home with the eight mares and ten additional horses they'd been given as a reward. Qachi and a group of his men escorted them.

When they came to the field of horses where the boys first met, Temujin whistled. His stallion broke from the other horses and trotted to his side.

Qachi, amused, laughed and clapped.

Temujin hopped from the black-headed gray. He moved his saddle to the stallion and then rounded up nine horses from their herd. "These are now yours, my friend," he said to Bo'orchu.

"That's almost all the horses we were given as a reward," Bo'orchu said.

"It's your fair share—half of the horses," Temujin said. "I came to you with only the stallion. I'm leaving with him along with my eight mares plus one. That's all I need."

"Keep them," Bo'orchu said. "I went with you as your friend, as friends we'll part."

In the field, a woman and young girl were milking the mares. Spotting Bo'orchu, they ran to his side. The woman turned to the girl. "Tell Naqa his son has returned."

As the girl ran off, Temujin scanned the gray-white gers dotting the valley. In the surrounding hills, he spotted several large herds of sheep and horses. "Your father is Naqa *the Rich?*" he asked.

Bo'orchu didn't respond. Qachi, however, nodded and smiled.

"You left all this . . . to help me?" Temujin asked.

A man rode up from the valley. Qachi rode to greet him.

The two men shook hands and talked briefly before riding toward the boys.

Bo'orchu dismounted. "Father," he said, bowing.

"You shouldn't have ridden away like that," Naqa said. "We found your milking bag and feared you were lost. Your mother, she was worried."

"I'm sorry, Father," Bo'orchu said.

Naqa looked toward the horses. "Qachi told me what happened," he said. "I'm not sure if I should believe him."

Bo'orchu remained in place, head bowed.

"You are my third son," Naqa continued. "In my eyes, just a boy. But the deeds Qachi describes are that of a man."

Bo'orchu looked up at his father, beaming with pride.

"You have shown, my son," Naqa said, his voice breaking, "you will become more than a simple keeper of my herd."

Bo'orchu turned toward Temujin. "Father, this is my friend, Temujin, a clan leader."

Naqa and Qachi exchanged glances. "And what clan might that be?" Naqa asked, smiling.

Bo'orchu began to speak, but then stopped. He looked toward Temujin, who gave a consenting nod.

"The Borjigin clan," Bo'orchu answered.

"You know they no longer exist," Naqa said. "And you should be careful using that name."

"The Borjigin men and their white-bone descendants were killed," Bo'orchu said. "But the Golden Emperor did not kill Kabul's third wife or Kabul's unborn son."

"Unborn son?" Naqa asked.

"Temujin's grandfather," Bo'orchu said. "His father's father."

Naqa, eyes wide, looked anew upon Temujin.

A direct male line?" Qachi asked. "*From Kabul?*"

"Temujin is Kabul's heir," Bo'orchu said, nodding. "Temujin is khan of the Borjigin."

21

Baabar sat in the hall of the Great Khural among the other seventy-five members of the Mongolian parliament. The members sat behind desks arranged in the shape of a horseshoe, an homage to the object upon which the country was built. At the open end of the horseshoe, Prime Minister Sanduin Khorloogiin and President Mandir sat on a raised stage along with the RDP's newly appointed Khural Speaker, Nambaryn Jambyn.

Speaker Jambyn rose and walked to a podium. "For our last order of business," he said, "Representative Onon will speak."

Baabar walked to a standing microphone. "Khural members, Mr. President, Prime Minister, Mr. Speaker," he began, taking in the room. His proud chin jutted forward. "In the recent elections, the people cast their vote in record numbers. They cast their vote for an independent Mongolia, a strong government, and conservation of our land and resources. Each vote was an affirmation of their faith in this parliament and in our Republic. But more than anything, the people cast their vote for change. Our nation's nomadic way of life has engrained change into our very character. In two decades, we've transitioned from a Soviet satellite state to self-rule, from socialism to capitalism, from communism to democracy. Significant gains have been made. But they are not enough."

Most Khural members stood and clapped while members of the People's Revolutionary Party, taking their cues from Prime Minister Khorloogiin and President Mandir, remained seated.

"That's why I must ask my fellow members of parliament

to vote 'no confidence' in respect to our prime minister," Baabar said.

With the Republican Democracy Party's victory in the elections, the vote of "no confidence" in the prime minister was the first step toward electing a new prime minister, which was determined by vote of the Khural members. With Laagan's resignation that morning, there'd been a flurry of activity among the members of the RDP. In the aftermath of the Khural elections, Laagan had edged out Jambyn and Puson as the RDP's favorite to replace Khorloogiin. Jambyn had then taken the open post of Khural speaker, while Puson was slated to be the party's candidate for the presidency, which would be decided in the next general elections. But now that Laagan and Puson were out, many thought Jambyn should resign his position as speaker and become prime minister. The names of other possible nominees, however, had begun to circulate. Baabar was among those being considered.

Baabar turned and walked back to his seat. Although the vote was a simple matter of parliamentary protocol, an uneasy rumble passed through the hall.

Speaker Jambyn rose. "Before we vote on this matter, our prime minister would like to address us."

A hush fell over the room as Khorloogiin stood and walked to the podium.

"Thank you, Mr. Speaker. Thank you, Mr. President. And thank you, members of parliament," Khorloogiin began. He scanned the hall. "Fellow Mongolians, I'm the proud father of seven children and twenty-three grandchildren. Over the years, my wife and I encountered numerous challenges while raising our children. The challenges were different for each child, for each age . . . and *never* stopped."

A few forced laughs echoed through the hall.

"Children question everything," Khorloogiin continued. "Sometimes they're obedient; sometimes they are not. Sometimes they take what you've taught them and do amazing things; sometimes they ignore you. They can break your heart, but they can also bring joys beyond comprehension."

Khorloogiin smiled. "I've been fortunate to see my seven

children grow up to raise their own children. My grown children have since come to me and told me they're thankful for the home we provided. They're thankful for the hard decisions we made, and for our sacrifices." He grabbed both sides of the podium, his smile dissipating. "During my forty years of public service, we were confronted with many difficult situations. Yes, some decisions could be second-guessed, but we led our country through the early years of independence. We survived drought and famine, double-digit inflation, and recession. When our people were starving and livestock dying, we made difficult choices. For *every* decision—"

Khorloogiin's voice broke. He paused to collect himself. "For every decision, there was a winner and loser," he said. "But decisions had to be made. They had to be made for the good of the majority and good of our country. Today, I look at our fledgling nation and am proud of our work. I'm proud of who we've become."

Throughout the room, the members of the People's Revolutionary Party nodded their heads in agreement. A few clapped.

"But instead of thanks for our service, I see malice in the eyes of those who've benefited the most from our work," Khorloogiin said. "For those desiring change, I commend you. Change is a part of life. Recognizing this, I hereby submit my resignation as prime minister. I plan to return to the steppe and my roots as a herder. I look forward to a *simple* Mongolian life."

Khorloogiin pulled an envelope from his suit coat pocket and handed it to Jambyn. With a bow, he walked from the stage.

* * *

That night, Mikou sat in the offices of the Republican Democracy Party. Around him, Baabar and the party's other members of parliament stood clapping.

Mikou waited until everyone quieted before speaking. "During the hunger strike of 1989, we sat in the cold of Sükhbaatar Square while Khorloogiin and the other

Politburo members peeked out from Government House and wrung their hands, threatening to put us in jail." His gaze narrowed. "The Soviets had left, but their puppet regime remained. The will of the people, however, was too strong. Led by Zorig, we fought and won. National elections were held. We had our democracy. Little did we know, however, the battle had just begun."

Sanjaasürengiin Zorig was the leader of the 1990 post-Soviet democratic reform movement that led to the downfall of Mongolia's one-party communist state and the beginning of multiparty elections. In 1998, a week before taking the post of prime minister, Zorig was killed in his apartment. Afterward, Mikou, a member of Zorig's Democratic Union, became disillusioned with the direction the party was taking. Breaking from the Democratic Union, Mikou formed the Republican Democracy Party.

Mikou looked over the room. "While the pursuit of democracy has brought out the best in our people, the pursuit of capitalism has brought out the worst. After the Soviet collapse, the international aid agencies and other ideologues poured into our country. They pushed forward a raw, unregulated capitalism—a form of capitalism that never existed in the West and never will. They held their money in front of us; naïvely, we chased it. We've allowed foreigners to shape our government, our policy, and us.

"For the real source of our problems, however, we must look within. Greed has reigned, providing fertile ground for the vultures of capitalism. Nowhere has this been more apparent than in the privatization of our state resources. Our state industries have slipped from Mongolian ownership at a fraction of their value. Our once indispensable state farms are gone."

Mikou paused. "Khorloogiin knows how to give a speech. For every decision, there is a winner and loser. But when you rule in the extreme, when you consistently turn a blind eye to fairness, the losers in Khorloogiin's world are always the same people. They become the oppressed. As leaders, even though you may be forced to make decisions unfair to some, you can still rule fairly. You *must* rule fairly. You must strive for balance."

Those in the room glanced at one another before their gaze returned to Mikou.

"Despite Representative Laagan's resignation this morning, today was a good day for the party—a day long in the making," Mikou said. A serene smile crossed the former monk's face. "Buddha once said: 'When the ruler of a country is just and good, the ministers become just and good; when the ministers are just and good, the officials become just and good; when the officials are just and good, the people become just and good.' With Khorloogiin's long-awaited resignation, we've said goodbye to the last living Politburo member. More importantly, we welcome in a new era."

Mikou's gaze settled on Baabar. "We must follow the lead of our representative from Ulaanbaatar. Corruption *must not* be tolerated. For if we are just and good, prosperity will follow."

22

Round this place a wall is built, enclosing a compass of sixteen miles, and inside the park there are fountains and rivers and brooks, and beautiful meadows, with all kinds of wild animals. Sometimes the emperor rides through the park with a leopard behind him. If he sees any animal that takes his fancy, he slips his leopard at it. This he does for diversion.

—Marco Polo, description of Xanadu

James stood in an ornate room. In front of him was a platform painted red and decorated with intricate gold carvings. In the middle of the platform was a glimmering, gold throne.

"It's hard to believe this existed two hundred years before Columbus discovered the New World, five hundred years before the United States was even founded."

He looked up. His father stood at his side. His father was smiling, his eyes warm.

Andrews stared up at his father, realizing this was something that had already happened. It was a memory. They were in Beijing.

A woman dressed in a multicolored, full-length *deel* appeared on the platform. She bowed and spoke softly. "Welcome to the Exalted Literature Pavilion," she said. "This was the library of the Imperial College during the Yüan dynasty. It also served as a lecture hall, where emperors once taught students." She smiled, scanning the tourists. "Now, let us return to the year 1355. Emperor Huizong ruled. It was a time of rebellion, drought, and famine."

The woman bowed and shuffled away.

A man with a wispy moustache and goatee dressed in a brilliant gold *deel* appeared from behind the throne. He walked to the front of the platform and looked sternly over his audience. "I am Emperor Huizong," he said, a guttural chop to his voice. "I am known to my Mongol brethren as Ukhantu Khan. I am a seventh-generation descendant of Chinggis Khan and fifth-generation descendant of the founder of this college, Kublai Khan."

He began pacing the platform, his hands clasped at his back. "Today, students, I will read to you from the *Tobchi'an*. I recommend you listen well. The *Tobchi'an*, also known as *The Secret History of the Mongols*, was an instruction manual for the future leaders of the empire, meant for only the eyes of my family members. It contains lessons on the art of war, but also imparts to the willing listener the wisdom necessary to rule. It teaches these lessons by telling stories of Chinggis Khan's youth."

The emperor paused, his gaze settling on the young Andrews. "For it's in the cauldron of our youth that trial and error shapes us into the adults we will become. Chinggis Khan hoped his descendants would be wise enough to learn from his errors without having to repeat them."

James looked up at his father, who was watching him and smiling.

"In the year of the Tiger, 1206 AD, Chinggis Khan was anointed as Great Khan by the steppe people in a *khurlitai* on Black Heart Mountain near Blue Lake," the emperor continued. "Making the Great Law, Chinggis cast it over the people. Using it like a bridle, he steered his new nation on a course of order and peace. Six years of prosperity followed. It was then the Jin emperor sent his emissary, demanding tribute and slaves. In his foolishness, the Jin emperor sparked a fire. It was a fire that would destroy him and burn hotter and brighter than any the world had ever seen."

The emperor picked up a scroll. "In his lessons on the art of war, Chinggis stressed five great principles: variety of tactics, iron discipline, ferocity, surprise, and speed." He looked up. "But the number of his tactics was as great as the number of days he did battle. Even the most ambitious scribe couldn't record them all: luring into ambushes, lightning attack, arc formation, chisel attack, outflanking, encircling." His gaze narrowed. "What's most ironic is that Chinggis wanted to live in peace with the kingdoms to the south and the Islamic kingdoms to the west. But they laughed at him. They maimed his emissaries. They slaughtered his trade delegations and did not pay him respect. They called *him* a barbarian."

He rolled up the scroll and set it next to the throne. "The enormity of what Chinggis Khan proceeded to do with just one hundred thousand men is beyond description. The great cities fell: Lingzhou, Zhongdu, and Ninghia along with Samarkand, Nishapur, Bukhara, Kashgar, Caffa, Otrar, and Merv. As the cities fell, so too did the kingdoms: the Khwarizm, Xi Xia, Song, and Jin. Hundreds of millions were conquered. Twenty-five million square kilometers of territory were acquired."

He fell back onto his throne and exhaled, shaking his head. "The collective fatigue of my ancestors worms its way through the decades and tires me. I need to get away, to rejuvenate myself in Xanadu."

The emperor looked longingly toward a window. "It's almost spring," he said. "Soon, the cranes will come. In Xanadu, there are so many it looks like an approaching rain cloud. At my signal, we release the falcons." His gaze turned skyward. "The falcons fly and meet the cranes. I've never seen anything like it."

He sat straight, suddenly energized. "During the hunt, I ride on a platform carried by four elephants," he said, holding the armrests tight. "The platform is decorated with sofas and silks and rugs of lion skin. We have trained leopards and tigers." He smiled. "Have you seen a leopard bring down a deer? Or a tiger bring down a bull?

"At the end of the day, we celebrate the hunt. The servants follow us and erect a movable palace. Musicians, acrobats, and singers entertain us as we eat and drink. My favorite meal is young eggplant stuffed with chopped mutton, orange peel, and yogurt. We drink the fermented milk from the white mares." He looked toward the window, his gaze distant. "You should see it," he said. "Xanadu." He glanced toward the audience. "Unfortunately, the shadows grow long. I'll return tomorrow, students, and we'll talk more of lessons regarding leadership."

The emperor stood and began walking away, but then stopped and looked back, adding an afterthought. "I must go and make plans to deal with the rebels to the south." A weary smile formed on his face. "Some say these peasants will overthrow me. They say I might be the last of my family's dynasty. I hope they're wrong. I must stay in power so I can pass on the lessons of my ancestors. I must keep our Xanadu alive."

The emperor took one last look around the pavilion. With head bowed, he walked away, disappearing behind the throne.

Andrews felt his father squeeze his hand. But when he looked up, his father was gone. So too were the other tourists along with the platform and throne. The entire pavilion had disappeared.

He was in a room of pure white. It was featureless—a cloud. As he strained to see, gray shaded areas appeared. The gray took on colors, the colors took shape, and the shapes melded into objects. The objects took form.

A woman sat before him. She held his hand, squeezing it, her lips moving. Her hair was long and red and pulled into a ponytail. Wearing a brilliant green robe, her eyes were large and bright blue. She opened her mouth. *"Pouvez-vous m'entendre?"*

He nodded.

"You've had a concussion," the woman continued, speaking slowly in French. "Your nose was broken. You were also shot in the back."

"Where am I?" he asked.

"Pitié-Salpêtrière Hospital in Paris," she said. "I'm your nurse, Tilly."

He tried to sit up, but collapsed back onto his pillow, wincing as pain arced through his back.

"Relax," she said. "You've just come out of surgery. The bullet only grazed your back, but the wound still needed to be irrigated and closed." When she stood and adjusted the stopcock on a bag of medicine, he saw she wasn't wearing a robe, but surgical scrubs.

A blurred figure moved from the back wall. The figure slowly came into focus. It was Abbey. Tears streamed down her face. She took his hand. "God, what you've been through."

"Is it true?" he asked. "*Sara?*"

"Yes," she said. "I'm sorry, James."

"What happened?"

"They stole the bone samples from your lab," Abbey said. "Sara was there when they came."

"*They?*"

"We're fairly sure it was the Chinese," she said. "They also took the samples from my lab."

Andrews's mind reeled. "Is anything Parker said true?"

Abbey took a deep breath. "Yes," she said. "He worked for the CIA."

"And you?"

She nodded.

Anger surged through Andrews. Summoning his energy, he sat up, swinging his legs over the side of the bed.

"What are you doing?" Abbey asked.

"I need to go back," he said, pulling the IV from his arm. "I need to tell Sara's fiancé what happened."

The electronic alarm on the IV pump began to sound.

"Ron already knows," Abbey said. "James, you need to rest!"

He set his feet on the floor. Standing, he wrapped his hospital gown tightly around him and began walking toward the bathroom. His legs moved slowly, his feet unsure.

Tilly blocked his path. "Dr. Andrews," she said. "You're still under the effects of your anesthesia. You have to get back in bed."

"I *have* to change," he said.

He sidestepped Tilly. As he did, his ankle turned. He began falling, but Abbey and Tilly were at his side, supporting him, directing him into a nearby chair.

Andrews felt a sharp pain in his shoulder. Tilly stepped back holding a syringe. She had injected something.

Andrews looked up at Abbey, a progressive numbness washing through him. "I need to teach my classes," he said.

"You need to get better," Abbey said. "Professor Herald and your grad students are teaching your classes."

He opened his mouth to speak, but couldn't. Moments later, he slumped to his side.

Once again, everything went black.

23

Baabar walked hurriedly between meetings at Government House. His cell phone rang. It was an old friend and former colleague, an economic writer from the *Ulaanbaatar Gazete*.

"It's been a long time," Baabar said, answering the call.

"It has been," the friend said. "Are the rumors true?"

Word was spreading that he might be the next prime minister.

"Before you tell me what you're talking about, let me inform you my answer will be no comment," Baabar said.

The friend laughed. "You're becoming the consummate politician."

"As you know, I don't take that as a compliment."

"Actually, I called for something else," the friend said. "I thought you should know about something that's happening on the stock exchange. The government just sold its shares in Khan Metals."

"By whose authority?"

"Khorloogiin's."

"He resigned," Baabar said. "He doesn't have any authority."

"Apparently he does," the friend said. "I know it's probably too late for you to do anything about it, but I thought you should know."

"Thanks," Baabar said, ending the call. He changed directions and walked toward Jambyn's office. Ignoring the objections of a secretary, he opened the speaker's door and stepped inside.

Jambyn sat behind his new desk. "Baabar," he said, standing. "What can I do for you?"

"The government's shares in Khan Metals were just sold on the stock exchange."

Jambyn walked to Baabar's side and closed the door. "They were only minority shares—30 percent," he said, calmly.

"You *knew* about this?" Baabar asked.

"Unfortunately, Khorloogiin has the power to do this," Jambyn said.

"He resigned two days ago."

"His resignation was dated to take effect today," Jambyn said, returning to his desk. "In his last act as prime minister, he signed an order for the state to sell the shares."

"And you didn't stop it?"

Jambyn looked down and patted at a small wrinkle in his freshly pressed shirt. "The important thing is Khorloogiin and the communists are out of power," he said. "The stock sale brought in needed revenue. *We'll* be the ones that benefit."

"Khorloogiin's family owns 25 percent of Khan Metals," Baabar said. "Do you think he was acting in anyone's interests but his own? Privatization is not in the best interests of our country. It's one of our party's basic tenets!"

Jambyn nodded thoughtfully.

"Can't you see what'll happen?" Baabar asked. "In a month or two, his family's shares will be bought out at an exorbitant price. The new majority owners, undoubtedly the Chinese, will bring in their own management and cheap labor. They'll divert the profits elsewhere and pay less taxes, recouping their money within three or four years. And we lose. The Mongolian people lose!"

"Someday, you'll learn to focus on the big picture, Baabar. We're in power. Things *will* change, but change happens slowly. If you focus on the negative, however, if you turn every issue into a battle, your career in politics will be very short."

"You're *defending* Khorloogiin?"

"As speaker, it's my job to ensure a smooth transition in power. It's important that we're civil to one another. The party that's in disfavor one year may be in power the next," Jambyn said.

"Parties *lose* favor when they stop acting in the people's best interests," Baabar said. "We're in power now. We have to act in the best interests of the people. *Now!*"

Baabar stepped around the desk. Furious, he reached out and grabbed Jambyn's tie.

"What are you doing?" Jambyn said, his voice a sudden, high-pitched squeal.

"I don't care about my longevity in politics, smooth transitions in power, or being civil," Baabar growled, tightening his grip. "What's the value of power if you don't follow your principles? We're representatives of the people. You should remember that."

Jambyn's face began turning red, his eyes widening.

"There's no excuse for what happened to Khan Metals today," Baabar said.

Saliva dripped from the corner of Jambyn's mouth onto his shirt. His neck veins began to bulge.

Baabar pushed Jambyn back into his chair. As Jambyn gasped, catching his breath, Baabar turned and walked from the office.

* * *

That evening, Baabar left Government House earlier than usual. In his apartment, he made a phone call. "Barcelona," he said into the phone.

Stepping outside, he passed the previous meeting site. When he was only a few blocks from the twelve-story apartment building, he felt a tap at his back. He spun.

The Russian wore his black skullcap and gray overcoat, his face half-hidden behind the coat's thick collar. "What took so long?" Baabar asked.

"In case you didn't notice, it's still light out," the Russian said.

Baabar glanced around.

"Don't worry," the Russian said. "You're not being followed. What's this about? I presume something important."

"Nambaryn Jambyn," Baabar said. "Do you have anything on him?"

"The new speaker? No, why?"

"The government's shares in Khan Metals were sold today based on Khorloogiin's directive. Jambyn knew about it, but didn't stop it."

The Russian grimaced. "I have nothing."

"Then find something," Baabar snapped. "Anything! I don't care what it is. I can't imagine going through the next four years with that impotent bastard as speaker, or worse, as prime minister."

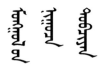

1179 Central Asia

When Temujin was seventeen, he took a wife, Börte. As dowry, Börte's father gave Temujin a black sable coat. It was custom for Temujin to pass the gift to his father; instead, he journeyed north to the land between the Black Forest and Orkhon River and presented the sable to his father's *anda*, Ong Khan.

Ong Khan slipped on the coat and ran his hands over the fur while Temujin knelt before him. Ong Khan stepped forward. "Rise," he said.

Temujin stood.

"Tell me," Ong Khan said. "Those many years ago, on the day of the winter hunt, did you catch your snow leopard?"

When Temujin nodded, Ong Khan laughed. "You have your father's perseverance. Yesugei would be proud." His gaze narrowed. "Did he ever tell you of my debt to him?"

"You shared the bond that cannot be broken," Temujin said.

"Yes, we shared the blood debt," Ong Khan said. "But there was more than that. After my father's death, when I became leader of the Kereyid, my exiled uncle returned. He and his mercenaries overthrew me. Your father led a group of men to the Qara'un Pass. He defeated my uncle and restored me to my position. For your father's deeds, I promised to repay not only him, but his children and their children."

"Your debt was to my father, not to me or my brothers."

Ong Khan reached out and lifted Temujin's chin. "As you did on the first day I saw you, you have a light in your face and a fire in your eyes. The steppe has not broken you, but changed you from a poor, black-boned boy into something more, something much more. For your gift of the sable coat, I'll bring together the people who abandoned you. I'll make you a leader of men."

Temujin motioned toward the coat. "Because you and my father whispered words that cannot be repeated and shared food that cannot be digested, I give you what belongs to you. I ask only that you think of me as a distant, but devoted son."

Ong Khan nodded. "If that's what you wish," he said. "But mark my words, Temujin. There'll come a time when you'll want me to do more than think of you as a distant son, but act as a father. When that time comes, I promise to do so."

24

James struggled to keep up with the long strides of his father. They were walking through the halls of the embassy in Beijing. At the front entrance, a uniformed guard stepped forward. "Sir," he said, saluting. "Will you be needing an escort?"

His father shook his head. "We'll be having lunch at the International Club. After that we'll be walking in Ritan Park."

"How about you, James?" the guard asked while writing on a clipboard. "Need anything?"

The young Andrews pointed at the guard's pistol and cleared his throat, summoning a deeper register. "In case terrorists threaten the ambassador."

The guard crouched and planted a forefinger in his chest. "When you become a marine, it's all yours," he said.

It was a sunny morning as he and his father stepped from the embassy. They turned left onto the Ritan Lu, neither taking notice as they walked past the International Club. At a busy street, they waited for a break in the passing rickshaws, bicycles, and cars, and jogged ahead, leaving behind Beijing's diplomatic quarter and entering the city proper.

Father and son passed through the outdoor market, enveloped by scents wafting from a cornucopia of food, the calls of shopkeepers, and the flow of pedestrians. In a clearing, his father pulled him aside. "The Temple of Heaven."

In Andrews's mind's eye, Beijing's street map unfolded before him. "It's south of the Forbidden City near Tiananmen

East," he said. He looked up, expectant. "Can we take the subway?"

His father dropped to a knee and smiled, holding up two passes.

He grabbed a ticket and ran down a nearby stairwell into the subway. They caught the next car. As they sped north along the counterclockwise loop circling Beijing, they struck up a conversation with a young couple next to them. The couple were students from Nanjing, visiting Beijing for the first time. They were headed to Tiananmen Square.

"You should get off the subway with us at Tiananmen East," James told them, speaking in Chinese. "It's the closest stop to the square. And you should visit Desheng and Qianmen Gates in the Forbidden City. They're the only remaining parts from the original wall. They were built during the Ming Dynasty."

"You're quite the expert," the young woman said, smiling. "Do you know what *Desheng* means?"

"Gate of Virtuous Triumph," he answered.

"And *Qianmen?*"

"Front gate."

The young woman looked up at his father. "Your son's Chinese is very good."

His father rolled his eyes. "I wish mine were as good."

When the car came to a stop, they all exited. Above ground, they said goodbye to the couple and headed toward the Temple of Heaven.

James and his father spent the next couple of hours touring the temple and grounds. Afterward, they walked to Tiananmen Square, where they bought bowls of noodles from a street vendor. Finding a bench, they sat and ate.

"What did you think?" his father asked.

"It reminded me of that church in Washington," he replied.

"The National Cathedral?"

"Yes, but instead of just having colorful stained glass, everything was colorful: the ceiling, the alters, the walls."

His father nodded. "While learning about China's

history and culture—the things that make them different than us," he said, "I can't help but see the similarities. In many respects, they're exactly like us. They want a peaceful, enjoyable life. And they're willing to work hard to achieve it. I was surprised to find the same thing in the Soviet Union. When you really get to know them, the Russian people were not cold and impersonal, but warm and friendly. They have families and children. They want a safe world and peace."

"Dad, on our excursions, why don't you tell the embassy guards the truth about where we go?" he asked.

"It's my job to learn as much as I can about the country," his father said. "It's important to do it firsthand. I can't do that with a phalanx of bodyguards following me around." His father elbowed him in the side. "Have you enjoyed our excursions?"

James didn't reply, his attention focused on a group of several dozen sitting not far away. "Look!" he said. "The teachers from the train." Setting aside his noodles, he hopped to his feet and ran ahead.

The couple, seeing his approach, stood.

"What are you doing?" he asked them.

"We're petitioning the government for the right to free speech," the young man said. "We also want to be able to publish our own newspapers." Bowing, the young man handed a pamphlet to his father as he jogged up.

"And we're petitioning for more transparency in our government," the woman added, handing a pamphlet to James.

His father scanned the group. "Is this a *protest?*"

The young man nodded.

"Is that allowed?"

The group suddenly began hissing as a policeman walked briskly toward them. "Can I see your identification?" the policeman asked his father.

His father opened his wallet and extended a card.

The policeman's eyes widened. "Ambassador Andrews," he said. He bowed and handed the card back. "I apologize."

A low groan came from the protestors. They were looking

toward the edge of the square where a canopied truck, a red star on its hood, had come to a stop. From the rear of the truck, soldiers emerged wearing olive-green uniforms, helmets, and shields.

The policeman turned to his father. "Sir, this way!" he said.

The protestors began whistling and shouting as the soldiers lined up, shoulder to shoulder.

"Please," the policeman said to his father. "You shouldn't be here. These people are criminals."

"What are they being charged with?" his father asked.

"Conspiracy to overthrow the state," the policeman said.

The young man extended a pamphlet. "We're petitioning the government for *basic* human rights," he said. "We haven't done anything wrong."

The policeman brushed the pamphlet aside. When the young man held his ground with the pamphlet extended, the policeman drew his club.

"He's unarmed!" his father shouted.

Shrill screams came from the protestors. The soldiers were marching forward.

"Stand firm!" someone yelled.

Several rocks arced through the air, clattering harmlessly against the soldiers' shields.

"James, let's go!" his father yelled.

He didn't move. He couldn't, his gaze transfixed on the approaching soldiers.

His father picked him up by the waist and began running. "Dad!" he yelled. "We can't leave them."

There was a gunshot.

His father dropped to the ground, covering him, as people ran in every direction.

"Listen," his father said. "When I say so, head toward the subway. Stay low. I'll be right behind you."

The soldiers threw canisters into the crowd. The canisters began spewing gray smoke. The policeman was on the ground, his hat off, his forehead bleeding. Raising his gun, he began shooting into the crowd.

"Now!" his father said. "Run! *Run!*"

Andrews's eyes flashed open. He was breathing hard. The memory was gone. So was his father.

He looked down. He still wore his hospital gown. The lime-green walls and white tiled floor of his room at Pitié-Salpêtrière, however, were gone—replaced by burgundy floral wallpaper and tan carpeting. He held up his forearm. Where his IV had been, there was a small, yellowish bruise.

He walked into an adjoining bathroom and looked into the mirror. His eyes were both blackened. His nose was straight. The doctors had fixed it. As he touched his nose, images of the Asian driving the gun's butt into his face came to him. Other memories followed: Abbey and then Parker coming into the hotel room, Parker grabbing Abbey's hair, the spit of Parker's gun, and the sharp pain in his back. He turned and lifted his gown. A bandage was across his back. He peeled it off, revealing a thin red incision closed by a neat row of blue sutures.

He showered and shaved. His clothes, cleaned and pressed, had been hung over the armrest of a bedside chair next to his duffel bag. He dressed. While packing his bag, there was a knock at the room's door. Tilly entered, wearing jeans and a white sweatshirt.

"Am I still at the hospital?" he asked.

In reply, Tilly walked across the room and opened the curtains, revealing a view of the Place de la Concorde. "You're at the American Embassy," she said. "You spent three days at Pitié-Salpêtrière. The last four here."

"*Seven days?*"

Tilly nodded. "You hit your head very hard, Dr. Andrews. There was some internal swelling. We had to keep you sedated until it diminished. For your safety, your government thought it best if you stayed here."

"Can I go now?" he asked.

"Yes," she said. "Your friend is here again. I'll tell her you're up." She walked to the door and turned, smiling. "Take care of yourself, Dr. Andrews."

"I will, Tilly. Thanks."

Moments after the nurse left, Abbey appeared in the doorway. She walked quickly toward him and wrapped her arms around him. When she looked up at him, Andrews wanted to lose himself in her eyes, in this moment, but couldn't.

He broke away from her and walked to the window, a million questions rushing through him. *Why am I at the American Embassy? Why did somebody take the bone? Why is Sara dead?* As he turned, however, one question pushed to the forefront.

"Is Abbey Conrad your real name?"

"James, I'm the person you've always known. I grew up in—"

He held up a hand. "Why did Parker do what he did?"

Abbey walked to his side. She looked out the window. "Parker took over as the CIA's bureau chief in Mongolia a few years before I arrived. There was little, if any, oversight. People were getting rich. Corrupt Khural members were making a killing privatizing government industries. Only Mongolians were given vouchers to buy shares in the companies, but there was nothing that prevented them from selling out to the Chinese. There was too much money, too much temptation, at least for Parker. He became Beijing's middleman." She turned toward him. "That was my first assignment—to get close to Parker, to find out what he was doing."

"Parker was your job?"

"He was, but he wasn't," Abbey said. "Things happened quickly between us. At the time, Parker seemed like such a man of the world. I looked past his many faults. Despite knowing he was working for the Chinese, I was attracted to him. For a while, I even thought I was in love." She shook her head. "Don't ask me why. Looking back, it all seems so crazy now. I'm not making excuses, James, but I was *so* naïve. I was a researcher, a molecular biologist. I had no idea what I was getting into."

"Did Parker know you were CIA?"

"Yes, but he thought my job was to indoctrinate new agents to the country."

"Your grad students?"

"And other western expats," she said, nodding. "The CIA had decided to make Ulaanbaatar a staging ground for operations in the Far East. The society began funding full-time health care workers, aide workers, even academic positions."

"Is that why you went?"

Abbey nodded. "The CIA wanted to build a network in Ulaanbaatar that was believable and one that would last. They began recruiting outside of the organization: engineers, lawyers, MBAs, PhDs. They were all young, like me. It was heady stuff. Nation building—that's how they billed it. And to be honest, they were right. Instead of coming out of school and taking starting positions at the bottom of some corporate or academic totem pole, we were heading our own design teams, starting our own businesses, and running our own labs."

"If Parker was a known double agent, why wasn't he arrested?"

"In the world of espionage, the evil you know is often better than the one you don't," Abbey said. "Parker has served as a good but unwitting source of information on China's activities. Six months ago, their activities in Mongolia began to accelerate. With Parker's help, the Chinese began buying out minority shares of Mongolia's twelve largest privatized companies. When we found out what they were doing, our people leaned heavily on the remaining shareholders, convincing them to not sell out. One by one, Parker's deals fell through. The Chinese ended up losing a lot of money. We believe that's why Parker was working for the Chinese. He probably didn't have a choice."

"What about Professor Herald?" he asked.

She nodded. "CIA."

Andrews ran his hands through his hair, groaning.

"Professor Herald never told you, James, not because he was trying to deceive you, but because he didn't want you involved."

"The Asian Historical Society funded my research. The Chinese tried to burn down the Archaeology Studies Building.

Sara's dead! Jesus, Abbey! I'm involved."

"I know, James. We wish we could go back. We wish we could do things differently."

"I was just a front," Andrews said. "A dupe!"

Abbey's eyes filled with tears. "It wasn't like that."

"It was *exactly* like that!"

Andrews stood in front of Abbey, his fists clenched, seething. With a loud guttural roar, he stormed from the room, slamming the door behind him.

1179 Central Asia

Temujin recruited other families shunned by the steppe tribes along with several friends, including Bo'orchu, to join him at the Borjigin camp at the base of Burkhan Khaldun. As the clan slowly grew, they began attracting unwanted attention.

One morning, the clan members woke to the whoop of a guard riding hard into the encampment. The clan members rose and hurriedly stuffed prized possessions into their knapsacks. While they bundled their babies and herded their children, they could hear the distant rumble of hoofbeats—the sound of approaching horsemen. Running from their gers, they hopped onto their horses and rode quickly up the mountain.

Temujin looked frantically back and forth. At his side were the other clan members, his family, and friends. But where was Börte? He turned back toward the camp, which was now swarming with horsemen.

"She's gone!" Bo'orchu yelled, blocking his path.

"I have to go back," Temujin said.

"If you do, we face certain death."

"*We?*" Temujin followed Bo'orchu's gaze up the hill to where his mother had come to a stop. Next to her were the heads of each of the families.

Sacrifice the individual to save the clan. When Temujin took control of the clan, it was the first thing his mother had told him.

His gaze returned to the camp. The horsemen were now riding up the hill toward them. With a furious yelp, Temujin spurred his horse up the mountain.

They rode to the hiding place. As planned, Temujin and several of the men then led the attacking horsemen across the steppe and away from the others.

After a few hours of riding, while the other men continued, Temujin circled back to the mountain. He found the clan members safely hidden. Börte, however, was not among them.

Temujin crept to a secluded area that overlooked their camp. Many of the attacking horsemen had given up the chase. They'd returned and were now plundering the encampment. From behind a cluster of thorny bushes, Temujin watched as a few horsemen passed nearby. The men were foreign.

Behind him, there was a subtle noise—a small twig snapping. He spun, drawing his knife.

It was his mother. She moved to his side and looked over the valley. Her eyes were red.

"What's wrong?" he whispered.

"This is all my fault," she said.

"What do you mean?"

"Those men are Merkit."

"Merkit?" Temujin said. "But they're wealthy and live far away. Why are they here?"

"For the oldest and most pointless of reasons," she said. "Revenge. When I was young, a Merkit boy came to our clan. He spent seven years in bride-service to our family. When we were both of age, we married. He was bringing me home to live with his family when your father and a band of Tayichiut attacked us. Seeing my husband was outnumbered, I told him to save himself and not forget me. Then he rode off. I haven't seen him until today. He was carrying the Merkit banner."

"Father *kidnapped* you?"

Hoelun nodded, smiling wistfully. "For months, your

father said I screamed so loudly, hawks fell from the sky. I wanted so much to return home. I had grown up with banquets and plenty of meat and milk while your father and his people survived on wild game and what they could dig from the ground. When you were born, however, everything changed. I decided to stay with your father. Life was hard, but I came to respect and love him."

"Do you want to return to your Merkit husband?"

She shook her head. "I've put thoughts of Chiledü aside," she said. "The pain I once felt is only a vague memory, just as the pain you now feel will also become a memory. With time, you'll forget Börte . . . and she'll forget you."

"This Merkit remembered you," Temujin said.

"I've been told Chiledü went on to have many wives and many children. But if he had stayed and fought your father, he would have died. Chiledü did what was necessary to survive that day, which is now what you must do. Put your feelings for Börte aside, Temujin. It's a woman's fate to be a spoil of war."

25

Andrews spent the next few hours walking briskly through the streets of downtown Paris, sweating away the inactivity of the last week. The toxic metabolites from the anesthetics, antibiotics, and assortment of other medications he'd been given slowly leeched from his system. His anger, however, wouldn't dissipate. Each step seemed to fuel it. He'd been the CIA's fool. But it was worse than that. He was Professor Herald and Abbey's fool. They had lied to him . . . for years.

It was dark when he bought a coffee at a café along the Rue Royale. Finding an open table outside, he sat back and sipped the coffee. He tried to relax. Instead his heart raced. It wasn't the effects of the caffeine or his persisting anger, but the sight of a wrought-iron streetlamp emerging from the pavement and curling above him. After tackling the Asian and falling over the balcony ledge, he woke looking up at a similar streetlamp.

He closed his eyes and let the sensations from that night return. He remembered Parker on the balcony, Parker falling from view, and the blond-haired man appearing over him. He remembered the overwhelming weakness, collapsing to the sidewalk, and the sensation of being lifted . . . carried by his arms and legs. There was a descent into darkness, but there was something else, something just out of reach. Throbbing pains came from his broken nose, concussed head, and injured back, but they mingled with other sensations: his body swaying back and forth, the scent of perfume . . . and something soft brushing against his face.

His eyes flashed open. Staring into the dull glow of the streetlamp, he saw wispy strands of hair waving in front of him. The hair was long . . . and blonde.

He pulled out his cell phone and went immediately to UCLA's website. He searched the faculty listings for the archaeology department and then the social studies, humanities, and history departments. *Nothing.*

He dialed the number listed for the archaeology department. As the phone rang, he checked his watch. It was one p.m. in Los Angeles.

"Hello, can I speak to Hayley Robbins?" he asked when someone answered.

"Who?" a woman asked.

"Hayley Robbins, an instructor in archaeology."

"I'm sorry," the woman said. "But we have no one on the faculty by that name."

"Could you please check?" he asked. "Maybe in another department?"

The woman gave a curt laugh. "Where are you getting this information?"

"What do you mean?"

"A few weeks ago, we received another call asking for a Hayley Robbins. The caller was quite sure she was on our faculty. But after I checked our department listings, two times I might add, I assured her there was no one here by that name."

Andrews walked from the cafe. Several minutes later, he entered his room at the embassy. Abbey, who was sleeping on the couch, woke.

"Hayley Robbins," he said.

Abbey sat up, bleary-eyed.

"That night at the Hôtel de Crillon, she was outside the balcony on the sidewalk," Andrews said. "Who is she?"

"We know she was at the conference during your presentation, but that's it," Abbey said. "We've tried to piece together what happened that night. We've reviewed the hotel's surveillance footage and interviewed hotel workers, but found nothing. No one saw anything. After Parker shot you, he knocked me out. When I came to, Parker was dead on the balcony, the Asian was dead on the sidewalk, and you had disappeared. A couple minutes later, we received word that someone had been found unconscious near the hotel entrance. It was you."

"Hayley and Dmitri carried me there," Andrews said.

"Dmitri?"

"He was one of Hayley's students from the mountain. He was outside the hotel that night."

"The voice from the balcony?" she said. "The voice that told the Asian to drop the gun?"

"Yes."

Abbey gave a knowing nod, a piece of the puzzle falling into place. "You're sure they were there?"

"Yes," he said. "The problem is a Hayley Robbins doesn't work at UCLA. But you already knew that, didn't you?"

"James, I—"

"Who is she?" Andrews interrupted.

Abbey's gaze turned sympathetic.

"Come on," he said. "With your resources, you must know by now."

Abbey stared back. After a few moments, she gave a reluctant nod. She stood and walked to an end table next to the couch. She opened a drawer and removed a folder. Slipping a photo from the folder, she extended it.

The photo was a blurry black-and-white portrait of Hayley. She was wearing a fur cap, a star in the middle.

"After you left this summer, I tried finding out more about her," Abbey said. "From Parker's e-mail picture, I ran her photo and the image of her two students through the Langley database. It took a while, but something finally turned up." She motioned to the photo. "Her name is Elena Lebedeva. The photo is from her graduation ceremony from the SVR's equivalent of boot camp."

"The what?"

"The *Sluzhbza Vneshney Razvedki*, the former KGB's first directorate," Abbey said.

"You're telling me she's a Russian spy?"

Abbey nodded. "She left the SVR several years ago and went back to school. After earning a PhD in Asian history, she started working at the Hermitage. It appears, however, she's been lured back to the SVR."

Abbey slipped another photo from the folder and held it up. "Have you ever seen this man?"

It was a color photo of a dark-haired man. Ruggedly handsome with a graying goatee, he was jogging across a street, wearing a black skullcap and gray overcoat.

"No," Andrews said.

"His name is Stasio Arganov," she said. "He's a career officer with the SVR. In the past year, he's been spotted several times in Ulaanbaatar."

Abbey raised two other photos—young men wearing berets.

"Hayley's foreign exchange students," Andrews said. He pointed. "Dmitri was from Moscow. Yao was from Hohhot."

"Petr Zhilkin and Anton Markovic," Abbey said. "They're Spetsnaz GRU, members of Russia's special forces. Both grew up in Moscow. Zhilkin is a lifelong Muscovite. Markovic's father was Russian and his mother was Mongolian. Markovic's parents met and married when his father was stationed in Ulaanbaatar before the fall of the Soviet bloc. When the Soviets withdrew, she returned with him to Moscow. Anton was born several years later."

"What were they doing on Burkhan Khaldun?"

"That's a good question," Abbey said. "I believe it all comes down to the bone."

"The bone?"

"You said you were with her when you found it?"

"Yes," Andrews said.

"I believe she brought it to the mountain."

"Why would she do that?"

"When you flew back to Ulaanbaatar, half of Mongolia's news media was waiting for you. At that point, nobody outside the excavation team knew about your find. Someone tipped off the media. It wasn't you. It wouldn't have been Parker. I think it was the Russians."

"Why?"

"Consider the timing," Abbey said. "After your find on Burkhan Khaldun and the demonstration in Chinggis Square, there was a surge in Mongolian nationalism. It was right before elections—elections that resulted in the pro-Chinese Communist People's Revolutionary Party being thrown from power. It's not a coincidence. Despite their recent actions in the Ukraine, Russia is no longer interested in Eurasian dominance. But like the United States, they don't want to be overrun by the Chinese. They prefer a strong Mongolia. An independent Mongolia benefits everyone except for China."

"Okay, hypothetically speaking, let's say she planted the bone," Andrews said. "The DNA markers match the Khan markers. The carbon dating matches with the time of death."

Abbey smiled. "You're the one that told me Stalin sent men into Mongolia to search for the grave."

"They never found it."

"They never *reported* finding it," she said. "If they found it, would they have told anyone? No. The last thing Stalin wanted to do was glorify Genghis Khan. Stalin's purges were an attempt to do the exact opposite."

"Still, why would the Chinese react like this over a bone?"

"For the same reasons the Russians gave it to us," Abbey said. "There's no greater symbol of Mongolian independence than Genghis Khan. If we confirm the bone belongs to him, the recent surge in Mongolian nationalism will likely continue, possibly turning into something more. The Chinese were trying to block that. Beijing realizes that if the surge in nationalism continues, it might not only mean the end of the Communist party in Mongolia, but the coup de grâce for Chinese ownership of Mongolian companies. In our growing cold war with China, it's the CIA's position that we do everything possible to assist the Mongolians in maintaining their independence."

Abbey walked to the window. "Unfortunately, there's something else," she said. "Over the past couple decades, China has been content to let its growing economy gradually swallow its northern neighbor. China's acquisitions, however, aren't happening as fast as they would like."

"What are you saying?"

"Over the past few weeks, a half-million Chinese troops have moved into bases along their northern border," Abbey said. "The Chinese are massing their troops. They want Mongolia and they want it now."

"Do the Mongolians know?"

"Not yet," Abbey said. "But with only ten thousand active troops, there's not much they can do to stop it."

"Manifest destiny," Andrews said.

Abbey nodded. "That's what the leaders in Beijing will claim," she said. "They believe Mongolia belongs to them. Less than a century ago, it did. In China's mind that's the blink of an eye. With Mongolia's untapped mineral deposits, open land, and potentially enormous oil and gas reserves, it's the answer to many of China's problems."

Andrews gave a thoughtful nod. He picked up his bag and walked to the door.

"Where are you going?" Abbey asked.

"I just bought an airplane ticket at an internet kiosk," he said. "In two hours, I leave for LaGuardia."

"James, you can't go."

"Why not?"

"We need you in Mongolia."

Andrews laughed. "It sounds like you need a few hundred thousand soldiers, not an archaeologist," he said.

"Actually, we do happen to be in need of an archaeologist," she said. "We need you to find Genghis Khan's grave."

"You just said you think the Russians already found it."

"Not officially," Abbey said.

"And you want me to *officially* find it?"

"We're currently making inquiries with the Russians," she said. "If they have the remains, as we suspect, then yes, you'll rediscover them."

"So, if finding one bone can push the communists from power, why not find the rest of him and see if the Mongolians will fight off the Red Army?"

"I believe it's worth a try," she said. "You, as much as anyone, know what Genghis Khan means to the Mongolian people. Public opinion may be our most powerful weapon."

"Why me?" he asked. "Anyone could do this."

"The institute is denying all requests for digging permits on Burkhan Khaldun, with one exception, that you lead it."

Andrews set down his bag. "Baabar," he said.

Abbey nodded.

"He probably thinks he's doing me a favor."

"He is," she said. "This summer, you left the mountain in pristine condition. The institute is rewarding you. If you go, the Asian Historical Society is also prepared to offer you substantial grant money."

"A herder or a hiker could just stumble across the bones," he said. "You don't need me."

"The find has to be as believable as possible," Abbey said. "Most Mongolians believe Genghis Khan is buried on the mountain. That's where we have to find him. As you know, there aren't many herders or hikers *wandering* the mountain."

Andrews shook his head. "No," he said. "I won't do it. In Paris, I lied to the media. I'm not doing it again."

"You don't have to. You'll be our ticket to get on the mountain, but once you're there, the remains you find will be sent to the institute. After that you can back out. I imagine the institute wouldn't be adverse to taking credit for the find."

Andrews walked to the window and looked outside. In the Place de la Concorde, lights at the base of the high-reaching Egyptian obelisk were directed up into the night sky. On either side of the obelisk were two large fountains bathed in lights—their spiraling streams of water shimmering as they arced through the air.

"Nothing seems like it was real," he said. "Professor Herald, the society, my research . . . you. Sara's dead. The person I thought I was doesn't exist anymore."

"Professor Herald wanted you to be able to pursue your dream of finding the grave without the political baggage he carried with him every single day," she said. "Your life, your research and teaching have been real, James. It's *our* lives that have been a lie. I'm here now as your friend. Whether or not you do this doesn't change that." She paused. "But Professor Herald, along with the hierarchy at the CIA, they feel bad about what's happened. They're offering three million dollars in grant money if you go back."

Andrews shook his head.

"What if the money could be used to set up scholarships in Sara's name?"

"I won't take society money in my name," he said. "I won't do it in hers!"

"What if it came from somewhere else: the National Academy of Science or the Smithsonian?"

"The same money, but with a different signature?" he asked.

"Yes, but to serve *your* purposes: a foundation for Sara, building a new lab, research projects. A lot of good can be done. Your name doesn't have to be associated with reports of any of the findings. You won't have to lie to anyone."

Abbey returned to the couch and sat. "It's your decision, but if this isn't handled right, what should be an incredible discovery for Mongolia may backfire. If they have a yak herder find the bones, trust me, he won't be ready for the attention. At some point, he'll crack. If the truth that the Russians found the remains comes out, this would turn into a complete farce. Instead of building Mongolian nationalism, it would be a huge embarrassment."

Andrews's gaze returned outside. He thought of Sara as she sat on his windowsill, looking toward the Rotunda.

I thought I'd sit in the gardens and read a good book. I never have.

He turned toward Abbey. She knew exactly what it would take to get him to go back.

"Instead of using the money for my research, I'd like to set up a foundation for Sara at the University of Virginia," he said. "The foundation will pay for two molecular biology majors a year—all expenses. I'd also like to set up a foundation for three Mongolian students to study at Virginia—the Battuulga Dashdevinjiin Foundation. Baabar will oversee it."

"What name was that?"

"Battuulga Dashdevinjiin," he said. "The Mongolian scholar who smuggled *The Secret History* from the country. The last one killed during the purges."

Abbey nodded, writing the name on a paper. "Is that it?" she asked.

"One more thing," he said. "I also want a donation made to the Rotunda Society at the University of Virginia. I want a bench in the East Gardens named after Sara. Whenever someone walks by that bench or sits to read a book, I want them to see Sara's face. I want them to think of her."

26

A man of tall stature, of vigorous build, robust in body, the hair on his face scanty and turned white, with cats' eyes, possessed of dedicated energy, discernment, genius, and understanding, awe-striking, a butcher, just, resolute, an overthrower of enemies, intrepid, sanguinary, and cruel.

—Minhaj al-Siraj Juzjani,
thirteenth century Persian historian,
eyewitness description of Genghis Khan when he was
sixty years of age

It was early morning when Baabar walked into his Khural office. His administrative assistant sat at her desk, her face buried in her hands.

"What's the matter?" he asked.

She looked up. She was crying. "He—he's dead."

"Who?"

"The speaker."

Baabar's stomach turned. "Jambyn? *How?*"

"They say he was stabbed. His body was found in his apartment this morning."

"Do they know who did it?"

The assistant shook her head.

Baabar, shell-shocked, walked into his office. He fell into his chair and ran his hands over his close-cropped hair, his own words ringing in his head. *Then find something. Anything! I don't care what it is.* With those words, had he ordered Jambyn's death?

Until now, the game he'd played with his enigmatic Russian visitor had worked to his advantage. He'd cleaned up Government House, creating a culture of nontolerance. He was doing the right thing. And he was in control. *Or was he?* He hadn't lied about the source of his corruption information, but he hadn't told the truth. If his source became known, however, there would be questions, inquiries, scandal. His political career would be ruined.

Baabar walked from his office and out of Government House. In the parking lot, he climbed into the jeep and drove away, dialing the Russian's number.

"Belfast," he said when the Russian answered.

He ended the call, his thoughts turning to the corruption of Laagan, Puson, and the others. In each case, their transgressions began small, but progressed until the borders between right and wrong had been blurred beyond recognition. Is this how it started? Was the Russian trying to destroy him?

He parked outside the twelve-story building and watched the entrance. Moments later, someone walked quickly past his door, rapping once against the window. It was the Russian.

Baabar climbed from the jeep and followed him down a sidewalk and into an alley.

"Why did you do it?" Baabar shouted.

The Russian turned and jabbed a forefinger into Baabar's chest. "You're the one that said you couldn't go through the next four years with him as speaker."

Baabar knocked the Russian's hand away. "I thought it would be like it was with Laagan," he said. "You'd find something from his past, something that would cause him to step aside. I didn't think you'd kill him."

The Russian glared back. "If anything, you should be thanking me for doing your dirty work."

"Who did it?" Baabar asked.

"A prostitute."

"*What?*"

"A young man," the Russian said. "They're regulars at Jambyn's apartment."

Bile rose in Baabar's throat. He bent over and spat. "Why couldn't we use that against him?" he rasped.

"*Les rubyat schepki letyat,*" the Russian said. "What's done is done."

Baabar straightened, wiping his mouth. "I don't know what you're planning, but I won't be blackmailed. I'll resign before—"

The Russian raised his hands. "We're done."

"*What?*"

"We're done, my friend. I have no more information for you," the Russian said. He shrugged. "As of this moment, our alliance is over."

"After cleaning out the Khural, you said we still had a lot of work to do."

"*You* have a lot of work to do," the Russian said. "You're a good man, Baabar. I wish you the best of luck." With a smile and nod, he walked back down the alley.

1179 Central Asia

After the Merkit left the mountain, the Borjigin returned to their camp and began rebuilding. Temujin, however, remained on the mountain, considering his next course of action.

His mother was right. He should try to forget Börte. This was the way of the steppe. Unless things changed, this would always be the way. But the clan would always live in fear. Whenever the larger clans desired, they could raid his camp and take their fill of livestock and women without fear of retribution.

Sacrifice the individual to save the clan.

In this case, his mother was wrong. If his people were to remain loyal, if the Borjigin were to prosper, each person had to know the full power of the clan stood behind them.

Leaving Börte behind had been the right decision during the raid, but now he had to save her. To preserve the clan, he had to save the individual.

After three days and nights on Burkhan Khaldun, Temujin rode north to the land of the Kereyid. He entered Ong Khan's tent and knelt before him.

"The time you've foreseen has come, my khan," he said. "The Merkit have taken my wife, Börte. I ask that you think of me as more than a distant son. In return, I will think of you as more than a distant father."

Ong Khan stroked his beard, eyeing Temujin. "Your *anda*, Jamuka, has also sworn his allegiance to me," he said. "You will both march to the Merkit camp. He will take his men on the right flank. You will lead your Borjigin and my men on the left. Together, we will defeat the Merkit."

* * *

Temujin and Jamuka led their respective armies along the opposing banks of the Selenge River. On the third day of riding, they came to the outskirts of the Merkit camp. While the others prepared for battle, Temujin rode by himself into the camp. He found the Merkit hurrying back and forth, packing their belongings.

"How far away are they?" an old man asked Temujin, mistaking him for a Merkit warrior.

"Less than a half day's ride away," Temujin said.

"Do we know who they are?" the old man asked.

"The Borjigin," Temujin replied. "They come for the woman."

"The woman, that's all?" the old man asked. He looked to a lone ger on a nearby hill. "Go. Tell this to Chiledü."

Temujin spurred his horse up the hill. He entered the ger, breathing a sigh of relief when he saw Börte packing clothes with a group of women.

In the back, a man loaded items from the altar into a crate. The man, who appeared to be his mother's age, was tall and strong and had an aristocratic look.

"Chiledü," Temujin called out.

The man looked up, glancing toward a sword leaning against a nearby crate.

"Toqto sent me," Temujin said, referring to the Merkit leader. "It's the Borjigin that approach. They come for Börte."

"The Borjigin?" Chiledü said. He smiled. "Then, we have nothing to fear."

"They come with their allies: the Kereyid and Jadaran."

Chiledü turned, hands on hips, and looked pensively toward Börte. "What does Toqto suggest?"

"That we avoid war."

Chiledü gave an accepting nod. "Leave me alone with her, for just a little while," he said.

"*You mean—?*"

"I must have my revenge," Chiledü said, his jaw clenched.

"She's been with you for *eight* nights."

"The more I try, the harder she fights," Chiledü said. "The more I tell her that her efforts are in vain, the louder she shouts her husband's name."

Temujin looked across the ger. The women had stopped packing. Börte stood frozen in place, staring back at him. "Temujin," he said.

Chiledü turned. "What did you say?"

"Temujin. Is that the name she calls out?"

Chiledü looked between Temujin and Börte. The Merkit lunged for his sword, but Temujin kicked it away. With one swift motion, he plunged his ivory-handled knife into Chiledü's gut.

Grabbing the older man's collar and pulling him close, Temujin stared into the Merkit's eyes.

"Who are you?" Chiledü hissed.

"I am the oldest son of Hoelun . . . and son of Yesugei." He paused, driving the knife farther in. "I am Börte's husband. I am Temujin."

27

"Is that it?" Abbey asked. She and Andrews stood by the window in the room at the embassy.

He nodded.

Abbey pulled out her cell phone. She dialed a number. A moment later, she was relaying Andrews's conditions for returning to Mongolia.

"That's great," she eventually said into the phone. "But that's not all. In addition to the money for the foundations, we want three million for James's research."

"No!" Andrews mouthed, stepping forward.

Abbey turned her back to him. "We want it in the form of individual grants for PhD students. Two a year for the next ten years, but nothing can be in his name."

Andrews grabbed Abbey's shoulder and turned her toward him. "No!" he said.

"Yes!" Abbey snapped, glaring up at him. "He's not asking for it, I am. I owe him. *We all do!* Take it out of my operating budget, the society's budget. I don't care where you get it. If you're not authorized, then find someone who is!"

There was a prolonged silence before Abbey gave a grim nod. She slipped the phone into her pocket and walked to the door, where she picked up his bag. "Let's go," she said.

"Where?"

She broke into a broad smile. "You're going back to Mongolia. You're going back to Burkhan Khaldun."

* * *

A few hours later, Andrews and Abbey sat at a table eating an early morning breakfast inside the concourse of Paris's

161

Le Bourget Airport. Abbey was talking on her phone with Munhtaya. When she finally ended the call, she looked up at Andrews. "You won't believe this, but Munhtaya just finished sequencing Baabar's X chromosome markers. They match with those in the bone."

"His X *and* Y chromosomes match?" Andrews asked.

Abbey nodded. "If the bone belongs to Genghis Khan that means Baabar's parents are both Genghis Khan's descendants."

"With his mother passing him the X chromosome and his father passing him the Y chromosome," Andrews said. "That's mind-boggling."

"Along with the fact that after over thirty generations, there have been no mutations at the marker sites in either gene," she said. She smiled. "Either that or Baabar really is Genghis Khan's reincarnation."

Andrews sat back. "Does the fact that it appears that you had Genghis Khan's bone and already have the X chromosome Khan markers change anything about your study?"

"Not really," Abbey said. "The real purpose of the study is to determine if Genghis Khan's daughters survived, if they thrived, and if so, where. We can still do that."

Andrews nodded. "To me, the interesting part about the Oxford study wasn't that they simply detected the Y chromosome Khan markers, it's what detection of the markers told us about their various study populations."

"The Hazaras?"

"Exactly," Andrews said.

After the Mongol Empire split into four parts, one of Genghis Khan's grandsons, Hulega, ruled the Ilkhanate—the Middle Eastern kingdom between Afghanistan and Turkey—until his death in 1265. Hulega's descendants then ruled the Ilkhanate for another eighty years before its collapse. In the subsequent power struggles, Hulega's descendants were thought to have been killed until centuries later when the Hazaras, a community in neighboring Pakistan, claimed to be his long-lost descendants. The Oxford study supported the Hazaras' claims since almost one-third of their men possessed the Y chromosome Khan markers.

Abbey nodded. "My hope is that detection of the X chromosome Khan markers in the general population will tell us something about the daughters and their offspring."

"Do you have more DNA from the bone?"

"It's gone," Abbey said. "Why do you ask?"

"No reason," he said. "But if the Chinese think you still have some DNA, they might come back. You should be careful."

Abbey smiled. "You're worried?"

"Sure," he said, grudgingly.

"That means you care."

"Old habits die hard."

Abbey set her hand over his. "I was hoping they wouldn't die at all."

Andrews recalled what Sara had said.

Besides me, Abbey Conrad is the only other steady female in your life . . . Every year, you always manage to keep a dialogue going after you come back. Either you leave something with her or she gives something to you.

He looked down at Abbey's hand. What she and Herald had done was wrong. He believed her, however, when she said they'd kept him in the dark, not out of indifference or malice, but concern for him. He also believed what she'd said about her relationship with Parker. She'd been young and naïve. Like himself, too naïve.

Their waitress approached. "Anything else?"

Andrews turned his palm skyward. His and Abbey's fingers entwined. "No," he said. "I think we'll be fine."

1179 Central Asia

A victory feast was held to celebrate Börte's return. As everyone ate, Hoelun walked up behind Temujin and wrapped her arms around him. Together, mother and son scanned the room.

"Did you think we'd ever gaze upon a feast like this?" Temujin asked.

The ger was full. Leaders from the Kereyid and Jadaran clans had joined with the members of the Borjigin.

"I'm not surprised we gaze upon a feast *or* company like this," Hoelun said. "When you were born, there was a light in your face and a fire in your eyes. In your eyes, I saw a determination, a determination not of this world."

"What you saw in my eyes was the reflection of your own," Temujin said. "When the Tayichiut abandoned us, you choked down your own hunger to feed us. With your juniper stick, you dug out roots of *chichigina* and *südün*, wild onions, and garlic. When father died, I was just a boy. But you taught me how to act with a pure soul and how to be a man. The way I am, what we've accomplished, it's because of you."

The room had quieted. Everyone was standing, facing them.

Börte stepped forward and raised a cup. "My husband," she said. "They told me you had ridden away, over many hills and many rivers. They told me no matter how loud I screamed, you would not hear me; no matter how much I longed for your embrace, you had forgotten me. But I never lost my confidence you would find me. And you repaid my confidence. For that I will be forever grateful." She bowed.

"My Börte," Temujin said, standing. "Tengri has bound us together. It is not man's right to break us apart." He scanned the room, raising his cup. "Tengri has bound all of us together: Kereyid, Jadaran, Borjigin. If we stick together, if we all stick together, we cannot be broken."

* * *

Late that night, Temujin stood outside, gazing up at the stars.

"There you are."

Temujin turned to see Jamuka walking toward him, holding a skin of airag over his shoulder. Jamuka lifted the skin, and they shared a drink.

Jamuka slapped Temujin on the back. "Let's renew our bonds of brotherhood."

The two walked up the mountain to a ridge overlooking the valley. Without the trepidation of their first ceremony, they pulled out knives and dug them into their palms.

"Men who are sworn brothers share one life," Jamuka said.

"They do not abandon each other, but become protectors of that life," Temujin added.

As they had before, they shared the food that could not be digested. "Brothers," they said in unison, slapping their palms together.

Temujin removed a gold sash from his robe and extended it. "This is from the Merkit that kidnapped Börte. A small sign of my gratitude."

Jamuka laughed. "We think alike, my brother." He removed a similar sash. "This is for you. I took it from Toqto."

Wrapped in their sashes, they fell onto the grass and stared up at the stars.

"It seems as though nothing has changed," Temujin said.

"What do you mean?" Jamuka asked.

"I thought I would be different when I grew older," Temujin said. "But inside me, the same voice speaks."

Jamuka sat up and looked over the valley, his eyes dancing with the flicker of countless campfires. "I wish everything was the same as when we were boys," he said. "When my father died and I took over the clan, however, life changed. It felt as though I climbed onto the back of a cart, a cart someone else was driving. I can see where I've been, but not where I'm going."

"But, you're a clan leader."

"Yes!" Jamuka said, his chin held high. "Khan of the Jadaran!" His gaze dropped to the cut on his palm. "Let's just say, my friend, it's not what I expected." His eyes darkened. "The expectations of our youth have served as only a burden. A burden the demands of leadership have required me to shed."

Jamuka looked up at Temujin and nodded. "Yes, I know

of this inner voice you describe. The same voice speaks to me, but I can no longer listen. And each time I don't listen, each time I ignore that voice, it becomes more distant."

"Why can't you listen?"

Jamuka smiled. "This was a great victory for you," he said. "The price of that victory, however, has yet to be paid. You are Ong Khan's new favored son, but someday he'll come to you and ask you to do something. He'll remind you of today, of your debt to him, and tell you the consequences if you do not obey him. When that time comes, you'll realize you're no longer driving your cart. You'll realize that for your clan to survive, you can no longer listen to your inner voice."

28

The army transport taxied across the tarmac. Andrews and Abbey sat in the back row of the passenger compartment. The compartment was filled with CIA agents, Andrews's supposed dig team. Each of the men wore crisp, new, long-sleeve plaid shirts, khaki pants, and hiking boots along with heavy pullovers or jackets. Trying to play the role of archaeology grad students, they looked instead as if they'd raided a Lands' End outlet.

A baby-faced man with dark, curly hair and thick glasses slid into the seat next to Abbey. He was the only one of the agents without a buzz cut and the only one that could have passed for a grad student. After fastening himself into the seat, he turned toward Andrews. "Why were you on Burkhan Khaldun this summer?"

"Pardon me?" Andrews asked.

The young man raised a dog-eared copy of Andrews's travelogue. "Your arguments for Genghis Khan being buried at Baljuna were so convincing. Why look anywhere else?"

Andrews pointed at the travelogue. "You read that?"

"I did," the man said. He extended his hand. "Joel Rosenthal."

"Joel is the commanding officer of your dig team," Abbey said.

The two men shook hands. Rosenthal's attention quickly returned to the book. He opened it and began thumbing through the pages. "It was right here . . ."

Andrews glanced toward Abbey. Smiling, she turned her attention to her cell phone.

The transport thundered down the runway and lifted into the sky, leaving Le Bourget for Ulaanbaatar.

Andrews looked out the window. During his and Baabar's travels over the Mongolian countryside, they'd used *The Secret History of the Mongols* along with other histories to find where Genghis Khan was born, where he called his great *khurlitais*, and where he defeated his enemies. The names of most locations in the ancient accounts were no longer in use, but by cross-referencing the histories, tracing the etymology of name locations through time, and correlating descriptions with landscapes, they'd been able to find many important sites that were only cryptically described in the histories: Back-Heart-Shaped Mountain, Spleen Hillock, Tilted Cliff, Seven Hills, Blue Lake, and Fox Pass. Of all the important sites they searched for, however, the one still eluding them was Baljuna.

For all *The Secret History's* detailed descriptions of important events in Genghis Khan's life, it never commented on the far-reaching events at Baljuna, where Genghis Khan and his followers established the bonds that would hold their future empire together. Accounts of Baljuna, nonetheless, seeped into the European, Chinese, Russian, and Persian chronicles. By the time the accounts were recorded, the preceding numerous retellings had warped the details. Baljuna was assigned different names and locations. It was described as a river and a lake.

The earliest source discussing the location of the covenant was the Chinese chronicle, *Memoirs of the Affairs of the Chung-t'ang*, which made reference to the "prime meritorious" who participated with Genghis Khan in the drinking of the muddy waters of the Hei-ho-tzu River. Subsequent Chinese histories made references to the *Yin-hun-shui:* the fortunate nineteen who shared in the drinking of the turbid waters.

A respected nineteenth-century Chinese geographer, Hsü Sung, believed the Baljuna River was located in the *Čečen'khan* territory, in the land of *Čžalaknor gin' čžabu*, along today's Kherlen River. At the site of the covenant, Hsü Sung wrote, the Baljuna River passed the rampart of the *Balasykutul myao*, a Buddhist monastery of the Yellow Hat sect. The monks at the monastery were reportedly descendants from one of Genghis Khan's daughters and a son of one of his most trusted generals.

A nineteenth-century Japanese historian, Li Wen-t'ien, placed Baljuna along the Lung-chü River at the site where Genghis Khan built Avarga, his capital city. Another Japanese scholar, T'u Chi, stated the covenant took place at Lake Pan-chu-ni. "Its water comes from branches from the lower reaches of the Kherlen," he wrote. "The lake overflows from the northeastern corner to form the Pan-chu-ni River."

Andrews's fascination with Baljuna had pushed him beyond the ends of his scholarly patience. After extensive forays throughout Mongolia, he and Baabar had never found the rampart of the *Balasykutul myao* in the land of *Čžalaknor gin' čžabu* or the Hei-ho-tzu, Pan-chu-ni, Lung-chü, or Lu-kou Rivers.

"Here," Rosenthal said. He held up Andrews's book and read:

> *At Baljuna, outnumbered and exhausted, Genghis Khan's followers risked their lives to follow him when all instincts for self-preservation screamed otherwise. Baljuna has been described as Genghis Khan's Henry V moment, his St. Crispin's day. Such a pivotal event, laced with such mystic devotion, would have made great fodder for* The Secret History. *But it was excluded. Why?*
>
> *Most historians point to Burkhan Khaldun as Genghis Khan's burial site because it was where he was born. I believe, however, Genghis Khan chose to be buried at Baljuna because it was the birth site of the Mongol Empire. The covenant at Baljuna, the most important event in Genghis Khan's rise to power, was excluded from* The Secret History *for the same reason the details surrounding his death and burial were excluded, because Genghis Khan wanted his burial site to remain a secret, because he wanted to rest in peace.*

Rosenthal looked up. "Did you ever find it?" he asked. "Baljuna?"

Andrews shook his head.

"Why'd you give up?"

Andrews smiled to himself. He'd spent six years in dusty corners of libraries, combing through long-forgotten Russian, Chinese, Arabic, Uighur, and Latin manuscripts, searching for clues to Baljuna's location, searching for clues to the burial site, believing they were the same.

"We chased down every clue, but came up with nothing," Andrews said. "I had to move on. To me, Burkhan Khaldun always seemed like a pretty good second guess. I presume that's where the Russians found his remains, which isn't surprising. Just about every historical account written near the time of Genghis Khan's death suggests he's buried there."

Rosenthal looked down at the open book. "Your argument for Baljuna is *very* convincing."

"And wrong," Andrews said. He shrugged. "But if you're really interested in the subject, I suggest you read more. Every Asian scholar has had a theory on where Genghis Khan was buried. Baljuna just happened to be mine."

PART
2

ᠬᠣᠶᠠᠷ

If my body dies, let my body die, but do not let my country die.

—Genghis Khan

ᠲᠡᠮᠦᠵᠢᠨ   ᠴᠢᠩᠭᠢᠰ

29

Four months earlier in Russia's northwest corner, Dr. Elena Lebedeva followed the bent figure of an elderly official through the corridors of St. Petersburg's Hermitage Museum. The museum, once the tsar's Winter Palace, had been meticulously restored to the Romanov's full, nineteenth-century neoclassical glory.

They entered a stainless steel lift, a conspicuously recent addition. The official hit the button for the basement.

"In the archives, I've come across several interesting documents," Elena said as the doors closed. "They may help the American."

The official, a former Gorbachev aide, shook his head. "The situation in Mongolia is accelerating," he said, peering at Elena above his bifocals. "We need to act faster than we thought. Much faster!"

When the lift came to a stop, the official hit a button on the panel. The doors remained closed.

The official turned toward Elena. "Your expertise in Asian history and previous experience with the SVR puts you in a unique position," he said, raising a thick, bushy eyebrow. "I'd like to make you an offer—one that extends beyond your current consultative role."

An assistant director of Asian artifacts at the Hermitage, Elena had recently been named as a consultant to the government's Asian Affairs Committee, which the official chaired.

"But if you choose not to accept my offer, you must forget everything you see and hear from this point on," the bureaucrat said. "In other words, before we proceed, I need to know you can be trusted."

"You've seen my record," Elena said, dismissively. "Have I ever done anything to suggest I can't be?"

The official grunted to himself. Removing his identification badge, he ran it through an electronic reader. A panel slid back on the lift's control panel, exposing a small glass window. He removed his bifocals and looked into the window. A thin light passed over his eye followed by an electronic voice. "What floor?"

"Three," the official replied.

The lift jolted. Instead of making its way up, however, the lift descended.

When the door opened, the official shuffled ahead. Elena walked with him through a maze of sterile, tan-walled corridors before they finally stopped at a door.

Sweating and out of breath, the official passed his badge through another reader. When the lock clicked, he pushed the door open and flicked a light switch. Several bare ceiling bulbs went on, illuminating a long, narrow room. A bulb hissed and then popped, going dark.

The official walked down a central aisle. Elena followed.

On each side of the aisle were dust-covered tables, piled high with old clothes, jewelry, knives, and coins along with countless books—their bindings split, their covers warped and stained. Numerous bins were filled with an ancient arsenal of swords and spears along with several poles that held faded banners. The room appeared to be a storage facility, a reject area for artifacts not meeting the Hermitage's criteria for public display.

The official walked to the end of the central aisle and then down an aisle to the right. He stopped in front of a glossy black casket. It appeared to be the only item in the room dating from this century. A tag hung from its lid.

Property of Soviet Science Academy, Genetics Division.

Rummaging in his pocket, the official removed a key. He inserted the key into the lock and turned. The lock clicked open. The official suddenly straightened, grimacing as he held his lower back. "Go ahead," he said, waving a hand toward the casket. "Open it."

Elena reached out and lifted the lid.

Inside the casket's shadowed interior was a skeleton. The bones, old and decayed, were colored a sickly yellow. The forehead of the pockmarked skull had collapsed on itself.

Elena's eyes passed over the bones. She reached out to touch one, but the official raised a hand. "They're almost eight hundred years old."

Eight hundred years. That was before the Romanovs. It was before Peter the Great and Ivan the Terrible.

Elena turned toward the official, who was watching her, smiling. "Think outside Russia."

Thirteenth century.

When her eyes widened, the official threw back his head and laughed. "Based on your recommendations to our committee, it's rather ironic, isn't it?"

"This summer," she said. "The mountain."

"Yes," the official said. "The American will be more successful than he ever dreamed."

Elena stared dumbfounded into the casket. *"How?"*

The official removed a handkerchief and wiped the sweat from his brow. "Before I tell you more or proceed with my offer," he said, "I need to know two things. Are you willing to rejoin the SVR? Are you willing to go to Mongolia?"

30

Elena Lebedeva stood on the balcony of a tenth-floor apartment, looking over downtown Ulaanbaatar. It was night. Petr walked from the apartment holding shot and wine glasses. He handed her the wine. "Pinot grigio. As ordered."

"Thanks," she said. She took a drink and then stared down into the swirling liquid.

"You seem preoccupied," Petr said.

"There's a lot going on," she said.

"Did Stasio end it with the Mongolian?"

She nodded. "Yesterday." She looked toward the apartment. "Are they back yet?"

Stasio and Anton had driven to the airport to set up the team's flight home.

"Not yet," Petr said. He threw back his vodka, gritting his teeth as it burned its way down the back of his throat. "When did you two meet, anyway?"

"A long time ago."

Petr gave a disgusted shake of his head. "He must have been *twice* your age. He must be—"

"Be nice," she interrupted.

Petr nodded. His gaze, however, remained fixed on her. "You're from St. Petersburg, right?"

"I grew up on the campus of St. Petersburg State."

"Was your father a teacher?"

"Yes, he still is—a physicist," she said. "And my mother was a historian."

"Was?"

"She died when I was young."

"Did you know her well?" he asked.

Elena turned and looked over the city. Petr and Anton had performed admirably as her students on the mountain. Petr had also done well in Paris, but he was still young and naïve—certainly too naïve to realize he didn't have a chance with her.

"No," she said. "Growing up, I knew two things about my mother. She was beautiful and crazy—at least according to my father. I also thought she was dead. But when I was twelve, my father took me for a drive to the outskirts of St. Petersburg. We stopped at an asylum. He told me that she had died there, two days earlier."

She paused, taking a sip of her wine. "Shortly after I was born, my father said he came home from work. I was in my crib. My mother was on the bed, nonresponsive, an empty bottle of painkillers next to her. She survived, but was admitted to the asylum. For twelve years, that's where my mother had been—less than ten kilometers from where we lived."

Elena shrugged. "Who knows what was really wrong with her. They diagnosed her as bipolar, but maybe she just had post-partum depression. Maybe she just needed counseling or time. Instead, they gave her electroshock therapy and a myriad of psychotropic drugs. My father said he visited her for the first year, but she only became worse. When she could no longer recognize him, he stopped going."

Elena turned back toward Petr, her eyes welling with tears. "That day when I was twelve, on the way home from the asylum, we dumped my mother's ashes into the Bolshaya."

"I—I'm sorry," he said.

The balcony door slid open. Stasio stepped outside. He looked between Elena and Petr. "Is everything okay?" he asked.

"Sure," Petr said. "Let me get you a drink." He slid past Stasio into the apartment.

Stasio walked to Elena's side. "Was he bothering you?"

She swiped at her eyes. "No."

Stasio stepped back toward the door, but Elena grabbed his arm. "I can handle Petr," she said.

"What did he do?"

"Nothing," she said. "He was just asking about how we met."

Stasio's gaze narrowed. "The bastard was wondering how an old man like me could—"

"No," she said, pulling him back. "We were making small talk. I ended up telling him about St. Petersburg and my mother. You know how I get."

Stasio remained fixed in position, staring toward the door.

"Please," she said. "Come here, Stasio. Take in the view of the city. It's nice."

He let her pull him to the railing, where they stood side by side. Only scattered lights illuminated the downtown region. Much of the city was in shadows.

Stasio frowned. "It's terrible. After St. Petersburg, I don't see how you can stand to even look at it."

She laughed. "It is rather desolate. But we've seen worse, haven't we?"

"Unfortunately, we have." Taking a relaxing breath, he set his elbows on the railing. "Did you remember how we met?"

"Of course."

He nudged her with his shoulder, smiling. "That was quite a night, wasn't it?"

"Yes," she said. "It was."

An academic prodigy and the daughter of the renowned physicist, Alexei Lebedeva, she started taking classes at the university when she was fifteen. By eighteen, she'd earned a history degree and begun graduate work. On her nineteenth birthday, her friends took her to a nightclub. They told her it would be an educational trip, an attempt to see how the other, less cerebral half lived.

At the nightclub, while her friends peered with academic detachment over the dance floor, her heart raced. The club was a combustible, living, breathing mass of pulsating flesh, lights, and music. When Stasio walked toward her with his devilish grin, something within her ignited.

After several dances and a few drinks, she and Stasio

left the nightclub as well as her friends and life as she knew it behind. Following visits to two more clubs, they ended up in Stasio's condo: a lavish construction of mahogany, steel, and glass adorned with leather sofas, plush carpets, and an expansive view of the Neva River.

The night with Stasio had been one of firsts. It was the first time she'd had too much to drink. It was the first time she'd done anything spontaneous or reckless. It was the first time anyone had made her feel beautiful or wanted. And it was her first time with a man.

Following their whirlwind night together, she and Stasio met regularly for dinner along the Bol'shevikov ulitsa or a late-night coffee capped off with bliss-filled sessions of lovemaking at his condo. Sophisticated, handsome, and exciting, he offered her a life she hadn't dreamed of: endless expense accounts, summer dachas, nightclubs, and travel. It was a life that wouldn't be relegated to the recesses of a dusty library, cramped office, or two-bedroom apartment, but one that played out on the world stage.

Against her father's wishes, she quit school and joined the SVR. Possessing an undergraduate degree, she was able to apply for officer training.

After three months of training, she and Stasio were a team. But she was soon disillusioned with their *grand* work. Stasio was an assassin and she was his lackey, lover, and cook. At the whims of their station chief, they moved from country to country, living in squalid flats in Belgrade, Helsinki, Hamburg, and Krakow.

After three years, it all came to an end when their station chief was linked to organized crime. Their work had not been for the good of the country, but the advancement of the Russian mob. In the fallout, Stasio took another field position. She went back to school.

The balcony door squealed open. Stasio and Elena turned. Anton stepped outside and handed a glass of vodka to Stasio.

"Petr and I are making a food run," Anton said. "Are either of you interested?"

"Yes," Elena said. "I'm starving. I'll be there in a second."

Anton nodded. "We'll wait."

When Anton closed the door, Elena turned toward Stasio. Four months earlier, after she agreed to rejoin the SVR and return to Mongolia, the elderly Asian Affairs committee chairman had taken her from the basement room back up to the first floor of the Hermitage and introduced her to the director of Mongolian SVR operations. It was Stasio.

"You said if I did this, if I came with you to Mongolia, you'd give me my space," Elena said. "And you have, Stasio. I respect that."

"I'm sorry," Stasio said. He extended his arms. "I love you, Elena Lebedeva. You know that. I always have."

She gave a consoling smile.

"I know, I know," he said. "We can't just return to the way we were." He paused. "Let me make a proposal, Elena. I'll continue giving you your space. All I ask is that when this is over, we have one last drink together. If your feelings for me haven't returned by then, we can go our separate ways."

She nodded thoughtfully. "That's a deal."

He raised his glass in salutation and downed it. "You want something more from life, Elena Lebedeva. What is it? Tell me and I'll give it to you."

"I wish I could, Stasio."

"Is this about the American? Is that why you went to Paris?"

"I'm not sure." She looked back over the city. "I feel like I did on that night we met at the club. If I hadn't gone with you, I would have burst. It's the same feeling now, just as intense, just as urgent. There's something out there waiting for me . . . I just don't know what it is."

31

Baabar woke to the sound of his cell phone buzzing. It was almost one a.m. "Berlin," the caller said.

Before he could respond, the line went dead. Only the day before, the Russian had ended their alliance. For some reason, it was back on.

He dressed and stepped outside. A cool September wind swept through Ulaanbaatar's streets. He pulled his jacket collar tighter around him and walked through the darkened back alleys, bracing for the Russian's approach. The Russian, however, didn't appear.

Baabar continued to the twelve-story apartment building. At the entrance, outside large wooden doors, he paused and looked around. Not seeing the Russian, he stepped inside.

Dimly lit, the lobby was spacious, but in ill repair, its walls cracked and peeling. A clerk, his face buried in a magazine, sat behind a worn reception desk.

Baabar walked across the lobby and took an elevator to the tenth floor. He followed the room numbers to Apartment 1022. As he knocked on the door, his cell phone buzzed. He answered the call.

"Baabar, where are you?" a woman asked.

"Who is this?"

"I'm a colleague of your contact. The man you've been dealing with."

"Then you should know where I am," he said. "He just called me."

"You're on your way to the apartment," she said, her voice suddenly panicked. "Something's wrong!"

The apartment door opened. Two men appeared. Both were Chinese. One of them motioned Baabar inside.

"I'm actually at the apartment," Baabar said, the phone still to his ear. "Someone just opened the door."

"Is it your contact?" the woman asked.

"No."

"Get out of there!"

Baabar extended the phone. "It's for you."

One of the men took the phone and lifted it to his ear. "Nǐ hǎo."

Baabar shoved the man back into the apartment and ran to the stairs. The men followed.

The stairwell filled with the squeak of rubber soles on concrete and the sounds of the men's exertions. Emerging onto the ground floor, Baabar sprinted toward the entrance and pushed through the front doors.

* * *

Elena stared down at her cell phone. Her call with Baabar had ended. "Drive faster!" she said to Petr.

Anton leaned forward from the car's backseat. "Did he say anything about Stasio?"

"No," Elena said. "Just that he'd knocked on the door and someone else answered."

Following her conversation with Stasio on the balcony, Elena had left with Anton and Petr. While they'd been on their food run, she'd called Stasio to see if he wanted her to bring him a late dinner. He didn't answer. After a couple more unanswered calls, she began to worry about him. She checked his cell phone activity. When she saw that he'd called Baabar, she'd called the Mongolian to see if Stasio was with him.

Elena pointed. "Go to the front," she said as they neared the apartment building.

Petr stopped at the entrance. The building's large doors swung open. A figure emerged.

Elena recognized him immediately. In addition to photos

from newspaper clippings and campaign material, she'd seen photos of Baabar as an infant, his yearly school and university portraits, and even his driver's license and passport photos. He appeared calm in the photos, in control. To her surprise, he appeared so now, even though he was running for his life.

She stepped from the car and waved. Baabar swerved toward her. Behind him, two Asian men emerged through the building's open doors, holding guns.

"Down!" Elena and Anton yelled together. Anton was at her side, his gun drawn.

Baabar dove to the pavement. Elena also dropped to the ground. There was a flurry of shots.

After a moment, Elena looked up. The men chasing Baabar were on the ground. Anton was still standing, but he was bent over, holding his abdomen. He looked toward her, grimacing, before he crumpled to the ground.

"Anton!" she yelled. She tried to lift him. "Petr, help me."

Petr was crouched behind the driver-side door, his gun raised. She followed his gaze toward the front entrance of the building, where Baabar stood over one of the Asian men, rummaging through his pockets.

Baabar pulled out a cell phone and slipped it into his own pocket, then turned and ran toward her. "I've got him," he said.

Grabbing Anton beneath the armpits, Baabar lifted him. They fell together into the backseat of the car. She slammed the door behind them and jumped into the front.

Petr was back in the driver's seat. He put the car in gear. In a screech of tires, they accelerated from the building.

In the back, Anton writhed in pain, holding his abdomen—an expanding circle of blood soaking his shirt. Baabar, kneeling on the floor, slid Anton's feet up onto the backseat. Baabar then removed his jacket and applied pressure to Anton's wound.

"Did you see Stasio?" she asked.

Baabar turned. "Who?"

"Your contact."

"No," he answered.

Elena looked toward Petr. "Stasio may still be alive," she said.

Petr shook his head. "They were *in* the apartment," he replied in Russian. "There may be more of them."

"We have to go back," she said.

"He's dead!" Petr said. "The apartment's been compromised."

Elena slammed her hand on the dash. "No!" she yelled. "It's Stasio. We can't just leave him. We won't!"

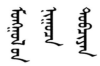

1181 Central Asia

After defeating the Merkit, the Borjigin and Jadaran clans lived together for the next two years. They shared the same campfires, hunted the same herds, and fought the same wars. The disparate tribes of the central steppe flocked to their camp, swearing their allegiance to Jamuka, Ong Khan's designated intermediary.

One day, the clans broke camp to search for new pastures. Temujin and Jamuka rode at the front of the procession. Jamuka pointed ahead. "Let us camp near the mountain, a suitable place for our horse-herders to pitch their bark-tents," he said. "Let us camp next to the river, a suitable place for our shepherds and their flock." Jamuka then spurred his horse forward.

The Jadaran began setting up camp near the mountain while the Borjigin continued to the river's edge. As Temujin looked back toward the mountain, Hoelun rode to his side.

"Does my brother mean what I think?" Temujin asked.

"His horses must have their tall grass while our sheep can eat short grass," Hoelun said. "The two cannot be pastured together."

"But we too have horses," Temujin said. "We too need tall grass. Since Jamuka and I renewed the vows of brotherhood, our animals have shared the same grasslands. Does he want us to separate? Does he *want* us to move away?"

"I believe so," Hoelun said.

Temujin scanned the river's banks. "Should we try and make the best of this?"

"I would say yes, we should stay, but I see the look in your eye when you're asked to follow and not lead," Hoelun said. "I would say yes, we should stay, but I see you hold your tongue when you should speak your mind. I would say yes, we should stay, if it were one of your younger brothers, Belgütei or Khasar, who led us. But it's you, Temujin! It's you!"

"I am loyal to Jamuka," Temujin said. "I am loyal to Ong Khan!"

"But your abilities are far greater than either," she said. "That is not only my opinion, but the opinion of the steppe elders. I believe it has also become apparent to Jamuka. For Jamuka, betrayal and deceit have become daily occurrences. Beyond his quest for power, he's been true to only one thing during our time with him—his bond with you. Now, he's even willing to throw that aside."

"There is good in Jamuka, I've seen it!"

"Jamuka has surrounded himself with those who speak only sweet words for his ears and done away with all others," Hoelun said. "If he hadn't already lost his way, these people would have led him astray. Temujin, you are blinded by your devotion to your *anda*. His soul was once pure, like yours, but it's blackened."

"To unite the steppe, we *must* remain together," Temujin said. He looked toward the mountain. "If the Jadaran and Borjigin cannot live together, who can?"

32

Petr, under Elena's glare, turned the car around and made the short drive back to the apartment. A crowd had already formed around the bodies of the two men at the front entrance to the building. He drove to the rear and parked.

In the backseat, Anton was pale and sweating, his eyes closed as the Mongolian hovered over him.

"I'll go up," Petr said to Elena. "Take Anton to the embassy. They'll know what to do."

"Once you're up there, give me a call," Elena said. She reached out and set her hand on his forearm. "Thank you."

Petr looked down at Elena's hand. With that simple gesture, he'd seen her control so many men. She thought she was controlling him now, but she would soon realize her mistake.

Petr exited the car. He opened the building's rear door and turned back, watching as Elena slid across the front seat and drove off. He then ran up the stairwell. On the tenth floor, he peeked into the hallway. It was empty.

He walked down the hallway. The apartment door was cracked open. Removing his gun, he slipped inside, closing the door behind him.

He walked through the apartment. Everything was in order until he reached Elena's bedroom.

The stench was unbearable. The sheets were torn away from the bed. A table was overturned, its lamp broken. He moved past the bed and stopped in front of the closet. The closet's light was on, its door ajar. Covering his mouth and nose, he reached out and opened the door.

In the closet, naked and gagged, Stasio hung from a rope tied around his wrists. His skin was covered with a myriad of blackened burns, dried blood, and cuts. Blood, vomit, and stool traveled in intersecting lines down his body, collecting at his knees in a pile on the carpeted floor.

He stuck a finger into the side of Stasio's neck, searching for a pulse. One of Stasio's blood-caked eyebrows fluttered open.

Petr removed Stasio's gag and cut through his bonds.

Stasio sank into his own filth, letting out a low groan.

"Let's get you up on the bed," Petr said, trying to lift him.

Stasio didn't respond. He looked down at his open palms, which Petr now realized were more than just covered with blood. All five digits on Stasio's right hand were gone. On his left hand, only the forefinger and thumb remained.

"What happened?"

"They broke in," Stasio said, his voice raspy. "The Chinese. They wanted to know my source."

"Did you tell them?"

"No," Stasio said. "That's when they started to—" He stopped, his attention drifting as he stared into his palms.

"What did you tell them?"

Stasio looked up. "Nothing!"

"They called your parliamentarian."

Stasio shook his head. "I did. I held out as long as I could. But I—" He choked, phlegm spouting from his mouth and nose.

"The Mongolian came to the apartment," Petr said. "They saw him. They have his cell phone number."

Stasio shook his head and pointed to the balcony with a crooked left forefinger. "After the call, I threw my phone. They couldn't stop me." His eyes suddenly widening, he directed a panicked look toward the hallway. "Where are they?"

"Dead," Petr replied.

Stasio thrust his fingerless right fist forward in victory, grimacing as he did so. The gesture drained his energy.

Within seconds, he was leaning back against the closet wall, drifting away.

Petr ran out onto the balcony. Two police cars were now at the building's front entrance. He dialed Elena's number. "It's me," he said.

"How is he?" she asked.

"I'm sorry. He didn't make it."

Petr heard Elena's breath catch. He waited for a few moments. "Before he died, I spoke with him. The Chinese know his contact in the Khural. The parliamentarian needs to be eliminated."

"But the corruption information has been passed on," she said. "The indictments have been made."

"Yes, but now the Mongolian knows who we are. That changes everything."

"No," she said. "Too much has been invested."

"Invested?" Petr said. "He's a liability. Bring him to the embassy, Elena. I'll meet you there."

The line went dead. Elena had ended the call.

"*Bitch!*" he screamed. Suppressing the urge to throw the phone, he instead dialed the embassy. After a brief conversation, he walked back inside the apartment.

Stasio was slumped against the closet wall, drunkenly wiping at a string of cigarette burns on the back of his left hand. He looked up at Petr, managing a stupid grin. "Elena always told me smoking was a bad habit," he said.

Petr dropped to a knee. "Listen, Stasio. You need to tell me the source of your information."

Stasio shook his head.

"What if something happens to you?"

With Baabar Onon's clairvoyant battle against corruption consuming Mongolia's national news, it was clear who was the recipient of Stasio's information. If Baabar Onon wasn't the recipient, however, another bureaucrat would be. It was the source of the information that was important. The source had not only provided the corruption information, but information that helped Stasio and his Mongolian counterparts block China's takeover of the country's industry, farming, and herding, of the land itself. For years, Stasio had kept his source a secret, not telling his SVR handlers, fellow agents, or even Elena.

Stasio smiled. "What could happen to me?" he asked, holding up his left hand, now a deformed claw.

Petr glared back.

"I'll make you a deal," Stasio said, his smile disappearing. "Give me your gun. Then, I'll tell you my source."

Petr shook his head.

"Please, Petr," Stasio said, holding out his hands. "You can't expect me to live like this."

Petr's gaze traveled from Stasio's swollen face to his burns and cuts, to the stubs of his amputated fingers. With a nod, he removed his gun and extended it.

Stasio reached for the gun, but Petr pulled it back. "First, tell me your source."

Stasio began coughing. It worsened until he choked and coughed out a large chunk of blood-tinged phlegm.

"Who's the source?" Petr asked, quietly.

Stasio, wheezing, slowly regained his breath. "It's an American," he said, his bloodshot eyes fixed on the gun. "The old academic from Charlottesville . . . Professor Herald."

"No," Petr said. "The Americans wouldn't have access to that kind of information. They must have another source—a Mongolian source. Who is it?"

"I agree," Stasio said. "But Herald is my source. I have no idea where he gets his information."

"How do you communicate?"

"Through the Asian Historical Society," Stasio said. "If you want to communicate with him, leave a message there. He'll contact you."

In Stasio's eyes, Petr saw pain and defeat, but also honesty. The old spy was telling the truth.

"Petr, please," Stasio said, extending his left hand. "We had a deal. Give me the gun."

Petr leaned forward. He set the gun in Stasio's open palm. As he did, there was a shrill whistling sound.

It took a moment before Petr realized the source of

the noise: electrical interference between the receiver taped to his chest and its transmitter, which had to be nearby. He looked up. The transmitter sat on the closet shelf. The Chinese agents had left it there.

When Petr looked down, Stasio was holding the gun securely between his left thumb and forefinger. "Lift your shirt," Stasio commanded, his gaze suddenly lucid.

"What?"

"Don't act stupid," Stasio said. "Lift your shirt!"

"You don't understand."

"That's why they came after the three of you left," Stasio said. "You're working with them. You let them know I was here alone."

"This didn't have to happen."

"Look what they did to me, Petr. Look at me!" Stasio screamed, phlegm spraying from his lips. "You did this!"

"If you just would have told us your source, they would have left you alone."

Stasio stood, the gun raised.

Petr backed away. "I didn't have a choice," he said. "They tortured me."

"Tortured you?" Stasio laughed. "Why do you still have your fingers? Where are your burns and cuts?"

"It—it was different."

"What did they offer you?" Stasio shouted. "Women? Money?"

"They offered me my life."

"Instead, you gave them mine!"

1181 Central Asia

The Borjigin left the Jadaran and the short grass by the river behind. They spent the night riding through Tayichiut territory.

In the dawn's first light, Temujin leaned toward Börte.

She was nursing their newborn son. He kissed her cheek, his nostrils filling with her sweet smell. When she suddenly brought her horse to a stop, he followed her gaze. In the distance, a line of horsemen studded the horizon. The Tayichiut had come to take their toll.

A year earlier, the Borjigin warred with Kiriltuk and the Tayichiut. Kiriltuk's son had been killed. *Sacrifice the individual to save the clan.* This time, his mother was right. The Tayichiut would be content with his life in return for the Borjigin's safe passage and as payback for the death of Kiriltuk's son.

Temujin spurred his red dun quickly up and down the Borjigin line, saying his goodbyes and giving his final orders. He then rode hard across the steppe.

Nearing the Tayichiut, who continued slowly but steadily forward, he pulled up his horse. He breathed in the crisp morning air and paused to take in the sunrise, realizing it would be his last.

The morning's stillness was broken by the sound of hooves. He turned. A single horseman approached. It was Bo'orchu.

"My last order was for you to lead them away," Temujin said.

"And I did," Bo'orchu said. He turned and pointed.

Temujin shook his head, unable to suppress a smile.

"Don't worry," Bo'orchu said. "Khasar will make a good leader." He matched Temujin's smile. "I hear he's a descendant of Kabul himself."

"The third son of Naqa the Rich would have also made a fine leader," Temujin said.

Bo'orchu raised an eyebrow. "Did you seriously think I'd let you do this alone?"

"No, but I hoped you would."

The two friends grasped forearms. After a mutual nod, they let out yelps and spurred their horses toward the Tayichiut. The line of horsemen, however, remained unbroken. At the last moment, Temujin and Bo'orchu swerved away.

They repeated the maneuver, this time whooping and hollering. Their voices rang high and clear through the morning air as they attempted to draw the Tayichiut away from the clan. But the Tayichiut continued forward.

The two young men circled for a third approach. Temujin drew an arrow. This time the Tayichiut would not ignore them. He rode directly at the lead horseman, taking aim.

The lead horseman suddenly waved and called out. "Temujin! Bo'orchu! What are you doing?"

It was not Kiriltuk that led the procession, but Qachi of the Jalayir.

Bo'orchu rode ahead to greet their old friend.

Temujin lowered his arrow and continued along the line of horsemen. After the Jalayir, there were the Barula, followed by the Mangqut, Arulat, and Besüd—all Jamuka's people.

Exuberant, he continued to the top of a nearby ridge. Beyond the ridge, the line of horsemen mushroomed into legions of yurt carts pulled by packhorses and oxen. The entire horizon moved toward him. Jamuka had not forsaken him.

He rode to the end of the procession, where he stopped and scanned the empty horizon.

A lone shaman approached, riding a donkey.

"Where is Jamuka?" Temujin asked.

The shaman brought the donkey to a stop. "Back at the mountain," he said. "His horses must have their tall grass."

"Why are you here?"

"The ancestors of these clans were born of the same womb as Jamuka," the shaman said. "Jamuka was born from the oldest son. It was heaven's mandate that we follow him. But yesterday, when you rode away, Tengri sent me a vision of a great white cow. The cow butted Jamuka and broke its horn. It then lifted the yoke of a yurt cart, harnessed itself, and walked in the direction you left us."

Temujin stared uncomprehendingly at the old man.

"We left Jamuka," the shaman said, "to follow you."

33

Baabar knelt in the back of the car. He pressed his jacket against the injured man's abdominal wound. The man's eyes cracked open.

"Your name is Anton?" Baabar asked.

The man nodded.

"You don't look like an Anton."

"Half Russian . . . half Mongolian," the young man said, his voice barely above a whisper. "My Russian father won out when it came to naming me." He looked down at his abdomen. "Sorry about your jacket."

"I shouldn't be so nice," Baabar said. "A few minutes ago, it looked like you were trying to shoot me."

"I was," Anton said. He smiled through gritted teeth. "I missed."

Baabar looked up. They'd stopped on a small side street outside a garage door. Baabar recognized the building. It was the Russian Embassy.

The blonde-haired woman, her hair tied back into a ponytail, had turned and was watching him.

"This summer, you were on the mountain," Baabar said.

She nodded. "You're a member of the Asian Historical Society," she said. "You recognize us from the newsletter photo."

"If I recall," Baabar said, "James said you were from UCLA."

"Yes," Anton said, a smile crossing his pale blue lips. "We're on extended summer vacation from Los Angeles."

The garage door opened. The woman drove ahead.

Men inside the garage rushed toward them and opened the car doors. Baabar helped lift Anton onto a gurney, which they slid into the back of a nearby van.

Baabar and the woman watched as the van left the garage. "They'll take him to the hospital," she said. "Thanks for helping."

"You must be hungry," one of the men said in Russian. He waved them toward a door leading into the embassy. "We have food."

"I need to get him back," the woman said, nodding in Baabar's direction. She looked toward the car. There was a bullet hole through the rear window. She walked across the garage to another car and peered inside.

"Petr called," the man said, following her. "He wanted you to wait for him. *Both of you.*"

"Our plan has changed," the woman said. She opened the car's door and slipped inside, motioning Baabar to the passenger side. He climbed in.

She started the car with keys that were already in the ignition. Rolling down the window, she reached out and grabbed the Russian man's forearm. "Thank you. I'll be in touch." After a smile and a reassuring nod, she drove from the garage.

Baabar looked back. The man, his brow knit, followed them to the garage door opening, where he stood with hands on hips, watching as they left.

"My contact," Baabar said. "He's dead?"

She nodded.

"Why? What's going on?"

"Those two men at the apartment were Chinese Red Army," she said.

"What were they doing there?"

"Let's just say the Chinese aren't very happy with you and Stasio regarding your recent indictments."

"How would they know about Stasio?" Baabar asked.

"You tell me. They must have been following you. They must have discovered he was the source of your information."

Baabar recalled Mikou's words.

But they also may be trying to manipulate you. If so, it's vital you figure out how and why as soon as possible.

"You could have turned the corruption information over to anyone: the minister of justice, another Khural member, the media," he said. "Why me?"

She glanced toward him. "We realized the power of the information—if placed in the right hands. We wanted to pave the way for your rise."

"*My rise?*"

"Yes, Baabar. You're in politics for all the right reasons. You're honest. You have integrity."

"What's in it for you?" he asked.

"Russia's interests are best served by having a strong Mongolian leader. We believe you can be that leader."

Baabar watched the woman as she drove, the city lights passing over her face. He couldn't help but stare. She was beautiful.

She parked a block from his apartment building. They walked in silence to the apartment. Inside, the lights and television were still on. She slipped out of her shoes, motioning for him to do likewise.

"Wait here," she whispered.

She removed a handgun from the small of her back. After circling through the apartment, she returned to the kitchen, where she turned off the television. She took off her jacket. There was a patch of blood on her shirt.

"Are you okay?" he asked.

"It's Anton's," she said, looking at the blood. "Can I borrow a shirt?"

They walked to his bedroom, where he pulled a shirt from the closet. "This is the smallest I have."

"It can double as a nightshirt," she said.

"You can't stay here," Baabar said, averting his gaze as she slipped off the soiled shirt.

"You *need* protection," she said.

"I can protect myself," he said. "If it becomes known I'm in league with Russian agents, the career you're hoping to accelerate will grind to an abrupt halt."

"Not as abruptly as it will if the Chinese find you," she said.

"If the Chinese want to kill me, there's nothing I can do to stop it," Baabar said. He turned toward her as she finished buttoning the shirt.

She picked up her gun. "Those two men killed Stasio. If you had gone inside the apartment, they would have killed you, too."

"But they're dead," Baabar said.

"Do you think they don't have colleagues? Do you think Chinese intelligence doesn't know where you live?"

"I haven't done anything wrong," he said. "I'm not running."

"They killed Stasio!" she said, glaring at him. "Are you that naïve?"

The woman held the gun stiffly at her side, her hands shaking. There was no point in pressing her further. He could figure out what to do next in the morning.

Baabar walked to a hallway closet and grabbed a blanket, sheets, and pillow. He returned to the living room and set them on the couch. "You can have the bedroom," he said. "I'll sleep here."

"I'll take the couch," she said, setting the gun on an end table. "I can keep an eye on the door."

He watched her as she began spreading the sheets over the cushions. "Why were you on Burkhan Khaldun this summer?" he asked.

She didn't respond.

"At some point you have to trust me," he said.

"We helped James find the bone."

"You planted it?"

"Yes," she said.

"Does he know?" Baabar asked.

"He didn't at the time, but he does now."

"Why would you do that?"

She turned toward him. "The biggest deterrent against Chinese aggression is Russia," But we're losing the battle. China is surging. Many of your countrymen feel they're missing out on China's economic boon. They want to be a part of it. We had to do something extraordinary. Finding Genghis Khan's grave would remind Mongolians of the principles of their founder, of his independence and tenacity."

"The bone belongs to Genghis Khan?"

She nodded.

"And what happened to Sara in Charlottesville and James in Paris, is it because of this?"

"The Chinese are responsible for both incidents," she said. She turned and continued tucking in the sheets.

He watched her for several moments before walking to the bathroom. He closed the door. Turning on the shower's hot water, he took off his shirt and looked into the mirror, assessing abrasions on his elbows and chin. He was lucky to be alive.

He held up a hand. It was steady. After everything that had happened, why wasn't *he* shaking?

He looked into the mirror, his thoughts turning to the phone conversation he overheard in the car.

The corruption information has been passed on. The indictments have been made . . . too much has been invested . . . I'm not doing it!

He thrust open the bathroom door. Billowing steam followed him into the hallway. "You told Petr you wouldn't do it," he said. "What wouldn't you do?"

The woman sat on the couch, reading something on her cell phone. She looked up, expressionless.

"You didn't wait for Petr at the embassy," he said. "On the phone, you were arguing with him. You're afraid of him. You were afraid of that man at the embassy. You say you're here to protect me from the Chinese, but you're also protecting me from your own people."

"They don't understand," she said softly. "Who you are, what you can be, it's more important than any of this."

Baabar's gaze narrowed. "What are you saying? You don't even know me."

"I do know you," she said. She stood. "The people will soon put their trust in you, Baabar. Lead them! Trust your instincts."

She unfastened a clasp on her ponytail and shook out her hair. Radiant, it fell out over his blue oxford.

"You're risking your life for me," he said. *"Why?"*

"I believe in you."

She moved closer. They were about the same height. Against him, her body was soft and warm. She bent her neck and kissed his bare chest. She then kissed his lips.

"I don't even know your name," he said.

"Elena," she said. "My name is Elena Lebedeva."

34

This is the end of the romantic phase of Mongolian democracy.
We entertained naïve thoughts that Mongolia could escape the
pitfalls of all the other post-Communist countries that are now
submerged in corruption and racketeering.

—Hashbat Hulan, 1998
Mongolian member of parliament

Baabar stood at a podium in the Khural's crowded pressroom. The minister of justice was at his side.

"As you can read in the summary, charges of embezzlement and fraud have been levied against *three* Khural members," Baabar said.

A reporter stood. "In your last two rounds of indictments, two Khural members from your own party have been charged," he said. "Do you expect backlash from your fellow party members?"

"As a member of the RDP, I'm disappointed," Baabar said. "As representatives of the people, however, we must realize that what's good for our country is ultimately what's good for our party."

The minister of justice stepped forward. "This speaks to the integrity of the corruption committee, the credibility of its new chairman, and the transparency of our new government."

"Can you provide insight into why Representative Laagan may have resigned?" a reporter asked.

"No," Baabar said. "You'll have to talk to him."

"Representative Onon," a reporter said. "The People's Revolutionary Party has criticized you for the timing of your first round of indictments, making them on the morning of elections. With respect to the last two rounds of indictments, did you have access to information on these individuals, particularly those from your own party, before they were re-elected?"

"We did not," Baabar replied.

"This makes a total of ten Khural members that have been charged by your committee," the reporter continued. "Are other Khural members under investigation, and do you expect more charges will be made?"

"If corruption is found, there *will* be more charges," Baabar said. "In no way will corruption be tolerated."

"Are you aware of the lessons learned by Zorig and his followers after *he* promised to eliminate corruption?" a reporter asked.

Sanjaasürengiin Zorig's assassination in 1998, prior to his appointment as prime minister, had been attributed to his vow to fight corruption.

"When I went into politics, I was under no delusion our national parliament was simply a debate society," Baabar said. "The Khural is the front line of change. I expected nothing less than a battleground. And it hasn't disappointed." His gaze narrowed. "But if you're suggesting that the lesson to learn from Zorig's death is to ignore corruption, then his life's work and the work of Mikou and the other democratic reformers has been for nothing. Zorig's assassination teaches us that change, true change, can be as tumultuous as any war."

Baabar's gaze scoured the packed room. "What's happened here today should send a message, not only to Khural members, but to every government official, every businessman, every Mongolian," he said. "No one is above the law. Justice may take time, but it will prevail."

***

Later that day, there was a knock at the door of Baabar's Khural office. The door opened. Mikou appeared.

As Baabar stood, Mikou waved him back down. "I'm fine," he said.

Mikou wheeled himself to Baabar's desk. "Can you be a pallbearer for Jambyn's funeral?" he asked.

"Me? Doesn't he have family?"

"Only his mother," Mikou said. "She asked me to pick six men from the party. Laagan has already agreed. And I know Jambyn thought very highly of you."

Baabar nodded. "Yes," he said. "Of course. I'll do it."

Both men quietly contemplated recent events. Only a couple of weeks after their rousing electoral victory, three senior party members were gone: Puson was awaiting trial on charges of corruption; Laagan had resigned; and Jambyn was dead.

Mikou removed his glasses and cleaned them. "Our situation reminds me of the elections of 1996," he said. "We had just ousted the communists. In our rush to obtain a Khural majority, we never thought about what came next. We still had to elect a prime minister, appoint a cabinet, and nominate a presidential candidate. Back then, we weren't allowed to pull Khural members for the top posts." He smiled. "Don't get me wrong. It was a good problem to have, but all of our best had run for the Khural. In the end, it was our youth and inexperience at the top that proved to be our undoing."

"I'm sorry for charging Puson," Baabar said. "It's—"

"Don't apologize," Mikou interrupted. He slipped his glasses back on. "I'd also prefer not knowing why Laagan resigned."

"Laagan?"

"That day you were outside his office, I saw something in your eyes," Mikou said. "I realize now it was pity."

"But—"

Mikou raised a hand. "There *is* a silver lining in all this," he said. "It's freed the way for your ascension. Your heart's pure, Baabar. You're passionate and relentless in your attack of those not as committed. Recent events have been unsettling, but I'm in no way concerned about your ability to lead us."

"But Mikou, you're our leader."

The former monk shook his head. "A few generations ago, at my age and in my state, I would have been thrown out to the wolves," he said, patting his legs. "I can last a few more years as party chairman, but I can't *lead* the nation. Our country needs someone with your charisma, your energy."

Baabar sat back. "I'm only a second-term parliamentarian."

"Today, at your press conference, you talked about change," Mikou said. "No one has more invested in the status quo than the old. No one has more to benefit from a better future, from true change, than the young."

"My only aspiration is to serve the people."

Mikou smiled. "Good," he said. "If that's true, the best service you can provide the people is to lead them. Which brings me to the other purpose of my visit. Earlier today, the Republican Democracy Party's senior members met. After a unanimous vote, we put forward your name as our nominee . . . for president of the Mongolian Republic."

35

In heaven there is but one Eternal God, and on earth there is but
one lord Genghis Khan, the Son of God, and his descendants who
ruled the Mongol Empire.

—**Möngke Khan,** 1255
Genghis Khan's son in a letter to the French king, Louis IX

James sat at the corner table at Pietro's in Charlottesville. His parents sat at the table across from him. Once again, he was embedded in a memory.

His parents had brought him and his college roommates along with Ben and Samantha out for dinner. The next day his mom and dad were leaving on an east coast car trip to Hilton Head and then Savannah.

His dad thrilled them with tales of important dignitaries and political intrigue. His mom—tall, attractive, and regal—corrected his dad when he strayed too far from the truth and humbled him when he sounded too self-important. Andrews had never thought his parents were interesting, but as he'd looked around the table and saw his roommates listening and laughing, he realized they were.

Andrews caught his dad watching him. His dad was smiling, a content look on his face, his arm wrapped around his mom. His mom's head was turned as she talked to Ben and Sam. It was this image of his parents, more than any remembrance or photo, that had been indelibly imprinted into his memory.

The image as well as the memory faded. Finally, only he and his dad remained. His friends and their other family members, the surrounding tables, and Pietro's were gone.

His dad was leafing through the pages of his travelogue. He stopped at the last page and read the concluding paragraph.

My search for Genghis Khan need go no further than a stroll through downtown Ulaanbaatar to see the multitude of consumer goods, businesses, schools, and streets named after him. My search need go no further than reading an editorial in the Ulaanbaatar Gazete *or discussing politics with Mongolian friends over a cup of coffee. More of Genghis Khan's essence can be found in these endeavors than in a thousand years of scouring the steppe. Over a half millennium of Siberian winds and rains have swept away Genghis Khan's remains, but his spirit is alive and well and living in Mongolia.*

His dad looked up. "Tell me about your studies."

"I spent my first two summers excavating Avarga, the Mongols' first city."

"Did you enjoy that?"

"No," he said. "Genghis Khan never lived there."

His dad nodded. "He was a nomad."

"After two summers of digging up bricks and mortar in Avarga, I went to Burkhan Khaldun," Andrews said. "Genghis Khan was born there. He fished the mountain's rivers, rode its trails, and hunted its meadows. In times of trouble, he disappeared into the mountain for sanctuary and advice, spending days at a time alone communing with his god. When he became ruler, he forbade anyone from setting up camp on the mountain. I hoped to find the grave, but more than that, I wanted to live where he lived, to experience what he experienced."

His dad held up the book. "You found him."

"I realize now that's what our excursions were really about," Andrews said. "To understand people, you taught me I not only had to know their past, but I had to walk in their shoes. Only then could I know their present. Only then could I envision their future."

His dad nodded and then looked down, his attention returning to the book. The book was open to the dedication.

To my father, Ambassador Michael James Andrews
Like one of our excursions, you've been at my side every
step of the way.
We did this, together.

His dad closed the book. He held it up, his eyes misty. He began to speak, but his voice caught. His dad then stood. After a silent nod, he turned and walked down a hallway toward a guard and pair of doors. As Andrews watched his dad step through the doors, the beginnings of dozens of excursions congealed in his mind.

"Where are we going today, Dad?"

His father dropped to a knee and held up two subway passes. "I don't know, James. We can go . . . wherever you want."

Andrews opened his eyes. He lay on his back, his head throbbing. His breath was condensing above him. He wasn't at the embassies in Beijing or Paris, but in Mongolia, in his one-man tent on the summit of Burkhan Khaldun. After arriving in Ulaanbaatar the day before, he and the CIA men had been taken by helicopter to the summit.

The throbbing was different than one of his post-concussion headaches. The pain had a rhythmic quality, synchronized with a pulsing sensation that seemed to emanate from the ground itself. He climbed from his sleeping bag and began dressing. As he did, the pounding stopped. So too did the pain.

He slipped on a jacket and stepped out into the cold mountain air. Most of the CIA men were huddled around a blazing campfire, where breakfast was cooking and coffee brewing. The others congregated around three small tank-like vehicles. Rosenthal stood on one of the vehicles, its engine running. He spotted Andrews. "Professor," he shouted. He hopped to the ground and jogged across the grass.

"What do you think?" Rosenthal asked, nodding toward the nearest vehicle. "Officially, it's an ATR-100, but I call it a Rover. Let me show you, it—"

Not really caring where Rosenthal was going with this, Andrews waved a hand. "I commend you on your enthusiasm; but please, whatever you're doing, continue." He turned and began walking toward the campfire and the inviting scents of bacon and eggs.

"You realize this may be your last chance on the mountain," Rosenthal called out.

"Let's get one thing straight," Andrews said, spinning toward Rosenthal. "I don't give a damn about the mountain or the grave or anything else that might be up here. Because of my fascination with this *goddamn* mountain, a friend of mine is dead."

Rosenthal nodded. "I understand that," he said. "But that's not why you're here this time, or why the rest of us are here. It's my understanding you came back because you're trying to commemorate your friend."

Andrews glared at Rosenthal. The young CIA agent was right. This time he was here for Sara.

Andrews rubbed his temples. "You do remember this whole production is a farce, Agent Rosenthal, don't you?"

"It's captain, sir," Rosenthal said. "I'm with the Army Corps of Engineers."

"And them?" Andrews asked, pointing toward the men around the campfire.

"All CIA," Rosenthal said. "I know the Russians already found the grave, but this doesn't have to be a complete boondoggle." He motioned around them. "This is Mongolia's holy mountain. It's probably loaded with artifacts. And you'll never find anything better for surveying than my Rovers."

"*Your* Rovers?"

"I designed them. They're why I'm here."

Andrews looked toward the vehicles. "It looks like you mated a tank with a four wheeler."

Rosenthal smiled. "That's actually not far from the truth. Can I show you?"

Andrews reluctantly nodded. He followed Rosenthal to the nearest vehicle.

"Based on experience in Afghanistan and Iraq, we realized we needed faster, more efficient mine sweepers," Rosenthal said. "While traditional mine sweepers assess only the top few feet of soil and a foot or so on each side, the Rovers can measure much deeper and a larger radius, allowing them to travel faster." He bent down and pointed to a V-shaped ridge running the length of the undercarriage. "Ultrasound monitoring devices are built into a spring-loaded keel that runs along the ground. With modifications to the signal transducers, they can measure as deep as twenty feet while traveling up to thirty miles per hour."

One of the men unscrewed a metal plate from the front of the vehicle.

"For safety purposes, they usually run by remote control," Rosenthal said. "But since we're not concerned with detonating mines, we're removing the protection plates to allow them to be manually driven."

The machine lurched forward, emitting the pounding noise that woke Andrews. When the vehicle stopped, so did the noise. "My God," Andrews said. "That's loud."

"It has to be," Rosenthal said. "It requires some pretty healthy shock waves to measure as deep as we'd like."

From inside the vehicle, fingers appeared through the open slits where the protection plate had been. "I can breathe," a voice echoed from inside.

"That's good," Rosenthal said. "Because you guys will be inside these things for the next few days." He turned to Andrews. "I'd like to cover as much of the summit as possible. I was hoping you could help point out the areas of interest."

"The summit is over twelve miles long," Andrews said. "There are several square miles of interest."

"Then we'd better get started," Rosenthal said.

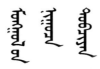

1200 Central Asia

After the Borjigin and Jadaran parted ways, two decades passed. Temujin and Jamuka continued as leaders of their respective clans. The steppe, meanwhile, remained divided into numerous factions, the size of each swinging back and forth as changing allegiances neutralized attempts to consolidate power. The result was a never-ending cycle of border wars.

Temujin sat in the Borjigin camp, watching his sons practice their archery. He and Börte now had nine children together: four boys and five girls. Their youngest daughter, Altani, sat on Temujin's knee.

"Let Alaqai compete," Altani yelled.

The boys continued their contests.

After another round of shooting, Altani called out again. "Let Alaqai shoot. She's better than any of you."

Ignored once again by her brothers, Altani turned toward her father, her lips pursed.

Temujin smiled. "Go," he said.

Altani ran off. She returned a few minutes later with Alaqai, who carried a bow and quiver filled with arrows.

"First, show me you can draw it," Temujin said.

Alaqai held out the bow with her left arm. She grabbed the twine with her right forefinger and pulled it slowly to her cheek. She held the twine for several seconds, unmoving.

"Very good," Temujin said.

Altani, stepping easily into the role of master of ceremonies, pointed at her oldest brother. "Jochi," she said. "You first."

Jochi drew an arrow. When he released it, the arrow struck the target, just off center. The boys cheered.

Alaqai stepped forward. Drawing her arrow, she fired, hitting the dead center of the bulls-eye.

Altani squealed, clapping her hands. "I told you," she said.

Chagatai and then Ogödei challenged Alaqai. Both lost.

Finally, there was only Tolui, the youngest. He lifted his bow and pulled the twine, his arms shaking. His shot, far from center, barely hit the target.

Alaqai took her turn. This time, her arrow sailed high over the target.

Tolui's eyes widened in surprise. "I won," he said. "I won!" His brothers slapped him on the back, congratulating him.

Altani turned toward her older sister, glaring. Alaqai

wrapped a consoling arm around Altani and whispered into her ear.

A broad grin spread across Altani's face. She suddenly took off, low and quick, running past the target and through the high grass. Stopping in the distance, she picked up her sister's errant arrow and lifted it over her head. On the end of the arrow was a marmot.

Temujin roared his approval, lifting his daughter in the air.

"I'd like to see you shoot against Khasar," Jochi mumbled.

"Who do you think taught me?" Alaqai asked, smiling proudly.

A horseman approached, a messenger from Ong Khan. He stopped at Temujin's side. "Jamuka has called a *khurlitai,*" the messenger said. "He's named himself Gur Khan, khan of all khans. He's trying to take control of the steppe."

Over the last two decades, Temujin had remained loyal to Ong Khan, but Jamuka had gone his own way.

Temujin recalled Jamuka's words from long ago.

Each clan has a white-bone leader who believes it's his destiny to rule the steppe.

"Father!"

Everyone turned. Altani held Alaqai's bow. She was trying to draw an arrow, but she was too small, the bow too stiff.

Temujin sprinted toward his daughter. But before he reached her, Altani let the arrow go.

The arrow spun and clattered against the bow, ricocheting away in a spray of blood. With a scream, Altani fell to the ground, holding the side of her face.

"Get your mother," Temujin yelled to Alaqai, who raced off.

Altani lay on her side, her eyes wide. Temujin knelt over her. "It's going to be okay," he said, assessing the cut.

The cut ran along Altani's jawline from ear to chin. It was long and deep, but straight and clean.

Börte ran toward them, holding a needle and thread.

"This will hurt, but I know you're a brave girl," Temujin said. "I need you to lower your hand."

Altani shook her head, her eyes welling with tears.

Temujin leaned forward and whispered. "I think you missed your marmot."

Altani smiled.

Temujin pushed back her hair and kissed her forehead. "We'll hunt later, Altani. We'll kill fifty marmots and save the skins. In the fall, we'll make you a coat. When winter comes, you can wrap yourself in the coat from head to toe. You'll always be warm."

Altani lowered her hand.

Temujin poked the needle through the skin. Altani's jaw muscles tightened, but she stared unflinchingly ahead.

"Several more just like that and then we're done," Temujin said.

"And then we can hunt the marmot?" Altani asked.

Altani looked up at him out of the corners of her eyes, her bottom lip jutting as she tried to hold back the tears.

Temujin looked proudly at his daughter. There was a light in her face and a fire in her eyes.

"Yes, Altani," he said. "Then we can hunt the marmot."

36

It was early morning as Andrews stood on a small rise on Burkhan Khaldun's summit. He removed a container filled with mare's milk from his pocket and flicked a few drops of the liquid into the air. He knelt and bowed nine times in the direction of the rising sun—performing the ancient steppe ritual of paying homage to Tengri, the Mongol god.

Baabar had taught him the rituals during their first summer in Avarga. Andrews found them relaxing.

When he finished, he sat back in the grass and looked over the valley. The view never ceased to amaze him. For as far as he could see, there was no sign of man's existence: no smoke curling from a distant chimney, no telephone poles, no buildings. The nearest paved road was in Möngönmört over sixty kilometers away.

From the time Genghis Khan united the steppe tribes in 1205 until Mongolia declared its independence in 1991, the mountain's Mongolian, Chinese, and Soviet overlords had kept the area secluded. Mongol and Chinese warriors had guarded the mountain, killing all intruders. The Soviets, to prevent Mongolians from traveling to the mountain, never built roads on Burkhan Khaldun or the surrounding lands, an area comprising over ten thousand square kilometers. It wasn't until glasnost when the mountain, known as the *Ikh Khorig* or Great Taboo, was declared a national park and opened to outsiders. Today, pilgrims came to worship and poachers to hunt, but no one had lived on the mountain for over eight hundred years.

Andrews stood and walked toward the camp. Rosenthal met him on the way. "We should finish today with the southern face," Rosenthal said, handing him one of two cups of coffee. "Where to next?"

For the last two days, the Rovers had combed the southern face of Burkhan Khaldun, generating ream after ream of ultrasound data. Andrews and Rosenthal had pored over the data, finding nothing of interest.

"Thanks," Andrews said, taking the coffee. "Remind me again. What are we looking for?"

"Whatever we can get through customs."

Andrews looked down at an *ovoo*—a small pyramid made of stone and wrapped in blue silk. Hundreds of the *ovoos*, built in dedication to Genghis Khan, covered the summit. In 1961, East German archaeologists found them when they visited the mountain. At the time, with Mongolia behind the Iron Curtain, pilgrims would have had to risk their lives to journey to Burkhan Khaldun and pay tribute to Genghis Khan's spirit. But they came, each adding something to the pyramids: candles, utensils, coins, more rocks, or silk.

"Well, we have a rusty pocketknife, a fork, a spoon, some bottle caps," he said as he bent over and scanned the pyramid. He shrugged. "To be honest, after the southern face, I don't know."

"I've been wondering," Rosenthal said. "What makes you so sure the Russians found Genghis Khan's grave?"

"Besides the fact they gave us one of his bones?" Andrews asked, laughing. "Well, for one, they had unlimited access to the mountain. And I'm sure Stalin provided their archaeologists with more than enough motivation to find the grave."

"Let me rephrase the question," Rosenthal said. "When the Soviets found the remains, how did they know it was Genghis Khan?"

Andrews sipped his coffee. "They wouldn't have known about the Y chromosome Khan markers. Carbon dating would have been available," he said thoughtfully. "But you've got a point. Simply dying at the right time wouldn't have been enough to make a definitive identification. There must have been something specific about the gravesite, something that correlated with one of the histories." He shrugged. "What that was, however, take your pick. Different historians have claimed Genghis Khan was buried with the treasures of Eurasia, his concubines, a young camel, forty virgins, and his saddle. One account says he was buried in a silver coffin. In another, a papal envoy wrote the Mongol kings are buried in their tent with a stallion and mare. A table is placed in front of them with a bowl filled with meat and a jar of mare's milk. In the afterlife, they have a tent to live in, food to eat, and a horse to ride."

"I almost forgot," Rosenthal said. Reaching into his pocket, he removed a paper. He began unfolding it. It was an ultrasound tracing. "Look at this. It's from the southeastern face."

At the deepest portion of the printout, the gray ultrasound tracing indicating solid ground gave way to an oval-shaped space. Rosenthal pointed toward the space. "What do you think?"

"That's over twenty feet deep," Andrews said. "The receptors might not be picking up a rebound signal at that depth, or it might be artifact."

"Didn't you write in your travelogue that Genghis Khan might have been buried in a cave?" Rosenthal asked.

Andrews nodded. "The *Ch'i-lien-ku.* The cave of Kinien."

Three separate historians living in the eighteenth and nineteenth centuries—Cordier, Gaubil, and Mailla—independently wrote that Genghis Khan was buried in the cave of Kinien. Paul Pelliot, a Harvard academic, believed the three historians had each misinterpreted the description of the burial site in the *Yüan-shih*—the Chinese history of the Yüan dynasty—incorrectly translating the ending phrase *ku* in *Ch'i-lien-ku* as cavern of the Ch'i-lien Mountain instead of *valley* of the mountain. In his 1959 compendium, *Notes on Marco Polo,* Pelliot hypothesized that "valley of the mountain" most likely referred to a lake, presumably the Ch'i-lien Lake.

Andrews handed the printout back. "If the space is real, it's only a couple of feet wide—not even large enough to qualify as a cave." He shrugged. "But who knows? Have the Rovers go back over the area. See what they find."

ᠵᠢᠯ ᠤᠨ

1200 Central Asia

Temujin returned with Ong Khan's messenger to the Kereyid camp. In the Golden Tent, Ong Khan sat on a throne among his court. Senggüm, Ong Khan's oldest son, paced at his side. "Jamuka has insulted you," Senggüm said to his father. "He's insulted all of us."

The now elderly Ong Khan looked toward Temujin. "Will you join me in battle against the Jadaran? Will you join me in battle against Jamuka?"

Although Jamuka had gone his own way, he had not warred against the Kereyid or Borjigin.

Temujin held out his hands. "I cannot strike down my brother at my father's bidding, any more than I could strike you down at his."

Senggüm thrust an accusing finger at Temujin. "Traitor!" he roared.

Temujin bowed. "Tengri has bound me to Jamuka. We've shared words that cannot be repeated, food that cannot be digested."

"My father is your khan!" Senggüm said.

"Do I honor my khan, or the promises I made in front of Tengri?" Temujin asked. "Tell me, Senggüm. *Who?*"

"Your unwavering devotions to your *anda* and your people are foolish," Senggüm sneered. "Are you sure they're as loyal to you? During her time with the Merkit, I've heard it said that your own wife welcomed several Merkit to her side. They say your oldest son, Jochi, is of Merkit blood."

In one swift motion, Temujin unsheathed his sword and swung, stopping the blade inches from Senggüm's forehead.

Senggüm stumbled back, pointing at Temujin. "Kill him!" he screamed. "Kill him!"

The royal guards looked toward Ong Khan, who raised a

calming hand. The old khan stood. He reached for his sword and unsheathed it, extending the hilt toward Senggüm. "If you want Temujin dead, then you do it."

Senggüm's eyes darted back and forth between the sword and Temujin before he stormed from the tent.

"I imagine I was that young once," Ong Khan said. "But I can't remember it." He turned toward Temujin. "Forgive his impetuousness."

Temujin nodded.

"As much as anyone, I understand the strength of *anda,*" Ong Khan said. "My promise to recognize you as a distant son, your position at my right hand, and Börte's presence at your side . . . along with the sons she has given you are testament to that. But Jamuka cannot go unpunished."

Ong Khan stepped forward. "Have you heard your former clan, the Tayichiut, are now allies of Jamuka?" he asked, a smile creasing his face.

"No," Temujin replied.

Ong Khan calmly scratched his beard. "Senggüm will lead the Kereyid against the Jadaran. Your Borjigin will ride against the Tayichiut. You will bring me Kiriltuk's head."

37

Andrews and Rosenthal stood on Burkhan Khaldun's southeastern slope. Nearby, a small backhoe was digging. The backhoe had been flown in that morning from Ulaanbaatar. After more ultrasound readings, Rosenthal's putative cave had proven to be a real space. But the area, about two feet wide, was something closer to a tunnel than a cave. Initially appearing at a depth of seventeen feet, it headed up the hill for fifteen feet before disappearing from the Rovers' view at a depth of twenty feet.

"It's not very efficient, but it's a start," Rosenthal said, nodding toward the backhoe. "In the meantime, my buddies at the base in Kabul are sending a DDA."

"A what?"

"Deep-drilling apparatus," Rosenthal said. "It's a modified well-drilling rig. In Afghanistan, the rigs were used to gain quick access to Taliban caves."

"You do remember this is just a boondoggle?" Andrews asked.

Rosenthal held out his arms. "I was told to make it look good."

A helicopter appeared from the east. They both looked skyward, shielding their eyes from the sun.

"Is that your rig?" Andrews asked.

Rosenthal shook his head. "No. It shouldn't be here yet."

Several CIA men jogged from the camp as the helicopter landed behind a nearby rise. "Is it one of ours?" one of them asked.

"It was unmarked," Rosenthal said.

The CIA man removed a handgun from beneath his coat. He checked the gun's clip and flicked off the safety. The others did likewise.

"Hold on," Andrews said.

The men followed Andrews's gaze to the top of the rise. One of the men gave a low whistle.

A woman stood at the top of the rise. She wore a fur vest, matching hat, and black leggings. From beneath her hat, long blonde hair spilled onto her shoulders.

* * *

Elena Lebedeva smiled, her arms folded and face crimson as Andrews walked up the hill. He stopped several feet away. He looked toward the helicopter and then motioned toward the backpack slung over her shoulder. "Is that for me?"

"Can we talk first?" she asked.

"There's not much to say."

"James, please. I need to tell you about this summer."

"I think I'm pretty clear on this summer," he said.

"I'd like to explain," she said.

Andrews turned, arms folded, and looked down the hill to where Rosenthal and the CIA men stared up at them. "Go ahead," he said. "I'm all ears."

"Some place *private?*"

He shrugged. "Sure."

They walked along the summit. After a few minutes, she stopped and set the backpack on the ground. Andrews looked down at it. "I always presumed if Stalin found the grave, he would have destroyed it, not kept the remains," he said.

"Stalin never found the grave," she said. "It was Andropov."

"Yuri Andropov?"

She nodded. "Before he became general secretary in the early 80s, he served for fifteen years as the KGB's chairman," she said. "His paranoia was legendary. Like Stalin, he was intent on destroying all forms of dissent. And, like Stalin, he was fascinated by Genghis Khan. In Andropov's younger years, Stalin impressed upon him not only Genghis Khan's brilliance as a military leader, but the importance of discrediting him. In 1975, Andropov sent a team of archaeologists into Mongolia to find Genghis Khan's grave. After four summers of searching, they found it."

"Where?"

"The second plateau—de Rachewiltz's site," she said.

"Then the rock formations *were* tombstones."

"One of them was."

"What did they find?" he asked.

"There was no coffin, but the body was encased in a coarse, thick cloth," she said. "The cloth was wrapped around him, almost like a cocoon. The body was dressed in a plain robe and wrapped in a sash."

"The golden sash," Andrews said. "The one Jamuka gave him after they defeated the Merkit."

She nodded. "The one he was wrapped in during his burial."

"Were there any artifacts?"

She shook her head. "Over the centuries, it's been a popular site for grave robbers. By the time Andropov's men excavated the site, anything of value, if it had been there at all, had been stolen."

"And the remains were then shipped to Leningrad?"

"Yes."

"And now you're returning them. *Why?*"

"I'm an assistant curator in the Hermitage's Department of Mongolian Artifacts. I have a PhD in Asian history, and I'm a member of Russia's Asian Affairs Committee. The committee asked me for the best way to block Chinese imperialism in Mongolia. My answer was to stimulate Mongolian nationalism. I recommended they find Genghis Khan's tomb, that they glorify Genghis Khan for all the reasons Stalin wanted to discredit him. When I made my recommendations, I didn't know the grave had already been found. That's when they brought me to a secret vault in the basement of my own museum. They showed me his remains."

"And now you're working for the SVR," he said.

"Even in today's Russia, academics are at the state's

beck and call. But really, James, I'm not much more SVR than you're CIA."

She slipped off her backpack and vest. Underneath, she wore a tight-fitting, white turtleneck. "I'm an academic. Like you, my research has led me, irrevocably, to Genghis Khan. And like you, I've read everything I could about him. But it was your travelogue that made him come alive for me. You were able to walk where he walked, think as he thought. You didn't just document your attempts to find the grave, but your journey to find his spirit. When the committee came to me, I told them you were the best bet to find the grave. I told them we should put whatever resources we had in *your* hands."

Andrews looked down and kicked at a patch of scorched earth and scattered cinders. It wasn't a coincidence she'd led him here. This was where they'd spent her last night on the mountain, where they'd built their campfire and wrapped themselves in their blankets and made love under the stars.

When he looked up, she was watching him, smiling, reading his mind.

"I'm sorry for what happened to Sara," she said. "I'm sorry for lying to you." She stepped closer, her body pressing against him. "But I'm not sorry for this summer, for what happened between us." She took his face in her hands and gently kissed him.

Andrews closed his eyes. He tried pushing back the memories: the star-filled sky, her hair sprawled over his patchwork fur blanket, her eyes and tanned skin glistening in the firelight. As she continued kissing him, his body stirring, the memories came faster: their bodies entwined, moving in rhythm . . . insatiable.

He began returning her kisses. His hands ran down her back, pulling her tighter. When she moaned her approval, he opened his eyes.

It wasn't Hayley looking back at him, but the black-and-white graduation photo of Elena Lebedeva—staring blankly into the camera, wearing a fur hat with a star in the middle.

"I—I can't do this," he said, backing away. He turned and began walking along the summit.

"James!" she called out.

He continued.

"James! *Wait!*"

As he stopped and looked back, she was jogging toward him, holding the backpack. "I don't know what you want, but—"

She raised a hand. "I know," she said. "I'm sorry. It was crazy. I—I just got caught up in the memories of this summer and—" She shook her head. Dropping to a knee, she set the backpack on the ground. She opened the pack and removed a small black case, which she held out.

He took the case and opened it. A yellowing, decayed bone sat in a foam casing. "Where are the rest of the remains?" he asked.

"They're being flown to Ulaanbaatar," she said. "They'll be there in two days."

* * *

"Is that it?" Rosenthal asked as Andrews walked toward him, holding the black case.

Andrews nodded. "It's a fibula. It's a down payment. In two days, the Russians are flying the rest of the remains to Ulaanbaatar." He looked toward the backhoe. "I imagine you'll want to call off your beast of burden."

"Those are my orders," Rosenthal said.

"Aren't you a little curious about what's down there?"

Rosenthal laughed. "We have what we came for," he said. "It's time to wrap things up."

Andrews looked up to the hill's crest.

Elena stood on the top of the rise, looking down at them. With a nod, she disappeared over the hill, heading toward the helicopter.

"Actually, we still have two days," Andrews said.

"Let me get this straight," Rosenthal said. "Now you're interested in what's down there? Would you like to tell me why?"

Andrews shrugged. "Like you said, we might as well make it look good."

1200 Central Asia

The Borjigin defeated the Tayichiut. Afterward, as ordered, Temujin brought Kiriltuk's head to Ong Khan. The head now lay on a white blanket in the Golden Tent.

The old khan watched as his first wife, Kiriltuk's sister, knelt at the edge of the blanket. Their fathers had arranged the marriage during better days between the two clans. The wife, insisting on paying obeisance to her brother, had surrounded the head with food, drink, and coins.

Senggüm entered the tent. His chin was high, fresh from his victory over the Jadaran. When he saw the head, he screamed in surprise. "It—it smiled at me," he said. "It's possessed!"

Senggüm ordered the shaman to take the head from the tent. Everyone then filed outside and watched as Senggüm rode his horse back and forth, trampling the skull.

Ong Khan turned to his wife. "While Temujin was pushed into the cold, you insisted our son stay by the hearth," he said. "While Temujin learned to hunt, you insisted our son play games with his sisters. While Temujin conquered the Merkit and Tatars, you insisted our son march at the front of parades and be given titles."

Ong Khan stepped forward and grabbed the trampled skull. He carried it to the river and flipped it into the water.

Senggüm rode to his mother's side. "Temujin did this," he said. "The evil spirit came from him. He must be punished. I'll ride east and capture the Borjigin."

Ong Khan, who was wiping his hand in the grass, looked up. "Capture them?" he scoffed. "Like you captured Jamuka?"

"His escape was unfortunate," Senggum said.

"Once you capture the Borjigin, what will you do then?"

"We'll take their quivers," Senggüm said. "We'll send

their men away and teach their women and children to clean and milk our animals."

"You'll have to cut off their hands before you take their quivers," Ong Khan said. "You'll have to tear out their hearts before they'll be subdued."

Senggüm bowed. "Then so be it."

Ong Khan and his wife watched as their son rode away.

"Will he war with Temujin?" the wife asked.

"For his sake, I hope not," Ong Khan said.

The wife turned. "You hope not? What do you mean? Senggüm is of the white-bone lineage while Temujin is of the black. Heaven favors our son."

Ong Khan pointed toward the river. Fish were swirling around the skull. "There is your white-bone lineage," he said. "*There* is heaven's favor."

38

The Mongols have succeeded by means of science.

—**Roger Bacon,** 1267, *Opus Majus*

On the day after Elena Lebedeva's visit to the mountain, members of the Army Corps of Engineers arrived on Burkhan Khaldun's summit with Rosenthal's DDA. Within a few hours, the drilling rig, situated in the trench dug by the backhoe, was up and running, its diesel engine belching oily black smoke into the air.

It was late afternoon when the lead drill broke into the space detected by the Rovers. After the rig was removed, Andrews and Rosenthal stood above the open shaft—a two-foot-wide hole. Rosenthal held a joystick controller. The controller was connected to a fiberoptic scope and monitor—all powered by an electrical generator, which was running.

Two of the engineers picked up the fiberoptic scope and threw its loops of black hose over their shoulders. One of the engineers raised the camera end of the scope. Rosenthal hit a button on the controller. A collaret of pinpoint light beams appeared from around the camera's lens. As Rosenthal moved the joystick, the scope's serpentine end turned back and forth. "Go ahead," he said.

The engineers fed the camera end of the scope into the shaft. Rosenthal and Andrews watched the monitor as the scope descended.

"Back it up a foot," Rosenthal said when the scope reached the bottom of the shaft. He turned the end toward the tunnel's opening. "Push it forward, slowly."

Over the next few minutes, the scope advanced over the tunnel's undulating, gravel-strewn surface. The image on the monitor suddenly froze. "We're at the end," one of the engineers announced.

Rosenthal moved the camera in a circle. The beams of light dissipated into darkness.

"Congratulations, it looks like your tunnel turns into a full-fledged cave," Andrews said.

Rosenthal continued moving the scope's head back and forth.

"Do you think there's enough room for someone to get down there?" Andrews asked.

"The tunnel is too narrow," Rosenthal said. "If we do manage to get someone into it, we'll never get them out."

"Let's dig another hole," Andrews said, looking uphill. "We can come down on top of the cave."

"We don't have enough time," Rosenthal said.

"Sure we do."

Rosenthal set down the controller. "Listen, Professor. I'm afraid we're done here."

"What do you mean?" Andrews asked.

"You were right. We had two days. The transport helicopter arrives tomorrow morning. We have orders to clear the mountain by eight a.m. We need to make it back to Ulaanbaatar before they can announce the remains were found."

"So, we should just fill the shaft and go home?" Andrews asked. "Don't you want to know what's down there?"

"We have our orders," Rosenthal said.

Andrews shook his head. "No," he said. "*We* don't."

* * *

Fifteen minutes later, Andrews stood above the shaft wearing a climbing harness. Rosenthal was at his side. Engineers and CIA men ringed the trench above them.

"The cave must open up somewhere," Rosenthal said. "We have some time. Let's search for the opening."

"If there was an opening, I would have found it by now," Andrews said.

Rosenthal shook his head. "No," he said. "I'm not letting this happen."

"Listen, Joel. I'm not living the rest of my life wondering what's down there."

"If you go down there, the *rest of your life* may be very short," Rosenthal said. "What happened to not giving a damn about the mountain?"

"When I said that, I didn't. But you were right. I'm here for Sara. I'm here for the right reason." He shrugged. "So, there's no point in sitting around and feeling sorry for myself. As you said, this could be my last chance on the mountain."

"If you're trying to pin this on me," Rosenthal said. "It's not working."

"*Essayon,*" an engineer said.

Andrews looked up. "What?"

"*Essayon,*" the engineer repeated. "It's the Corps's motto. It's French for—"

"He knows what it means," Rosenthal snapped. "He speaks five goddamn languages."

"Let us try," Andrews said. "Why is your motto French?"

"The Corps was created with France's help during the War for Independence," the engineer replied, smiling as Rosenthal glared up at him.

"*Essayon,*" several of the others called out, laughing.

Rosenthal fumed. "All right," he said. "Go!"

"If you say so," Andrews said, grinning. "Thank you."

Two engineers stepped forward. One snapped a rope to Andrews's harness; the other gave him a hardhat fitted with a headset.

"If the tunnel's too small, you have to let us know," Rosenthal said. "We'll pull you back up."

Rosenthal slipped on a matching headset and pointed toward a button on the mouthpiece. "Push this when you want to speak. And here, take these." He handed Andrews the camera end of the fiber-optic scope and a flashlight.

Andrews looped the scope through a belt buckle and clipped the flashlight to the harness. "Thanks."

"You're crazy, you know that?" Rosenthal said.

"You discovered a cave on Burkhan Khaldun, Mongolia's holy mountain," Andrews said, holding out his arms. "It would be crazy for me not to go."

Andrews knelt and stared down into the shaft. Bending over, he slipped headfirst into the hole.

Blood drained into his head. With his body blocking the light, it became dark immediately. He turned on his headlamp. As the men slowly lowered him, his shoulders scraped against the walls, dislodging clods of dirt and rock. When he neared the bottom of the shaft, he hit the button on his mouthpiece. "Stop," he said. "Hold me here."

He looked into the tunnel. The opening was too small. For the next few minutes, hanging upside down, he knocked away dirt at the angle between the shaft and tunnel.

When the opening was large enough, he reached into the tunnel and dug his fingers into the sidewalls. He pulled himself forward. His torso slid into the tunnel, but his legs remained in the shaft, angled skyward.

He spun onto his back. Curling one leg and then the other toward him, he pushed with his feet against the opposite wall of the shaft. He slid farther into the tunnel, but the sidewalls pressed in on him. He tried turning onto his belly, but couldn't. Rosenthal was right. The tunnel was too narrow.

The brim of his hardhat had knocked dirt into his face. He turned his head back and forth, blinking the dirt from his eyes and blowing it from his mouth. When he finally opened his eyes, his headlamp illuminated the roof of the tunnel, inches from his nose.

"Christ!" came Rosenthal's voice in his earpiece. "It looks like you're burying yourself. Crawl back. We'll pull you up."

The air was thick. He was gasping from his exertions. He tried to slide his hand up to press the transmitter button, but his arms were trapped at his sides. Closing his eyes, he breathed deeply, trying to suppress the panic welling within him.

1201 Central Asia

Temujin peered across the Daljun plain unable to suppress the sensation that he was staring at his own reflection. In the year since the Jadaran's defeat, Jamuka had scoured the steppe, searching for allies. He'd successfully united thirteen previously disparate tribes. Desperate to mark his newfound ascendancy, he led his army of the thirteen tribes across the Ala'u'ut and Turqa'ut Mountains. Jamuka and his army now sat on horseback on the other side of the plain.

Ong Khan had ordered Temujin and the Borjigin to ride out and meet Jamuka. This time, Temujin was not given a choice.

"What shall we do if they attack?" Bo'orchu asked.

On the other side of the Daljun plain, the Jadaran's banner flew alongside thirteen banners. Temujin looked up at his own Borjigin banner flapping high in the wind. "Jamuka won't. He can surely see our colors."

Moments later, a distant battle cry sounded. Jamuka's army began their advance.

"My brother," Temujin said. "Why do you forsake me?"

When the approaching horde reached the plain's midpoint, Bo'orchu turned toward Temujin. "What are your orders?"

Temujin's gaze narrowed. "Retreat," he said.

"And lure them into ambush?"

"No. Tell the men to disperse. Tell them not to fight."

"And what of Ong Khan's orders?" Bo'orchu asked.

"If there is a penalty to pay for not fighting, I alone will pay it," Temujin said. "But I refuse to pit Mongol against Mongol, family against family . . . or brother against brother."

39

Rosenthal directed a flashlight down the shaft. Only a small pile of dirt remained where Andrews's feet had been. Andrews was moving through the tunnel slowly but surely. Rosenthal checked the gradations on the hose and then his watch. After eight minutes, he'd moved a total of ten feet.

Rosenthal's earpiece crackled with static. "What's going on?" Andrews asked.

"What do you mean?"

"Can't you feel that?"

Rosenthal listened. Over the hum of the generator, there was a low, rumbling noise. As the noise became louder, Rosenthal felt a vibration in his feet. "Yes," he said. "I do."

"Here come the Rovers," an engineer said. "All three of them."

"Stop them!" Rosenthal yelled.

The engineers ran from the trench, hollering and waving. Moments later, the vehicles stopped.

Rosenthal looked down the shaft. Several clumps of dirt had fallen to the bottom of the shaft, but the wall remained largely intact. He pressed the transmit button on his headphone. "How's that?"

Rosenthal waited for a reply, wondering if his inner ear was playing a trick on him. The rhythmic hammering of the Rovers had stopped, but the vibration continued. If anything, it was worse. "Professor?" he said. *"Professor?"*

There was a loud roar. Dust jetted up through the shaft, blinding him. He collapsed to his knees, covering his eyes. It was then he heard a low rumbling sound followed by the men yelling. Wiping the dust from his eyes, he looked up just in time to see the trench wall falling toward him. The wall of dirt knocked him back, pinning him flat to the ground.

There was a sudden silence. The crushing weight of the dirt pressed down on him, squeezing the air from his lungs. Entombed, unable to breathe, he fought the urge to scream. He tried to move his arms and legs but couldn't.

He felt himself drifting slowly away, his oxygen levels dropping. In the distance, he heard scratching noises. The scratching came closer. Hands were suddenly grabbing him and rolling him over, slapping his back.

He retched out a mouthful of dirt. On his side, he coughed and spat. When he could finally breathe, he wiped his eyes and looked around.

The men were digging furiously. The entire trench wall had collapsed. He pushed the transmit button on the mouthpiece. "Can you hear me?" he asked. "Andrews! Can you hear me?"

There was no response.

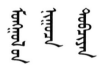

1201 Central Asia

Jamuka and his army of the thirteen tribes pursued Temujin's retreating army from the Daljun plain. They captured a few dozen warriors, but the full-scale battle that Jamuka envisioned didn't materialize.

As his anticipated conquest went unrealized, Jamuka grew increasingly frustrated. To mark his victory, he finally ordered the few prisoners they'd captured to be boiled alive. Afterward, he rode among his men, dragging the prisoners' severed heads behind him.

The following morning, Jamuka rode with his shaman through the camp. They stopped in front of an open area, its grass matted. "Where are the Qongqotads and Mangquts?" Jamuka asked.

"They left," the shaman said. "Along with the Ubchiqs and Uru'uts."

"*Why?*"

"By destroying the prisoners' souls, you prohibited their transition into the Eternal Blue Sky, angering their forefathers," the shaman said. "By spilling Mongol blood, you desecrated the steppe, angering Tengri."

"Where did they go?" Jamuka asked.

"They pledged their allegiance to Temujin," the shaman said.

"Temujin?" Jamuka said. "But why? We won! *I won!*"

"This morning, when the people of the steppe tribes woke, their sons were alive because of Temujin's decision not to fight," the shaman said. "Temujin ran, but he did so in the interests of the people. He ran, but he did so with Tengri's blessing."

"The Borjigin wear the furs of marmots and rodents," Jamuka said. "They eat what they can dig from the dirt: seeds and nuts and roots. Does that sound like a people *blessed* by Tengri?"

"When the Borjigin defeated the Tayichiut, Temujin distributed the spoils evenly among his men," the shaman said. "The Tayichiut people were not kept as prisoners or slaves, but allowed to live among the Borjigin as equals. Temujin took a Tayichiut wife. His mother adopted a Tayichiut child. Yes, their lands became his, but his lands became theirs. When he conquered the Jurchen and Tatars, he did the same with them."

The shaman's gaze traversed the camp. "When the steppe people look at the Borjigin, they see fellow Mongols. When they look at Temujin, they see a savior."

40

When he conquered a province he did no harm to the people or their property . . . And when those whom he had conquered became aware how well and safely he protected them against all others, and how they suffered no ill at his hands, and saw what a noble prince he was, then they joined him heart and soul and became his devoted followers.

—Marco Polo, 1300

The derrick of the drilling rig rose high into the night sky above Burkhan Khaldun. The air was filled with the sharp cough of the rig's diesel engine, the whir of the gearbox, and the subterranean hum of the drill.

Rosenthal covered his ears as he approached the rig's operator. "How deep?" he yelled.

"Twenty feet," the operator shouted back.

After the shaft collapsed, they'd spent the time since drilling a new hole uphill from the trench. It was now just after midnight. Andrews had been underground for over six hours.

"Can't this go any faster?" Rosenthal asked.

"The motor is burning a quart of oil every half hour," the operator yelled. "The hydraulics are going to hell, and the bearings and seals are shredded. If anything, we need to slow down."

"Keep drilling!" Rosenthal shouted. "When this is over, we'll build you another one."

Rosenthal walked down the hill to the trench. One of the engineers, a lieutenant, sat on the ground in front of the monitor. The monitor was dark.

"Anything?" Rosenthal asked.

The lieutenant shook his head.

1203 Central Asia

"He insults you by offering his bastard Merkit son," Senggüm said, standing in front of his father.

"How can I forsake Temujin?" Ong Khan asked. "He's been a loyal son."

Temujin had proposed a marriage between his eldest son, Jochi, and Ong Khan's daughter.

"*Loyal?*" Senggüm asked. "Right now, he conspires against us. He's sent emissaries to the Naiman."

"The Naiman?" Ong Khan asked. "Who spreads these lies?"

"Temujin's own *anda*—Jamuka."

After the incident at the Daljun plain, the alliance of the thirteen tribes had disintegrated.

"Why is Jamuka with us?" Ong Khan asked.

"He's become a valuable ally," Senggüm said. "He, more than anyone, understands Temujin's true motives."

The old khan gave a dismissive wave. "Jamuka will say anything to gain favor. Greed and envy have warped him into something that I'm sure his own father wouldn't recognize."

"Jamuka is of our white-bone lineage," Senggüm said. "In front of Tengri, in front of his ancestors, he's sworn his loyalty to us."

"Upon my order, Temujin has warred with the Tayichiut, Jurchen, and Tatars," Ong Khan said, his voice rising. "He's fought admirably—in my name!"

"But in *his* interests, Father. He slew their white-bone leaders and made their people his own."

Ong Khan's gaze narrowed. "Why do you insist that Temujin is our enemy?"

"He's openly defied you, Father. He ignored your order to war with the thirteen tribes. He's repeatedly ignored your orders."

"I should never have asked him to war against Jamuka," Ong Khan said. "That was a mistake. Besides, the thirteen tribes now belong to me."

"They belong to him!" Senggüm said. "How many from the thirteen tribes has he sent us as servants? How many from the Tayichiut, Jurchen, or Tatars? *None!*"

"They're not his servants," Ong Khan said. "He treats them as equals."

"Call it what you will," Senggüm said. "But the Tayichiut, Jurchen, and Tatars no longer exist. Temujin has absorbed them and made them his own. They're Borjigin, not Kereyid. They're his, not yours!"

The old khan stared ahead.

"When you're gone, he'll do the same to us," Senggüm said, dropping to a knee. "Your grandsons will grow up sleeping at the doors of his black-bone families. Don't you see, Father? If you agree to this marriage, it means you have chosen his people over yours, him over me."

41

The greatest legacy of the Mongol Empire bequeathed to the Chinese is the Chinese nation itself.

—**Hidehiro Okada,** Japanese poet

The Chinese vice premier stood at the Khural's podium as the members of the Mongolian parliament clapped. Peering above bifocals, he smiled and nodded, waiting patiently until everyone sat.

"Respected Mongolian neighbors, it's with pleasure we celebrate the birthday of our common forefather, Kublai Khan. As khan, he ruled the Mongol nation. As emperor, he united China." The vice premier paused and scanned the room. "While Genghis surpassed all others as a conqueror of nations, Kublai's genius was as a governor of those nations. As leaders of our respective countries, we can learn much from the grandson."

Baabar seethed. At the time of Genghis Khan's birth, the lands comprising modern-day China were a patchwork of separate kingdoms. By the time Kublai Khan became ruler, the Mongols had conquered Manchuria, Turkistan, Xinxiang, and Tibet. They'd brought the Tangut, Uighur, Sung, and Jin kingdoms under their rule. After defeating his brother to gain control of the empire, Kublai Khan then proceeded to commit the gravest of Mongol sins. He became more Chinese than Mongol. Moving his capital to Dadu, modern-day Beijing, he surrounded himself with Confucian advisors. Under his governance, the empire began its decline, breaking into four parts: the Chagatai khanate in Central

Asia, the Great Horde in modern-day Russia, the Il-Khans of the Middle East, and Kublai Khan's eastern empire, which would become modern-day China. Baabar glared at the vice premier. The Chinese should be thankful to Mongolia. Instead, they believed that since Kublai Khan was emperor of China, he was Chinese. If Kublai Khan was Chinese, extrapolating backward, then so was his grandfather, Genghis Khan. With this myopic view of the world, it was not too difficult for the Chinese to conclude that since Genghis Khan was Chinese, then so was Mongolia.

The Chinese imperialists had used similar, convoluted lines of reasoning to lay claim to the many divergent cultures and people held hostage within their borders: not only the Mongolians in Inner Mongolia, but Muslims in eastern Turkistan, Uighurs in Xinxiang, Manchu in northeastern China, aborigines in Taiwan, and Buddhists in Tibet. In all, a total of fifty-five of China's ethnic minorities, many desiring secession, many not even speaking Chinese, were, according to Beijing, ultimately Chinese.

Infuriated, Baabar stood and raised a fist. All eyes turned toward him.

The Chinese vice premier spoke louder, trying to drown the growing buzz spreading through the hall. In response, Baabar began chanting, pumping his fist into the air. "One Mongolia! One Mongolia! One Mongolia!"

The vice premier backed from the podium. Khural guards descended on Baabar. Baabar pushed them away and continued his chant, fighting and kicking, until he was overwhelmed and muffled by the guards.

The room grew eerily quiet. One and then another Khural member stood and watched, in shock, as one of their own was gagged and dragged from the floor.

"One Mongolia!" a parliamentarian shouted. Others did likewise.

Within moments, the entire Khural, including members of the CPRP, was standing. The parliamentarians, raising their fists in collective furor, turned toward the Chinese vice premier and resumed Baabar's chant, "One Mongolia!"

ᠵᠢᠯᠤᠭᠤ   ᠨᠤᠲᠤᠭ   ᠮᠣᠩᠭᠣᠯ

1203 Central Asia

Temujin led his family and an entourage from their camp at Burkhan Khaldun. Ong Khan, who'd accepted Temujin's proposal of marriage between their children, had invited the family to a betrothal feast.

When the entourage was one day's ride from the Kereyid camp, a man approached on horseback. "I came to warn you," he said. "In the morning, Kereyid warriors will come for you."

"Yes," Temujin said in good spirits. "My khan sends a greeting party."

"A greeting party comes, not with open arms, but with closed fists," the man said.

"I am Ong Khan's adopted son, his right arm and sharpest blade," Temujin said, undeterred. "Tomorrow, we feast in the Golden Tent. My son is to marry Ong Khan's daughter."

"I know who you are," the man said. He slipped from his horse and bowed. "You are Temujin. My name is Badai. My father was Chava of the Ne'udeis."

Chava, Temujin's former friend and ally, had been taken prisoner at Daljun. Chava had been one of the men beheaded by Jamuka.

Temujin returned Badai's bow. "I deeply regret your loss," he said. "I have prayed your father's spirit escaped Jamuka's cauldrons. But your feud is with Jamuka, not Ong Khan."

"Yes, my feud is with Jamuka," Badai said, nodding. "But he now rides at Ong Khan's side."

"That can't be," Temujin said.

"I'm afraid it's true," Badai said. "Jamuka now speaks from the back of the Golden Tent. And Ong Khan listens. Together, they have formed an alliance against a common enemy. That enemy is you."

Badai's eyes glowed with anger. "And yes, my father's spirit did escape Jamuka's cauldrons. He ascended into the Eternal Blue Sky and now visits me in my dreams. In my sleep, my father calls out for vengeance. He tells me Tengri favors the Borjigin. He tells me Tengri favors you."

42

Elena held herself up by the lift's railing as it ascended, her knees weak. She stared at the text message sent by her Russian embassy contact.

RIP Anton.

It had been one week since Stasio's death. His body, surprisingly, had still not been found. Mongolian police had discovered Petr's body inside the apartment, a bullet through his forehead. Now, following an operation for complications related to his gunshot wound, Anton was dead.

The lift stopped. The bell rang and the door opened.

Elena stood frozen in place, staring into the hallway. The SVR team should all be back in Russia. Instead, they'd decided to stay, to finish one last job.

She took a step forward, but then stopped. No. She couldn't do this, not by herself. She hit the lift's down button. As the door began to close, a hand appeared, sweeping past the sensor. The door opened. A policeman stepped inside.

"I—I'm sorry," Elena said, sliding past him, speaking Mongolian. "This is my floor."

The officer remained in the opening. "Are you okay?" he asked. He was holding a roll of yellow restraining tape.

Elena summoned her best smile. "I'm fine," she said. "You caught me daydreaming."

"Do you live here?"

"Just visiting," Elena said, motioning vaguely down the darkened hallway.

When she turned back toward the officer, his gaze was locked on her tight-fitting sweater. She pointed toward the roll of yellow tape. "Is the building safe?"

"Yes," the officer replied.

"If not," she continued, "maybe I should call my boyfriend."

The officer gave a sheepish grin. "You'll be fine," he said. With a quick tip of his hat, he stepped back into the elevator. The doors closed.

Elena waited for a moment and then strode down the hallway, stopping at the door to the apartment. She stared down, amazed. Restraining tape over the doorframe, which the officer had presumably just placed there, was already cut—its loose edges hanging to the ground.

She looked up and down the hallway. It was empty. She reached for the doorknob. It turned. Removing the handgun from her back holster, she pushed the door open.

She was immediately hit by the stench of human waste. She moved through the apartment. The kitchen, living room, and hallway bathroom along with the men's bedrooms were untouched. Approaching her room at the end of the hallway, she heard a noise.

A figure was huddled on the floor by the window. The compartment beneath the window had been opened. Rifle parts were strewn over the floor.

"*Khöl-dökh!*" she commanded, gun raised.

The figure, wearing a black skullcap, looked up. Elena's mouth dropped open. "*Stasio?*"

"Help me with this," he said. His beard was long and unruly.

She looked around the room, her nose burning, the reek overwhelming. Police tape marked the outline of a figure on the ground, presumably where Petr had been found. Large patches of blood stained the carpeting, walls, and bed.

Stasio swore as he dropped the trigger. As he fumbled for it, she saw his hands were bandaged and bloody. Most of his fingers were gone.

She dropped to her knees. "What did they do to you?"

"Please," Stasio said. "We don't have much time."

She took over the rifle assembly. Stasio stood and

opened the window. "They're already on Sükhbaatar Street," he said. *"Hurry!"*

She assembled the bolt and breech and connected them to the stock. Snapping the scope into place, she extended the assembled rifle.

Stasio held up his bandaged hands. "You've got to do this, Elena. I can't."

Diverting her gaze from his mutilated hands, she slid toward the open window and lifted the rifle to the windowsill. She peered through the scope.

The motorcade, black and shiny in the midday sun, was on Sükhbaatar Street. The vehicles, three SUVs and a limousine, turned left onto Khuvsgalchid Avenue. They continued slowly for a couple hundred meters before stopping in front of the Historical Museum. She directed the rifle up the museum's steps to where the curator was waiting. Behind him was a television crew.

A couple of weeks earlier, several days before the SVR team was scheduled to return to Russia, they were informed of the Chinese vice premier's visit. The visit had been kept secret in the hope the events surrounding the signing of the Goodwill Treaty would not be repeated. The Chinese were scheduled to fly in that morning. After the vice premier spoke to the Khural, the delegation would make the short drive from Government House to the Historical Museum, where they would present several artifacts for display. By the time news of the visit was broadcast on Mongolian television, the delegation would have returned to the airport and be on their way back to Beijing.

Delegation members and security men from the rear SUVs surrounded the limousine. After several moments, three men emerged from the crowd, each holding a box.

Elena moved the scope's crosshairs between the three men as they began walking up the steps to the museum, their backs toward her. From behind, they appeared identical. Each wore a black overcoat, gray pants, and polished black dress shoes.

"Which one's the vice premier?" she asked.

Stasio stood behind her, holding a pair of binoculars. "I can't tell," he said.

"What should I do?"

"Take all three," he said. "Start in the middle."

Snapping two more bullets into the magazine, she aimed. She fired, then fired twice more. As she let the rifle drop to the floor, Stasio closed the window.

They walked quickly from the apartment and took the lift down to the lobby. They exited the building and climbed into Elena's car. In the distance, they heard the wail of sirens.

"Where have you been?" she asked as she drove them from the parking lot.

"In the safe room."

They'd set up an efficiency apartment on the ninth floor in case of emergencies.

"You should have called me," she said. "You should have let somebody at the embassy know you were alive."

"I didn't have my cell phone, and there was no landline," Stasio said. "You should have known I would have gone there. I thought I was going to die. I've barely been able to make it out of bed for food and water. You never came, Elena. *Why?*"

"Petr told me you were dead," she said. "Why would he do that?"

"Petr was a double agent."

"I know you didn't like him, Stasio, but—"

"There's no gray area here, Elena. That night, the Chinese showed up shortly after the three of you left. Petr alerted them. After the Chinese left, Petr came back up to the apartment. He confessed to working for them. He offered me money. He was wearing their wire."

"The Chinese left the apartment?" she asked, surprised. "All of them?"

"Yes."

"There were only two?"

He nodded.

"Then who killed Petr?"

"I did," Stasio said. "He didn't give me a choice. What

happened that night, Elena? Why did only Petr come back up?"

"While we were out, I called to see if you wanted anything," she said. "When you didn't answer, I knew something was wrong. On our way back to the apartment, I checked your cell phone calls. I saw you had called Baabar, so . . . I called him."

"You did what?"

"Baabar said you had initiated the meeting protocol," she said. "He'd walked all the way to the apartment and had just knocked at the door. One of the Chinese agents answered. I told Baabar to leave. By the time we got back to the building, he was running outside. The Chinese were chasing him. Anton shot both of them, but he was hit. Afterward, Petr went back up to check on you. I drove Anton to the embassy. They took him to the hospital. That's why we weren't there."

"How's Anton?"

She took a deep breath. "He's dead."

Stasio gritted his teeth. "This is Petr's fault. He was undisciplined. I should have replaced him this summer, before we moved out of the embassy." He turned toward her. "The embassy. Is that where you've been staying?"

"No, I had to drive Baabar back to his apartment."

"You took Baabar to the embassy?"

She nodded. "He helped with Anton."

"Where have you been staying?"

Elena brought the car to a stop at a light, her hands wrapped tightly around the steering wheel, her knuckles white. She turned. "I stayed . . . with him. He was in danger— from the Chinese, from Petr."

"*Baabar?*"

"Yes," she said. "Petr wanted to kill him. I didn't understand why until now."

When the light turned green, Elena pulled ahead, avoiding Stasio's gaze.

They continued in silence. Elena drove from the downtown region to a small airfield east of the city. She parked outside a hangar. Inside, they found a uniformed pilot standing by the wing of a small jet, writing on a clipboard, going through his preflight checks. Next to the jet was the helicopter that Elena had taken to the mountain.

"Right on time," the pilot said as they approached. "But I thought there were *four* passengers."

"Only two," Stasio said. "Could we leave as soon as possible?"

The pilot nodded. He hit a button on the wall. The hangar door began to open. "We're cleared for a direct flight to St. Petersburg," he said. "We're ready to go." He jogged up the stairs leading into the jet and disappeared inside.

Stasio followed the pilot up the stairs, but then stopped and looked back.

Elena remained on the hangar floor, looking up at him. He walked back down the steps. "What's wrong?"

"I can't leave," she said. "Not now."

"You can't stay, Elena. They'll trace the shots to the apartment. That policeman you were talking with in the elevator will be able to describe you. In a few hours, everyone in Ulaanbaatar is going to be searching for a tall Caucasian woman with long blonde hair."

She ran a self-conscious hand over her hair.

"Elena, there's nothing left to do here. You've given the American the bone. We've turned over the corruption information. The vice premier is presumably dead. It's time to go home."

"You're right, Stasio. We've accomplished everything we wanted and more. You should go."

He folded his arms, unmoving. "Is this what you thought was out there? Is this what you've been looking for?"

She nodded. "I think so."

"Is this about *who* he is?"

"What are you saying, Stasio?"

"Have you told him who he is?"

She shook her head.

"He's still just a man, Elena. A politician. Nothing more. He may bed you, but he knows what being with you, truly being with you, would mean to his career."

"Stasio, don't be mean."

"Do you love him?"

"Just go," she said. "Please."

Stasio's face creased into a smile. He shook his head and laughed. Reaching into his pocket, he pulled out a glass flask of vodka. "You promised me one last drink." With the palm of his hand, he unscrewed the lid and raised the flask in salutation.

After a long drink, he looked her squarely in the eyes. "You're still the same naïve girl I met in that nightclub." Before she could respond, he clamped his bandaged palms to her face and kissed her firmly on the lips.

With a reflexive jab, she knocked him back. He fell hard to the stairs, holding his abdomen.

"Stasio!" she said, leaning over him. "I'm sorry."

Sprawled over the steps, he looked up at her. "You'll wrap those skinny legs around anybody, won't you?"

She slapped him hard across the face.

Stasio ran a hand over his cheek and smiled. "Thank you," he said. "That makes this so much easier."

Elena turned and walked away.

Stasio began laughing, the sound echoing through the hangar.

When she neared the door, there was a loud crash—the flask shattering against the wall above her. Showered with shards of broken glass and vodka, she shook off both and left the hangar, not looking back.

1203 Central Asia

Temujin took Badai's warning to heart. He sent his family back to Burkhan Khaldun. He and a small band of nineteen men then spent the night waiting on the southern side of the Mau Heights.

At sunrise, they saw an approaching dust cloud and hid as the horsemen passed. Senggüm rode at the front of the procession with Jamuka at his side. The Kereyid's fiercest warriors followed.

"There is your greeting party," Badai whispered to Temujin.

Temujin nodded to Khasar, who held a bow and arrow. Khasar raised the bow. When he released the arrow, it struck the warrior behind Senggüm.

Temujin and his band then took off on horseback with the Kereyid warriors in pursuit.

For the next nine days, Temujin and his band stayed just beyond Senggüm's grasp. With their rations depleted, they rode over a ridge into a secluded valley. A muddy, winding river split the valley.

"When I was a boy, my uncle lived here," Bo'orchu said. He pointed. "His ger was on that hill. The mares grazed here and the sheep there. He called it Baljuna."

A gust of wind moved in a rolling wave across the valley. Pushing back the grass, it leaped over the river and swept up the hill, dissipating in the shimmering leaves of a large tree.

"We used to climb that tree," Bo'orchu said. Spurring his horse ahead, he rode into the valley.

"We have to keep moving," Khasar said, riding at Temujin's side. "They're not far behind."

Temujin held out his arms. "Look at this place, Khasar. And look at them. So easily they could ride away and be done with us."

The brothers' mutual gaze settled on those assembled around them. The men's faces were gaunt with fatigue and hunger, but their eyes glowed with determination.

"Why do they endure this?" Temujin asked.

"Because they believe in you," Khasar said. "They believe you'll lead the steppe people to something better."

"I cannot ask them to go farther," Temujin said. "Our fate is with Tengri. If it's his will that we join him, then so be it. We'll die here in this valley."

A white boar appeared in the reeds near the river.

"There's another reason they follow you," Khasar said, grabbing his bow. "Tengri favors you. He always has."

Khasar let loose an arrow that killed the boar. Within minutes, the men had gutted the animal and started a fire. Using the skin as a kettle, they boiled the flesh. At the river's edge, they dipped their cups into the muddy waters.

"Tengri has brought us to this, our lowest point, for a reason," Temujin called out. "This moment marks the beginning of something important. With our outcome in doubt, our bond of friendship has held strong. Unifying the steppe takes more than mere words or handshakes, but a bond forged from adversity, a bond blessed by Tengri himself."

Temujin looked into the eyes of his companions. He then raised his cup. "If we accomplish our great work, I promise to share the bitter and the sweet. If I break my word, then let me be as this water."

The men raised their cups and drank.

43

Rosenthal fell into a sea of darkness. Above, the enveloping blue of the morning sky was now only a distant pinhole, framed by the dirt walls of the newly drilled shaft. He looked down. The light from his headlamp reflected off glistening stalagmites as he settled on the cave's floor. Walls were visible downhill and to each side. Uphill, his light dissipated into darkness. "Andrews!" he yelled out. His own voice echoed back.

He spotted Andrews's rope on the rock-strewn ground. Unfastening his C-clamp, he followed the rope downhill to a rocky wall and the now dirt-filled tunnel. The dull, glassy-eyed camera end of the fiber-optic scope emerged from the base of the passage. The scope's lights were off.

Rosenthal looked at the dirt-filled space—tall, long, and irregular—and realized it wasn't a tunnel, but a fissure, a fault line. The Rovers had induced a mini-earthquake.

He scanned the ground. Andrews's hardhat sat nearby. He picked it up and flicked the lamp's switch on and off. The battery was dead.

"Lieutenant, can you hear me?" he asked, speaking into his mouthpiece.

"Yes," the lieutenant said.

"It looks like Andrews made it into the cave."

"Do you see him?" the lieutenant asked.

"No, but it's big. I'd better start moving."

Rosenthal began walking uphill. The cave widened and then narrowed. Near the point where the hill crested, he came to a wall.

The light from his headlamp moved across the wall, disappearing briefly into a shadowed opening. He stepped toward the opening, which was largely covered with vines. He pushed aside the overgrowth and directed his light inside. The opening was large enough to walk into. Looking down, he saw a footprint in silt. The tread on the bottom of his boot was identical. Andrews, who'd been wearing the same boot, had been here.

Rosenthal stepped past the vines. As he did, he heard a voice. "Hello, Captain."

Surprised, Rosenthal took a step back. As he did, he tripped and fell. All the while, the voice continued. "Where are you? . . . Captain? . . . Captain?"

Rosenthal pushed the transmit button. "*Andrews?*"

"Speaking," Andrews said.

"Where are you?"

"I'm currently standing around with a bunch of engineers. We're looking down into a long narrow hole, wondering where you are."

* * *

Andrews sat in the grass, chewing a granola bar, his face scraped and muddy, a bottle of Gatorade in his lap. He watched as the engineers pulled Rosenthal to the surface.

Rosenthal unfastened his C-clamp and walked toward him. "Are you okay?"

Andrews held out his arms. "Considering everything, yeah."

"What happened?"

Andrews took a swig of the Gatorade. "I thought I was stuck down there, but then I was able to inch slowly forward," he said. "When the vibrations started, the tunnel began to collapse. I was able to flip onto my belly and crawled forward as fast as I could. When I could stand, I ran. By the time I realized everything wasn't coming down, I was lost. Then, I just started walking."

"How'd you get out?" Rosenthal asked.

"It seemed like I walked for hours," Andrews said. "But it was probably a lot less. When my flashlight ran out of power, I couldn't see anything. I laid down and fell asleep. When I woke, I saw a ray of light coming from the surface." He held up his hands, showing off his dirt-caked fingers. "I dug my way out."

A few of the men came with bottles of water, a sweatshirt, and towels.

Andrews stood. He took off his shirt and opened a bottle. After taking a gulp of the water, he dumped the rest of the bottle over his head. "Were these in a freezer?" he asked, shivering. He opened another bottle and dumped it over his hands, which he scrubbed together and wiped in the grass.

In the distance, there was the sound of a helicopter. Several seconds later, the helicopter appeared along the eastern horizon.

"It's one of ours," someone said.

The helicopter landed nearby. While the rotors were still turning, the door opened. Abbey jumped out and ran toward the group. "Where is he?" she asked.

The men parted to reveal Andrews. Now wearing the sweatshirt, he was toweling his hair dry. "I was wondering what it would take to get you up here," he said, grinning.

Abbey ran and jumped into his arms. She squeezed him tight.

A few of the men whistled.

"All right, guys," Rosenthal said. He waved the men back toward the camp. "We have a lot of work to do. Let's start with the tents. This place has to look pristine, ASAP."

Rosenthal began leading the men back toward the camp.

Andrews set Abbey on the ground. She looked up at him, continuing to hold him tight. "James, if you were hurt, I don't know what I would have done."

"Everything's fine," he said. He smiled. "I'm actually glad you're here for this."

"For what?"

"Can you hold on?" he asked.

She nodded.

Andrews took Abbey's face in his hands and kissed her. He then turned toward Rosenthal's retreating figure. "Joel, hold on," he called out.

Rosenthal and the other engineers turned.

"You forgot to ask me something," Andrews said.

"I've just been trying not to say I told you so," Rosenthal said. "That maybe it wasn't the best idea to go down there."

Andrews didn't reply. He just nodded and smiled.

"Okay, I'll bite," Rosenthal said. "What did I forget to ask you?"

"If I found anything while I was down there."

Rosenthal laughed. "Besides a lot of dirt?"

"*Did* you find something?" Abbey asked.

Andrews reached into his pocket and then held out his hand. In his open palm were several white, cuboidal objects. He threw one into the air.

Rosenthal caught it. He held the object up between thumb and forefinger. "A bone?"

"A sheep's knucklebone, to be exact," Andrews said. "Mongolian children used to play with them, like dice."

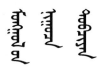

1203 Central Asia

Renewed in strength and spirit at Baljuna, Temujin and his small band eluded the Kereyid. After returning to their camp at Burkhan Khaldun, Temujin sent a message to Ong Khan.

As a child, I was thrown into the cold. You took me in and warmed me. But now, you've pushed me back outside. Why? By forsaking me, you not only turned your back on me, but the memory of my father, your sworn brother. I have never held you to the debt you owed him. But how can you ignore it? Was my father not a good brother? Have I not been a good son? Let us return to the way we were.

Ong Khan's return message came three days later.

You have been our prop, Temujin. If I favor you, however, I must look past Senggüm. My heart will split in half. It must be one or the other.

Temujin then sent word to Senggüm.

Brother, when the Naiman plundered your clan and took your wife and sons, I sent my four warhorses and restored your family. I've earned a position by the hearth, but have been pushed outside. As our father grows old, do not worry him with talk of succession. Let us reunite. Let us turn our backs to one another and fight the outsider.

Senggüm's response came three days later.

Brother?! When have you called me brother when you weren't trying to position yourself closer to my father? And why would I worry him with talk of succession? My father's succession was determined the moment I was born.

Temujin sent word to Jamuka.

As young men, we were brothers and shared one life. Your soul was like the wolf, Börte Chino. Today, however, you are no longer like the wolf, standing strong in the wind, but like the leaves of a tree, your people the branches. During the summer, you enjoy the sun's warmth. With the cold, you'll fall away. Soon your people will stand naked and cold. Prepare yourself, Jamuka. Winter approaches.

44

Andrews, Abbey, and Rosenthal stood on the southwestern slope of Burkhan Khaldun, shining flashlights into the open mouth of a cave. Moments earlier, the backhoe had cleared out the crevasse that Andrews had dug his way through earlier that morning. After several feet of dirt, the backhoe struck a brick wall, intact portions of which were over four feet thick.

"Someone didn't want us to get in here," Rosenthal said.

They stepped over remnants of the wall and walked single file into the cave, their flashlight beams leading the way. The cave, with its occasional stalactites and stalagmites and gravel-strewn floor, was similar to the cave on the southeastern side of the summit, but narrower.

They walked for over a minute. The air became cooler, their breaths condensing in front of them. The passage finally opened into a large cavern. As they stepped into the cavern, Rosenthal and Abbey leaped back.

Their lights illuminated dozens of figures.

Abbey turned toward a grinning Andrews. "You're evil," she said.

"I'm sorry," he said. "I should have warned you, but if it's any consolation, I was ten times more startled when I walked in here last night, by myself, with only half a light."

Throughout the cavern, medieval soldiers stood in formation, holding crossbows, spears, and swords. Several were missing heads or arms. Some lay on the floor, their body parts turned to rubble.

"It's a terracotta army," Andrews said to an open-mouthed Rosenthal.

"A what?"

"In 1974, farmers in China's Lintong District were digging for a well and discovered an underground necropolis built in the third century BC for China's first emperor," Andrews said. "Archaeologists subsequently discovered over eight thousand, life-size clay statues built near the emperor's mausoleum for the purpose of protecting and entertaining him in the afterlife."

The three of them walked among the gray figures.

"The Chinese mass-produced the statues," Andrews said. "The parts of the body were all made separately. The faces were made from several different molds. The pieces were then put together in one of history's first mass-production assembly lines. At the site, there were more than 8,000 soldiers, more than 100 chariots, and more than 500 horses."

Abbey poked at the armor covering the chest of one of the soldiers. "This looks real."

"It is," Andrews said. "The statues are made of clay. But the helmets and armor are real. So are the weapons."

Rosenthal peered into the face of one of the soldiers. "What are they doing here?"

Abbey turned toward Andrews. "They're protecting something," she said. "What is it?"

Andrews directed his light toward numerous shadowed openings in the back of the cavern. Covered by a tangle of roots and hanging vines, the openings were each about seven feet high and seven feet wide. They stepped past the vines into the nearest passageway.

From the wall, Rosenthal tore away a patch of moss, exposing gray-white rock. His fingers settled into small, regular cuts. "This is man-made," he said.

Andrews nodded, waving them forward. They soon emerged from the passage into a room. The room was circular. The ceiling, carved from the rock, was smooth. With their flashlights, they followed the ceiling to a central peak.

"It looks like the inside of a ger," Abbey said.

"It is," Andrews said. "At least a replica."

Andrews directed his flashlight to a large rectangular

structure on the far side of the room. Rosenthal walked quickly toward it and brushed away some of the moss and vines, revealing a smooth, glistening white surface. He circled the structure and swept away the remaining overgrowth and dirt, exposing a marble vault.

Rosenthal turned, his eyes wide. In response, Andrews nodded, laughing.

Rosenthal raised his arms and howled. Andrews and Abbey embraced. Rosenthal began running around the vault, continuing to howl.

The sounds of the celebration, resonating against the walls, were punctuated by an abrupt, cracking noise.

All three whirled. Their flashlights illuminated a partially collapsed wooden frame. An equally fragile wooden horse stood next to it.

"A tent to live in and a horse to ride," Andrews said. He removed the knucklebones from his pocket and set them on a bench inside the collapsed tent. "And games to play."

Rosenthal opened a nearby wooden chest, its hinges creaking. From inside the chest, he pulled out handfuls of silver and gold coins.

"And more than enough money to spend in a thousand afterlives," Andrews said.

"James, this is incredible!" Abbey said.

They directed their lights around the room, illuminating other chests and artifacts along the wall. As Abbey and Rosenthal stared in amazement, Andrews began backing toward the entrance. "Let's go," he said.

Rosenthal laughed. "What's the hurry?"

"We have a lot of work to do," Andrews said. "Everything has to be photographed and documented. No one's been down here for over 680 years."

"Joel has a point," Abbey said. "Enjoy the moment. It's not every day you find the treasures of Eurasia."

Andrews gave a nonchalant shrug. "I just thought you might want to see the others."

"*Others?*" Abbey asked. "Other what?"

"Tombs," Andrews said, smiling.

"There are more?" Rosenthal asked.

Andrews nodded.

"How many?"

"In all . . . eleven."

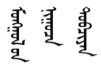

1203 Central Asia

Temujin never thought he would battle against Ong Khan and the Kereyid. He certainly never thought he would war against Jamuka. Mongol fighting Mongol, however, was the way things had always been. Until there was one master, it was the way it would always be.

Temujin sent word over the steppe for his people to unite. Warriors from the Tayichiut, Jurchen, and Tatars, along with those formerly in Jamuka's clan—the Mangqut, Jalayir, Arulat, Barula, Besüd, and Tarqut—all made their way to the Borjigin camp.

Temujin led his army west. They met the Kereyid at the Khökh Nu'ur, where they fought for two days. On the morning of the third day of fighting, the Kereyid fled in disarray.

Temujin and his army rode into the Kereyid camp. He lit a torch and threw it onto the Golden Tent. As flames enveloped the tent, the flap swung open. Two stretchers were carried high on shoulders through the opening. The stretchers held the bodies of Ong Khan and Senggüm.

Temujin and Bo'orchu sat on horseback. They watched the khan's family pour from the tent, screaming and crying, circling the two bodies.

One of Ong Khan's grandsons glared at Temujin. The boy's fists were clenched, his eyes filled with hatred.

"Kiriltuk should have killed me when he could," Temujin said.

"What do you mean?" Bo'orchu asked.

"I was that boy's age when the Tayichiut left us," Temujin

said. "That day, I vowed I would kill Kiriltuk. And I did. I cut off his head and brought it to Ong Khan." He paused. "Like we've done with the others, we'll make the Kereyid people our own. But these people are Ong Khan's grandchildren, his daughters and sons. If we, if our sons and daughters, are to survive, all of Ong Khan's people must die."

"*Everyone?*" Bo'orchu asked.

"Look at him," Temujin said. "That kind of hatred cannot be appeased by horses or silk, rank or prestige. It must be us or them, one or the other."

45

The Imperial coffin is sent north to the burial ground, where it is deeply interred.

—**Yeh Tzŭ-chi,** 1378, Chinese historian

"When the Borjigin wanted to disappear, they would ride up into Burkhan Khaldun," Andrews said. "Over the years, as I've walked the mountain, I've always wondered where they went. I've seen areas where a few men could hide, a crevasse here or there, but certainly nowhere a whole clan would be safe."

Andrews stood once again with Abbey and Rosenthal on the southwestern slope. They watched as the CIA men and engineers filed from the passage, carrying chests of jewels and coins, gold-plated helmets, shields, knives, and spears.

The Mongolian Institute of Geography, after being alerted of the discovery, requested that everything of value be removed for safekeeping. Andrews had subsequently divided the men into eleven teams, one for each burial chamber. Before anything was touched, each artifact was photographed and catalogued. The tombs would remain in place until the institute decided what to do with them.

"Not to be greedy, but weren't there more than eleven khans?" Rosenthal asked.

Andrews nodded. "There were thirty-nine."

"Then why only eleven tombs?" Rosenthal asked.

"And," Abbey interjected, "if the Soviets already found Genghis Khan's remains, who's in them?"

"Last night, while I was trapped down there, I wondered

the same things," Andrews said. "Then I remembered statements from two separate sources. The *Yüan shih* states the Chinese emperors were brought back to Mongolia and buried *near* the funerary mounds of their ancestors, while Rashid al-din, a Persian historian, wrote Kublai Khan and the Chinese emperors were not buried *with* their ancestors."

"That's contradictory," Abbey said.

"That's what I thought," Andrews said. "This morning, however, as I was digging out of the cave, I realized both statements are correct. The Chinese emperors were brought back to Mongolia, but they were not buried with their ancestors."

"If they went through the trouble of bringing them all the way back, why not?" Rosenthal asked.

"The khans' reigns can be divided into three periods: pre-Chinese, Chinese, and post-Chinese," Andrews said. "Once you understand the differences in the periods, you can begin to see what might have happened.

"A few years after Genghis Khan's death, Chinese ambassadors were taken to his gravesite. In their accounts, the ambassadors wrote the grave had no funerary mound. They wrote that the Mongols, to keep the location a secret, had replaced the grass over the site and stampeded the area with horses. Most believe the Chinese ambassadors were taken to a false gravesite. Regardless, I believe that's exactly how the pre-Chinese khans would have been buried—without markers."

He looked toward the cave. "The burial of the Chinese khans, however, would have been different. Kublai Khan was the first of the Chinese khans. Nine others followed, all serving as both Mongol khans and Chinese emperors. To govern, they used a hybrid of Mongolian and Chinese customs. Their burials would have been the same. To honor Mongolian tradition, they would have chosen to be buried near their ancestors, who everyone believed were on Burkhan Khaldun. To honor Chinese tradition, they would have been buried with the pomp and circumstance of an emperor."

"That would account for the terracotta soldiers," Abbey said.

Andrews nodded. "Which is definitely a Chinese touch."

"Kublai Khan was followed by nine more Chinese khans," Rosenthal said. "If there were only ten Chinese khans, why eleven tombs?"

"Ratnadhara, the prince and heir-apparent to Emperor Wên-tsung, died as a child," Andrews said. "The emperor was so distraught over his son's death he gave him an emperor's funeral. Like the emperors, he was reportedly brought north and buried with his ancestors."

"You said no one's been down there for 680 years," Rosenthal said. "Is that when the last Chinese emperor died?"

Andrews nodded.

One of the engineers emerged from the tunnel wearing a vest and helmet.

"No souvenirs," Rosenthal shouted. "Officially, we're not even here."

The men whistled as the engineer modeled the medieval garments before sashaying back into the cave.

Abbey turned toward Andrews. "And the post-Chinese khans?"

"They ruled Mongolia, but didn't serve as emperors of China," Andrews said. "They would have reverted to traditional Mongolian burial methods. Out of respect for their ancestors, they would have left the tombs of the Chinese khans intact." He motioned toward the cave. "To prevent their desecration, they might have even gone so far as to brick them up."

1203 Central Asia

"Swear your allegiance to Temujin, and there will be no bloodshed," Jochi called out.

After the Golden Tent burned to the ground, the Borjigin pursued the remnants of the Kereyid army. Temujin and his three oldest sons were chasing three horsemen.

Thus far, every Kereyid warrior given this offer had sworn his allegiance.

Two of the three Kereyid pulled up their horses, hopped to the ground, and dropped to their knees. The third horseman, however, continued.

"Bring these two back with the others," Temujin said. "I'll get the third."

Temujin rode ahead. He found the third man tending to his horse at a river. As he approached, he saw it was Jamuka.

Temujin slid from his horse and advanced, his blade flashing. Jamuka retreated, blocking Temujin's blows.

"My brother," Jamuka said as they wound in and out of the river. "What's wrong?"

"When we rode to the mountain and river, why did you want our clans to separate?"

"I didn't," Jamuka said. "You were the one that left."

"Why did you march against me at the Daljun plain?"

"I knew you would ride away," Jamuka replied.

Temujin swung, but Jamuka blocked the blow.

"Why did you desecrate the steppe with my men's blood?" Temujin asked.

"I had to conclude the battle," Jamuka said. "My men would have continued fighting. They wouldn't have stopped until they hunted you down and the Borjigin were defeated.

"You lie!" Temujin yelled. He swung hard.

Jamuka slipped to the side, avoiding the blow. Temujin's sword hit a rock and broke, leaving him with only the hilt.

Jamuka stepped purposefully forward, sword raised. "I was hoping you would join me against the Kereyid," he said as Temujin retreated. "I knew Ong Khan would never step aside. But together, we could defeat him. We could realize our dream of unifying the steppe."

"You wanted me to betray Ong Khan?" Temujin said, laughing. "To join you and the *thirteen* tribes?"

Jamuka leaped forward and swung. Temujin blocked the blow, but its force tore the hilt from his hands. Jamuka raised his sword again.

Temujin, defenseless, felt an inner peace wash through

him. Time slowed as he closed his eyes, acquiescing to his fate. Long after the imagined slice of the blade, he heard the pounding of hooves. He opened his eyes. To his surprise, Jamuka was riding away.

Temujin ran to his horse and grabbed the bow from his saddle. Raising an arrow, he aimed at the middle of Jamuka's back.

Jamuka suddenly slowed his horse to a trot. Sitting upright, he extended his arms.

Temujin's sons rode up. "That's Jamuka," Jochi said. "You can't let him get away."

"Kill him, Father," Chagatai called out. "He's your greatest enemy."

Temujin lowered his arrow. He looked down at his palm and the scars he shared with Jamuka, reminding himself of things he'd forgotten. "No, he's not," he said. "Not anymore."

Jamuka continued across the field, arms extended.

"What's wrong with him?" Tolui asked.

"After all these years, my brother can finally see in front of the cart," Temujin said. "After all these years, he's finally listening to his inner voice."

46

All the Grand Khans, and all the descendants of Chinggis their first Lord, are carried to a mountain that is called Altay to be interred. Wheresoever the Sovereign may die, he is carried to his burial in that mountain with his predecessors; no matter the place of his death were 100 days' journey distant, thither must he be carried to his burial.

—Marco Polo, 1300

Andrews sat in a transport helicopter, the last to leave the mountain. He looked across the valley to a nearby hill. His thoughts turned to his first trip to the mountain, seven years earlier.

It was an overcast, rainy day. He and Baabar had driven from Avarga into the heart of the previous Highly Restricted Area—the four thousand square miles of unchartered thicket surrounding Burkhan Khaldun. Baabar brought their jeep to a stop on the top of a rise.

"The mountain is on the other side of that hill," Andrews said, pointing across a water-soaked valley, a map spread over his lap. "We'll have to backtrack and find another way."

They stepped outside into the rain and walked down the rise. Baabar paced back and forth at the edge of the valley before they returned to the jeep.

"We can make it," Baabar declared. He put the transmission in gear and jammed his foot down on the accelerator. As they sped downhill, Andrews braced himself.

Forty kilometers per hour . . . fifty . . . sixty . . .

Baabar was better than anyone at navigating the hills and bogs of the Mongolian countryside. Definitively Mongolian in his driving, he was, in a word, shrewd.

Seventy . . . eighty . . . ninety . . .

As they transitioned from hill to valley, Baabar turned the wheel to avoid a pool of water. A small mound, however, loomed ahead.

"Hold on!" Baabar yelled.

The jeep launched into the air. They came down hard, slamming into their seats, mud slapping against the windshield.

Baabar jerked the wheel back and forth as they moved through the quagmire, the tires spinning. "If you see grass, let me know," he yelled.

"I thought you mapped this out," Andrews yelled back.

"I never thought we'd make it this far."

They limped from one patch of solid ground to the next, the tires kicking up water, peat, and mud. Halfway across the valley, their path was blocked by another pool of water.

With a flick of the wheel, Baabar gained momentary traction on an unseen surface. The jeep shot forward, but made it only halfway across the pool before coming to an abrupt stop.

In the rain, stuck in the middle of nowhere, Baabar started whooping, rocking back and forth in his seat, his foot down on the accelerator. Andrews joined him. With the engine redlining, the two hollered and bounced against the walls of the jeep as the smell of burning rubber and smoke filled the cabin.

In rhythm with their gyrations, the jeep began moving back and forth. The front wheels suddenly caught. They lurched forward. With its engine whining, its tires spitting rooster tails, the jeep spun its way up the hill.

At the hill's crest, Andrews and Baabar stepped outside and ran through the rain, still whooping and hollering. Soaking wet, they collapsed against the side of the vehicle, laughing. Their laughter came to a stop as they stared ahead. Spread before them was Burkhan Khaldun.

There was the sudden shrill whine of the helicopter's engine followed by the pull of the rotors. As the helicopter ascended and the summit unfurled beneath him, Andrews's thoughts wound through the mountain's subterranean passages. Reliving the moment of discovery, he knew the exultation washing through him would eventually seep away. But he could already feel what would replace it—something more profound. Satisfaction.

He didn't know if he would ever make full professor. He didn't know if he would ever publish another research article or make another significant find, but he knew the satisfaction of this moment would stay with him forever.

He looked toward the campsite. The area had been cleared. The trench dug out by the backhoe, the newly drilled shaft, and the passageway into the cave had been refilled. Once again, the mountain was left at peace.

PART

3

ᠲᠡᠮᠦᠵᠢᠨ

*Where is Genghis Khan? He is not dead. He slept
and from that sleep he has never awakened. But
would not Holy Genghis heal himself: When he is
healed, he will awake and save his people.*

—Owen Lattimore,
Mongol Journeys

47

The helicopter approached Ulaanbaatar's International Airport. Andrews scanned the tarmac for news trucks or television crews, relieved to see neither.

After landing, Andrews walked with Abbey and Rosenthal toward the US Army transport that had flown them from Paris. The transport was taking Rosenthal, his fellow engineers, and the CIA men back to Washington, D.C. Andrews was leaving the next day on a commercial flight.

At the base of the steps leading into the transport, Andrews and Rosenthal turned toward each other. The engineers and CIA men circled around them.

"You turned our boondoggle into the trip of the century," Rosenthal said. "None of these guys will forget this. I know I won't."

"It wouldn't have happened without you," Andrews said. He turned, scanning the group. "Without all of you. Thank you."

One by one, the men shook hands with Andrews before filing up the stairway. Finally, only Rosenthal remained.

"Thanks for coming after me while I was down there," Andrews said.

"Even though you escaped on your own?" Rosenthal asked.

"It's the thought that counts."

The two embraced. With a nod, Rosenthal jogged up the stairs.

"You know, you've ruined archaeology for me," Andrews called out.

Rosenthal turned, smiling. "How's that?"

"I can't imagine a dig without your Rovers."

"Whenever you need them, they're yours." Rosenthal said. "Just give me a call." With a last wave, he disappeared inside the plane.

Andrews and Abbey walked toward the terminal.

A black SUV with tinted windows pulled up alongside them. A man wearing sunglasses leaned from the open driver's window. "Abbey," he said, nodding. "Dr. Andrews."

Andrews recognized the driver. A few years earlier, he'd been with Abbey on a couple summer hikes. At the time, Andrews had thought he was Abbey's boyfriend.

"Can we get a car for James?" Abbey asked. "He's not leaving until tomorrow."

"No problem," the driver said. "Hop in."

They made the short drive to the terminal and pulled into a small garage. The garage was empty except for another black SUV with tinted windows and Abbey's car. The driver switched off the ignition and handed the keys back to Andrews. "When you fly out, bring it back here," he said. "Just leave the keys inside."

"Thanks," Andrews said.

The driver motioned toward the black case that Abbey was holding. "If that's the bone, I can take it to him."

Abbey handed over the case.

"Also, he'd like to see you," the driver said. "Both of you."

The driver exited the SUV. He walked across the garage and climbed into the front passenger seat of the other SUV.

Abbey turned and met Andrews's inquisitive gaze. "Professor Herald," she said.

He shook his head. "No, Abbey."

"James, he feels terrible about what happened. He wants to apologize. He *needs* to apologize."

"I'm *not* meeting with him," Andrews said.

"If he thought anyone would have been hurt by all of this, he never would have done it."

"But he did do it," Andrews said. "And someone was hurt."

The rear door of the other SUV opened. Herald

appeared. His snow-white hair and pale, almost translucent skin stood in sharp contrast to the rich brown of his beret and a matching wool scarf.

"He loves you like a son," Abbey said. "I know I don't deserve it, but please, do this for me. I beg you."

After glaring out the window for several moments, Andrews took a deep breath. "I guess this has to happen sometime."

"Thank you," Abbey said.

Andrews opened the door.

The old professor stepped penitently forward, head bowed. *Scholar . . . teacher . . . mentor . . . friend.* Each pedestal Andrews had placed him on had been knocked away.

"James, I'm sorry," Herald said. "I wanted to protect you from all of this. What I did, however, was the exact opposite."

Herald held out his arms. "In the beginning, I planned on telling you everything. In fact, I hoped you would take my place, not only as an Asian scholar at the university, but with the society. When you published your travelogue, however, everything changed. I realized your *potential*." His voice broke. "You had absorbed my teachings and moved on, immersing yourself in the writings of de Rachewiltz, Rashid al-din, Juvaini, Cleaves, Pelliot." Herald's eyes lit anew with each name. "You spoke not only for me, but for a whole field of academia, for a lost generation of Mongol scholars. But more than that, you spoke for Mongolia, for Genghis Khan and his lost empire."

Herald slipped off the beret. "I've been content to spend my career studying Genghis Khan. But you! To you, history was not something passive or dusty and old, but something alive. You befriended Genghis Khan. You shared the warmth of his campfire, rode his horses, and walked his trails. You came to know his thoughts and desires, his secrets." His gaze narrowed. "In today's world, we don't need more spies. We need more people like you, people who understand Asia. People who can take that understanding and make a difference. Because I was more historian than spy, I kept everything a secret from you. I believed your greatest contribution would be as a scholar. With your knowledge and abilities, I believed you were capable of turning their past into something important, something more than purely academic." He smiled. "With this find, you have."

"You chose to live a lie," Andrews said. "For decades. *Why?*"

"When I founded the society, it was legitimate," Herald said. "We had a single office in Tokyo along with a small staff that organized sabbaticals for visiting professors traveling back and forth to Asia. When the CIA came to me, we were the push of a button away from the end of the world. I wondered, what could I do? I was a 145-pound weakling with a fondness for tweed jackets and bow ties. But they told me I could make a difference."

"Did you make a difference?" Andrews asked. "The kind you wanted?"

"I've tried," Herald said. "There's been good and bad. Yes, I've had to lie to you about the society and myself, but there's nothing disingenuous about my respect for you. Because of that respect, I've kept this a secret from you." He paused. "No matter what happens from this day forward, you *must* know that."

The two looked at one another, neither speaking.

With a nod, Herald slipped the beret back on. He took a step toward the SUV and then turned. "James, you're what a teacher waits his whole life for, someone motivated, someone gifted. But I failed you. I failed Sara." He held his arms out wide. "I'm sorry. Apologies aren't nearly enough, but they're all I have."

Andrews wanted to be angry. He wanted to rant and rave at the old professor. Instead, he suppressed a pang of guilt as he watched Herald, looking very old and very frail, shuffle away and climb into the SUV.

48

Herald closed the SUV's door and nodded toward the driver. They drove from the garage and across the tarmac, leaving Andrews and Abbey behind.

They entered another garage on the other side of the terminal. Herald, holding the black case, exited the vehicle and stepped through a door into the airport proper.

Herald spent the next few minutes walking. He spotted an elderly man sitting peacefully by himself. The man was in a wheelchair, ignored by the passersby as he looked out a plate-glass window onto the tarmac.

Herald stopped several feet away from the wheelchair-bound man. Together, they watched the mammoth US Army transport plane rumble down the runway and lift into the sky.

"You look good, my old friend," Herald said, turning.

Mikou met his gaze. "Who would think we would wear the last ten years so well?" he asked.

"Or the last forty?" Herald asked.

The old men smiled.

"Tell me," Mikou said. "How did it go?"

"Not well."

Mikou nodded. "It's hard for the young to forgive their elders."

"Perhaps they shouldn't," Herald said.

The two men looked back out the window, lost momentarily in their thoughts.

"How are the Chinese delegation members?" Herald asked.

"The foreign minister and ambassador are dead," Mikou

said. "The vice premier will die soon." He turned. "Why did you bring the Russians into this?"

"There was no way to foresee they would do this."

"But they've always been heavy-handed," Mikou said.

"True," Herald said. "With respect to Ulaanbaatar, however, we're both on the same team. Mongolia is also a much higher priority for Moscow than it is for Washington. Russia is far from their glory days, but their intelligence service is still first rate." He glanced toward Mikou. "Besides, you got your wish. The Khural has been cleaned out. And, by giving the corruption information to the Russians, it made it nearly impossible for anyone to trace the information back to you."

"But the information came so full circle," Mikou said. "I wanted to distance myself from it, not to protect myself, but because I was afraid someone close to me might be hurt."

"You're afraid of what might happen to Baabar?"

Mikou nodded. "What I don't understand is why the Russians gave it to him—a first-term parliamentarian? Don't get me wrong. It's a good use for the information. I thought of giving it to him myself, but in the end I decided against it."

"Because of what happened to Zorig?"

"Yes, and so many others."

"I presumed it was because he was the only one on the corruption committee that was clean," Herald said. "Maybe the Russians gave it to him because they see what you see— that someday he'll make a good prime minister or president."

"He doesn't need the push," Mikou said. "He's on track to do that already."

For several moments, the two men remained at the window looking out onto the tarmac. Herald turned. His back to the window, he casually scanned the travelers. "So, it's here?"

"It arrived from St. Petersburg a few hours ago," Mikou said. "I'd like you to take a look. I want your opinion on something."

Herald handed the black case to Mikou and grabbed the handles of the wheelchair. "Which way?"

Mikou set the case on his lap. He then directed them to a quiet corner of the airport.

They passed down a side hallway and through branching corridors to where an armed guard stood in front of a door. The guard passed a handheld metal detector over Herald and then opened the door.

Herald wheeled Mikou through the doorway. A black casket with silver handles sat in the middle of a small, windowless room. Another armed guard stood next to the casket. After a nod from Mikou, the guard unlocked the casket and lifted the lid.

"We'll be fine," Mikou said to the guard, who nodded and left the room.

Herald stepped forward. "Remarkable," he said, peering through his bifocals.

A skeleton lay inside, embedded deep within a pillowy down. The bones, thin and yellowing, were placed in correct anatomical position. A few bones were missing, including the portion of pelvis they'd given to James this summer. Many of the larger bones were pockmarked with holes of uniform circumference and depth. Herald leaned closer. "It seems the Russians were collecting bone marrow," he said.

"That's what I wanted to show you," Mikou said. "Why would they have taken so many samples?"

"I'm not sure," Herald said. "The edges of the biopsy sites are worn. It appears they were taken a while ago."

"How should we explain it?" Mikou asked.

"I'm afraid you can't," Herald said. "They're obviously man-made."

"What would you suggest?"

Herald thought for a moment and then pointed. "Remove the remainder of the pelvis and both femurs. There are too many holes. Say they weren't with the remains or had turned to dust."

"What do we do with the bones that still have holes?" Mikou asked.

"Drill out larger holes," Herald said. "You can say the

institute took bone marrow samples for analysis. Abbey could do it. I'll talk to her."

Mikou nodded.

Herald reached into his breast pocket and pulled out a package containing a pair of sterile gloves. He opened the package and slipped his hands into the gloves.

Mikou opened the black case. Herald gently removed the fibula from the case and placed it into its proper place in the casket.

"Who will announce the find?" Herald asked, slipping off the gloves.

"The minister of the institute," Mikou said. "But the unearthing of the eleven tombs complicates things. The minister believes it will add authenticity to his announcement if he reports the discoveries together: Genghis Khan's remains and the eleven tombs. He's delaying the announcement until a team flies back to the mountain."

"When will that happen?" Herald asked.

"They're assembling a team now," Mikou said. "They should have men back on the mountain in three days."

49

"*Sain bainuu,*" Andrews said. It was nightfall as he stood in the parking lot outside Baabar's apartment.

"*Sain ta sain bainaa,*" Baabar said as he stepped from his jeep.

After leaving the airport with the SUV, Andrews called Baabar, who'd been on his way home from work. Baabar, through connections at the Mongolian Institute, had already heard about the discovery.

The two men embraced.

"You look good for someone who spent last night underground," Baabar said. He pointed across the street to a park. "Are you up for a walk? My apartment's a mess."

"Sure," Andrews replied.

"Tell me everything," Baabar said as they jogged across the street to a sidewalk. "Where were the tombs?"

"The entrance to the cave was on the western face of the summit's southern tip," Andrews said. "But caves and tunnels extended all the way to the southeastern face." He shook his head. "I don't even want to think about how many times we walked over that area."

They began walking, their way lit by streetlamps.

"And the tombs were untouched?" Baabar asked.

"Yes."

"And the site was at a different location than where the Soviets found Genghis Khan's remains?"

"They found his remains at de Rachewiltz's site on the second plateau," Andrews said. "Or at least that's what the Russian's representative told me."

"*Representative?*"

275

"The woman who was on the mountain this summer," Andrews said. "The blonde in the photo."

Baabar nodded. "Then, who's in the tombs?"

Andrews proceeded to explain his theory about the tombs being the final resting places for the Chinese khans. As he and Baabar talked, they circled the park. They finally came to a stop back outside Baabar's apartment building.

Baabar laughed. "At the institute, they had to find a larger scale to weigh all the coins," he said. "When the Chinese hear about this, they'll claim the treasure belongs to them. All I can say is thank you, James. Thank you!" He patted Andrews on the shoulder. "Which reminds me, the institute is assembling an official excavation team that will return to the mountain in a few days. They want you to lead it."

"I can't," Andrews said.

"What? James, this is *your* find. It's big. Unlimited press! Research funding! Book deals! You should get the credit."

"Will this team be announcing that they found Genghis Khan's grave?" Andrews asked.

"You know they have to," Baabar said. "The tombs are an incredible find, but we can't ignore the fact that we have his remains."

"I can't, Baabar. I told Abbey I'm not going to lie about this."

"I heard about the scholarships for Sara and the foundation. They're admirable, James, but none of it's for you. You deserve something."

A hooded figure appeared from behind the back corner of the apartment building.

"I didn't find Genghis Khan's grave," Andrews said. "I'm not going to take credit for it."

"But you found the other tombs, the treasure!"

Andrews watched over Baabar's shoulder as the hooded figure opened the side entrance to the apartment building and disappeared inside.

"Listen, James," Baabar continued. "Don't make a decision now. You have a couple of days to think about it. You—"

Andrews suddenly began running. He ran past Baabar and threw the side entrance door open.

The hooded figure stood outside Baabar's apartment, holding a bag. Andrews sprinted down the hallway.

The figure, spotting him, unlocked the door and slipped inside.

Andrews lowered his shoulder and banged through the door just before it closed. The door flashed open, knocking the figure to the floor. The hood slid back—revealing a woman with short jet-black hair.

"Elena?"

She looked up at him, her eyes glaring.

Baabar rushed through the door. Bending over Elena, he took her hand and helped her up. "Are you okay?"

"I'm fine," she said. "Thank you."

"Jesus!" Andrews said. "Do you know who she is?"

Baabar closed the door behind him. "Yes," he said quietly. "Elena has been honest with me. I know she's with the Russians, but she has Mongolia's best interests at heart. I know she's trying to help me."

Andrews picked up one of the spilled items from the bag—a black silk negligee. *"Help you?"* he said. "Do what?"

Elena snatched the negligee away.

"You don't understand," Baabar said.

"Yes!" Andrews said. "I finally do! Everyone's together on this: the Republican Democracy Party, the Russians, even the CIA. Everyone except me!"

50

Our findings nevertheless demonstrate a novel form of selection in human populations on the basis of social prestige. It is fortunate that events of this magnitude have been rare.

—Tatiana Zerjal and colleagues, 2003

Abbey was in her lab, engrossed in her work, when Andrews walked to her side.

"How was Baabar?" she asked, glancing up from the bench.

"Insane, absolutely insane!"

"What happened?"

He told her about his visit.

"Associating with a Russian agent could end his political career," Abbey said.

"That possibility doesn't seem to bother him."

"I don't know," Abbey said. "Baabar is pretty levelheaded. Even under the circumstances, I'm sure he understands the risk he's taking."

"Come on, Abbey. You're with the CIA. You must see this isn't good."

She shrugged. "It sounds to me like he might be in love."

"More likely lust," Andrews grumbled.

"Either way, there's likely nothing you or I or anyone else can do about it."

Andrews folded his arms. "You're probably right." He looked at his watch. "Are you hungry? Let's get out of here. I'm buying."

"I was *hoping* to make you a nice, home-cooked meal."

"Home-cooked? I would love that."

"Good," she said. "Let me wrap this up, then we can go." While Abbey finished her work, Andrews strolled through the lab. He stopped at a framed poem on the wall. "You kept this!"

Andrews had sent her a poem, *The Squire's Tale.* Written by Chaucer, it was a fictional story about Genghis Khan and one of his daughters. The daughter had magical powers over animals and knew the use of every plant. The tale, which was unfinished, ended with the line, "And where I left I will begin again."

"Of course," Abbey said. "I thought it was perfect. I couldn't think of better motivation for my research than to begin where Chaucer left off, to finish the real-life story of Genghis Khan's daughter."

"How *is* your research?"

She pointed toward a stack of papers on a nearby bench. "Take a look."

Andrews picked up a set of stapled papers.

X CHROMOSOME KHAN MARKERS was typed at the top of the first page. Listed beneath it were twelve markers.

"You found them?" he asked.

"We think so," Abbey said.

He turned the page.

Time to Most Recent Common Ancestor Calculations Using BATWING program

807 years ± 27 years

"Eight hundred and seven years," Andrews said. "This matches perfectly with the period when Genghis Khan's daughters would have started having children. Abbey, this is amazing."

"But also depressing," she said.

"Why?"

"Look at the frequency of the markers in the various locations," she said.

He turned the page.

Frequency of X chromosome Khan Markers

Choibalsan	27%
Mongolia	4%
Inner Mongolia	1%
Western China	1%
Northern Mongolia	<1%
Xinxiang	<1%
Southern China	<1%
Hazaras	0%
Pakistan	0%
Kazakhstan	0%
Uzbekistan	0%
Europe	0%
US	0%

Andrews nodded as he read. The frequency was low in most locations where the daughters might have lived. Genghis Khan's daughters were known to have been ruling queens of the Karluk, Onggud, Uighur, and Oirat kingdoms—respectively located in today's Xinxiang, northern Mongolia, Inner Mongolia, and Kazakhstan. In the table, at each location, the frequency of the X chromosome Khan markers was 1 percent or less.

"The daughters must not have had a lot of children, or they and their offspring were killed in the power struggles after Genghis Khan's death," Andrews said.

"Either way, the daughters didn't benefit from the same selective advantage Genghis Khan's male offspring enjoyed," Abbey said.

"Except in Choibalsan," he said. "At least one of the daughters must have flourished. Twenty-seven percent have the markers."

"I did a little research into Choibalsan," Abbey said. "It isn't so large now, but it was once a bustling trade center located on a major caravan route through Central Asia. What makes the Choibalsan population even more interesting is that only 2 percent of their men possess the Y chromosome Khan markers—the lowest in all Mongolia."

"One of Genghis Khan's daughters flourished, but not a son," Andrews said.

Abbey nodded. "The problem is, since this daughter wasn't a queen of the Silk Road and likely never left the steppe, we'll never know anything about her."

"Probably true," Andrews said. He held up the stapled papers. "But still, this is impressive, Abbey. To be honest, I thought the X chromosome Khan markers might still exist in today's population, but I didn't think their frequency would be high enough to detect. You found them, however. Congratulations."

"Thank you," she said. "But after what I tell you next, you'll doubt that I did."

"What do you mean?"

"Our X chromosome Khan markers," she said. "They're different from those in the bone."

"*Really?*"

Abbey nodded. "Either I didn't find the Khan markers... or the bone doesn't belong to Genghis Khan."

1204 Central Asia

After the Kereyid were defeated, Jamuka sought refuge with the Naiman, the richest of the steppe clans. On the sixteenth day of the first month of summer, the Naiman army rode east to Mount Qangqarqan. That night, after the Naiman set up camp, their leader, Tayang Khan, summoned Jamuka to his side. Together, they scanned the valley.

"When we arrived on the mountain, the valley was empty," Tayang Khan said. "Now, there are more fires than stars in the sky."

Jamuka smiled. He'd sent an envoy to Temujin to warn him the Naiman were riding against them. The Borjigin had ridden out to meet the Naiman army. "Temujin's horses ride the wind, eating nothing but the dew," he said.

Tayang Khan continued looking over the valley. He nodded thoughtfully. "Our geldings are fat while theirs are lean," he said. "Let's move to higher ground. The pursuit will tire their geldings."

The Naiman moved to higher ground.

Afterward, Tayang Khan again walked with Jamuka. "Why do the Borjigin surround us and herd us like sheep up the mountain?" the khan asked.

"They slaver upon themselves with the anticipation of killing Naiman soldiers," Jamuka said.

"Before engaging these men, let's move to higher ground," Tayang Khan said.

The Naiman moved higher up the mountain.

The Borjigin followed. From the middle of the Borjigin army, a group of horsemen rode forward.

"Why do those men frolic like that?" Tayang Khan asked.

"Temujin has released his Four Hounds," Jamuka said. "On killing days, they feast on human flesh."

"Who is that following them?" Tayang Khan asked.

"Temujin's brother, Khasar. He has the strength of a three-year-old ox. His arrow can pierce twenty men."

"And the man behind him?" Tayang Khan asked. "The one that looks like a starved falcon."

"That is Temujin," Jamuka said. "His body is forged from iron and stitched with cast copper. He cannot be struck down by sword or arrow."

"Let us stand at a distance from these men," Tayang Khan said.

Late in the day, after Tayang Khan had led his men to the summit of Mount Qangqarqan, Jamuka left the Naiman.

* * *

Temujin sat on horseback, holding a torch above his head. He peered into the darkness.

Earlier, as they'd made camp and set their fires, he

ordered his men to leave a path open from the mountain's summit through the corridor along the Naqu-kun Cliffs. As expected, the Naiman were attempting a late-night escape.

Temujin turned toward Jamuka's envoy. "If Jamuka's allegiance is with us, why isn't he here?"

"Jamuka desires to rejoin you, but he's ashamed," the envoy said. "He cannot wipe the dirt from his face."

Temujin extended his torch. He lit Bo'orchu's torch to his right and then Khasar's to his left. Each passed the flame to the men next to them.

After a thousand torches were lit, forming a line of fire, a row of archers stepped forward and lit their arrows.

When Temujin signaled, wave after wave of arrows rose into the sky. The line of fire transformed into a canopy that blanketed the Naiman.

After the arrows were exhausted, Temujin turned to his men. "The Naiman are many and will lose many," he shouted. "We are few and will lose few."

The Borjigin army stormed ahead. Without resistance, they reached the edge of the cliff.

"Where are they?" Bo'orchu asked.

Temujin looked over the side of the precipice. He threw his torch into the oily black. The others did likewise.

The torches fell through the darkness and landed far below, illuminating the Naiman carnage.

51

ndrews and Abbey sat at the kitchen table in her condo north of Ulaanbaatar. They ate by candlelight, enjoying a dinner of lamb khuushuur with braised shiitake mushrooms. Music played softly in the background.

"This is absolutely delicious," Andrews said. He raised his glass of cabernet. "To the cook."

"Thank you," Abbey said.

They clinked glasses and drank.

"Before I forget," Abbey said. "The next time you talk to your brother, you should thank him."

"Ben knows what happened?"

She nodded. "Professor Herald called him when you were hurt in Paris. You were initially taken to the nearest ER, but Ben insisted you be transferred to Pitié-Salpêtrière."

Andrews sat back. "Ben had me transferred, from Manhattan?"

Abbey nodded. "He told Herald that Paris's leading head trauma unit was at Pitié-Salpêtrière. Within an hour, you were on your way. I thanked Ben on your behalf, but he said he owed you."

"Owed me?"

Abbey took a sip of her wine and smiled. "He said you gave him the most important physician's tool he has."

"And that is?"

"His bedside manner."

Andrews shrugged, laughing. "I have no idea what he's talking about."

"In high school, you both volunteered at a nursing home?"

He nodded. "My mom worked full-time as a nurse before she married my father. After we moved back to the United States, she did volunteer work at the home. One summer, she signed us up. Our jobs were to talk to the residents, wheel them around, and help with less pleasant tasks: changing their bedpans and giving them baths. It was terrible. And I was terrible at it. But Ben was a natural. That's when I first realized he'd make a great doctor."

"Your brother's story was a *little* different," Abbey said. "He told me you saw each of the residents as individuals with their own personalities and histories. While he could compartmentalize their humanity and go about changing their bedpans or diapers, he said you couldn't. He said you felt their humiliation, that you cared *too* much. Ben said he still reminds himself of that summer. He never wants to forget he's treating people, not just an illness."

Abbey set down her wine. "Ben said that's why you're such a good archaeologist. Even though the people you study lived a thousand years ago, somehow, you have the ability to see the world through their eyes."

"Ben said that?"

She nodded. "In Paris, I talked to him every day; Baabar too. Baabar was going to fly to Paris, but I told him not to, that you were sedated and wouldn't even know he was there."

"You know, you're making it hard for me to stay mad at anyone," Andrews said. "First, you. Then, Herald. Now, Baabar."

"Sorry," she said.

On the stereo, a new song started, "I'll Stand By You."

"The Pretenders," he said, smiling. "You love them."

"You remember?"

"*Remember?*" he said. "I still haven't recovered."

"Was it that bad?"

"Bad enough I promised myself I'd never make the first move with you again."

She took a sip of her wine. "And all these years, you haven't," she said. "Does this promise explain the hike to the Almsgiver's Wall?"

"It does."

During Andrews's second summer in Mongolia, he posted notification of the summer's final hike on the society's web page. As usual, the plan was to meet outside the Asian Historical Society's offices and drive to the site. Usually five to ten expatriate members participated in the hikes. That day, only Abbey showed up. They drove to Avarga and hiked to the Almsgiver's Wall—a stone wall built on a hill. At the hill's crest, Abbey spread out a blanket, and they had lunch beneath a tree. He couldn't keep his eyes off her. They talked and laughed, flirting unabashedly. Their mutual attraction was almost palpable, but he'd resisted the urge to make a fool of himself again, sticking to his promise.

"I thought I sent out every positive vibe I could," Abbey said. "But you didn't bite."

"Believe me, I wanted to," he said. "But I'd also thought you sent out a few positive vibes that first night at the club."

Abbey ran a finger along the side of her wine glass. "You know, Parker and I used to fight about you," she said. "He'd get *so* mad at me during the hikes. He thought I paid too much attention to you."

"I was the guide."

"That's what I told him," she said. "That day, when he found out we were alone at the Almsgiver's Wall, he thought you should have cancelled the hike. I told him you offered to, but I insisted we go."

"Which isn't true."

"He was furious," Abbey said. "By then, however, I had already decided to end it. Although it would have been 'strategically advantageous' for me to stick with him, as one CIA strategist put it, I couldn't do it. Long after I stopped caring for Parker, I realized I could no longer keep pretending to."

"If you were interested in me, after you two broke up, why did you always bring someone else along on the hikes?" Andrews asked. "There was always *someone* at your side."

"As I said in Paris, I was responsible for indoctrinating new CIA agents. After the breakup, that became my sole responsibility. Your hikes were a good excuse to show them around."

"They were all CIA?"

Abbey nodded. "When nothing happened between us at the Almsgiver's Wall, I thought nothing ever would. I started to believe your advances that first night at the club were an aberration. And we'd become such good friends. I didn't want to do anything to ruin that." She smiled, looking toward the stereo. "At the end of the song, do you remember when I looked up at you?"

He nodded.

"That line about being at the crossroad," she said. "It hit too close to home. I had just started working for the CIA and living a double life. I was so overwhelmed. But that night, you made me feel at ease. I imagined you were singing to me, telling me you would take care of me, not to hold it all inside."

They sat and listened to the rest of the song. As it ended, Andrews walked to his coat. From a pocket, he removed a white box topped with a red bow. He set the box on the table in front of her.

"What's this?" she asked.

"A memento from my subterranean travels."

"James, you weren't supposed to take anything."

"Don't worry," he said. "It's not made of silver or gold. Your colleagues at the institute would understand."

She peeled away the bow and paper and opened the box. Inside was a small round case made of hammered tin. She took it out and lifted the case's lid. "A compass?"

He nodded. "The needle is gone, but you can still see the etchings."

"So I won't get lost?" she asked.

"No," he said. "So we won't get lost."

Abbey looked down at the compass.

"Sorry," he said. "It's a little corny."

Abbey's hand went to her mouth. She looked up at him, her eyes filled with tears.

Andrews knelt in front of her. He took her face in his hands and softly kissed her.

She smiled, wiping her eyes. "That was almost like a first move."

"I've made a new promise," he said. "To live in the present."

"I like that promise better."

They continued kissing. When Abbey wrapped her arms around his neck, he lifted her from the chair and carried her into the bedroom. He set her gently on the bed. He leaned down to kiss her again, but she raised her hand, pressing a forefinger to his lips.

"James, I—I'm sorry," she said.

"For what?"

"There's one more thing you need to know."

"You're serious?"

She nodded.

Andrews fell back into a bedside chair. He bowed his head and set it in his hands, bracing for the news. "What is it?" he asked.

"Professor Herald," she began.

Andrews looked up. "He lied again?"

"No," she said. "Everything he said today was true, but he didn't tell you everything. He didn't tell you how he was recruited into the CIA. He didn't tell you who recruited him."

"What difference does it make?"

Abbey smiled. "A world of difference." Her eyes glistened. "It was a person he was close to, someone he respected and trusted."

"Who?"

"James, you've been through so much. I don't—"

"*Who is it?*"

Abbey looked silently back, a sympathetic look on her face. After several moments, she gave an accepting nod. "The person that recruited Professor Herald into the CIA . . . was your father."

1205 Central Asia

After Temujin subjugated the Naiman, Jamuka found refuge with the Qatagins. When Temujin subjugated the Qatagins,

Jamuka found refuge on the open steppe. When Temujin subjugated the remaining tribes and the steppe belonged to him, Jamuka was brought before him and made to kneel.

Temujin ordered his guards away. He then turned toward Jamuka. "Brother, stand," he said.

Jamuka remained kneeling, head bowed.

"Look at me," Temujin said. He held his arms out wide. "I live in the same ger I lived in as a child. Against the wall are sacks filled with roots of *chichigina* and *südün*, elm seeds, onions, and garlic. I ride the same mountain trails, hunt the same forests, and make the same sacrifices as when we were boys. Inside me, the same voice speaks." He stepped forward. "I have not changed. Neither has my bond with you."

Jamuka didn't respond.

Temujin continued. "My brother, on the Sa'ari steppe you warned me of the Naiman's approach. Your words struck down Tayang Khan and his army. Come, Jamuka. Let us be companions again. Let us remind ourselves of things we've forgotten."

Jamuka spoke, his eyes lowered, his voice gravelly and flat. "Don't concern yourself with things that have been forgotten, but with things that will be remembered."

"You set yourself apart and spoke mouthfuls against me, but never did you intend to hurt me," Temujin said. "When we fought at the river and were locked in fair combat, you could have killed me. Instead, you rode away and left me unmarked. *Why?*"

Jamuka looked up, his gaze distant. "As I rode away . . . the future stretched clearly in front of me," he said. "The people of the steppe were together. We were walking in the same direction. And you were leading us." He focused on Temujin. "You've united the People of the Felt Walls. Now that the world is ready for you, what use am I? If you favor me, put an end to me."

"You were the outsider who became a friend, a friend who became a brother," Temujin said. "Let us travel this path again."

Jamuka's face darkened. "Since birth you've been better

than me. From the time we shared the words not to be forgotten and ate the food that cannot be digested, I've been overwhelmed by you. I'm no longer worthy to look upon the face of my far-sighted brother."

"The Borjigin and Jadaran now live as one," Temujin said. "If our people can live together, we too can be companions again."

"You ask me to be your companion, but at night I would only haunt your dreams," Jamuka said. "Honor me by putting an end to me. Kill me without shedding my blood. Lay my bones in a high place where I can watch over you and the seed of your seed."

Temujin dropped to a knee. "My brother, I offer you life, but you insist on death. I ask to be your companion, but you say it can't be."

Jamuka clenched his fist, his eyes radiant. "The throne of the Khan is before you. Take it!" he said. "You've realized the dreams of our childhood. You've become more than khan of all khans. You've become master of earth and sky, a true *Chinggis* Khan!"

52

Andrews and Abbey sat at her kitchen table, eating breakfast. The night before, they'd stayed up late, talking.

Andrews had learned that after his father graduated from Georgetown's law school, he spent four years working for the CIA in Langley before starting his career as a law professor in Charlottesville, where he continued his work for the CIA. Recruiting academics like Herald with access to foreign countries, he built a large intelligence network with ties in every major country. His experience with the CIA coupled with his expertise in international law made him a natural candidate for ambassador. After twelve years as a diplomat, his father returned to Charlottesville and served as dean of the law school, never resuming his affiliation with the CIA.

Abbey looked across the table, her eyes warm, concerned. "Are you okay?" she asked.

Andrews stared down at his coffee. "I'm numb," he said. "I keep thinking I should feel something: anger or betrayal or—" He gave a helpless shrug. "I feel nothing. I can't blame my dad for not telling me. This all happened so long ago, before I was even born."

"When your father and Professor Herald started working for the CIA, we were in the middle of the Cold War," Abbey said. "What they did was heroic."

"Why didn't Professor Herald ever tell me about my dad?" Andrews asked. "Or about the society?"

"I believe he would have eventually. But they were linked. Herald couldn't tell you about your father's involvement with the CIA and not tell you about his own involvement or the society."

Andrews nodded.

"I really believe he was always acting in your best interests," Abbey said. She reached across the table and squeezed his hand. "I'm sorry to drop all of this on you, but I felt I had to. I didn't want there to be any more secrets between us."

The night before, they'd fallen asleep at each other's side, but they hadn't resumed their intimacy.

Abbey stood. Dressed for work, she carried her plate to the sink. "I don't want to go in," she said. "But the department is having their annual budget meeting. If things don't go my way, I may lose funding for my lab techs, even Munhtaya."

"Your position at the university is real?"

"Too real," she said. "A few years back, there were large-scale cutbacks at the CIA. I lost the funding for my research. I'm not sure if Parker was behind that, but he certainly didn't help. To stay, I had to get outside funding. That's when I started working for the institute."

He walked to her side, carrying his plate. "Go ahead," he said. "I'll clean up."

She wrapped her arms around him. "Breakfast, and now this," she said, smiling. "You're a pretty useful guy to have around."

"I try," he said. "After your dinner last night, it's the least I could do."

Abbey took his hand and led him to the door. In the doorway, they embraced and kissed. "I'm sorry for my part in all of this," she said. "If you can ever forgive me, if you think we have something, I'll be here waiting."

He pulled her closer. "Abbey, I . . . I—"

She set her open palm on his chest. "No promises, not now," she said. "Your world has turned upside down, James. Like you said, you're numb. You need time to figure it all out."

Abbey gave him a quick kiss and then walked away. Halfway down the hallway, she spun, her eyes filled with tears.

"Abbey!" he said.

"I'll be fine," she said. "Just come back. Soon!"

With a wave, she disappeared around the corner.

Despite the endless lies and half-truths, the sight of Abbey crying made his heart ache. He remained in the doorway, looking down the empty hallway. He wanted to run after her. He wanted to tell her he didn't hold her responsible for everything that had happened, that he loved her.

But something held him back. She was right. He needed time, time to think, time to figure out what came next.

He closed the door.

* * *

After cleaning the table, Andrews packed his bag and headed toward the door. He passed through the kitchen, where the television was still on.

On the screen was a crowded room. The camera moved to a podium and a doctor wearing a white coat and scrubs. "At 5:23 a.m. this morning, the Chinese vice premier was pronounced dead," the doctor said.

The video, recorded an hour earlier based on the time at the bottom of the screen, switched to a reporter standing outside a building identified as Ulaanbaatar's Yonsei Hospital. "The assassinations of the Chinese diplomats have shocked the country," the reporter said. Behind him, three hearse limousines passed through the hospital's gates. "The bodies of the three diplomats are being taken to the airport. They'll be flown to Beijing for burial."

The screen suddenly went blank, filling with static. Andrews turned through the channels. All the channels were static—a frequent occurrence in Mongolia.

He turned off the television. He picked up his bag and walked to the door, where he stopped and looked back over the apartment.

He wasn't sure if he still knew the entire truth about Abbey and her involvement with the CIA. He wasn't sure he ever would. But he was sure of one thing. He loved her.

He grabbed the doorknob. As he did, he noticed it was vibrating. He placed his hand against the wall. The wall, the floor . . . the entire building was shaking.

He walked across the room and pulled open the patio door. People stood in the streets, pointing to the south, panicked looks on their faces.

Andrews stepped out onto the ground floor patio. To the south, plumes of smoke rose above the city.

There was a sudden, deafening roar. The ground shook as a silver needle-nosed jet thundered overhead. The jet banked and rose into the sky—a red star on its wing.

The Chinese were attacking the city.

He jumped over the patio railing and ran to the SUV. He raced from the parking lot, heading downtown.

As he drove, he turned on his cell phone and checked his messages. Over the last seven minutes, there were four calls from Abbey.

"James!" she answered when he returned her call.

"Are you in your lab?"

"We're all down in the basement. Where are you?"

"I'm coming to get you."

"I'm safe," Abbey said. "Please, James. Just stay away from the downtown area."

In the opposite lane, a steady stream of cars was leaving the city.

His phone beeped. He checked the caller ID. "Baabar is calling. Can you hold on?"

"Sure."

"Baabar!" he said, answering the call.

"James, I was walking into Government House . . . when everything collapsed," Baabar said, his voice groggy.

"I'm heading downtown," Andrews said. "I'm not far away. Where exactly are you? Baabar? . . . *Baabar?*"

The call had ended. Andrews hit the call-waiting button. "Abbey?"

The line was dead. Seeing there was no reception, he flipped the phone onto the passenger seat.

When he looked up, two cars sped toward him, occupying both sides of the two-lane road.

53

The People of Mongolia are not important, the land is important.
Mongolia is larger than England, France, and Germany.

—Bohumír Šmeral, 1880-1941
Founder of Czech communist party

Andrews opened his eyes. Slowly regaining consciousness, his head ringing, he pushed back the air bag and opened the door. The front bumper of the SUV was curled around a lamppost. As his head cleared, he remembered the oncoming cars. He'd been on his way to Government House. Baabar was in trouble.

He began jogging, then running, dodging people and cars. After several blocks, he came to Chinggis Square.

In the center of the square, the equestrian statue of Sükhbaatar was gone, replaced by a rubble-filled crater. The State Opera and Ballet, along with the Palace of Culture, were on fire. Most of Government House had collapsed.

"James! *James!*"

He turned toward the voice. A dark-haired woman stood in front of Government House, waving. It was Elena. He ran to her.

"Baabar is in a hallway on the other side of this doorway," she said. "He called me before the cell phones went dead." She began picking up rubble that blocked the doorway and throwing it aside.

Andrews looked up at the front façade of Government House. Screams echoed from inside. A slab of concrete fell to the ground and shattered.

Andrews helped Elena. Together, they feverishly tossed chunks of the concrete and debris aside, ignoring the building's façade as it tottered above them. When there was enough space, they squeezed under the doorframe.

The hallway beyond was an undulating tunnel of bent girders and collapsed walls. From the decimated rear of the building, rays of daylight pierced the darkness.

"Baabar!" Andrews yelled.

To his surprise, there was a reply. "Here!"

Andrews and Elena wound their way down the hallway. They found Baabar on the ground, his legs buried under a collapsed wall.

Several feet beyond, a man lay on the floor, a large gash on his forehead. Andrews set a finger on the man's carotid. There was no pulse.

"Can you feel your legs?" Elena asked.

"Unfortunately, yes," Baabar said, gritting his teeth.

Andrews tore a metal bar from the exposed wall and wedged it between a piece of concrete at Baabar's feet and the fallen wall. He put all his weight on the end of the bar. The wall slowly rose. Elena pulled Baabar by the shoulders. He howled in pain as his legs slid from beneath the wall.

Baabar grimaced as he stood on his right leg, holding his left foot in the air. He wrapped his left arm around Andrews's shoulders. With a three-legged gait, they made their way back down the hallway.

The opening where they'd entered, however, was already blocked by more rubble.

"We'll have to dig our way out," Elena said.

The building creaked as the walls swayed back and forth. There was a metallic groan followed by a crash.

"We don't have enough time," Baabar said. He pointed toward a nearby stairwell. "There!" He hopped forward. Alternating his weight between his hands on the railings and his right leg, he levered his way down the stairs.

Andrews and Elena followed, small emergency lights illuminating their way. At the bottom of the stairwell, they came to a door. Baabar ran his badge through an electronic reader. When the lock clicked, he pulled. The door didn't move. He and Andrews pulled together. The door screeched open, scraping against the distorted frame. Beyond lay a long, narrow room. On the far side of the room was a door.

"It leads to a tunnel that connects with the hospital," Baabar said.

Baabar wrapped his arm around Andrews. They followed Elena into the room. On the wall to the left was an electronic console with several screens. A voice sounded from the console, speaking in Mongolian but with a thick Indian accent.

"*Bainuu? Bainuu? Khen be? Ta naash ir!*"

"Let me sit," Baabar said.

Andrews helped him into a chair.

"This is Government House's transmission center," Baabar said, scanning the console. "They had something like this at the *Gazete.*" He pushed a button. His image appeared on a dust-covered screen. He hit several more buttons. On other screens, different views of Chinggis Square appeared.

"My God!" Baabar said. "What happened?"

"The Chinese are bombing the city," Andrews said.

"*Khün guai! Tany ner khen be?*" the voice continued in choppy Mongolian.

Baabar hit another button. "This is Representative Baabar Onon," he said, speaking in English. "You're coming through loud and clear. To whom am I speaking?"

On a screen, the image of a middle-aged Indian man appeared. "My name is Adi Pilay," he said. "I work for Delhi Satellite Television, provider of Mongolia's satellite services. Per emergency protocol, I'm authorized to relay broadcasts from Government House."

"To where?" Baabar asked.

"Anywhere in the world," the Indian said. "Do you have any preferences?"

"The United States?" Baabar asked.

"The White House?"

Baabar shrugged. "Sure."

"Hold on," Adi said. He disappeared from the screen.

"Baabar!" Elena called from the open doorway. "This isn't safe. We need to go."

"She's right," Baabar said to Andrews. "Go ahead, both of you."

"Not without you," Andrews said.

Adi reappeared on the screen. "Look into the camera and say who are you."

Baabar turned toward a lens embedded within the console. "I'm Khural Representative Baabar Onon from Ulaanbaatar's northern district," he said.

Adi typed on a keyboard. On the screen, he was replaced by the image of an empty leather chair. Moments later, a familiar figure swept into view.

The American president, wearing an open-collared red shirt, looked into the camera. "Representative Onon," he said, "we understand your country is under attack."

"Yes, Mr. President," Baabar said. He flipped a switch.

The president's image was replaced by a series of real-time images of collapsed and burning buildings. "I'm currently in Government House," Baabar said. "These are live shots from Chinggis Square . . . the State Opera and Ballet . . . the Palace of Culture. And if you recall your visit two years ago, Mr. President, this is what remains of Sükhbaatar's statue."

"My God!" the president said. "It's gone."

The image on the screen changed again.

"What's that?" the president asked.

"Government House," Baabar replied.

"You're inside *that*?"

"A few stories beneath it," Baabar said. He hit a switch. The president reappeared.

Above them, the remaining supporting beams of Government House gave a prolonged groan. Plaster fell from the ceiling. "It's coming down!" Elena yelled. "We need to leave!"

"That sounds like good advice," the president said. "Do you have a way out of there?"

"An emergency tunnel," Baabar said.

"You'd better leave," the president said. "Before you do, however, can you tell me who attacked you? We have a pretty good idea, but we have no eyewitness accounts."

"I'm told it was the Chinese," Baabar said.

"You were told?"

Baabar glanced back toward Andrews, who stepped forward. "It was the Chinese, Mr. President."

"Who are you?"

"James Andrews. I'm an associate professor at the University of Virginia."

"Ambassador Andrews's son? The archaeologist?"

"Yes."

"You're sure it was the Chinese?" the president asked.

"I saw one of their fighters," Andrews said. "It looked like an F-15, but it had Chinese markings with a red star on the wing."

"A J-10," someone off-camera said to the president.

There was a loud cracking sound. More plaster fell.

"You'd better go," the president said. "Thank you." His face faded from the screen.

Andrews stepped to Baabar's side. Baabar held up a hand. "Hold on," he said. He hit a button on the console. "Adi, are you there? *Adi?*"

"Come on!" Elena pleaded. "Hurry!"

The Indian reappeared.

"Can we do one more broadcast to all the Mongolian outlets?" Baabar asked. "As if it were a normal telecast?"

"Sure," Adi said. He typed on the keyboard and then began flipping switches on his own console.

There was a deep rumbling. Another shower of dust fell from the ceiling. Baabar looked up at Andrews. "Go, take Elena."

Andrews stepped back and pointed at the camera. "Do this. *Quickly!* Then we'll get out of here."

"Are you ready?" Adi asked.

Baabar turned toward the camera. "Yes."

Adi raised three fingers. "You're on in three . . . two . . . and one." He pointed.

"One hour ago, Chinese planes swept from the sky and

bombed our beloved capital city," Baabar began, speaking in Mongolian, his voice calm. "Government House, from where I'm now broadcasting, has been hit. Chinggis Square is in flames. Our country is at war."

He sat forward. "As China looks to the north, they see our natural resources, our untouched lands, and our open steppe. They wish to fill them with their cities, industry, and pollution. I just spoke with the American president. The world is rushing to our aid. In the meantime, we must defend ourselves. We must make it clear Mongolia will not be the next pearl on China's necklace."

Baabar looked intently into the camera lens. "Fellow Mongolians, we *will* persevere. We must find our courage in each other, in the depths of our character, the beauty of our steppe, and the eyes of our children." He paused. "Sükhbaatar's statue no longer stands. Let's hope his words do: 'If we, the whole people, unite in our common effort and common will, there will be nothing in the world we cannot achieve.'"

Another rumbling passed through Government House. The building gave a deep, metallic groan. The lights in the room flickered. Adi's image, along with the images on the console screens, went black.

Baabar stood. He wrapped an arm around Andrews. Together, they hobbled across the room and through the door. Elena pointed to a wheelchair. "Get on!" As Baabar flung himself into the chair, Andrews pushed. He followed Elena down a narrow, sloping tunnel.

Above and behind them, the building's death knells continued. There was another groan followed by the high-pitched screech of shearing metal and a series of loud, thundering explosions. Tiles from the ceiling fell, buffeting them as dust jetted through the tunnel. The lights in the tunnel went out. They continued blindly forward, their progress slowed as the sides of the wheelchair inadvertently scraped and bumped against the tiled wall. Finally, in the distance, a misty square of light appeared.

They emerged into a corridor, continuing until the air cleared.

A hospital orderly appeared. "Are there more coming?" he asked.

Wiping their eyes, coughing and choking, they looked back toward the tunnel. A hazy cloud of dust—the aerosolized remains of Government House—obscured the darkened opening.

Andrews, bent over, shook his head. "No," he said, catching his breath. "That's it."

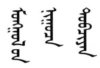

1205 Central Asia

Temujin made his way on horseback up the mountain. A second horse followed behind, tethered to his saddle. When Temujin reached the summit, he hopped to the ground and lifted his bow. He let an arrow fly and watched it arc through the sky. He then began walking, leading both horses.

He stopped on the sunny side of a small hill. From where he stood, he could see the origin of the three rivers and the site on the banks of the Onon where he grew up. He could see the fields where he and Jamuka spent their youth—hunting, fishing, and riding—and the clearing where they first met.

He'd tried convincing Jamuka to choose life. If Jamuka didn't desire to be his companion, then he could live a peaceful life in the forests to the north or the mountains. But Jamuka had chosen death.

Temujin reached down and pulled the arrow from the ground. He removed a shovel from his pack and began digging.

When he finished, he walked to the second horse and untied a rug, which was fastened to the saddle. The rug was wrapped around Jamuka's spiritless body. He hefted the rug onto his shoulder and set it into the hole. Filling the hole with dirt and carefully replanting the sod, he carried the extra dirt far away and spread it where it couldn't be seen. He then walked the horses back and forth over the gravesite until the area was flat.

When Temujin finished his work, he sat in the grass and opened a flask of airag. He drank until the flask was half empty. As he lay down and looked skyward, he and Jamuka were boys once again sitting in the upper branches of the large tree in the clearing, dreaming of what could be.

"If you became ruler of Earth and Sky, what would you do then?" Temujin asked Jamuka.

"Send my armies in every direction," Jamuka replied.

"To do what?" Temujin asked.

"Rule the world."

"Ruling the steppe wouldn't be enough?"

"My younger brother wishes to be me, so someday he can be khan," Jamuka said. "My father is khan, but wishes to rule the steppe. Kabul ruled the steppe and was khan of all khans, but even that wasn't enough. He crossed the Gobi and rode against the southern kingdom."

"Do you think Kabul would say warring with the southern kingdom was worth it?" Temujin asked.

"Probably not," Jamuka replied. "But it's only human nature to want more."

Temujin looked toward the horizon. "Kabul watched as his wives and sons and daughters were slaughtered in front of him. If he could do it again, he would easily push aside his lust for power. Kabul would tell you if your family is free from persecution, if you do not live in fear and have enough, you should be content with that."

They sat in silence, staring skyward.

"After you sent your armies in every direction and ruled the world, what would you do then?" Temujin asked.

Jamuka grinned. "Whatever I want."

"If you strive to conquer the world, it has to be for something better," Temujin said. "What do you want that you don't already have? What would you do that other khans aren't doing? If your people are going to ride to the ends of the world, if they're going to fight and die for you, they have to believe it's for a good reason."

Jamuka shrugged. "When I become khan, I'll figure something out." He turned. "How about you, Temujin? If you ruled the world, what would you do?"

"I don't want to rule the world. Having more isn't always better."

"Yes," Jamuka said. "But having less never is . . ."

As memories of Jamuka and the clearing faded, Temujin fell asleep in the grass over the gravesite.

In the morning, he rose and faced the sun. He held his hands in prayer and knelt, bowing nine times. He then sprinkled mare's milk over the ground. He sat back in the grass and began eating a piece of dried meat.

After finishing half of the meat, he set the remainder in the grass with the half-finished flask of airag. He removed his father's ivory-handled knife from his waist scabbard. Holding the knife above his palm, he jabbed it into his skin. He let the blood drip from the cut onto the flask and meat.

He walked to Jamuka's horse and removed the saddle, bit, and reins. With his knife, he sliced off part of the horse's tail—now Jamuka's spirit banner.

The horse flinched but didn't run away.

Temujin slapped the horse on the backside. The horse became agitated but didn't move. With a yelp, he slapped the horse again.

This time, the horse reared up, kicked, and galloped away.

54

Mongolia must be Mongolian.

—Bimbaev Richen, twentieth century
Mongolian intellectual

Andrews stood at a hospital window, looking up into a whirling maze of exhaust trails. The sky was momentarily devoid of jets.

"James!"

He turned. Abbey ran down the hallway. He'd called her earlier after cell phone service had been restored. They hugged. "How's Baabar?" she asked.

Andrews looked to a nearby door. "He's just coming out from his anesthesia."

She brushed at dust on his hair and clothes. "And you're okay?"

"I'm fine," Andrews said. He shook his head. "Actually, while I've been standing out here, I can't stop thinking about what you said yesterday."

She smiled. "We covered a few topics."

"We did," he said. "It's what you said at the lab—about the bone not containing the X chromosome markers. If the Soviets didn't find Genghis Khan, I've been trying to figure out who they did find."

"You didn't just presume I didn't find the Khan markers?"

"No," he said. "Come here." He took her hand and led her into the adjacent, empty room. "When Elena came to the mountain with the second bone, the distal head of the fibula was missing and the shaft torsed. The bone had been broken, but Genghis Khan died peacefully. From the moment I saw the bone, that's bothered me."

"Is that why you were so intent to see what was in Rosenthal's tunnel?"

He nodded. "Partially."

"If the bone doesn't belong to Genghis Khan, who does it belong to?" she asked.

"Elena said when the Soviet's found the body, it was wrapped in a coarse cloth and wearing a sash. After Genghis Khan and Jamuka defeated the Merkit, they exchanged sashes. Genghis Khan was reportedly buried in this sash. Besides the sash, Elena didn't describe anything specific about the burial site." He shrugged. "I didn't expect there to be markers or treasure, or for there to be anything elaborate or grand about the burial site, but I always thought there would be something, something intensely personal about the site. I still believe that. Given everything we now know, I can think of only one other person who died within the range specified by the carbon dating studies, who could have had a broken bone, and who might have been buried on the mountain, wrapped in a coarse cloth and sash."

"Who?"

"Genghis Khan's childhood friend, Jamuka," Andrews answered. "When he died, he was wrapped in the sash Genghis Khan had given him."

"But Jamuka wasn't a member of the royal family," Abbey said. "He wouldn't have been buried on Burkhan Khaldun."

"When Genghis Khan took control of the steppe, he wanted to reunite with Jamuka, but Jamuka couldn't live with the shame of his betrayals," Andrews said. "In *The Secret History*, it says Jamuka asked to be put to death, specifically for his bones to be placed to rest in a high place. I believe Genghis Khan would have buried his friend as he wished— in a high place. Jamuka was also a member of a white-bone family. At the time of his death, he was considered steppe royalty. A mountain burial would not have been unreasonable."

"Why was the bone broken?" Abbey asked.

"When the Mongols executed someone of white-bone lineage, they'd wrap them in a rug to prevent the spilling of their blood, which was considered taboo," Andrews said. "The person was then stampeded by horses. The coarse cloth the body was wrapped in might have been one of these rugs. The horses could have caused the broken bone."

"Why couldn't the remains belong to one of Genghis Khan's sons or another male relative?" Abbey asked.

"The carbon dating study indicates a time of death between 1203 and 1233," Andrews said. "Jamuka died around the time Genghis Khan united the steppe in 1205. Genghis Khan's sons died after 1233. Same with his brothers, except his half-brother Begter, who died before 1203. Genghis Khan wasn't close to any of his more distant relatives. It's unlikely any of them would have been buried on Burkhan Khaldun."

Abbey nodded thoughtfully. "If the bone belongs to Jamuka, then he and Genghis Khan must be paternal cousins or true brothers," she said. "They have the same Y chromosomes."

"It's possible."

"Then how do you explain Baabar having the same X and Y chromosome markers as Jamuka?" she asked.

Andrews shrugged. "All of our previous hypotheses about Baabar's relationship to Genghis Khan simply transfer to Jamuka. He might be Jamuka's descendant, not Genghis Khan's."

There was a sudden noise from the hall. They turned.

Baabar sat in a wheelchair in the doorway. Elena stood behind him. She pushed him into the room.

"I'm cured," Baabar said, patting his cast leg. He was smiling. He apparently hadn't overheard them.

Abbey walked toward Baabar and hugged him. "You're lucky you escaped with only a broken ankle," she said. "I saw your telecast from Government House. You're lucky to be alive. You're all lucky to be alive." She looked toward Elena and extended a hand. "Hi, I'm Abbey Conrad."

Elena tentatively took her hand. "Hi."

An awkward moment of silence was broken as a white-coated doctor entered the room. "Representative Onon, you should hear this," he said, turning on the television. "They're broadcasting again."

As the screen came to life, a newscaster sat behind a desk. "The eyes of the world are upon us," he said. "This morning, the Chinese submitted a document to the United Nations stating the lands comprising present-day Mongolia were unfairly taken from them during the Soviet Revolution. They said they would take actions to restore the pre-Soviet era borders of 1910. Shortly after the document was submitted to the UN, Chinese planes crossed into Mongolian airspace and bombed Chinggis Square. Chinese troops also crossed the Mongolian border near Zamyn-Üüd."

The screen filled with grainy video of Chinese trucks and tanks swerving around smoking vehicles.

"China's declaration was immediately denounced by the international community," the newscaster said as the video played. "The Secretary General of the United Nations issued a statement proclaiming the full power of his organization would be directed toward maintaining Mongolia as an independent, sovereign nation. Meanwhile, the Russian president has said he considers any encroachment on Mongolian airspace or soil as a direct attack on the Russian border. He gave Chinese troops thirty minutes to reverse course; otherwise, he would consider the Chinese advance as an act of war on the Russian nation."

The newscaster reappeared. "Twenty-seven minutes ago, the Russian president's deadline passed," he said, somberly. "Despite encouraging shows of support from the United Nations, Russia, and a spirited display of opposition by Mongolian civilians, the Chinese troops continue their advance."

The hospital room had filled. More doctors, along with orderlies and nurses, had poured in to listen to the broadcast.

Someone handed a sheet of paper to the newscaster. The newscaster raised it. "President Mandir has just officially declared war against the People's Republic of China." He set down the paper. "We are now officially at war with China. The almost one hundred year peace between our two countries has ended."

He looked off camera and raised a hand to his earpiece. "We're receiving reports that a squadron of Russian bombers, reportedly with nuclear capability, has lifted off from a Kyzyl airbase. They are heading south from the Siberian base toward China. I repeat, Russian bombers are heading toward China."

A feeling of dread settled over the hospital room. Andrews wrapped an arm around Abbey. A nurse began crying.

"For much of the day, air battles have raged over the city," the newscaster continued. "Our Ulaanbaatar airbase was attacked. Several of our fighters, however, were able to engage the Chinese. The dogfighting has since drifted south. We have live footage from a film crew in Maanit."

On the television screen, blue sky appeared, interrupted by smoke and swirling vapor trails. The hand-held camera fixed on a plummeting fireball, following it until it disintegrated into shards. The camera then moved skyward before tracing the downward path of another tumbling object that crashed in a cloud of dust.

"I've been told the two planes shot from the sky were Mongolian," the newscaster said. There was a moment of silence as the video continued playing, showing the dust cloud rising into the sky.

"We now go south . . . to the city of Choyr."

Video appeared of people sprinting past burning cars. The camera moved to a reporter. "Minutes earlier, a stream of Chinese troop carriers entered Choyr, heading north from Bayant-Ukhaa toward Ulaanbaatar," he said. He pointed behind him. "Moments after driving through this civilian blockade, they turned around. Chinese ground troops are now heading south! I repeat, Chinese troops are heading south."

The newscaster appeared. He was sitting upright, his eyes wide. "We have just received word that officials from Beijing and Moscow have been in communication," he said.

He spoke slowly and deliberately, his voice cracking with excitement. "Beijing has agreed to pull back their forces. In response, Russian bombers have been ordered to return to their Siberian base."

There was a loud cheer from the room.

The newscaster sat back in his chair, grinning. He glanced off camera and nodded. "This has been confirmed with contacts in Moscow. I repeat, Chinese troops are withdrawing from Mongolian soil. Russian bombers are returning to their Siberian base."

The camera feed from Choyr reappeared. The camera was still directed toward the blockade, where a crowd had assembled.

The camera focused on a toothless, old man. The old man's weather-beaten face filled the screen. Tears streamed down his cheeks as he chanted rhythmically, thrusting a pitchfork into the air. When the reporter extended a microphone, the old man's words became discernible.

"One Mongolia! One Mongolia! One Mongolia!"

Baabar raised his fists and joined the old man from Choyr. Everyone in the room did likewise, their collective voices resonating up and down the hallways. "One Mongolia!"

55

*You may conquer an army with superior tactics and men, but
you can conquer a nation only by conquering the hearts of the people.*

—Genghis Khan

After news of the Chinese retreat spread, hundreds of
thousands of Mongolians streamed into the streets
of Ulaanbaatar. In Chinggis Square, in front of a
decimated Government House, President Mandir and Khural
members spoke to the crowd and a nationwide television
audience, exhorting the country to overcome the destruction
around them.

Baabar, with the aid of crutches, was the last to take the
microphone. As if he'd just risen from the rubble around
them, the crowd went delirious.

From the time the photo of Baabar fighting the fire
at Government House appeared on the front page of the
Ulaanbaatar Gazete, he'd been thrust into the public eye. His
one-man assault on corruption had dominated the recent
news, and the Khural's tape of his show of defiance against
the Chinese vice premier had replayed countless times on
Mongolian television. His telecast from Government House
earlier that day had rallied the country.

"Today, we have looked into the sky above our capital
city," Baabar began. "We have seen bombs falling and smoke
rising. We have seen jets come . . . and go."

The crowd cheered.

Baabar scanned the square. "Unfortunately, we have also
seen Government House crumble. We have seen our beautiful

State Opera and Ballet and our Palace of Culture burn." He shook his head, his gaze narrowing. "But why is it that today, today of all days, I feel our republic is stronger than ever? Why is it, I feel our people are more determined than ever?"

The crowd stirred. There were whistles and shouts.

"It's because Mongolia is not that building, or that building." Baabar pointed, his voice rising. "It's because Mongolia is standing before me. Mongolia is there and there." He paused and placed his hand over his heart. "It's because Mongolia is here. Our buildings may have fallen, but we have not. You . . . me . . . We are Mongolia!" He threw aside his crutches and raised his fists.

The crowd erupted.

* * *

Late that night, Baabar lay in bed in a room at the Ulaanbaatar Hotel. He looked up at the ceiling, his eyes wide, while Elena's head rested on his shoulder.

Following the speeches in Chinggis Square, a late-night Khural meeting had been called at the hotel—the new makeshift Government House. After the meeting, the hotel's rooms were parceled among the parliamentarians. Baabar was given a two-room suite.

"The Chinese plan backfired," Baabar said. "Instead of crushing Mongolian nationalism, the attack unlocked something dormant in the people. It's made us stronger. We believe in ourselves again."

"The people believe in you," Elena said. "You've given them hope."

"At best I've been a catalyst," he said.

"A catalyst?" Elena sat up. "If it weren't for you, Mongolia would belong to China. Moscow would have bombed Beijing. Right now, we'd be in the middle of World War III." She moved over him. "Are you serious? A *catalyst?*" She began kissing his chest and neck.

Baabar started laughing, holding her back. "We need to rest," he said. "I need to rest."

She stopped. "I suppose," she said. Looking down at

him, she ran a finger along his chest. "It's not every day you rally a nation, have a building fall on you, and break your ankle." A smile crept across her face. "It's just . . . I thought we should make love while we can."

He propped himself up onto an elbow. "*Why?*" he asked, suddenly serious. "Are you leaving?"

"Only if you want me to." She gave an indifferent shrug. "And, someday, you might not find me attractive."

He fell back to his pillow. "That'll never happen."

She remained over him, continuing to smile.

"What is it?" he asked.

She shook her head, pursing her lips.

"You're not telling me something," he said. "What is it?"

"It can wait," she said.

He playfully rolled her over onto her back. "Something's going on inside that beautiful head of yours," he said. "What is it? Hit me. If I can't take it now, in my current state of bliss, I'll never be able to."

"Okay," she said. "But remember, you asked for it." She paused. "While we were at the hospital, I took a test."

A concerned look crossed his face. "Are you okay?"

"I'd like to think so," she said. "In your hospital room, in the bathroom, there were test kits . . . *pregnancy* test kits."

The color drained from his face.

She looked into his eyes and nodded. "Yes."

"How?" he asked.

"How?"

"I mean, isn't it too early?"

"The tests can turn positive as soon as seven days after conception. This is our ninth night of being together. Our ninth straight night."

Baabar looked away, his gaze suddenly distant.

"I'm sorry," she said, sliding from bed. "This is bad news."

"No, not at all," he said.

She turned. "It's not?"

"Do you love me?" he asked.

"Yes, Baabar. You know I do."

"And I love you."

"What are you saying?" she asked.

"We should get married."

She laughed. "Now, isn't that a *little* early?"

"Not if we love each other."

She moved back against the headboard, pulling the bedsheets tightly around her. "What if it becomes known I'm with the SVR?" she asked.

"You're an academic, a PhD who works at the Hermitage," he said. "Our countries are allies now. Together, we fought off the Chinese. Marrying you would be a badge of honor."

"You're serious?"

"I am," he said. He climbed to his knees and wrapped the bedsheet around him. Assuming an air of formality, he took her hand. "Elena Lebedeva, will you marry me?"

She looked back, her eyes wide.

"Do I need to repeat that?" he asked.

"Baabar, are you sure about this?"

"More sure than anything in my entire life."

She continued staring at him. After several moments, she nodded. "Yes, I will marry you."

They hugged, holding each other tight. Losing their collective balance, they fell onto the bed, laughing. He moved over her. He bent down and kissed her.

"I thought you wanted to rest," she said, smiling.

He reached out and pushed back a strand of dark hair from her forehead. "It can wait."

There was a sudden, electronic beeping—Baabar's cell phone. For a few seconds, they tried to ignore it before Elena turned toward the bedside clock. "It's four thirty in the morning," she said. "Who could it be?"

He picked up the phone and looked at the caller ID. "It's an unidentified number."

"Let it go," she said.

"I'd better answer it," he said. He lifted the phone to his ear. "Hello."

"Stockholm."

The word hit Baabar like a sledgehammer.

"What is it?" Elena mouthed, seeing his reaction.

He shook his head.

"Can you get away?" the voice asked. It was Stasio. His voice was muffled, emotionless.

"If I have to," Baabar said. "But—"

"I'm waiting in a car outside the hotel lobby," Stasio interrupted. "Don't tell anyone I called, including Elena." The line went dead.

"Who was it?" Elena asked.

Baabar, his heart pounding, rolled from the bed. "They've called another Khural meeting," he said, trying to sound calm.

"Now?"

"They said it's urgent."

He began dressing, his cast foot raised.

Elena watched. "Do you need help?"

"I'm fine," he said.

She extended her foot and ran it along his thigh. The bedsheet fell away from her, exposing her naked torso. "Are you sure?" she asked, pouting her lips.

"I think I'll make it," he said. He slipped his shirt over his head and then looked down at her, taking her in. "I'm crazy for leaving you."

"You are," she said. "Stay in bed. Make love to me."

He took a resolute breath. "I need to do this." He leaned over her and kissed her. "I'll be back as soon as I can."

Baabar made his way on crutches from the room. He took the elevator down to the first floor. At the entrance, guards asked if he needed a ride, but he waved them off.

He spotted Stasio huddled behind the steering wheel of a two-door white car across the street. Stasio swung the car around to the curb. Baabar climbed in.

Stasio, unshaven, was wearing his black skullcap and gray overcoat along with a thick pair of gloves. He put the car into gear and pulled ahead. He appeared fatigued.

"Everyone thinks you're dead," Baabar said.

"Let's keep it that way," Stasio said.

"Elena would be ecstatic to know you're alive," Baabar said. "Why couldn't I tell her?"

"She knows I'm alive," Stasio said. "We met two mornings ago."

"You're lying."

Stasio didn't respond.

"How did you know she was with me?" Baabar asked.

Stasio turned toward him. "She told me."

They drove in silence for another minute before Stasio swung the car into an empty lot and parked. From their vantage point, they overlooked the dry bed of the Selbe River.

"Ulaanbaatar was founded in 1639 when your country-men were still nomads," Stasio said, staring ahead. "The city moved on an almost yearly basis before settling by this river in 1778. The city was known as the *Ikh Khüree*, or 'Great Camp,' until Mongolia became independent from China in 1911, when they changed the name to Urga. Then, when the Soviets took control in 1924, it was changed to Ulaanbaatar, which means—"

"Red Hero," Baabar interrupted. "You didn't bring me here to tell me what every Mongolian school child already knows."

Stasio held up a hand. "My question is why don't you change the name back to Urga or *Ikh Khüree*? Red Hero is so Soviet. Even Russia has done away with the city names of Stalingrad and Leningrad."

Baabar shook his head, irritated. "Why am I here?"

Stasio smiled. "You never were big on small talk," he said. "First of all, I wanted to apologize for calling you that night, for initiating our meeting protocol."

"Don't worry about it," Baabar said. "I'm sure the Chinese agents didn't give you much of a choice."

Stasio extended his gloved hands in front of him and stared into his open palms. "I'm returning to Russia," he said. "Before I go, however, I believe there are some things you deserve to know: the truth about why we're here and the truth about why we gave you the corruption information." He turned. "But mostly, you deserve to know the truth . . . about yourself."

56

*Its appearance was brief—some would say ephemeral.
But it changed everything.*

—**Joel Achenbach,** *Washington Post,* December 31, 1995

Elena woke, a smile on her face. After Baabar had left, she'd fallen back to sleep. She sprang from bed and pulled back the curtains, letting the morning sun spill into the room. The vapor trails and smoke filling the skies over Ulaanbaatar had dissipated. It was a new day for Mongolia, a new beginning for her.

She showered and dressed. As she walked from the bathroom, she found Baabar sitting in a bedside chair. "How was your meeting?" she asked.

Baabar, unmoving, glared back at her.

She sat on the edge of the bed. "Are you okay?"

"You knew who I was," he said. "From the beginning."

For the first time that morning, her smile disappeared. "What happened at your meeting?"

"There wasn't a meeting," he said. "The call this morning was from Stasio."

"*Stasio?* Why didn't you tell me?"

"Then, you knew he was alive?"

She nodded. "Yes, but not until a couple days ago. I went back to the apartment building. Stasio was there. He was alive. Petr had lied to me. That day, I dropped Stasio off at the airport. I didn't tell you about Stasio because I didn't think you'd ever see him again. He was supposed to fly back to St. Petersburg." Her gaze narrowed. "What did he tell you?"

Baabar laughed. "What did he tell me? He told me *everything.*"

"There are things I haven't told you, but I haven't lied to you," she said. "I've never lied to you."

"The truths you've neglected to tell me are far worse than any lies."

"The truth?" she said. "The truth is what's happened between us: the last nine nights . . . this morning." Her eyes filled with tears. "Baabar, I love you."

"Love me? By what definition?"

"*Any definition!*"

"You let yourself get pregnant, knowing this?" Baabar said. "And you were *excited* about it. It's sick!"

"It wasn't intentional, Baabar. But I am pregnant. It's something we have to deal with."

"You say you went back to the apartment. To do what?"

Elena didn't respond. She looked toward him, her eyes pleading. Tears began streaming down her cheeks.

"You killed them," he said, his jaw clenched. "The three Chinese delegation members. You started *all* of this."

"No, Baabar," she said. "If it hadn't been me, it would have been someone else. Stasio would have done it."

"*How?* I saw what they did to him. He didn't have any fingers."

"The Chinese were mounting troops along the border," she said. "The invasion would have happened anyway. They—"

Baabar waved a hand at her. Propping himself up on his crutches, he began walking from the room.

"Where are you going?" she asked.

"I can't listen to any more of your lies," he said. "I'm leaving. When I come back, I want for you to be gone."

* * *

Andrews and Abbey lay together. After Baabar was given the two-room suite at the Ulaanbaatar Hotel, he'd invited Andrews and Abbey to stay in the second bedroom.

"What are you thinking?" Abbey asked.

"That this, us being together after all these years, is right," he said.

"I agree," she said. "It's always seemed right. It just took a while."

They kissed.

"I can't promise the backdrop will always be as earth-shattering as last night," he said.

Late the previous night, after the Khural meeting at the hotel, Baabar gave a speech from the suite's balcony to a crowd outside. Afterward, Baabar led the crowd in an emotional rendition of the national anthem.

"You mean we won't always make love to the sound of a hundred thousand people chanting and singing outside our bedroom window?" Abbey asked.

"Maybe a few fireworks on the Fourth of July, but that's about it."

Abbey smiled, nuzzling closer. "I'm fine with that."

"Can you believe it?" he asked. "When Baabar spoke, did you see the people?"

"They were delirious."

"It seems like just yesterday Baabar was a college student, looking for a summer job," Andrews said. "Now, he's an icon."

From outside the bedroom door there was shouting. A door slammed. They jumped from bed and quickly dressed.

Andrews opened the bedroom door and stepped out into the suite's common room.

Elena sat on a couch. She glared beneath her black-dyed bangs toward the door leading into the hallway.

"What's going on?" Andrews asked. He moved to a chair across from the couch while Abbey remained standing in the bedroom doorway.

"Baabar found out," Elena said, blankly.

"Found out?" Andrews asked. "About what?"

Elena didn't respond. She continued staring toward the door.

"*Elena?*" Andrews said.

She turned toward him, her gaze suddenly lucid. "He

found out the truth," she said. "On the mountain, do you remember when I told you about Yuri Andropov?"

Andrews nodded.

"In 1982, Andropov succeeded Leonid Brezhnev as general secretary of the Communist Party," Elena said. "The following year, the polymerase chain reaction for amplifying DNA was developed. When Andropov learned of it, he ordered his scientists to extract and purify the DNA from Genghis Khan's bones."

"He wanted to *clone* Genghis Khan?" Andrews asked.

"Yes," Elena said. "Andropov died before his project was finished, but his protégé and hand-picked successor as general secretary, Mikhail Gorbachev, continued to fund the work. It took a year for the scientists to learn how to extract DNA from the bones, and another year to install the DNA into embryo cell lines. After countless attempts, the scientists obtained a dividing cell line of human embryos. In December of 1985, three successful in vivo fertilizations were performed. Nine months later, the boys were born."

Elena's gaze returned to the door. "The boys were given the best of everything. But it was the early nineties. When the Soviet Union collapsed and their funding disappeared, the scientists disbanded. Gorbachev didn't want the boys' existence to be known. He buried the paperwork and moved them to Mongolia, placing them with immigrant Russian families. The boys went on to lead relatively normal lives. One died in a car accident as a teenager. One works in the copper mines in Erdenet." She looked toward Andrews. "And Baabar's the third."

The hallway door opened. Baabar appeared on his crutches. "So, she's told you the news," he said, a manic look in his eyes. "I'm the result of a twisted, perverted—"

"It can't be," Abbey said, stepping into the middle of the room. She looked toward Baabar. "Do you remember giving me a blood sample for my study?"

Baabar nodded.

"Your Y chromosome markers match Genghis Khan's," Abbey said. "But not your X chromosome markers."

"X chromosome markers?" Elena said.

"Abbey found Genghis Khan's X chromosome markers," Andrews said. "Baabar doesn't have them. Neither does the bone. Andropov's men found someone else."

"You made a mistake," Elena said. "Repeat your testing."

"Elena," Andrews said. "Every detail of the burial site you described on the second plateau matches with the burial of Genghis Khan's *anda*, Jamuka."

"*Every* detail matches with what we know about Genghis Khan's burial site," Elena said. "Andropov's men wouldn't make that kind of mistake." She stood and grabbed Baabar's arm. "Look inside yourself. You have the same DNA as the greatest man who ever lived. It explains so many things: the intelligence, the ability to lead, the capacity to read men's souls."

Baabar tore his arm away.

"This doesn't have to change our plans," Elena said. "Mongolia needs a great leader. You can be that leader. I can help you!"

"Stop!" Baabar yelled, raising his hands. "Leave!"

With his crutches, Baabar walked toward the bedroom.

Elena remained in place. "No!" she said.

The sudden control in her voice made Baabar turn.

"We're going to be married," Elena said, her voice suddenly soft. She spread her hands over her abdomen. "We're going to have a baby. We have to raise it, together."

Andrews and Abbey, relegated to bystanders, watched, wide-eyed.

"No," Baabar said, shaking his head. "You planned this. You planned this all along."

"I didn't."

"Yes!" Baabar roared. "You did!" Letting his crutches fall to the floor, he hopped back toward the hallway door and opened it. "*Leave!*"

Elena stepped toward Baabar. She bowed her head. She set the side of it gently, almost apologetically, on his chest. They remained that way for several moments.

Baabar, his gaze softening, set a hand on her head. When

she looked at him and smiled, they stared contentedly into each other's eyes.

Elena, having apparently won Baabar over, moved closer. She went to wrap her arms around him, but Baabar stepped quickly aside and pushed her through the open door.

Elena stumbled into the hallway. Gaining her balance, she looked back just as Baabar slammed the door shut.

Baabar fell back against the closed door and slid to the floor. From the hallway, Elena screamed and pounded the door. With each kick, Baabar shuddered, absorbing her fury.

When there was silence, Baabar's mouth bent into a half smile. "Most parents tell their kids if they work hard, they can accomplish anything," he said. "My adoptive parents always talked about my destiny. *My destiny!*" He shook his head. "They spoke of it reverently, as if it was some sort of pre-ordained truth. Now, I know why."

Andrews walked to Baabar and held out a hand, helping him to his feet.

"You've made yourself into the person you want to be, regardless of whose genes you have," Andrews said.

"Nurture over nature," Abbey added. "Over time, millions of people have had Genghis Khan's genes. Yet, there's been only one Genghis Khan."

"But I don't have his genes," Baabar said. "From what you're saying, I have Jamuka's genes—the genes of a cruel, deceitful warlord."

"Don't do this to yourself," Abbey said.

"I'm like Jamuka," Baabar continued. "I am Jamuka! I've made bad decisions, terrible ones! I knew Elena was a Russian agent, but I couldn't stay away."

"Learn from your mistakes and move on," Andrews said. "You have to."

"You don't understand," Baabar said. "Because of me, because of my mistakes and the bad decisions I've made, reputations and families have been ruined."

"I hope you're not talking about your work on the corruption committee," Abbey said. "Your work has been heroic. Those representatives broke the law."

"Heroic?" Baabar said. He laughed. "I was simply passing on information from the Russians. And they only gave me the information because I was their sick little experiment."

"Yes, they might have used you," Andrews said. "Just like they used me. But what happened because of it isn't our fault."

"Someone was killed, someone innocent," Baabar said. "And it *was* my fault. If I was heroic, truly heroic, all of this would have been avoided: the deaths of the Chinese delegation members, the Chinese invasion, the—"

There was a loud knock at the door. Baabar spun. "Go away!" he yelled.

The knocking continued, however, followed by a male voice. "Representative Onon . . . Representative!"

Baabar looked through the peephole. He opened the door.

A man wearing a suit and tie stood in the hallway. "Representative Onon," the man said. "I'm the hotel manager. I hate to bother you, but—" He pointed into the room toward the balcony doors. "May I?"

Baabar stepped aside. The manager walked to the balcony and pulled back the curtain.

The street in front of the hotel was a spur from Chinggis Square. Beyond the street was a grassy park with a statue of Lenin—a holdover from the days of Soviet rule. Outside, the street, the park, even the base of the statue was carpeted with people.

As the manager pushed open the balcony doors, the crowd began cheering. "They asked me to give you this," the manager said, extending a microphone.

Baabar turned toward Andrews and Abbey.

"Whatever you're describing, I'll never believe you wanted to hurt anyone," Abbey said. "Whatever happened, I'm sure you simply did what you thought was right."

"Regardless of our genes, we're all human," Andrews said. "We make mistakes. We're ambitious, jealous, and petty. Everyone knows what we're capable of, the good and the bad, but it's our actions that define us." He looked toward the balcony. "And like it or not, my friend, you've trained yourself for this: your time in Charlottesville, your job at the *Gazete*, the last four years. Everything you've worked for has led toward this moment."

Baabar gave a reluctant smile. "Maybe it's the expectations of the people you respect, your friends, that drives you to do the right thing," he said.

"You've built those expectations," Abbey said.

Baabar looked toward Andrews, who nodded. "She's right, Baabar. Don't blame yourself for the past. Focus on your future, Mongolia's future."

Baabar hugged Andrews and then Abbey.

"We believe in you," Abbey said. She pointed to the balcony. "Your people believe in you."

The cheering continued.

Baabar turned. Taking a deep breath, he extended his hand toward the manager, who still held the microphone. "I think I'm ready for that."

57

Elena slumped to the hallway floor and stared at the food tray next to her. On it were scraps of scrambled egg, a crust of bread with jam, and a half-empty juice glass. Up and down the hallway, similar discarded trays stood sentinel outside other rooms.

This couldn't be happening. Andropov's experiment was proceeding better than he could have ever dreamed. The Mongolian people were prepared to follow Baabar. And he was capable, more than capable, of leading them. But he would do it without her.

"May I help you?"

Elena looked up. A man wearing a blue suit stood above her. "May I help you?" he repeated.

Ignoring him, she picked herself up and began walking down the hallway. Behind her, there was knocking. She turned expectantly. The man was at Baabar's door.

"Go away!"

Baabar's hatred knifed through the door. She doubled over, a wave of nausea sweeping through her.

"Representative Onon," the man said, knocking. "Representative!"

Elena heard Baabar's door open and then close. After a few moments, the nausea dissipating, she straightened and walked slowly to the lift.

She emerged from the lift onto the first floor, which was packed. She made her way through the crowded lobby to the entrance. Outside, there were people as far as she could see.

A sudden roar came from the crowd. People began

pointing and shouting. She followed their gaze to where Baabar stood on his second-floor balcony, smiling and waving.

Didn't he see it? If it weren't for her, he would be dead, three times over: killed by the Chinese agents in the apartment, shot by Petr and dumped in a back alley, or buried in the ruins of Government House. Genghis Khan prized loyalty above all else. He never would have pushed away someone like her, someone so devoted, the mother of his first child.

Baabar began to speak. It was then that it hit her. James was right. Andropov's men had made a mistake. They'd found Jamuka, not Temujin. She was carrying Jamuka's baby, not Temujin's.

Another wave of nausea swept through her. She collapsed to her knees and vomited.

An old woman materialized at her side, patting her on the back. The woman leaned down and gave her a sympathetic smile. "Morning sickness?"

Elena coughed and spat, eventually catching her breath as the cramp dissipated. She climbed to her feet and wiped her mouth. All the while, the old woman's hand remained on her lower back. "What's this?" the woman asked, her hand patting the gun holster.

Elena reflexively pushed the woman's hand away. "Nothing," she said. She looked up at Baabar on the balcony. "But thank you . . . I'll be fine."

* * *

"In 1991, just down the street, a hunger strike was held for independence and democracy," Baabar said, his voice booming from speakers outside the hotel. "These revolutionaries changed our nation. We must, once again, declare our independence from tyranny. We must remember the qualities that make us *uniquely* Mongolian: the strength to take the difficult path when the easy one pulls us forward, the wisdom to act in the interests of the group rather than the individual, and the same abilities that were once used to build the greatest empire the world has ever seen."

Andrews stood a few feet from Baabar, holding back the balcony curtain. Baabar turned toward him and smiled.

There's a light in his face and a fire in his eyes. Baabar was more Temujin than Jamuka. Andrews recalled a rainy day and a water-soaked valley. Once again, Baabar was in control. Instead of driving a jeep, however, he was guiding a nation.

"Our best days are ahead of us," Baabar said. "We must again become like Genghis Khan, the starved falcon, willing to fight to the death to defend our lands and way of life."

The crowd erupted. Baabar scanned his audience. When the cheering stopped, he continued. His smile, however, was gone.

"We must build our future from our present, not our past. No matter how much we'd like to, we cannot recreate Genghis Khan . . . or his times."

A hush fell over the crowd. The fervor in Baabar's voice had been replaced by grim certainty.

Andrews followed Baabar's gaze to the front entrance of the hotel. Elena stood among the crowd. She was glaring up at Baabar, her eyes filled with hatred.

"For all Genghis Khan's accomplishments, the one thing he never achieved was peace," Baabar said, his amplified voice now echoing over a silent crowd. "Today, Mongolia must live in harmony with our fellow nations. We must find our future through diplomacy, not war. We must pursue peace and prosperity and independence with the same tenacity Genghis Khan and his armies pursued victory. We will not reach our goals through more war, but through an unwavering commitment to avoid war, to a commitment to civility and negotiation."

The conclusion of the speech was met by more silence.

Baabar remained at the balcony's edge. He firmly grasped the railing, his gaze unflinching as he looked over the crowd.

Someone began clapping. The sound of each firm, validating clap resonated crisply through the morning air. Others joined in.

Andrews peered out from behind the curtain. He saw realization course through the people's eyes. Yes, their collective gaze seemed to say, here was someone with ability, someone with intelligence, discipline, and courage. Here was someone who appreciated their past, understood their present, and envisioned a better future. Here was someone to follow.

The building crescendo of cheering was broken by a single, high-pitched crack. Cheers were followed by silence and then screams.

The expanse in front of the hotel turned into a sudden sea of churning people. Heads turned, searching for the source of the noise.

Andrews spotted Elena in the middle of a clearing. She held a gun. The clearing around her quickly collapsed. Moments before she disappeared beneath a pile of men, she slipped the gun into her mouth. From deep within the pile, there was another crack, this time muffled, followed by another volley of screams.

Andrews turned toward Baabar. He stood motionless, his eyes wide.

"Are you okay?" Andrews asked.

Baabar tilted his head as if listening for something in the distance. He opened his mouth in reply. As he struggled for words, a defect—a small, barely perceptible tear—appeared on the right side of his neck. Blood pooled in the defect and began running down his neck. He gasped—a wet, gurgling intake of air.

"Baabar!" Andrews said.

Backpedaling, his chest heaving, Baabar's heel hit the balcony step. He tripped. Andrews caught him before he hit the ground.

"Get an ambulance!" Andrews yelled as he sat on the floor, cradling Baabar's head. The manager ran from the room.

Abbey brought a bathroom towel, which they pressed over the neck wound. The white towel quickly turned pink and then red. They didn't have time to wait.

Maintaining pressure on the wound, Andrews picked Baabar up, cradling him tight to his chest. He carried him into the hallway. Abbey ran ahead and held the elevator. They all moved inside.

In the sudden calm of the elevator, there was only the sound of Andrews's breathing. Baabar, his eyes glazed, stared up at Andrews.

"Hold on," Abbey said.

When the elevator door opened, they emerged into chaos. People were cramming into the hotel, trying to avoid the shooting outside. Women, seeing Baabar and the blood-soaked towel, began screaming.

The manager appeared, waving them forward. They followed him outside and through a gauntlet of onlookers. "Where's the ambulance?" Andrews yelled.

In reply, there was the distant chirp of a siren. They ran toward it, the crowd parting in front of them. When they reached the ambulance, the rear doors swung open. Two emergency technicians leaped out with a stretcher. When Baabar was situated on the stretcher, the technicians lifted him into the ambulance. Andrews and Abbey followed, slamming the doors behind them.

The ambulance began making its way slowly through the crowd, its siren blaring. Andrews and Abbey watched the technicians dress Baabar's neck wound. Despite the pandemonium around him, Baabar appeared calm. His skin was pale, however, his lips blue.

"Can't you go faster?" Abbey asked the driver.

"There are too many people," the driver said.

Baabar extended his hand toward Andrews. Andrews grasped it.

Baabar pulled him closer. "Bury me in the traditional manner," he whispered.

"They've stopped the bleeding," Andrews said. "You're going to be fine."

On the street, men ran ahead of the ambulance, shouting and pushing people aside. The crowd parted. As the road opened, the ambulance began to accelerate.

"We'll be at the hospital in less than a minute," Abbey said.

Andrews squeezed Baabar's hand. "Hang in there," he said.

Baabar choked and then swallowed. "Bury me as Genghis Khan buried Jamuka, in a high place, so I can watch over my people."

"You're not like Jamuka," Andrews said. "You want to live. You're going to survive."

"Bury me on the hill, my friend, where we first gazed on Burkhan Khaldun," Baabar said. "When you return, we can make the observances, together."

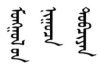

1210 Central Asia

When the kingdom south of the Gobi proclaimed a new emperor, an emissary was sent north from their capital city of Zhongdu.

"The Golden Emperor will confer upon you the title of *Ja'utquri*—keeper of the frontier," the emissary told Temujin. "In return, he asks for thirty of your maidens. And, in a public ceremony, you will kneel, face the Zhongdu palace, and pronounce your devotion to the emperor."

"And if I do not agree to this?" Temujin asked.

"Another will be appointed to take your place," the emissary said. He grinned. "For countless generations, the barbarian leaders of the steppe have struggled with this question. In the end, they either submitted or were destroyed."

Temujin turned his back on the emissary. He climbed onto his horse and rode away, ascending Burkhan Khaldun. He knew war with the southern kingdom would be difficult. They lived in walled cities on the other side of the Gobi and outnumbered the steppe people twenty to one. In the time since he'd united the steppe, however, his armies had grown restless. Accustomed to marching beneath colored banners, they had not easily transformed into shepherds and huntsmen.

When Temujin reached the summit, he looked skyward. "We've united the steppe, but only to bend a knee to the south? If we submit, it will diminish us. But if we war with the southern kingdom, there will be no end of it. Do we abandon the dream of a unified steppe? Or should we see this through to its end, even if to our deaths?"

Temujin spent three days and nights on Burkhan Khaldun. When he came down from the summit, he found Bo'orchu waiting on an overlook.

"The Eternal Blue Sky, Tengri, our ancestors. They were all silent," Temujin said, eyes downcast.

"Look inside yourself," Bo'orchu said. "Tengri will guide you. He always has."

"The burden is too much for one man," Temujin said. "The decision must lie with the people. Whether or not we war with the southern kingdom will affect their children and grandchildren, maybe countless generations."

"The people *have* decided," Bo'orchu said.

"What do you mean?"

Bo'orchu motioned him to the edge of the overlook. Before them, bowed heads stretched in every direction as chants of meditation and prayer hovered over the valley.

"I called a *khurlitai*," Bo'orchu said. "Not for peace or war, but in your name. The people came, from every clan and every family. They've agreed to follow you, whatever your decision."

The people of the steppe were all together . . . and you were leading us.

"Trust your instincts," Bo'orchu said. He nodded toward the valley. "They do."

The emissary approached on horseback. He stopped at Temujin and Bo'orchu's side and looked over the valley. "Our armies are like the ocean," he said. "Yours are but a handful of sand."

Temujin bent his knees and ran his hand through the grass. "On the steppe, grass stretches to every horizon," he said. "In our Gobi, sand stretches as far as the eye can see. Is it possible we are oceans of grass and sand, and you are but a handful of water?"

"Is that what you would like me to bring back to the Golden Emperor?" the emissary asked. "Questions, and not answers? You should consider yourself fortunate the Golden Emperor sent me and not his army."

Temujin stood and looked over the valley. In that moment, he sat with Jamuka in the front of the cart, the future stretching clearly in front of him. He saw past this moment, past the people in the valley, and past the emissary. He saw past the Golden Emperor and the southern kingdom, envisioning countless distant kingdoms.

"Tell your master, he will not have his tribute or maidens," Temujin said. "Tell him, he'll soon suffer the greatest of humiliations. He will wake to the sound of hoofbeats, be pulled from his throne, and made to bow at the feet of barbarian horsemen. In that moment, the moment before I take his head, he'll realize he's not a god, but a man. He'll wish he never ascended to his throne. He'll wish he never heard my name."

58

Chinggis Khan went against a certain castle, and there he was
shot with an arrow in the knee, so that he died of his wound.
A great pity it was, for he was a valiant man and a wise.

—Marco Polo, 1300

Mikou sat at his office desk, typing at his computer. When he finished, he sat back and stared at the screen. His gaze wasn't focused on the words in front of him. His thoughts had instead traveled to a different office, to a different place and time.

Wheeling himself down a narrow corridor in the basement offices of the *Ulaanbaatar Gazete,* he turned into a small windowless room. In the corner, a young man typed furiously at a computer. After watching for a couple of minutes, Mikou finally spoke. "If you continue at that rate, you're going to break your keyboard."

The young man spun. Mikou had seen his face in photos, but they didn't do him justice. The face was more handsome, the cheekbones higher, the chin more jutting. As the eyes widened in recognition, he saw the gaze was more intelligent.

"Mikou," Baabar said, standing. He walked around the desk and bowed. "To what do I owe this honor?"

Mikou lifted a stack of newspapers from his lap and set them on the desk. "I wanted to commend you on your descriptions of our nation's problems," he said. "They are both accurate and eloquent."

"Thank you," Baabar said. He returned to his chair and sat. *"But?"*

Mikou smiled. "But, I was wondering if you had plans to do anything about them?"

"That's why I wrote about them. And why I outlined methods to solve them."

"You did," Mikou said, nodding. "But each editorial neglected one important element—who will implement them?"

"Parliament can fix each problem with the right legislation," Baabar said.

"You expect someone in the Khural to be inspired by your editorial, to push aside their own agenda along with his party's agenda, and dedicate himself to implementing your plan?" Mikou asked.

Baabar grinned. "Since you put it that way, yes, I guess so."

Mikou quietly assessed the young man. "You believe your ideas are that good?"

"I do," Baabar said.

"Actually, so do I," Mikou said. "The problems you describe, however, have existed for years, even decades. Unless someone goes to work to fix them, I mean *really* goes to work, they won't go away."

"What are you saying?" Baabar asked.

"I would like for you to join the Republican Democracy Party," Mikou said.

Baabar sat back in his chair. "I'm honored you would ask," he said. "I certainly agree with your platform regarding most issues. As a political writer, however, it's probably best that I not affiliate myself with a party."

"I'm not asking you to continue writing about the country's problems," Mikou said. "I want you to fix them. I want you to be our nominee to represent Ulaanbaatar's northern district."

"I'm a writer, not a politician," Baabar said.

"I believe you're more than either."

Baabar steepled his fingers in front of him. "The northern district is the most populated in the country."

"And the most important," Mikou said.

"Malder has the machinery of the CPRP behind him."

Mikou nodded. "Defeating Malder is a daunting task," he said. "But this is a key battleground. If we can win the northern district, we can turn the tide against the CPRP. In four, maybe eight years, the RDP can become the majority party."

Mikou's reflections were broken by an electronic crackling. His assistant's voice sounded over the intercom. "Sir, it's Laagan. He's calling from the hospital."

"Take a message," Mikou said.

When the intercom light blinked off, Mikou turned a weary eye back to the computer. He read through the letter and made his last edits. As he typed his name at the bottom, the office door opened. His assistant appeared.

Mikou closed his eyes. He tried to retreat to an inner state. But there was nowhere to hide, not from this.

"He's gone," the assistant said, falling into a chair. "Baabar died ten minutes ago."

Mikou took a deep breath. He opened his eyes. Reaching out, he hit the computer's print icon.

"It's not fair," the assistant said. "He was so full of life, so gifted."

After the paper scrolled from the printer, Mikou signed his name to the bottom of the letter and slid it across the desk.

"Don't make this decision now," the assistant said, knowing the nature of the letter. "Wait a few weeks, a month."

"The people need hope," Mikou said. "Unfortunately, I can't give it to them."

"If you can't, who can?"

"Someone will rise," Mikou said. "Someone will have the energy and vision. For me, however, a light has gone out. I'll find it in the only place an old man can—in the past. And that will not do this country or this party any good."

The assistant shook his head. "Your retirement from public service should be a celebration."

"My coming or going is inconsequential," Mikou said. "In a few months, it will only be more so." He wheeled himself to the door.

"Where will you go?" the assistant asked.

Mikou stopped and took a last look around the office. "Believe it or not, I'll take my cue from Khorloogiin. I plan to return to a more simple life, the life of my youth."

59

I have lost Xanadu.

—Ukhantu Khan, the last Yüan emperor

On the day of Baabar's burial, six transport helicopters carried mourners and Baabar's body west from Ulaanbaatar to a hill near Burkhan Khaldun. The ceremony was broadcast on national television. President Mandir oversaw the service and announced that rebuilding had begun on Government House and the other buildings surrounding Chinggis Square. In addition to restoring the equestrian statue of Sükhbaatar, a new statue would be placed. The statue would be based on a photo taken of Baabar as he stood in front of a fallen Government House, his crutches tucked under his left arm, his right hand over his heart. Engraved on the base of the statue would be the words, "Mongolia is here."

"Baabar strove for greatness," Mandir concluded. "It's clear to me, he achieved it."

After eulogies by Baabar's Khural and *Gazete* colleagues, his casket was lowered into the ground. The mourners stood and knelt nine times. The dirt was returned to the hole and the turf rolled back over the site. The mourners then circled the area, stamping the grass into place. The extra dirt was carried far away and spread where it couldn't be seen. Afterward, the shaman sprinkled mare's milk over the site. While the shaman beat a drum, the mourners passed single file over the gravesite and said their final goodbyes.

Andrews and Abbey were the last in line. As they made their way to Baabar's gravesite, Andrews's gaze settled on a large tree in a clearing between the hill and mountain. He pictured two boys in the upper branches of the tree. The boys were watching him. He wished they would look away. They shouldn't be concerned with gravesites and death, but with playing knucklebones, climbing trees, hunting, fishing, and riding.

When it was their turn over the gravesite, Andrews crouched and ran his hand through the grass. "We were right here, leaning against the jeep," he said. "It was raining. We were soaking wet." He looked toward Burkhan Khaldun. "Because the mountain was so untouched, so pristine, I said it was a conduit to the past. Baabar said it was a conduit, but a conduit to something pure, something defying time. I had a respect for the mountain and its history, but Baabar felt something more, something spiritual. Every time we came back, he had that same reverence."

Andrews stood and lifted a skin of airag from his shoulder. He took a drink and then set the airag on the grass. He turned and looked back over the once rain-soaked valley.

"If you see grass, let me know."

"I thought you mapped this out."

"I never thought we'd make it this far."

Andrews smiled. "You made it, my friend. You made it this far . . . and further."

1211 Central Asia

Temujin led his steppe army across the Gobi against the southern kingdom. His army adapted quickly to city warfare, learning how to use siege machines, trebuchets, and catapults. They learned how to exploit a city's weaknesses, choke off its supply lines, and how to strike fear in the peasantry—causing them to flee behind a city's walls, consume its food stores, and clog its roads. After four years of war, Temujin and his army marched triumphantly into Zhongdu and overthrew the Golden Emperor.

It was fall when Temujin finally journeyed home, making a grateful return to the rhythms of steppe life. At dusk following a day of work, he entered his ger. Börte put aside her sewing and motioned for him to sit near the fire. When he sat, she began rubbing his shoulders.

"Where is Altani?" he asked.

"Foraging near the Onon."

"It's late," he said, starting up.

"Sit," Börte said, pulling him back down. "No one would dare harm *your* daughter. And Altani can take care of herself. Besides, she's with Sechin."

"Who?"

"Bo'orchu's youngest son."

"The small one?" Temujin asked.

"He's not so small anymore," Börte said. "They say he's considering becoming a monk."

Temujin relaxed. He closed his eyes as Börte worked her way down his neck.

"I should warn you," Börte said. "Altani wishes to speak with you."

Since his return, he and Altani hadn't spoken. "Isn't she worried I might have chosen a husband for her?"

"I think she just wants to know, one way or the other."

On cue, the felt flap swept back. Altani entered. She walked toward them and bowed deeply, her ponytail almost brushing the ground.

"The herd is as strong as ever," Temujin said. "And none of the grazing lands appear depleted. You've moved them well."

"Thank you," Altani said.

During Temujin and his sons' absence, Börte had run the affairs of the steppe while Altani had run the affairs of the ger.

Altani remained before them, her brow knit. "Father," she finally said. "In the time you've been gone, I've grown up."

"I can see that," Temujin said.

"I think I deserve to know if you've chosen a husband for me."

"I haven't," he said.

Altani ran a hand along her jawline. "Is it because of my scar?"

Temujin popped to his feet. He took his daughter's face in his hands. "If you had a hundred such scars, it would not hide your beauty." He smiled. "You have no idea how many clan leaders have asked if they or their sons could marry you."

"But still, you've said no to them," Altani said. "*Why?*"

"Are you anxious to be married?" Temujin asked. "Are you anxious to move away from your mother to a foreign land?"

"My sisters are all married," Altani said, pulling away. "They have all moved away. Why should I be different?"

"But why should you be the same?"

Börte had trained her daughters in the traditions of the women of her Khongirad tribe. Khongirad women, known for their beauty and intelligence, often married powerful men. After their husbands' deaths, they served as female khans, or khatun.

"What about the southern kingdom?" Börte interjected. "Khatun of the Jurched would be a fitting position. They must have an eligible son?"

"The people of the southern kingdom are like cattle," Temujin said. "They'll follow whoever holds the whip. Altani's talents would be wasted."

"And they're not wasted here?" Altani asked. "What will become of me, Father? You haven't raised me to lead an idle life beneath my mother's roof. You've raised me to be khatun. You've raised me to rule."

Temujin nodded. He began pacing. Altani and Hoelun watched. After several moments, he stopped. "I do see a possible role for you," he said. "When I'm away, I need someone to stay here, someone I can rely on to rule our most precious possession—our homeland."

"But when you're gone, Mother is khatun," Altani said.

Temujin turned toward Börte. "I haven't told you, but

Alaqai requested that you visit her," he said. "I suspect she needs your advice. In the spring, I'll go north to deal with the forest tribes. You could head south to the Onggud."

Börte smiled. "I would like that."

Temujin turned toward his daughter. "There," he said, holding out his hands. "We're now in need of a khatun."

"But what of a husband?" Altani asked.

"You'll be khatun!" Temujin said. "You don't need a husband!"

"Mother was married with two children by the time she was my age," Altani said. "Am I not to marry? Am I not to have children and give you grandchildren?"

Temujin folded his arms. "We'll have one of your sisters pick someone suitable," he said. "He'll have to be someone educated, someone who can read."

"If I'm to remain on the steppe, I should marry someone from the steppe," Altani said.

Temujin turned to Börte. Seeing his frustration, she stifled a laugh. "If you insist," he said. "Your mother and I will select someone for you."

"As khatun, with all its responsibilities, shouldn't I be entrusted with picking my own husband?" Altani asked. "I know all the steppe families and all their sons."

Altani was negotiating as if her life depended on it. As Temujin looked into his daughter's eyes, he realized it did.

"Yes," Temujin said. "If you remain on the steppe and learn to be khatun, it would be acceptable for you to marry someone from the steppe." He ran a hand over his face, exasperated. "And . . . for you to pick your own husband."

With a shriek of joy, Altani wrapped her arms around her father. She kissed him on the cheek and then danced toward the entrance, where she pulled back the felt door.

Temujin's jaw dropped as a young man stepped inside. It was a young Bo'orchu.

Altani ran back to her father. "Sechin would like to talk to you regarding a certain matter." She stepped closer and whispered. "By the way, he can read."

"I—I thought he wanted to be a monk," Temujin said.

Altani smiled brilliantly. "Only if he can't marry me."

Temujin, catching a knowing glance pass between mother and daughter, realized he'd been outmaneuvered. He shook his head and smiled to himself, wondering if Alaqai's request for Börte's visit had anything to do with this. It didn't matter. This was one battle he didn't mind losing. "How did you get to be so smart?" he asked.

Altani bowed her head. "I've been told by some I am my grandmother's granddaughter," she said. "I've been told by others, I am my mother's daughter." She looked up, meeting her father's gaze. "But most say I am my father's daughter."

Temujin's throat clenched. He kissed his daughter on the forehead and hugged her. He then turned toward Sechin.

The young man stepped forward, head bowed. "Sir," he said. "I would like to ask your permission, your most esteemed permission, to be joined in marriage with your daughter."

Temujin reached out and lifted the young man's chin. "When your father and I met, we were boys not much older than you. In the time since, we've shared sweat and tears. Now, we will share blood."

"Thank you," Sechin said. "I will not disappoint you or my father."

"Does he know you're here?"

"No."

"Then we'd better go talk to him," Temujin said. He wrapped an arm around Sechin's shoulders and walked him toward the ger's entrance. "Did he ever tell you how we met?"

Sechin glanced toward Altani and smiled. "No, he never did."

"When I first met your father, I was searching for eight stolen mares," Temujin said. He pushed back the felt flap at the ger's entrance. While Sechin stepped through the opening, Temujin looked back.

Altani was beaming. So was Börte.

Temujin returned their smiles and bowed deeply. He then followed Sechin outside. "Your father was milking a vast herd of horses, but he set aside his milking bag—"

60

She united with her ravishing beauty such a cultivated mind that she not only knows everything which it is customary to teach persons of her rank, but even the sciences which are only learned by men.

—Francois de la Croix, 1765,
description of one of Genghis Khan's daughters
in *Arabian Nights*

The minister of the Mongolian Institute of Geography stood at a podium, gazing intently over Ulaanbaatar Hotel's packed conference room. "For centuries, the people of Mongolia have been asked two questions," he said, his words almost drowned by the rapid-fire clicks of camera shutters. "Where are the ancient treasures of Eurasia? And where is the royal burial ground? These questions can finally be answered."

The minister scanned the room. "Genghis Khan and his descendants built the largest empire the world has ever known. In the centuries since, Chinese emperors, Russian czars, and Soviet dictators, along with countless treasure hunters, archaeologists, and scholars, have searched for the khans' treasure and tombs. Until now, their efforts have been unsuccessful."

He removed a handkerchief from his pocket and wiped his brow. "Two days ago, an institute-sponsored archaeology team was excavating Burkhan Khaldun's southeastern face. They found an underground necropolis. Among a maze of man-made tunnels and natural caves, eleven separate rooms were found. Each room contained a tomb. Each room was filled with treasure."

The reporters began shouting questions. Along the back wall of the conference room, Andrews turned toward Abbey. "Ready?"

She nodded.

They slipped through a rear door and climbed into a waiting taxi. It took them through downtown Ulaanbaatar.

Andrews and Abbey had spent the week since Baabar's funeral grieving together. With no emotions left to feel or tears left to shed, they stared silently ahead, holding each other's hand.

Abbey shook her head. "I keep asking myself, why would he do it? Why would Andropov want to clone Genghis Khan? What would he gain? I keep coming back to the same answer. He did it because he could. He did it because the temptation to play God was too much."

"I've heard it said that Andropov was a throwback to Lenin, an ideologue," Andrews said. "He must have wanted to raise the boys himself. He must have thought he could influence them. He just died too soon." He nodded. "But I think you're right. He did it because he could. His justifications for doing it, whatever he hoped to accomplish, were likely secondary."

The taxi headed north of the city to the airport, stopping outside the main terminal. While the car waited, they stepped together to the curb. Andrews dropped his duffel bag to the pavement and spread his arms out wide. Abbey moved into him. They held each other tight.

Cars began lining up behind the taxi. Someone honked. "I should go," Abbey said. She handed him a box.

He removed the lid. Inside was the compass he'd given her. "Abbey, no. I—"

"I know where I am, James. And I know where I want to be. I just hope your path leads back to me."

She gave him a kiss and slid back into the taxi. As the vehicle pulled away, Abbey looked through the rear window and waved.

Andrews raised a hand. He stood frozen, paralyzed by the sudden possibility of not seeing her again, wondering if she would ever leave Mongolia, wondering if he'd ever return.

Long after Abbey and the taxi had disappeared from view, Andrews picked up his bag and walked into the terminal.

1215 Central Asia

In the spring, Temujin and his men went north and warred with the rebelling forest tribes. Börte went south to the Onggud kingdom to visit Alaqai. Altani remained behind as khatun of the steppe. When Temujin and Börte returned to the steppe in late summer, Altani and Sechin were married.

In the winter, Temujin and his armies moved south, crossing the Gobi. With the spring, they marched south and then east, conquering the larger Sung and Tangut kingdoms. Caravans returned to the steppe from the conquered lands carrying mathematicians, translators, engineers, teachers, and weavers. As the steppe population grew and became more diverse, they needed more furniture, jewelry, spices, books, and silk. They needed more of everything. It was this hunger for more that fueled the Mongol juggernaut.

After four years in the east, Temujin and his armies turned west and wrought havoc on the Muslim world: a rich mosaic of Persian, Arabic, and Turkic civilizations. Over the next decade, as Temujin's armies marched across most of the known world, his vision of a united steppe transformed as he attempted to establish a global order with a universal language, universal currency, common law, and free trade.

While campaigning in the south, in the midst of his seventh decade, Temujin was injured after being thrown from his horse. His condition gradually worsened.

One morning, as Temujin lay feverish and rasping for breath, Bo'orchu came to his side. Bo'orchu lifted a flask of airag and held it up as Temujin drank.

"I once would have hopped right back onto my horse after a fall like that," Temujin said, fatigue crossing his face. "Now, I can't even breathe."

"You'll soon be riding again," Bo'orchu said.

Temujin smiled as Bo'orchu's worried gaze passed over him. "Those many years ago, when you dropped your leather milking bag to help me, I knew here was someone of substance, here was someone to make my friend."

"Can you believe it?" Bo'orchu asked. "We risked everything to chase eight stolen horses."

"You risked everything," Temujin said, laughing. "I had nothing."

Temujin took another drink from the flask. "Do you remember when we drank the muddy water?"

Bo'orchu nodded.

"That day remains with me more than all others," Temujin said. "Everything we have and everything we are grew from the brotherhood forged at Baljuna."

"And you've been true to your word," Bo'orchu said. "You've shared the bitter and the sweet, but mostly the sweet."

"When we unified the steppe, I thought it was the end of something," Temujin said. "Little did I realize it was just the beginning."

"The beginning of something good," Bo'orchu said. "Something we can be proud of."

"Is that true?" Temujin asked. "Did we do more than just conquer? Was our vision worth so much sacrifice, so many lives?"

Bo'orchu considered his reply. "Yes, it was," he said. "There were too many tribes, too many leaders and borders and gods, too many small-minded men. You moved us ahead, closer to something better, to a time when everything good is not destroyed by the next border war, to a time when we can work with each other, not against each other."

Temujin stared into his old friend's eyes. "I'm tired," he said.

"Your work is almost finished," Bo'orchu said. "The world is almost yours!"

"A kingdom, a city, not even a clan can belong to one man, certainly not the world," Temujin said.

Bo'orchu knelt and grasped his hand. The old men gazed into each other's eyes, a lifetime of memories passing between them.

"In war, there's no good in anything until it's finished," Temujin said, his breathing labored. "A life is no different."

"You tore down the walls separating our people," Bo'orchu said. "You breathed life into the steppe and pointed us in the same direction."

"Yes, but we've had our time," Temujin said. "It's time for our sons and daughters to have theirs." He summoned a rueful smile. "Bo'orchu, my friend, bury me at Baljuna where we made the covenant. Bury me at Baljuna under the tree you played in as a boy."

"You've been Tengri's loyal servant," Bo'orchu said. "Ask him for more time."

"Bury me near the river, so I can once again drink the muddy waters," Temujin said. "Bury me without ceremony or markers, so I can rest in peace."

Bo'orchu's eyes filled with tears.

Temujin looked up at him, his gaze pleading. "I'm tired," he said.

It was several moments before Bo'orchu gave a reluctant nod. "You deserve to rest, my friend."

Temujin, returning the nod, closed his eyes.

Bo'orchu remained at the bedside, still clutching Temujin's hand. "Because you shared the bitter and the sweet, I will bury you as you wish," he said.

Temujin's grip relaxed.

Bo'orchu, tears streaming down his face, leaned forward and whispered. "Because you kept our covenant, my descendants and I will remain loyal," he said. "We'll watch over you, my friend. We'll watch over you until the end of time."

61

Next to the River they swore an oath and split the tallies.
When you spread out the map, there appear their fiefs.

—**Yüan Chiehmm,** fourteenth century Japanese poet

The following summer, Andrews walked across the steppe's undulating sea of green, enveloped by the simmering heat and chirp of cicadas. Along these grasslands, set between the Siberian tundra to the north and Gobi to the south, Genghis Khan and his Mongols had ridden off to conquer the world. As Andrews's thoughts turned west, traveling over four hundred kilometers to Burkhan Khaldun, he recalled Baabar's words.

One day there can make you forget everything.

He wished it were that easy. In Charlottesville, a day hadn't passed that he didn't imagine Sara walking unannounced into his office, sitting at his window, and looking out toward the Rotunda. A day hadn't passed that he didn't picture her sitting next to the gene sequencer in the newly-constructed lab, hear her laughter emanating from a group of students, or imagine her reading a book on her bench in the Rotunda. In his first trip back to Mongolia since Baabar's death, he'd seen his old friend in the reflection of every Mongolian's eyes. Baabar was waiting at every bus stop, driving every taxi, and walking every trail. As much as Andrews tried to forget, he couldn't forget anything.

A week earlier, he'd visited Baabar's gravesite. After making the observances, he sat on the hill and recalled their times in Charlottesville, their discussions over newspapers and coffee, and their days exploring the steppe. He hadn't returned to Mongolia to remember, however. He'd spent the last nine months remembering. He returned because it was time to move on.

Abbey now walked at his side. As part of her work for the institute, she'd confirmed his theory that the remains in the eleven tombs belonged to the ten Chinese khans and Prince Ratnadhara. The remains each contained all fifteen Y chromosome Khan markers. Carbon dating analyses matched with the known times of death.

After Abbey identified the remains, she'd turned her attention back to her study looking for the X chromosome Khan markers. Attempting to learn more about her Choibalsan study group, she traveled to the city in eastern Mongolia and interviewed those possessing the X chromosome Khan markers. She discovered a common thread. At some point in their histories, all had ancestors from Bala, a small community north of Choibalsan.

Andrews and Abbey had spent the last week camping out and hiking the steppe, looking for Bala. They hadn't found it, but they didn't mind. After not seeing each other over the past nine months, they were happy to spend their time, however listlessly, together.

"All this time, you haven't said a word about your research," Abbey said. "Do you have any plans?"

"Right now, I'm content with just teaching," he said.

After Andrews returned to Charlottesville, his department chairman informed him he'd been promoted to full professor. The chairman told him that a certain emeritus professor had insisted on making a presentation to his tenure review committee. Andrews was subsequently named as the University of Virginia's inaugural Battuulga Dashdevinjiin Chair of Asian History. The three yearly research grants accompanying the chair were endowed by a donation from the Smithsonian Institute. Separate donations from the National Sciences Foundation funded scholarships in Baabar's and Sara's names.

"I'll eventually start doing research again," Andrews said. "I'm just not sure what it'll be."

"Will you continue looking for the grave?" Abbey asked.

Abbey had informed the hierarchy at the Mongolian Institute that the bones the Russians transported from the Hermitage did not possess the X chromosome Khan markers. The bones, which had largely been forgotten, now resided in a storage room at the institute. Andrews still believed they belonged to Jamuka.

"I may have to stand in line," Andrews said.

Recent events had sparked an incredible amount of interest in Mongolia. Every major newspaper and magazine had published stories about Burkhan Khaldun's underground necropolis and speculated on the location of Genghis Khan's still-unknown final resting place. Many major archaeology departments were now funding research into finding the grave. National Geographic Society had funded a satellite survey of the Mongolian landscape and identified thousands of "archaeological anomalies" possibly corresponding with the burial site. The Mongolian Institute had granted permits for five digs this summer on Burkhan Khaldun in addition to continuing their excavation of the royal burial ground. A Hollywood filmmaker had offered a ten-million-dollar reward for the discovery of Genghis Khan's tomb and first rights at filming a documentary of the story behind the find.

"I've come to terms with not finding the grave," Andrews said. "The problem, as Professor Herald and I have discussed, is that every other endeavor pales in comparison, which is the reason I started looking for it in the first place."

"I'm glad you two are talking again," Abbey said.

With time, Andrews had forgiven Herald. He'd come to believe Herald's reasons for not telling him about his father or the society, like Abbey's, were altruistic. It had also been much harder to hold a grudge against Herald knowing that it was his father who had recruited him into the CIA.

"We meet once a week for lunch," Andrews said. "It's been good."

Across the grassy plain, they spotted two people. As Andrews and Abbey approached the figures, they saw it was a woman and small girl. Both wore large rice paddy hats and were picking berries near a stream. Andrews and Abbey introduced themselves, speaking in Mongolian.

"I'm Tuya," the woman said. "This is my daughter, Nasan."

"Maybe you can help us," Abbey said. "We're looking for a village called Bala."

"We're from Bala," the girl said, beaming.

"We were just heading back," the mother said, pointing across the plain. "Would you like to join us?"

"We'd love to," Abbey said.

Andrews and Abbey walked with the mother and daughter, following the meandering stream. Andrews carried their collected berries in one of the baskets on his shoulder.

They eventually passed from the open steppe through a winding collection of hillocks.

"No wonder we couldn't find it," Andrews said to Abbey. "It's a maze."

"Where are you from?" Nasan asked.

"I'm from Ulaanbaatar," Abbey replied. "And James is from Virginia in the United States. We're here to do some tests. We hope to test people from your village."

"What kind of test?" the mother asked.

"A DNA test."

"Does it hurt?" the girl asked.

"It's just a swipe along your lip," Abbey said, showing her.

"Can you test me?" the girl asked.

"If it's okay with your mother."

Nasan looked expectantly toward Tuya, who smiled pleasantly and nodded.

The stream led them through the hillocks to a small lake. Beyond the lake were dozens of gers and a grassy plain. Spotty collections of sheep could be seen throughout the surrounding hills.

"This is beautiful," Abbey said.

"Thank you," Tuya said. "We'll have to go around the

lake. During the rainy season, the river swells and this lake forms. In the summer, it slowly retreats."

"And turns black," Nasan added.

Andrews pointed to a cluster of stone buildings on a hill across the lake. "It looks like a monastery," he said.

"It is," Tuya said. "Our village is named after it."

"Is it active?" he asked.

"Yes," Tuya replied. "Several monks live there."

After circling the lake, they stopped in front of an empty ger. Andrews lifted the basket of berries from his shoulder.

"Thank you," Tuya said, taking the basket.

"No problem."

"You can stay here," Tuya said. "Stay as long as you want. If you need anything, please ask."

* * *

Late that afternoon, Andrews and Abbey sat outside the ger, reading. Abbey leaned back and scanned the hills. "It's like a postcard," she said.

"We're in the middle of nowhere," Andrews said. "But right now, I wouldn't trade places with being anywhere else." He reached out and squeezed her hand. Since he'd left Mongolia, they'd kept in close touch, texting at least daily and skyping frequently. Still, he'd missed her. Until the last week, he hadn't realized how much.

"What are you reading?" she asked.

"Herald's translation of *The Secret History*," he replied. He handed her the open book and pointed.

"'The son of Bodonchar was Jajiradai,'" she read aloud. "'The son of Jajiradai was Tugudei. The son of Tugudei was Buribulchi.'" She smiled. "This sounds like something from Genesis."

"It is," Andrews said. "The Mongolian version. Keep reading."

"'The son of Buribulchi was Qara-qada. The son of Qara-qada was Jamuka.'" She looked up.

Andrews nodded. "It explains why Genghis Khan and

Jamuka had the same Y chromosomes. Bodonchar is the common male ancestor linking them. With a different wife, Bodonchar had another son, Qabachi, a sixth-generation ancestor of Genghis Khan."

Abbey closed the book. They sat back and took in their surroundings. In the monastery on the nearby hill, a door opened. Two monks emerged wearing yellow robes, one pushing another in a wheelchair. They stopped beneath a sprawling tree.

"Baabar and I visited many ancient monasteries, but not this one," Andrews said, picking up a map.

"It's not exactly along the beaten track," Abbey said.

Andrews looked at the map. "The river must be a branch from the Kherlen. It's the only major river in the area. And I'm not surprised the area floods. This is the lowest point above sea level in all Mongolia."

Nasan approached carrying a tray of food.

"*Sain ta sain bainuu,*" Abbey said.

"*Sain bainaa,*" Nasan replied. She set the tray on a table. "This is for you. This is a bowl of *tsuivan*. Here's some *buuz*. And—"

"*Banshan,*" Abbey said, pointing at a large bowl of creamy soup.

"Yes," Nasan said. She lifted a skin from her shoulder and handed it to Andrews. "And airag."

"Thank you," Andrews said. He handed money and a candy bar to Nasan.

The girl shook her head. "Mother says I shouldn't take anything."

"Tonight, just set the money on your altar," Andrews said. He winked. "And we don't have to tell her about the candy."

Accepting the offerings, Nasan tore the wrapper off the candy bar and took a bite.

"How old are you?" Abbey asked.

"Seven," the girl said, her mouth full.

"What are your favorite things to do?"

"Ride horses and explore the hills," Nasan said. "I also like to visit the monastery. The monks are our teachers."

"What do they teach you?"

"Math, science, reading," Nasan said. She sat and folded her legs. "Even meditation. *Watch!*" Closing her eyes, she took a deep breath. She then slowly exhaled.

"Excellent!" Abbey said. "Are you thinking deep thoughts?"

Nasan didn't reply, but remained in her meditative state. "Very deep," she finally breathed.

Andrews and Abbey laughed and clapped.

Nasan popped to her feet and looked toward the lake. "I also like to swim," she said. "Mother tells me to enjoy the lake now. In a month, it will dry up." She frowned, her voice filling with melancholy. "Then we'll have only the river—the little Pan-chu-ni. In the winter it freezes. We take our skates and—"

"*The what?*" Andrews interrupted.

Nasan looked blankly back.

"You called the river something," Andrews said, his heart pounding. "The little what?"

Nasan smiled sheepishly. "I'm sorry." She glanced toward her family's ger. "My parents have many names for the river, but they tell me not to speak of them."

"What else do they call it?" Andrews asked.

"James!" Abbey said.

Andrews held up his hands. "Abbey's right," he said. "Let's play a game, Nasan. I'll say a name, and you tell me if you've heard it before. That way you don't have to say the names, and you won't get into trouble. Okay?"

The girl blushed, but nodded.

"Pan-chu-ni?" Andrews said, avoiding Abbey's glare.

Nasan smiled. "I already said that name."

"Just testing," he said. "Black River?"

She shook her head.

"Hu-lun Nao-erh?" he asked.

"No."

"Banjur?"

"No."

"Lung-chü?"

Nasan paused, then nodded.

"*Lung-chü?*" he said. "You're sure?"

"Yes."

Andrews glanced toward Abbey, who was now staring wide-eyed at Nasan.

"Hei-ho?" he asked.

Nasan nodded again.

"And . . . Baljuna?"

Biting her lower lip, the girl glanced toward her ger and then at Abbey. "Go ahead," Abbey said. "Be honest, Nasan. You won't get into trouble."

The girl nodded.

"Baljuna?" Andrews said, trying to remain calm. "You're sure?"

"Yes."

Andrews smiled. "That's it, Nasan. Thank you." He held up his hands. "No more questions."

Nasan popped the remainder of the candy bar into her mouth. She then looked toward Abbey. "When will you give me the test?" she asked, pulling at the corner of her mouth.

"Tomorrow," Abbey said, setting her hand on the girl's shoulder. "We'll do it tomorrow."

Andrews held out an open hand. Nasan placed the crumpled candy wrapper in it. "Remember, tonight, set the money on the altar," he said.

"And tell your mother thank you for the food," Abbey said.

Nasan nodded. She tried winking at Andrews, but instead clamped both eyes shut. She then ran away.

Andrews stood and looked in disbelief toward the lake.

"James!" Abbey said, hugging him. "You found it! Baljuna! Your search is finally over."

"It is," Andrews said. "It's a river . . . and a lake."

* * *

Andrews walked up the hill to the monastery. The wheelchair-bound monk sat by himself in the shade of the tree.

"*Sain bai-na uu,*" Andrews said, bowing.

The elderly monk returned the greeting. The other monk, a young man, appeared from a side door. "*Karma Gendun Chöpel,*" he said.

The older monk waved him off. "*Karma Tsöndru Rabten.*" After a quick bow, the young monk disappeared back inside.

"The enlightened one who spreads the teachings," Andrews said, interpreting.

"My young brother does me undeserved honor," the monk said. "I'm but a humble servant of the monastery, trying to find my way."

"This is a nice place to search," Andrews said.

The monk smiled, nodding peacefully.

They spent the next several moments looking over the valley. Finally, the monk spoke. "He said you would come."

Andrews turned. "Excuse me?"

"He said you would come," the monk repeated.

"You know who I am?"

"Professor James Andrews from the University of Virginia."

"Who told you I would come?"

"Baabar Onon."

"You knew him?"

"Yes," the monk said. "He told me this four years ago."

"Baabar knew about this place?"

"No, I never told him," the monk said. "Baabar said you understood what you were up against. He told me you thought of your quest to find the grave as a personal battle— between you and Temujin. He believed you would win." The monk smiled. "When I first read your book, I agreed. You understood the significance of the covenant. But then you strayed from your convictions. You went to Burkhan Khaldun. You gave in to your impatience."

Andrews stared incredulously at the yellow-robed monk. "Who are you?"

"Someone who has given in to his own impatience. As a young monk, I was unable to find my nirvana. No longer capable of ignoring the sentients, I went into the world and elevated myself to a high place. I tried to control the paths of other men. I failed. I've since returned to the monastery of my youth. After all these years, I've finally found my nirvana."

The old monk looked down the hill toward the river and reeds, his eyes flashing with distant memories. "Now, I simply try to help the young monks find their nirvana." His gaze returned to Andrews. "I tell them not to ask questions, but to contemplate their answers. If they do, they'll find their own truths."

Andrews, feeling the monk's stare, contemplated his own question. *Who are you?* He looked back toward the monastery, the writings of Archimandrite Palladii, a Russian historian, coming to mind. In Palladii's work, he referenced the unpublished works of Hsü Sung, a Chinese historian.

> *The burial took place in the Čečen'khan territory, in the land of Čžalaknor gin' čžabu. There even now is a rampart called Balasykutul myao at the site.*

Andrews looked toward the valley and the collection of gers. Bala was the name of the village. *Myao* was a Chinese word meaning "temple."

"*Balasykutul myao,*" Andrews said, putting them together. "The village, it's named after your monastery."

The old monk nodded. "Hsü Sung knew more than any of the outsiders. Palladii gained access to his writings before they could be destroyed."

Andrews's mind raced. Members of *Balasykutul myao* were Buddhists of the Yellow Hat sect. The founding members of the sect were said to be offspring of one of Genghis Khan's daughters.

"You're descendants of Genghis Khan's daughter," Andrews said.

The monk bowed his head. "I'm of the thirty-eighth generation of the union of Altani and Sechin."

"That explains why people from this area have Genghis Khan's X chromosome markers, but not his Y chromosome markers," Andrews said.

"Is that what you learned from your friend's studies?" the monk asked.

Andrews looked toward Abbey. She sat outside their ger, reading. As she'd hoped, finding Genghis Khan's X chromosome markers had provided insight into her study population. Her research had led them to the monastery of *Balasykutul myao* and the living members of the Yellow Hat sect. Her research had led them to Baljuna. It had led them to . . .

Andrews's heart raced. The full impact of what Abbey had done coursed through him. She hadn't simply replaced the missing pages of *The Secret History* or added a few stanzas to Chaucer's tale, she'd written the final chapter, penned the concluding verse. He looked up, barely able to control his excitement. "Is this the tree?"

"Over the centuries, these hills and valleys have changed like the waves of the ocean," the monk said. "There have been many trees. This is the ninth."

A light breeze passed over the valley. The monk breathed it in. "Genghis Khan did everything he could to erase the events occurring here from the scrolls of history, but time and his own success conspired against him. The legend of the covenant was passed by word of mouth from generation to generation and soon seeped into the histories. It eventually became recognized for what it truly was—the defining moment of Genghis Khan's life."

The monk paused as he looked over the valley. "When Genghis Khan died, he made two requests. He wanted to be buried here and he wanted to rest in peace. Bo'orchu brought his remains here. To honor Genghis Khan's wish to rest in peace, Bo'orchu had an empty casket brought to Burkhan Khaldun—accompanied by a thousand guards. To solidify the deception, Bo'orchu and three generations of his descendants stayed on Burkhan Khaldun and guarded the false site. Of Genghis Khan's family members, only Altani knew the true burial site. She and Sechin came here and built this monastery. Their offspring, members of our Yellow Hat sect, have spent their lives guarding the site. Our monastery has survived time and the elements, three centuries of Chinese rule, and seventy years of Soviet rule."

"Why are you telling me this?" Andrews asked.

"Baabar said you would continue searching until you knew the truth," the monk said. "When I asked him if you would respect the burial site, he said you would. When I received word you were north of Choibalsan looking for Bala, I sent Tuya and Nasan to find you. You might not have found us this trip, but I knew you'd eventually piece it all together." He smiled. "And, with a little prodding, you did." He shrugged. "I'm an old man. I don't have much time. I wanted to be here when you came. I wanted to be able to look into your eyes to see if our secret would be safe."

The monk reached beneath a fold in his robe and removed an ornate wooden box from his lap. He opened the box. Inside, an intricate silver binding held together a shock of coarse black hair. Most of the hairs had fallen from the binding and lay in the bottom of the box. "Along with protecting the burial site, my ancestors have guarded this with their lives," the monk said.

"The *black* spirit banner?" Andrews asked.

The monk nodded. "The one he flew during times of war."

"The banner that was lost?"

"Yes," the monk said. "To history, but not us."

Next to the binding was an ivory-handled knife studded with blue stones. The monk removed it. He slid it from its leather scabbard and held it up. The blade gleamed under a thin layer of oil. Sheathing the knife, he held it out. "In the past, it's brought me luck. Maybe it will do the same for you."

"I—I couldn't," Andrews said.

"I'm aware of what you did with your reward from the institute," the monk said. "Baabar would be honored to know of the endowment in his name. Please, think of it as a gift from a grateful nation."

Andrews took the knife. He looked down at it as it sat in his open palm. Baabar was right. He would be content simply knowing the truth. He set the knife back in the box. "It must have meant something to him," he said. "That's why it belongs here with you."

The monk, nodding his appreciation, closed the box.

Andrews recalled a quote that had been on the wall of Baabar's Khural office. "'Pain and grief can last a lifetime while happiness can be fleeting. Seeking nirvana is the struggle to reverse that,'" he recited.

The quote was attributed to the chairman and founder of the Republican Democracy Party, Navaandorjiin Mikou. Baabar once told him Mikou had been a monk. Next to the quote, Andrews vaguely recalled a photo. In the photo, Baabar was bent down with his arm around an older man. Andrews didn't realize until now why the older man was sitting.

"Baabar had a gifted mind, but more than anything a pure heart," the monk said. "You and I have lost something special."

"We have," Andrews said.

They looked back over the valley.

"What's next?" Mikou asked.

As the wind blew and leaves of the great tree shimmered, Andrews looked toward Abbey. His thoughts turned to his parents and his image of them from that last night at dinner. His dad's arm had been wrapped tightly around his mom, but there was something stronger, much stronger, that bound them together. The love they shared was not something that could be given or taken. It was part of them. Andrews thought he'd never be capable of that kind of love. But he was wrong. Abbey was now part of him. Whatever the future held, he couldn't imagine one without her.

He pulled the compass from his pocket. Holding it in his palm, he pushed back the lid. A ring sat inside, its diamond sparkling. Abbey had hoped that his path would lead back to her. It had.

Andrews looked toward Mikou. The old monk was watching him, his eyes gleaming. The monk bowed.

Andrews returned the bow. He closed the compass and slipped it back into his pocket. Without a word, he hurried down the hill.

BIBLIOGRAPHY

Achenbach, Joel. "The Era of His Ways; In Which We Choose the Most Important Man of the Last Thousand Years." *The Washington Post* [Washington D.C.] 31 Dec. 1995, Style sec.: F.01.

Cleaves, Francis Woodman. "The Historicity of the Baljuna Covenant." *Harvard Journal of Asiatic Studies* 18 (1955): 357–421.

Hartog, Leo De. *Genghis Khan, Conqueror of the World*. New York: St. Martin's, 1989.

Kohn, Michael. *Mongolia. 4th Edition*. Lonely Planet, June 2005.

Man, John. *Genghis Khan: Life, Death, and Resurrection*. New York: Thomas Dunne/St. Martin's, 2005.

McRae, Michael. "Genghis on My Mind." Outside. July 1996.

Onon, Urgunge, trans. *The Secret History of the Mongols: The Life and Times of Chinggis Khan*. Richmond, Surrey: Curzon, 2001.

Pelliot, Paul. "138. Cinghis." *Notes on Marco Polo*. Paris: Impr. Nationale, 1959. 281–363.

Rossabi, Morris. *Modern Mongolia: From Khans to Commissars to Capitalists*. Berkeley: University of California, 2005.

Sabloff, Paula L. W. *Modern Mongolia: Reclaiming Genghis Khan*. Philadelphia: University of Pennsylvania Museum of Archaeology and Anthropology, 2001.

Weatherford, J. McIver. *Genghis Khan and the Making of the Modern World*. New York: Crown, 2004.

Weatherford, J. McIver. *The Secret History of the Mongol Queens*. New York: Crown, 2010.

Wikisource contributors, "The Travels of Marco Polo," Wikisource, https://en.wikisource.org/w/index.php?title=The_Travels_of_Marco_Polo&oldid=4510593 (accessed August 22, 2015).

Zerjal, T. "The Genetic Legacy of the Mongols." The American Journal of Human Genetics 72.3 (2003): 717–21.

ACKNOWLEDGMENTS

I would like to thank Jack Weatherford, John Man, and Leo de Hartog for writing incredibly vivid biographies and travelogues on Genghis Khan that captured my imagination and provided the inspiration for this novel. I would also like to thank Lisa Akoury-Ross from SDP Publishing Solutions for making this book a reality and for her patience while working with a first-time author. I am much in debt to Shannon Miller and Stephanie Peters for their expert editing of this novel, and to Howard Johnson for his creative layout designs and making countless changes to the text.

I would like to thank my early readers: Jane McAndrews, Kevin Kuske, and Lauren Pelkey. Their advice and words of encouragement have been greatly appreciated.

I would like to thank Ganbat Badamkhand for creating the cover art and Batjavkhaa Batsaikhan for providing the Classical Mongolian script. I would like to thank my high school math teacher, Jim Phelan (deceased), for giving a teenager access to his library of hardbound Robert Ludlum books. I would like to thank my parents, Jim and Win, for their never-ending support. I am also grateful to my professional partners: Drs. Kim Mills, Sam Attal, Bob Knapp (deceased), and Dave Graham. I couldn't work with a better group of guys.

Most of all, I would like to thank my wife, Leslie, for listening to my ramblings about writing well beyond the point when it could have seemed even remotely interesting, for reading numerous versions of this novel, and for her boundless encouragement.

ABOUT THE AUTHOR

Tim Pelkey is married and the father of two. He lives in Michigan. *The Baljuna Covenant* is his first novel. He is currently working on his second novel, *The Ottoman Excursion.*

The Baljuna Covenant
Tim Pelkey
Publisher: SDP Publishing
Also available in ebook format
Available at all major bookstores.

 **SDP Publishing**

www.SDPPublishing.com
Contact us at: info@SDPPublishing.com

Recommended Reading Lists

Kirkus Reviews

US Review of Books

Stevo's Reviews on the Internet

CPSIA information can be obtained
at www.ICGtesting.com
Printed in the USA
LVOW12s1800301117
558159LV00005B/929/P